TALISLANTA

WORLDBOOK

Fantasy Role Playing Game Supplement

by Stephan Michael Sechi

Additional text provided by W.G. Armintrout, Anthony Pryor, & Stevie McBride.

Editor: W.G. Armintrout

Cover Art: P.D. Breeding-Black

Interior Illsutrations: P.D. Breeding-Black, Ron Spencer, Todd Cameron Hamilton, Larry Dixon, Sandra Santaro, & Victor Wren

Cartography: P.D. Breeding-Black (with Czeslaw Sornat & Tamerlin), Larry Dixon

Graphics: Patty Sechi

Talislanta Logo: P.D. Breeding-Black & Todd Cameron Hamilton

Proofreading: Anthony Pryor

Creative Director: SMS

Dedicated to Jack Vance, pre-eminent author of fantasy and science fiction.

TABLE OF CONTENTS

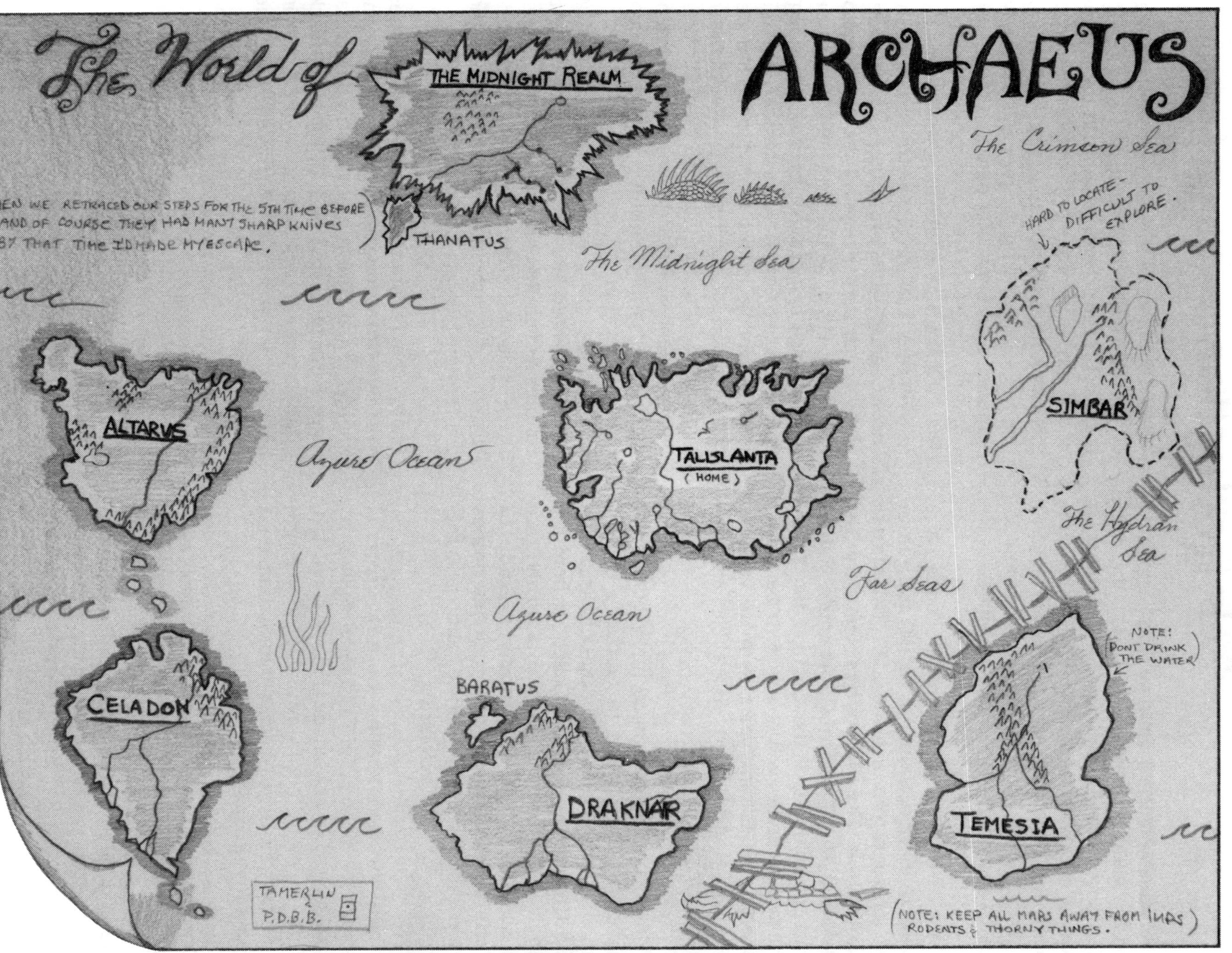

The World of
ARCHAEUS
THE MIDNIGHT REALM
THANATUS
The Crimson Sea
HEN WE RETRACED OUR STEPS FOR THE 5TH TIME BEFORE
AND OF COURSE THEY HAD MANY SHARP KNIVES
BY THAT TIME I'D MADE MY ESCAPE.
The Midnight Sea
HARD TO LOCATE -
DIFFICULT TO
EXPLORE.
SIMBAR
ALTARUS
Azure Ocean
TALISLANTA
(HOME)
The Hydran Sea
Azure Ocean
Far Seas
CELADON
BARATUS
DRAKNAR
NOTE!
DON'T DRINK
THE WATER
TEMESIA
TAMERLIN
&
P.D.B.B.
(NOTE: KEEP ALL MAPS AWAY FROM IMPS)
RODENTS & THORNY THINGS.

Scale: 1" = 825 miles.

Introduction

The fantasy land of Talislanta first appeared on the gaming scene in 1987, with the publication of **The Chronicles of Talislanta**. It was a eccentric book, filled with the rambling and disjointed accounts of an itinerant wizard named Tamerlin, plus the fabulous illustrations of artist P.D. Breeding-Black.

Since that time, eight further books have been published about the **Talislanta** game. At present, the list includes **Talislanta Handbook, The Naturalist's Guide to Talislanta, The Talislanta Sorcerer's Guide**, and six volumes of the **Cyclopedia Talislanta**. The series will continue to be developed in the coming years, as more volumes of the **Cyclopedia** and related titles are added to the line.

With the publication of so many books, we have had the chance to gradually expand upon the original description of Talislanta in the **Chronicles** — in the Gazetteer from the original **Cyclopedia Talislanta**, in the race descriptions from **A Naturalist's Guide to Talislanta**, in the arcane societies entries from the **Sorcerer's Guide**, and in further volumes of the **Cyclopedia**.

While the proliferation of new material helped to define the Talislantan milieu, it also led to a certain degree of confusion. With so many books available, it was becoming difficult to access information on a given region or culture.

Our solution has been to create **The Talislanta Worldbook** — a single reference work covering the entire world of Archaeus, from the continent of Talislanta to the Unknown Lands. In it you'll find all of the geographic information from the **Chronicles**, plus the map references which appeared in the Gazeteer section of the first **Cyclopedia Talislanta**. This material has been completely reorganized, revised, and updated to reflect the most recent developments in the **Cyclopedia** series. In order to facilitate the use of this book as a world atlas, the accounts of the wizard Tamerlin were excised, to be compiled again at a later date.

The Talislanta Worldbook also features all-new entries covering the mysterious Unknown Lands — the previously uncharted regions which lay far beyond the continent of Talislanta. Here, you'll find information on places which before were known only in legend: the Lost Continent of Simbar, the miraculous Flying Island of Alcedon, the demon-haunted isle of Temesia, the dreaded Midnight Realm, the wild continent of Altarus (mistakenly referred to on certain ancient maps as Alhambra), and the lush green continent of Celadon.

Also presented are the various races and cultures which inhabit the Unknown Lands. These include the giant Drakken, the aquatic Hydrans, the amphibious Batrachians, and the Demon Hunters of Thanatus.

Finally, the **Talislanta Worldbook** includes over two dozen new city, regional, and continental maps. The regional and continental maps were produced by P.D. Breeding-Black — purportedly in collaboration with a certain itinerant wizard, whose travels continue even to the present day...

Hope you enjoy it —

Sincerely,

Stephan Michael Sechi
Creative Director
Bard Games

A Note from the Editor

How to use this book:

You won't find any rules in this book, for the simple reason that we've placed them all in another volume (the soon-to-be-published **Talislanta Guidebook** will contain the third edition of our rules). Instead, this book contains background information which can be used with the **Talislanta** game, or with any other fantasy role-playing system.

If you haven't played **Talislanta** before, then you might start by borrowing a few races or creatures from this book and adding them to your existing fantasy campaign. That's perfectly all right with us — take as much as you like (but if someone asks where you found such great ideas, give us credit, OK?).

Later on, you may decide to bring your regular adventurers to Talislanta for a brief visit — you might let them stumble through a transdimensional gate, arrive on a dimension-spanning schooner, or have a magical mishap propel them into a new world.

Suddenly, your players will find themselves in a totally original fantasy world: a place where there are no elves, no dwarves, and nothing that's been described in anyone else's monster compendium. Having visited Talislanta once, there's a good chance that you and your players won't want to leave.

In short, the **Talislanta Worldbook** gives you the world of Archaeus (including the continent of Talislanta) in a form that you can use in a variety of ways. You can mine this book for ideas to be used in your own fantasy campaign world; you can use this world as a setting for your favorite role-playing rules-system; or you can combine this book with the **Talislanta Guidebook** for a complete, stand-alone game system.

Credit where credit is due:

The fantasy setting of **Talislanta** could never have been created without the inspiration of several of the authors of the best in fantasy literature. At the top of this list is Jack Vance, to whom this book is dedicated — if we have created even half the sense of wonder and awe which his fantasy inspires, we will consider ourselves successful.

Thanks are also due to the authors and artists who have worked not just on this book, but on the entire series to date: Joe Bouza, P.D. Breeding-Black, Larry Dixon, Jan and Rollin Ehlenfeldt, Rick Emond, Anthony Herring, Tom Kane, Spencer Kipe, Barry Link, Kevin Murphy, Anthony Pryor, Joel Roosa, Sandra Santaro, Curtis Scott, Patty Sechi, Craig Sheeley, Czeslaw Sornat, Ron Spencer, Richard Thomas, Nathan Verrilli, Stewart Wieck, and Victor Wren.

However, the largest debt of gratitude is due to our faithful readers, those who have driven us to continue to produce new **Talislanta** products. Thanks from all of us for your support — we appreciate it.

And lastly, a note about *Black Savant*, the Talislanta newsletter. If you'd like to find out what's new with Bard Games and the **Talislanta** game, or if you want to know what other Gamemasters and players are doing in their campaigns, then subscribe to *Black Savant*. For a free copy, send your name and address to:

Black Savant
c/o Bard Games
P.O. Box 7729
Greenwich, CT 06836

The World of Archaeus

Of the Thirteen Realities which comprise the Omniverse, the Prime Material Plane — known as *Primus* — is the one within which mortal lifeforms dwell. Of the infinite number of worlds on this plane, this volume is concerned with only one: Archaeus.

Archaeus is a sphere, though few of its inhabitants perceive this fact. Scholars know of nine celestial objects which revolve around Archaeus, though a tenth has sometimes been theorized. Two of these are the twin suns of Archaeus, which rise and set in unison. The larger of these is blood red in hue, and is known as the Greater Sun. The smaller, a mass of golden fire, is called the Lesser Sun.

Also in orbit around Archaeus are its seven moons, each of which reigns in its full phase over one of the 49-day months of this world. These moons (and months) are — purple *Ardan*, the moon of romantic love; amber *Drome*, which is associated with protection and conjuration; crimson *Jhang*, whose light shines kindly on hunters and warriors; blue *Laeolis*, the Moon of Sorrow; green *Phandir*, sphere of mystery and reputed to be a home of Destiny; silver *Talisandre*, a capricious influence; and black *Zar*, an ally of Death. Each of the seven months consists of seven weeks, each of which has seven days.

There are two events of astrological significance which occur yearly. The first is the *Conjunction of the Twin Suns,* which happens on the last day of Phandir — at noon on this day, one of the suns eclipses the other for a period of up to an hour. Astrologers have proven unable to predict the length of the eclipse or which sun will impose over the other for a given year, making this celestial event of great interest to gamblers and speculators.

The *Septenarial Concordance* is just as famed an occurrence, for during these two weeks the seven moons of Archaeus remain in alignment. The Conjunction of the Suns is a time of feasting and dancing for many of the inhabitants of Archaeus, but the time of the Concordance is considered to be ill-aspected.

The Continents

Of the several land masses of this world, one is of more importance than the others. This is the continent of Talislanta, which has traditionally been the seat of civilization and knowledge upon Archaeus. It is inhabited by a fabulous array of intelligent races, organized into both civilized nations and primitive tribal-states. The chief nations are the *Seven Kingdoms,* a peaceful coalition of disparate peoples; the *Quan Empire,* a despotic realm which dominates the eastern portion of the continent; and the rival lands of *Zandu* and *Aaman,* two halves of the once-great Phaedran Empire, which dissolved following the Cult Wars of the first century, NA (*New Age*).

The inhabitants of this continent, known as the Talislantans, have little knowledge of the actual state of their world. To them, the other continents are lands of legend; this lack of knowledge is reinforced by the difficulty of travel on and over the sea. Of the races of Talislanta, the only true sailing peoples — those who deliberately cruise beyond sight of the shore — are the Imrians and the mysterious Parthenians. The Sunra also once freely sailed the seas, before they fell under the domination of the Quan.

The other continents of Archaeus, which constitute the territories known to Talislantans as the *Unknown Lands,* are:

Altarus, the flying island which was thrust into the skies during the cataclysm known as the Great Disaster. Before the upheaval, this landmass was part of the Sinking Land, in Talislanta.

Alcedon, a continent which has been ravaged by continual warfare for untold thousands of years. It has been confused by Talislantan scholars with the mythical continent of Alhambra.

Celadon, a paradise where Nature (and the Green Mandarin) rules supreme. The Dendrads who dwell here appear to be plants by daylight, but in the night take on the semblance of Men.

Draknar, the last refuge of a species of reptilian giants which once ruled this world. Nearby is Baratus, formerly the home of a race of fierce windship pirates now thought to be extinct.

The Midnight Realm, which lies in the far north, is a place of continual darkness. The chief inhabitants are Night Demons, but the associated isle of Thanatus is the dwelling place of a race of devils.

Temesia, a volcanic and mist-hung continent, is possessed of an environment hostile to the other lifeforms which dwell on this world.

There may have been other continents and major islands in the history of the world, but the only one which survives in memory is Simbar, often called the "Lost Continent." This land broke nearly in two and subsided beneath the waves at the time of the Great Disaster, and now marks the shallows between the two eastern seas of Archaeus.

World History

Archaeus is an ancient world, littered with the ruins of a succession of past ages. Modern Talislantan scholars have divided the history of this archaic world into the following periods:

THE TIME BEFORE TIME

Almost nothing is known of this lost epoch, when time dawned on the world. The legends of Sursia and Acimera may originate from this period, though scholars remain uncertain as to this point. These two warring civilizations reportedly ended in a terrible holocaust, which some scholars believe was followed by an age of ice.

The mystical beings known as the Ariane may also have come to Archaeus at this time, migrating from elsewhere in the Omniverse.

THE FORGOTTEN AGE

Tribes of primitive sub-men were extant during the *First Millennium* of the Forgotten Age, and wandered the barren ice plains of what is now known as the continent of Talislanta. While foraging for sustenance, one of the clans chanced to stumble upon the wreckage of a ship of some sort. Inside, they found a crystal orb, within which were stored the secrets of a lost and forgotten art – Magic.

Armed with their new-found knowledge, the sub-men were able to protect themselves from the depredations of hostile races and beasts. Two great settlements were founded, one in the territory which is modern Aaman, and the second in ancient Hadjistan (now in the Wilderlands of Zaran).

The *Second Millennium* was marked by the rapid expansion of the Archaeans (as the evolving sub-men now called themselves). They spread across the Talislantan continent, driving out the other races. The giant Drakken were among their victims, leaving behind such artifacts as the Watchstone, the City of Kharakhan, and the tomb of the great dragon, Orrix, whose mummified remains lie buried beneath the ruins of Four Nations.

By the *Third Millennium*, the Archaeans had established an empire comprised of numerous citystates, each ruled by a master magician. Among these were Ashann, Aurantium, Elande, Erythria, Farnir, the Four Nations, Jalaad, Kasraan, Numenia, Osmar, Phandril, Sharna, Thanatus, and Xambria.

A single governing body ruled over this sorcerous civilization – the Archaean Cabal, a group comprised of representatives from each of the Archaean states. The Cabal mediated disputes and enforced the First Law, which prohibited direct conflict between magicians. Otherwise, the citystates were allowed to govern themselves as they pleased.

The Third Millennium was the Golden Age of the Archaeans, marked by fabulous achievements in the arcane arts. The mages used magic to alter their physical appearance, and to create new lifeforms of their own design. They built floating cities, automatons, and bridges of light. Sailing in their windships, they explored new and uncharted lands, returning with cargos of precious stones, exotic beasts, magical herbs, and artifacts from dead civilizations.

The *Fourth Millennium* saw the onset of the decadence which eventually overcame the Archaeans. Allowed to do as they pleased, the rulers of the citystates became corrupted by greed and the desire for power. The Archaean Cabal, preoccupied with its own petty interests, failed to impose any meaningful restraint upon the member states.

The Elandar became elitists, regarding those who lived on the ground as their inferiors. The Numenians, under the demagogue Solimorrion, became fanatical symbolators. The Necromancer-Kings of Quaran consorted with devils and demons; the Phandre became addicted to exotic stimulants and hallucinogens; the Thane became morbid and reclusive. The Erythrians and others created armies of surrogates, and sent them into battle to resolve disputes with rivals, or for their own amusement.

THE GREAT DISASTER

Most scholars of the New Age believe that The Great Disaster was caused by the excessive use and general misuse of magic. They speculate that this resulted in a weakening of the dimensional fabric, which in turn allowed extradimensional entities to invade Archaeus. Great upheavals followed, resulting in the sinking of Simbar and the flight of Alcedon. Central Talislanta became a wasteland, and the North Sea drained away (becoming the modern Lost Sea).

THE AGE OF CONFUSION

An untold number of years passed, during which the survivors of the Disaster began to establish new settlements. None lasted for very long until the establishment of the Phaedran Empire.

THE NEW AGE

The founding of the Citystate of Phaedra marked the beginning of the current age – present time, in the Talislanta game. It is now the year 600 N.A. The Phaedran Empire has collapsed, but other civilizations have risen in its place.

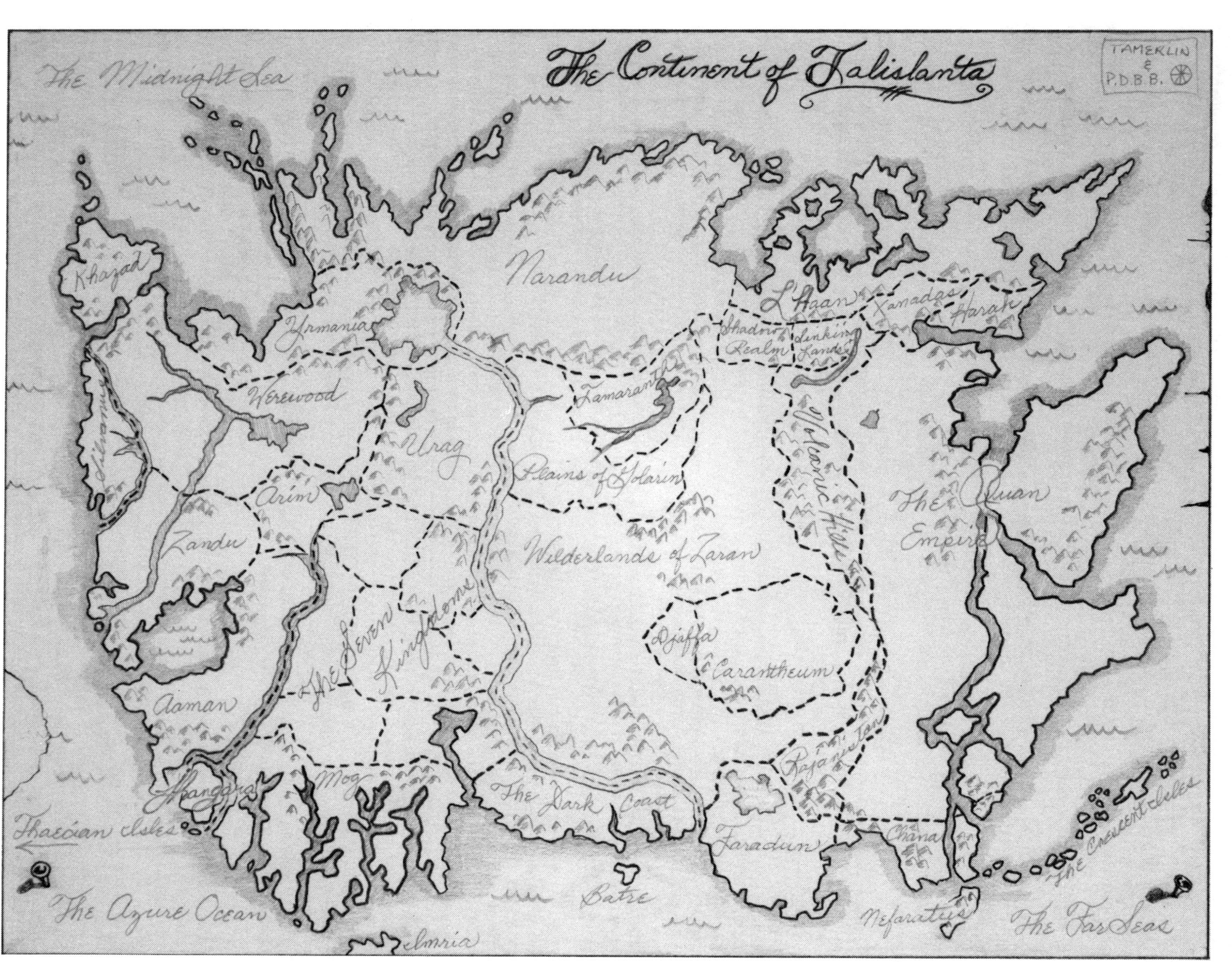

Scale: 1" = 210 miles.

The Continent of Talislanta

Since the time of the Great Disaster, the inhabitants of Archaeus have struggled to regain the degree of civilization and enlightenment which their ancestors knew at the height of the Forgotten Age. Nowhere has the climb from barbarism been more successful than on the continent of Talislanta, though even here the advances pale compared with the achievements of the ancient Archaeans.

The Post-Disaster Age

Scholars of the New Age can only estimate the span of time which passed between the onset of the Great Disaster and the founding of the Citystate of Phaedra – the period known as the Age of Confusion. The Archaeans of the Forgotten Age either vanished during the Disaster, devolved into certain of the modern races, or fled elsewhere in the Omniverse…and perhaps all three of these theories are correct.

Other survivors may have come from those races which the Archaeans fashioned as their servants and minions. Their descendants may include such warrior peoples as the Thralls, Kang, Araq, Shadinn, and Ahazu; specialized races like the subterranean Vajra, the aquatic Sunra, the Yassan (born with twin opposable thumbs), and the metalic-skinned Parthenians; and possibly such servitor peoples as the Ispasians, Thaecians, Bodor, Callidians, Batreans, Kasmir, the Green Men, Monads, and Thiasians.

Whether the modern, unspecialized races of Men (the Cymrilians, Zandir, Aamanians, Phantasians, Quan, and so forth) are descended from Archaean stock, or from the sub-men who inhabited the wilderlands even during the height of the Archaean Age, is unknown. If the Archaean sub-race survived, its knowledge of magic certainly did not – the Talislantans of the New Age have had to piece together their arcane lore from whatever incomplete legends were passed on by their ancestors, and from the scraps of information recorded on scrolls and tablets from ancient times.

Modern history begins with the founding of Phaedra. Therefore, historians have knowledge of the many civilizations which rose and fell in the intervening years since the Great Disaster. It is known that the war-like Mazdaks (now extinct) ruled in the East before the rise of the Quan. For a time, the Yassan Technomancers reigned over a modest kingdom in the Sanctuary Mountains of modern Carantheum. The Mandalans had an advanced culture from an early date, and the Ariane built the Maze-City of Altan long before Phaedra arose.

The New Age

The Phaedran tribes, triumphant in their wars against the Wildmen of the West, marked the beginning of the current age with the founding of their first citystate, Phaedra. What followed was an explosion of culture and knowledge unparalleled in known history. In little more than a century, the Phaedran Empire matured into a complex array of castes and factions, rediscovering along the way the ancient arts of the Archaens.

But by the year 110 N.A., the Phaedran Empire lay in fragments, disrupted bya series of religious conflicts called the Cult Wars. The fighting lasted for four centuries, after which a truce was finally declared; the modern descendants of the first New Age empire are the rival states of Zandu and Aaman, and the pirate stronghold of Gao-Din.

Quan and Carantheum. Meanwhile, two other civilizations were on the rise. In the East, the barbaric Quan became the masters of the lands once held by the Mazdaks, who brought about their own extinction through ceaseless warfare. Within a century, the Quan ruled an empire mightier than Phaedra's, populated by the warrior Kang, the mining Vajra, the seafaring Sunra, the mercantilist Ispasians, and the philosophical Mandalans. Only the Mondre Khan sub-men remained unconquered.

Meanwhile, the nomadic Dracartans stumbled upon a cache of ancient tablets in the heart of the Red Desert. The knowledge gained – supposedly a boon from their reclusive god, Jamba – gave the Kingdom of Carantheum the secrets of thaumaturgy, including the ability to create red iron from the sand which surrounded them. They erected the Citystate of Dracarta in the central desert, which became a major commercial center.

Developments in the North. In the frozen Northlands of Talislanta, the Mirin tribes erected their first cities, L'Lal and Rhin, under the direction of their Snow Queen. Despite the pressures of a constant war against the Ice Giants of Narandu, the Mirin kingdom of L'Haan developed an advanced culture based on the science of alchemy. Due to the cold and its remoteness, however, L'Haan remained isolated from the other Talislantan states.

The gradual but irresistible advance of the Ice Giants – a race which appeared in Talislanta after the Great Disaster, and which brought arctic cold with it as it advanced to new territories – displaced other civilizations of the North. Farnir, one of the few Archaean citystates to survive the Great Disaster in any form, fell to the onslaught of the Giants. Another northern race, the Ur, fled to the south. Conquering the despicable Darklings and uniting with the avian Stryx, the refugees founded the Kingdom of Urag. Shortly thereafter, they began to ravage their new land of its mineral resources.

The Union of the Seven Kingdoms. The rise and fall of the Phaedran Empire had an effect far beyond its own borders. Exiles, driven East by the early conquests and the later civil war, founded such diverse nations as the Kingdoms of Vardune and Cymril (in the Seven Kingdoms), and the Wilderlands citystates of Hadj, Maruk and Danuvia. The end of the second century of the New Age brought with it a threat which changed the course of Talislantan history — a unified Beastmen army, surging out of the Plains of Golarin under the leadership of a brilliant and charismatic general, Tyranus.

In order to survive, seven of the western kingdoms — Cymril, citystate of the exile mages; Taz, kingdom of the Thrall warriors; Sindar, the mesa homeland of the dual-brained Sindarans; Vardune, the forest kingdom founded by the Ardua; Durne, beneath which live the subterranean Gnomekin; Kasmir, kingdom of the money-lenders; and Astar, the home of the peaceful Muses — were forced to cooperate in a defensive war. After their eventual triumph, the military coalition became a political union known as the Seven Kingdoms.

The Seven Kingdoms might best be considered the spiritual descendant of the Phaedran Empire, for it has become the primary guardian of knowledge and culture on the continent. Likewise, its Grand Army and fleets of windships maintain the tradeways, allowing commerce to prosper. Fortunately, the intolerance of the ancient Phaedrans is replaced here with a degree of cultural and religious tolerance seldom matched elsewhere on the world of Archaeus.

The Death Cultists. For a time, the nations of Talislanta appeared to have reached a political balance. The Quan attacked and failed to conquer the barbarous Harakin, and the Ur were repulsed by the Wildmen of Yrmania. The only developments of note were the alliance of the Ariane of Tamaranth with the Gryphs, and the founding of the first settlements in Jhangara.

The fourth century of the New Age witnessed the rise of another power: Rajanistan. The various subraces of Rajans — the Rajanin, Shadinn, Zagir, Aramut, and the mongrel Vird — fled to the deserts of southeastern Talislanta during the wars of the Mazdak Empire, but remained hostile and divided.

In the third century of the New Age, the Rajanin allied with the Shadinn giants and brought the Zagir and Aramut tribes under their dominion, but the union was precarious at best — the subject tribes were prone to revolt, and the Rajanin chieftains often squabbled among themselves.

This changed in the year 390 N.A., when the necromancer Urmaan rose to power among the Rajanin. The Rajan leader had somehow learned the secrets of the arcane art of Necromancy, and he taught the magical rites to those who would follow him.

Urmaan treacherously attacked and conquered his Shadinn allies, then led the united Rajan tribes in the subjugation of Virdistan. After erecting the fortified Holy City of Irdan, the Necromancer decreed one final attack: the conquest of Carantheum. When the Rajans were repulsed, Urmaan vowed revenge...but the mage mysteriously disappeared shortly afterward.

After the death of Urmaan, a cabal of Rajanin Necromancers founded the Black Mystic Cult of Rajanistan as a tool through which to rule the Rajan nation. The cultists promoted a religion which worshiped Death, and which taught a virulent form of fanatical intolerance toward other races and deities. The nation of Rajanistan is currently one of the greatest threats to the stability of modern Talislanta.

Talislanta Today. Little has changed politically in the two centuries since the founding of Rajanistan. The balance of power seems to be proven by the record of failed conquests — the defeat of an Ice Giant advance at the hands of Ariane mystics, in 493 N.A.; the failure of the Ur to conquer the Arimites in 553 N.A.; and the defeat of Imrian raiders by the Grand Army of the Seven Kingdoms, in 570 N.A.

The Regions of Talislanta

Geographers divide the Talislantan landmass into ten districts, each of which shares certain characteristics or qualities. These regions are:

The Seven Kingdoms. This western nation, composed of seven very different races and societies, continues to thrive politically and commercially. The Seven Kingdoms is a beacon to exiles and refugees who appreciate its standards of tolerance, and its Lyceum Arcanum is the foremost institute of the arcane arts on the continent.

The Wilderlands of Zaran. Practically the opposite of the Seven Kingdoms, this wilderness in central Talislanta is an ungoverned district still blighted by the effects of the Great Disaster. Ruins litter the sands and wastes, where the Za bandits, Kharakhan Giants, the Saurud, and other militant tribes raid caravans and one another for the goods needed to survive. The only outposts of civilization are the citystates of Hadj, Danuvia and Maruk, and the trade fortresses (Akmir and Karfan) maintained by the Seven Kingdoms.

The Western Lands. The states which formed out of the self-destruction of ancient Phaedra, Aaman and Zandu, are absolute opposites. The Aamanians are Orthodoxist cultists, devoted to a strict worship of the deity Aa, while the Zandir are Paradoxists, resistant to any attempt to regiment their lives. Silvanus, the home of the gypsy Sarista, is considered somewhat of a wilderness preserve by the Sultan of Zandu, but the northern woodlands of Werewood are justly feared by Zandir and Aamanian alike. The Kingdom of Arim, nestled in the heights of the Onyx Mountains, is a nation of miners held in thralldom by the tyranny of the Revenant Cult, a secret society.

The Eastern Lands. The Quan Empire remains firmly entrenched in the East, though experts disagree as to whether it is poised to invade Carantheum or Rajanistan, or if the decadent Quan are about to be ousted from power by one of their subject races. To the south, the jungles of Chana are divided among three strange and sinister tribes. In the north, the cold-hearted Harakin remain unchallenged in their desolate homeland. Somewhere in the northern mountains lies the Temple of the Four Winds, from which the Savants of Xanadas are said to document the affairs of the continent.

The Desert Kingdoms. The nations which inhabit the sandy wastes of central Talislanta are bitter enemies. Carantheum, which lies astride the trade route between the Quan Empire and the Seven Kingdoms, is at the height of its commercial success. Its fleets of duneships patrol the deserts against the incursions of the fanatic warriors of Rajanistan, which has never retreated from its goal of subjugating the Red Desert. Djaffa, a small desert nation of nomad tribes (some of which are said to be bandit clans), remains an ally of Carantheum.

The Northlands. The threat which dominates the north lies within the Kingdom of Narandu; a frigidland ruled by the enigmatic Ice King and his minions, the Ice Giants. Narandu's slow but inexorable encroachment into neighboring territories, bringing with it the onset of an arctic climate, remains a threat to all Talislantans. The Mirin of L'Haan have successfully resisted the Giants for centuries, but alone they have no chance to reverse the tide. The Wildmen of Yrmania are too disorganized to stop the arctic advance, while ancient Khazad lays in ruin, uninhabited except by necrophages, scavengers, and vermin.

The Central Regions. Urag, depleted by centuries of despoliation by the Ur clans, is a barren land polluted with toxic wastes. Soon, the Ur must again try to expand into new territories, to replenish their depleted stores of food and natural resources. Across the Dead River Canyon live the Beastmen of the Plains of Golarin, who have remained disunited since their defeat in the Beast Wars centuries ago. Tamaranth is a sylvan forestland, shared by the winged Gryphs and the Ariane, a race possessed of extraordinary mystical abilities. In the east, the Shadow Realm and the Sinking Land are twin mysteries, one inhabited by shadowforms and the other by mud-swimming Snipes; to the south lies the hostile terrain of the Volcanic Hills, where dwell such hostile races as Saurans, Raknids and Satada.

The Wild Coast. The southern coast of Talislanta is a tropical land where jungles and swamps predominate. The three western nations are differentiated primarily by the races which dwell within them: Jhangara is home to the primitive Jhangaran tribesmen; Mog is the land of the Mogroth, the slow-moving sloth-beings who dredge the swamps for amber; and the Dark Coast is the habitation of the agricultural Green Men, the brutish Mud People, and the fierce Ahazu tribesmen. Three islands are of particular interest: Gao-Din, the Phaedran penal colony which has become a pirate stronghold; Imria, the home of the Imrian slavers; and Batre, the isle from which come some of Talislanta's most beautiful women. In the east is Faradun, a nation where unscrupulous monopolists control the price of all trade goods and services.

The Far Isles. The final geographical district of Talislanta consists of two island chains, on opposite sides of the continent. The Crescent Islands, in the east, include the homelands of the Mangar Corsairs, the peaceful Sawila, and the Na-Ku cannibals. Adjacent to the end of the chain is Nefaratus, the mysterious island of the mages known only as the Black Savants. The Thaecian Islands are in the west, and are inhabited by such races as the Parthenian seafarers, and the cultured Thiasians and Thaecians. South lies the isolated isle of Phantas, where a flying castle of Cabal Magicus bears witness to the lost arts of the Archaean sorcerers.

Traveling in Talislanta

Those desiring to journey from place to place on this continent must take into account not only the features of terrain, but the motives of those who inhabit the land as well.

Ground Travel. Four primary roadways link the continent from east to west. In the West, the Phaedran Causeway runs throughout Zandu and Aaman; it is in disrepair, but caravans still manage to use it. Zandir traders often leave the causeway in Zanth and head along the trails into Arim, rather than cross the border into Aaman.

At Vashay of Vardune, the Phaedran Causeway meets one of the six tendrils of the Seven Roads which link the Seven Kingdoms. These highways link Cymril to each of the other capitals in the nation, and are well maintained and constantly patrolled.

The Wilderlands Road, a relic of the Forgotten Age, winds east from Kasmir of the Seven Kingdoms, and continues across the wastes and deserts until it climaxes at Hadran of the Quan Empire. This route is amazingly well preserved given its age, but not even the Seven Kingdoms' outposts can keep the highway clear of marauders and bandits.

At Hadran, the traveler encounters the Emperor's Road, which is the longest highway in Talislanta. The roadway nearly circles the Quan Empire, ranging from the jungled Wildlands of the south to the Vajran Hills, and as far east as the Citystate of Ispasia.

Two other routes are worthy of brief mention. The dry canyon of the Dead River, which runs from the Lost Sea almost to Faradun, is popular with certain caravan masters. Ramps at Nankar, Kasmir and the Dracartan Bridge allow wagons to exit the sheer-walled ravine. Lastly, there is the Maruk Road, a northern extension of the ancient Wilderlands Road. Unfortunately, few are interested in traveling to this place, which is believed to be cursed.

Daring travelers should note two interesting options when traveling overland. The duneships of the Dracartans sail the desert sands on red-iron runners, and the schooners and sleds of the Mirin perform a similar feat on ice utilizing runners of adamant.

Water Transport. Two waterways are extensively used for transport by the Talislantans. One of these is the River Shan, which is a convenient arterial for trade within the Quan Empire. The other is the Axis River, which is traversed by Imrian slavers bound to Arim, and Zandir merchants eager to bypass Aaman.

Most Talislantans exhibit a superstitious fear of the open sea — only the Imrians, the Sunra, and the Parthenians willingly sail beyond sight of shore. The Aamanians are strictly limited by their religious beliefs from sailing far from their homeland. Among the few merchant fleets in operation are the coast-hugging ships belonging to the Farad, the Zandir, and the Quan. Preying on the coastal trade routes are Imrian slavers, Mangar Corsairs, and the Rogues of Gao-Din.

Air Travel. The unique technology possessed by the Cymrilians and the Phantasians allows them to operate fleets of windships, capable of levitating and catching the wind in their sails. Passenger flights operate regularly out of Cymril, but the ships are seldom on schedule. The fragile windships are subject to frequent breakdowns, requiring costly repairs. Nor is aerial travel free of danger, for the skies above Talislanta abound with avian predators.

Languages

The language spoken by most Talislantans is the tongue called Talislan, which has two dialects: *Low Talislan* is spoken by commoners, while the ability to speak the more flowery *High Talislan* marks one as a person of elevated status, advanced education, or extreme snobbishness.

In the East, the *Quan* language is the only tongue permitted to be spoken in public. The Quan actually "stole" the language from the Mazdaks, who acquired it from even more ancient origins; it is interesting to note that the Savants of Xanadas employ Quan script to record their observations.

A universal language of hand gestures, known simply as *Sign,* is used by the primitive tribes of Talislanta to communicate with one another. Unusual variants are used by the Monads and by the Black Savants of Nefaratus.

Two dead languages are in common use by certain factions. Western scholars write their manuscripts in the *Phaedran* language and script, valuing tradition above practicality. Similarly, the *Archaean* tongue is employed by Talislantan mages when casting magic or inscribing spells.

The following languages are also employed in certain portions of the continent: Ahazu, the Ancient Tongue (spoken by dragons), Avian (spoken by the Gryphs), Bodorian (a musical tongue), Chanan (spoken by the Witchmen, Manra, Nagra, Batreans, and Sawila), the Elder Tongue (used by the Ariane and the Mirin), the secret language of plants (spoken by the Green Men), Amphibian (spoken by the Mud People and Imrians), Nomadic (spoken by the Djaffir and Dracartans), Northron (tongue of the Ur, Darklings and Stryx), Rajanin, Sarisa (the coded tongue of the Sarista), Sauran, Sea Nomad (used by the folk of Oceanus, the Mangar Corsairs, and the Rogues of Gao-Din), Sylvan (the language of the Whisps), Thaecian (an elegant language preferred by poets and authors), and Xambrian.

Currency

The standard coin of Talislanta is the gold lumen, but other coinage is in circulation: Adamants (rare and valuable Mirin coins), Coppers (from Aaman), Crescents (half-moon golden coins of Zandir), Emperors (minted by the Quan), Pentacles (the golden coins of Cymril), and Pyramids (the red-iron coins of Carantheum). When traveling to a distant land, bring lumens, as they are accepted nearly everywhere.

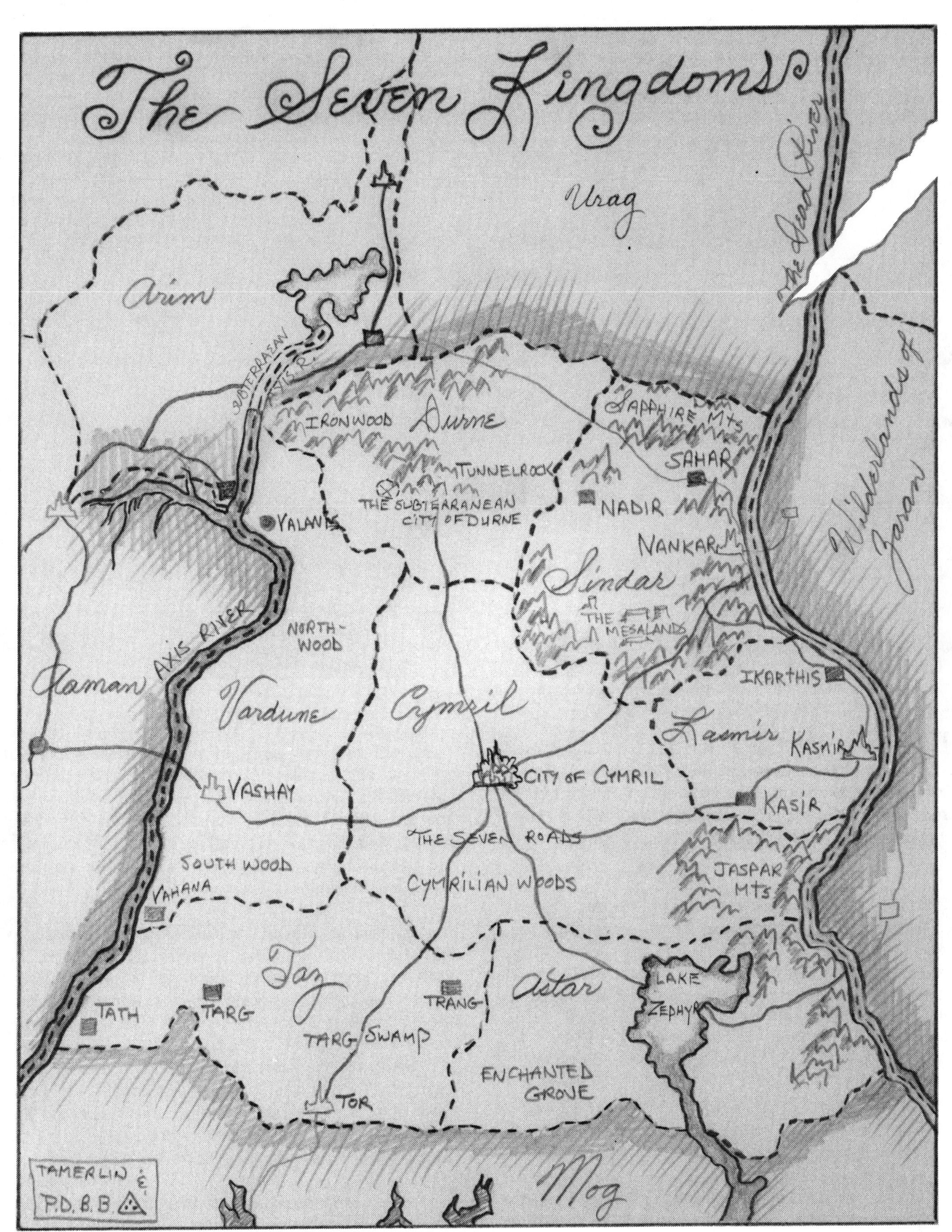

Scale: 1" = 75 miles.

THE SEVEN KINGDOMS

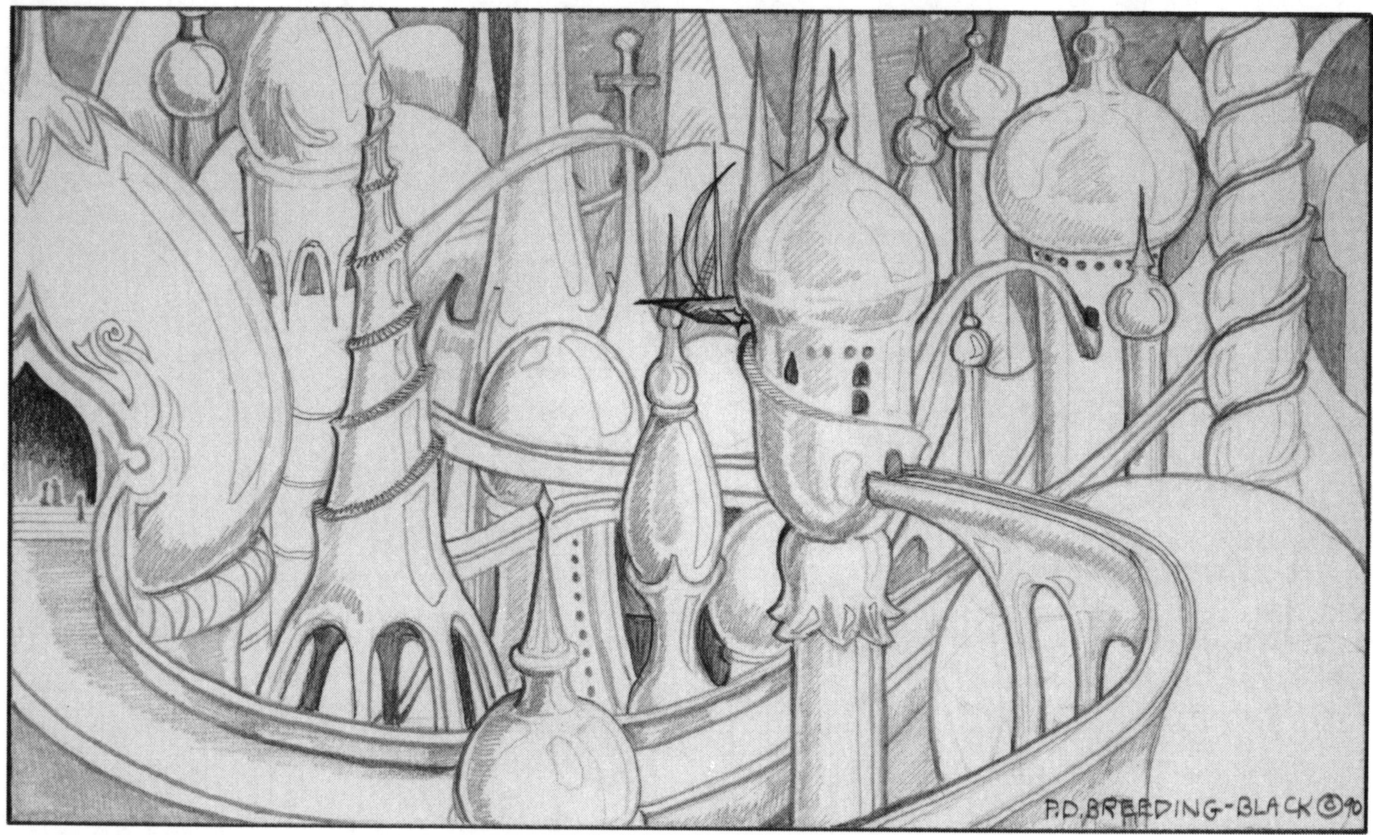

The City of Cymril, capital of the Seven Kingdoms

The Seven Kingdoms may not lie at the geographical center of the continent, but that doesn't stop it from being the heart of civilization on Talislanta. The freedoms enshrined by this commonwealth of semi-autonomous states attract all kinds of people, from curious visitors to eager immigrants.

Established during the New Age by the descendants of various peoples displaced by the Great Disaster, the territories now designated as the Seven Kingdoms were once separate nations, each ruled by its own king and distrustful of the others. It took a nearly fatal threat from outside — the invasion of the Beastmen (at the close of the second century N.A.) — to unite the disparate societies.

Today, the Seven Kingdoms is ruled by the Council of Kings. which is composed of the rulers of the separate states. Each kingdom has its own national color, and retains all the customs and traditions peculiar to its inhabitants. The Seven Roads link the capitals, and are a vital east-west link for the trade caravans of Talislanta.

A superb national army of mercenaries, small but well-trained, guarantees the liberty of the commonwealth. The Grand Army comprises seven regiments and a fleet of windships, plus barge-fort squadrons on the Axis River. A separate organization, known as the Legion of the Borderlands, mans three vital outposts on the fringes of the Wilderlands.

The land ranges from the rocky, desert wastes of Sindar and Kasmir to the dense forests of Astar and Vardune; from the tropical jungles and swamps of Taz to the lightly-wooded open country of Cymril. The Axis River forms the western border, keeping the Aamanians at bay. The waterless Dead River canyon performs the same function in the east, discouraging the raids of bandits and Beastmen. The mountains of southern Urag, and the dense swamps and mountains along the borders with Mog and Jhangara, likewise provide protection on those frontiers.

The seven member-states of this unique confederation are: Astar, Cymril, Durne, Kasmir, Sindar, Taz, and Vardune.

The Kingdom of Cymril

"First among equals" within the Seven Kingdoms, the Kingdom of Cymril is a rich land ruled by the descendants of an ancient race of magicians.

Sweeping hills and light forest dominate much of the Cymrilian countryside, which is largely uninhabited. The greatest part of the population lives in the enchanting City of Cymril, a metropolis of convoluted spires and archways constructed almost entirely of green glass. The city is divided into six districts ("hextants") around a hub of scenic parklands.

Cymril is the continent's leading supplier of magical wares, and of such commodities as amberglass and aquavit. Being at the nexus of the Seven Roads means that caravans from many lands pass through here.

The kingdom is also the center of Talislanta's windship industry. The secrets behind the construction of levitationals and gossamer sails are carefully guarded by the powerful Windship Guild. The Air Men of Cymril man the sky fleets, and have a reputation for adventurous derring-do.

The city is also known for the Lyceum Arcanum, Talislanta's foremost institute of magic. Here the Cymrilian magicians learn their arts, creating wondrous potions, powders and other magical adjuncts.

The Cymrilians

Three different peoples dwell in the kingdom, all descended from the Phandre — a race of wizards and mages exiled long ago from the now-defunct Phaedran Empire (located where Aaman and Zandu now rule).

The Koresians are the dominant sub-race, and are also known as "Cymrilians." Tall and slender, they have pale green skin and hair, with golden eyes and placid features. They have few prejudices regarding fashion — all types of exotic apparel are in vogue, though their mages continue to favor the high-collared cloaks worn by their ancient ancestors.

Once the ruling class among the Phandre, the Tanasians comprise Cymril's other sub-race. They proved disloyal during the Beast Wars, and many were exiled into the woodlands. The few Tanasians who remain in the citystate are regarded with some suspicion, but are respected for their mastery of the more obscure of the arcane arts.

Cymrilian magicians

The third Phandre sub-race left the citystate long ago, protesting against the discriminatory practices of the Wizard King — both the Koresians and Tanasians have skin of pale-green hue, while the Pharesians are of a darker lime-green shade. They are now nomadic peddlers, traveling the continent but regarding the woodlands of Cymril as their home.

Customs

All Cymrilians are enamored of magic in any of its myriad forms. Most citizens own a lesser talisman or two, and there is a brisk trade in minor charms, elixirs and potions. There is always a market for enchanted items and magical tomes in Cymril, particularly those of ancient origin.

Though practicing magicians make up less than one-tenth of the populace, the ruler of Cymril is always a mage. Usually the most capable of Cymril's spell-casters, the Wizard King is elected by popular vote, and serves a term of three years.

Once each year, the city of Cymril hosts the Magical Fair, a colorful two-week spectacle attended by folk from all across Talislanta. The magical competitions are especially fascinating to view (from a safe distance, that is.)

City of Cymril

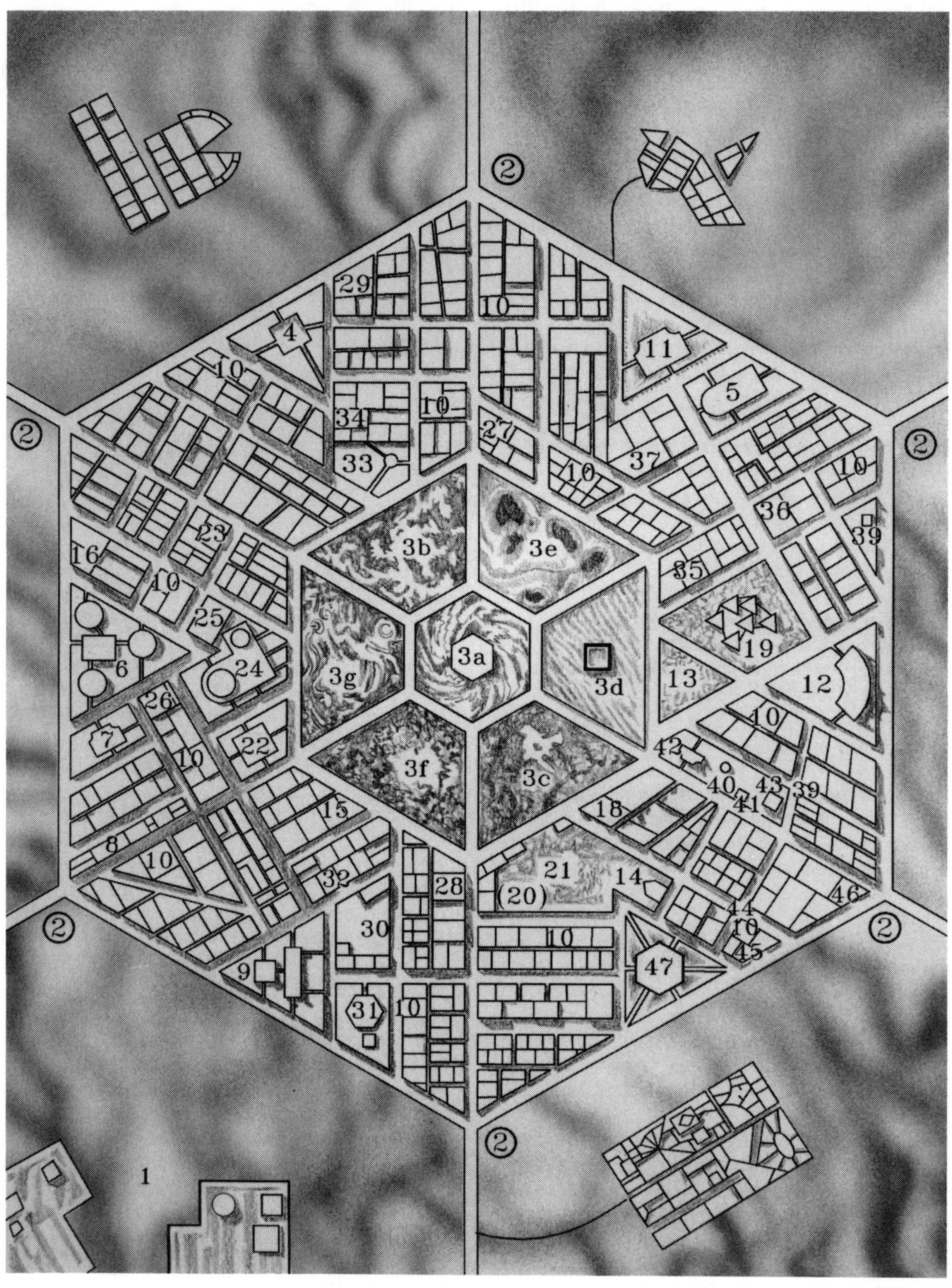

The City of Cymril

Every adventurer worthy of the name visits Cymril at least once in his lifetime. The fabulous city of convoluted spires, geodesic domes and arched promenades is uniquely, uniformly green — chiefly crafted from blocks, slabs and beams of translucent green crystal. Those structures which aren't constructed from crystal are at least lacquered green. The building materials are brought from Cymril's mines in Faradun, on the shores of the Sea of Glass. For reasons which should be self evident, it is illegal to throw stones anywhere within the boundaries of the city proper.

Citizens customarily attire themselves in raiment colored to complement the city's hue: lemon yellow, sea green, lime, canary yellow, aquamarine, saffron, or vermillion.

1. City Outskirts

Surrounding the city are many small farms, vineyards, and country estates. Most of these are owned by Green Ardua, who work the land with exceptional skill. The fruits of their labors are transported by wagon to Cymril, though a small percentage of the crop is sold at roadside stands.

Thrall Warriors mounted on mangonel lizards patrol the roads leading to Cymril. Pharesian peddlers, bandits, troupes of Bodor Musicians, Djaffir merchant caravans, Sarista gypsies, and the occasional lone itinerant wizard may also be encountered along these thoroughfares.

2. Sentinel Stations

Each of these one-story structures houses a contingent of 20 mercenaries (predominantly Thralls) from the city's Legion, armed with greatswords, heavy crossbows, and garde. Mangonel lizards are stabled outside, a provision intended to discourage wandering bandits and predatory woodland beasts.

Patrols from the inner city check in at these stations on a regular basis, keeping the sentinels appraised of security concerns. It is a mistake to underestimate the capabilities of these forces: the Thralls stationed here are all experienced veterans.

3a. Cymril Park

This attractive garden is landscaped with crystalline shrubs, trees and flowers, all fashioned of colored glass. Walking paths paved with green-glass tiles lead to a central commons. Here stands a crystal statue of Pharos, the first Wizard King of Cymril, whose extensive writings on magic are preserved at the Lyceum Arcanum (see below).

3b. Durne Park

Built to resemble an underground cavern, this enclosed area is complete with scenic grottos, and gardens where amber crystals are grown. An amber statue of Sabo Orabio, the Gnomeking who led his people to victory over the Darkling hordes of Urag, stands here. Phosphorescent fungi illuminate the cavern-park, lending a definite Durnean ambience to the surroundings.

3c. Astar Park

A sylvan preserve replete with fields of rainbow-hued wildflowers, copses of willowood, and a pond which is a scaled-down version of Lake Zephyr, the Astar Park is one of the most peaceful sites in the city. In the middle of the lake is an island, upon which stands a statue fashioned of lavender-blue stone and hung with garlands of blossoms. The statue depicts a Muse; possibly Twysk, a remowned maker of gossamer harps in ancient times, though the Muses claim not to recall precisely.

3d. Kasmir Park

Sweeping dunes of yellow-gold sand serve to represent the arid land of Kasmir. Within a windowless stone tower at the center of this area is a gold-plated statue of Abn Kadan, acknowledged as the wealthiest merchant in Kasmir history. At the peak of his power, Abn Kadan is said to have owned four-fifths of the gold in Kasmir. Regrettably, the tower is almost always kept under lock and key — a measure intended to keep thieves from stripping the statue of its gold plating.

3e. Sindar Park

In this unusual setting, built to resemble the wind-worn mesas and rock spires of Sindar, stands a 14-foot basalt statue of Nadir Saluu. An esteemed collector, he is credited as the inventor of the complex game known as Trivarian, the favored pastime of the Sindarans. The Nadir's fabulous collection of ancient artifacts is considered a national treasure of Sindar, and is periodically on display at the nearby Museum of Antiquities.

3f. Taz Park

Overgrown with tangled vines, fronds and dendrons, this park is designed to resemble the wild junglelands of Taz. The landscape is quite authentic, if perhaps a trifle overdone — the inclusion of poisonous serpents, man-eating plants, and other hazards indigenous to Taz, while popular with visiting Thralls, may give less-adventurous tourists cause to consider avoiding this particular attraction. Somewhere in the interior is a lacquered iron statue of Zar, greatest of all the Thrall military heroes, who freed his people from the Imrian conquest.

3g. Vardune Park

These splendid terraced gardens, through which visitors pass on elevated walkways fashioned of woven vines, shelter myriad forms of plant life. In the central garden stands a towering statue made from a single, living viridia plant, which has been tended constantly by Green Ardua for several centuries. The statue depicts Viridian, the great magician who created the viridia hybrid, which is the national plant of Vardune.

4. Consulate

This large two-story structure has quarters and offices for ambassadors from each of the Seven Kingdoms. Separate facilities for visiting dignitaries and their entourages are also available. Sentinels patrol the grounds regularly. The current representatives of each of the Seven Kingdoms are:

- **Astar:** Moonseed (2nd Level), but she threatens to leave in a few weeks
- **Cymril:** Corolian (19th Level), a merchant-mage who has voyaged the continent
- **Durne:** Ebo Aban (22nd Level), a wounded veteran who saved the Gnomeking from a Darkling ambush
- **Kasmir:** Hassan il Dune (17th Level), an aged counselor to the King of Kasmir
- **Sindar:** Nared Motas (19th Level), the famed Peacekeeper and collector of Snipe shells
- **Taz:** Rann (14th Level), one of the rare Thralls who has survived to reach old age
- **Vardune:** Ki-Kya (21st Level), a senior member of the Great Council of Vardune

5. Hall of Records

The offices of Cymril's tax collectors, assessors, and related functionaries are found here, as are all records pertaining to tariffs, trade duties, real estate holdings, registrations to practice magic, and so on.

*Profile: **Avir K'Ya***
Green Ardua Administrator, 9th Level
Head Archivist at the Hall of Records, Avir is very old – his once-green plumage has faded to yellow. He tries to accommodate every request for information, but is often swamped with work. Avir is hard of hearing, so it is advisable to speak loudly when addressing inquiries to him.

6. Court of the Seven Kingdoms

Seven judges (one from each of the Seven Kingdoms) preside over this court, which handles disputes arising between the member nations. Criminal and civil cases of importance are referred from one of the lower courts (numbering 49 in all – seven for each kingdom).

7. College of Law

A university and guildhouse for arbitrators and legislators, legal representatives from across the Seven Kingdoms and beyond are available here for hire at costs of 100 gold lumens per day or more. Sindaran litigators, due to their unique mental faculties, usually command fees of up to twice the standard rate.

*Profile: **Uru Nadar***
Sindaran Litigator,16th Level
Renowned as the most skillful litigator in all of the Seven Kingdoms, Uru's fees are commensurate with his reputation – as high as 1,000 gold lumens per day. Some claim that his obsession with artifacts from lost Khazad is extreme, even for a Sindaran.

8. City Gaol

One of the city's few stone structures, the gaol serves as a place of incarceration for felons, miscreants and other undesirables. Heavily-armed Thralls are employed as guards, with Kasmir Trapsmiths acting as gaolers.

All locks used here are of Kasmir make, each device having between two and eight separate locking mechanisms. Maximum security facilities are available to house spell-casters and members of those races requiring special attention. By Talislantan standards, these facilities are deemed quite tolerable. Still, conditions in the subterranean levels leave something to be desired.

*Profile: **Ibn Asheel***
Kasmir Trapsmith, 7th Level
A shriveled Kasmir barely four feet in height, Ibn Asheel is the head gaoler. He is said to be scrupulously honest, and cannot be bribed. Attached to his belt by a chain is a great key-ring which holds the keys to every cell in the City Gaol.

9. Citadel

A fortified installation with facilities for over a thousand mercenaries (chiefly Thralls and Blue Ardua) as well as a Cymrilian Warrior-Mage troop, the Citadel serves as the barracks, armory and training camp for Cymril's private Legion.

*Profile: **Varn***
Thrall Warrior, 14th Level
As Commander of the Watch, Varn is in charge of coordinating security for the citystate. He is a veteran officer of the Legion of the Eastern Borderlands, and is not one to be trifled with. Varn bears a +3 True Sword, a ritual greatsword that outwardly appears ordinary, but is of great worth to a Thrall.

10. Sentinel Stations

Each of these two-story outposts is manned by a mixed contingent of heavy and light infantry, typically 20 in number, and a pair of Cymrilian Warrior-Mages. Platoons of five sentinels patrol their designated areas in four-hour shifts. If a platoon fails to report on time, alarm gongs sound and additional units respond.

11. Palace of the Wizard King

This is the dwelling place of Rabian, the current Wizard King of Cymril, who lives here with his family and a retinue of advisors. He is guarded day and night by a personal guard of elite Thrall warriors and Cymrilian Warrior-Mages, all attired in ceremonial battle armor. The palace is splendid rather than ostentatious, featuring a large banquet hall, canopied terraces, scalloped balconies, a solarium, a library, and private chambers of varying size and utility.

*Profile: **Rabian***
Cymrilian Magician, 28th Level
Rabian is an aging Cymrilian with a long beard, and emerald-green skin and hair. He is a benevolent ruler, though perhaps a bit addle-brained as a result of excessive indulgence in Phantasian dream essence, a weakness of his.

12. Council of Kings

This is the great hall of the Seven Kings, who gather here once every month (seven weeks, in Talislantan chronology) to rule on issues pertaining to the Seven Kingdoms. Facilities for each of the kings and their entourages are contained in an adjoining structure. At present, the Seven Kings are:

- Astar: Starshine, a male Muse (but his term of office is only seven weeks, or until he grows bored)
- Cymril: The Wizard King, Rabian (see above)
- Durne: The Gnomeking, Anio Orabio, a direct descendant of the famed Sabo Orabio
- Kasmir: The King of Kasmir, Naji al Aran, younger brother of the Patriarch of House Aran
- Sindar: The Nadir Absolute, Ezarud, a proud daughter of the ta Benit clan of Nadir
- Taz: The Warrior King, Marr, a 50-year veteran of the Grand Army
- Vardune: The River King, K'Yan, a Blue Ardua warrior

13. Cymril Bazaar

This open-air market is where merchants from across the continent come to offer their wares. Numerous types of goods are available in the shops and stalls, including seeds, plants and viridian linen from Vardune; weapons and armor from Taz; gossamer and intricate musical instruments from Astar; amber crystals and precious stones from Durne; locks, fetters, and trap mechanisms from Kasmir; alchemicals and skoryx from Sindar; magical paraphernalia and aquavit from Cymril; and much more. Travelers are advised to keep an eye out for unscrupulous charlatans, who attempt at every given opportunity to foist inefficacious remedies and tonics upon gullible wayfarers. Djaffir merchants, selling beasts of various sorts, usually occupy the southern sector of the bazaar.

Profile: *Darual the Morphosite*
Cymrilian Magician, 11th Level
An odd and eccentric individual, Darual is known for his habit of magically altering his manner of dress, skin coloration, and gender, as the mood suits him (hence the name, Darual the Morphosite). He is a seller of exotic potions and charms, and operates from a small booth festooned with gaudily-colored silks and baubles. As strange as he may seem, Darual is quite friendly, and is a well-known figure both here and at the Magical Fair.

14. The Emerald Pentacle

An unusual five-sided structure built of translucent green crystal, furnished with tables and chairs of polished lemon-yellow glass, the Emerald Pentacle is an inn and tavern catering primarily to travelers and magicians. Curtained booths are available for those seeking privacy; a spacious common room and outdoor terrace suit the needs of individuals inclined to more sociable behavior. The accommodations are first-rate in all respects, and the prices reasonable. House specialties include steamed rock urchin in a sauce of leeks and truffles, Zandir wine, and aquavit of the first order.

Profile: *Atherian*
Cymrilian Magician, 20th Level (retired)
Atherian is the proprietor of the Emerald Pentacle. He was once a magician of some note, until an ill-advised wager with a powerful Shaitan purportedly impelled him to change professions. He wears a charm said to ward devils, hidden somewhere on his person, and reportedly owns an interesting collection of magical paraphernalia.

15. The Double-Edged Sword

This inn and tavern caters to mercenaries and men-at-arms, especially Thralls. Hearty food and Tazian fire-ale served in red-iron mugs are the house specialities. Sparsely furnished rooms and ample stable facilities are available at standard rates. A Zandir swordsman named Qefanque tends bar, and an immense Monad named Ord delivers food and drink to the patrons. Tazian combat (with garde) and other contests of a martial nature are held here on a nightly basis. All weapons except garde must be checked at the door – a stipulation suggestive of the nature of the Double-Edged Sword's typical clientele.

Profile: *Gann*
Thrall Warrior, 17th Level (retired)
A disabled Thrall Warrior, Gann is the owner of the Double-Edged Sword. He is a veteran of many years' service in the Eastern Borderlands. Gann walks with a limp, using an old broadsword as a cane. He refuses to discuss how he came by the injury, but those who know say it had nothing to do with his military service. Embittered by his experiences, the old warrior does little but sit and drink.

16. The River Inn

Catering exclusively to Blue and Green Ardua, this inn is furnished with tables, lounges, hammocks, and elevated walkways fashioned of woven vines. The fare (seeds and pods, fermented vinesap, and giant waterbugs broiled in a savory swamp-sauce) and accommodations (tiered tree-dwellings situated behind the tavern) are likely to hold little appeal to non-Ardua. A stream flowing through the common room helps sustain the viridia-plant decor and adds a touch of authentic Vardune atmosphere. Prices are one-fourth higher than standard rates.

Profile: *Cha-Chik*
Green Ardua Horticulturist, 9th Level
The proprietor of the River Inn grows hybrid plants as a hobby, and has an extensive knowledge of Talislantan flora. She is aided by an enchanted and fully mobile Bombo Tree.

17. Sindar Pavilion

An inn and tavern catering mainly to Sindarans, though also frequented by scholars, antiquarians, and curio dealers, the decor here is in the Sindaran style: open-walled, with diaphanous curtains dyed in oranges and deep browns, and furnishings of smoothly polished hardwood or stone. In the central common room Sindarans play Trivarian, a game incomprehensible to single-brained beings. Wagering is often brisk, the players being stimulated by rainbow-hued skoryx served in spheres of frosted crystal.

A collection of one sort or another is usually on display (the demented Sadaan's compilation of skulls and necromantic regalia always draws a sizable crowd). Aspiring thieves would do well to consider other prey – the Sindarans ward their money satchels with clever devices, and are exceptionally vigilant with regard to their treasured collections. A further concern is Sadaan, who is always in the market for skulls, bones, and other morbid collectibles. The inn's prices are average.

Profile: *Kahutan*
Sindaran Collector, 15th Level
The owner of the Sindaran Pavilion is known for his collection of antique jewelry, much of which dates back to the Forgotten Age. The Sindaran often appears in public ornamented with priceless rings and bracelets, seemingly oblivious to his danger. Kahutan is also a Trivarian player of some note (he is a Nadir of the Fourteenth Degree). He considers himself a guardian of sorts for a Sindra named Sadaan, who collects necromantic adjuncts.

18. Astar Gardens
This nympharium and pleasuredrome was built to resemble the sylvan glades and scenic woodland vistas of Astar. An admittance fee of 100 gold lumens is charged at the entrance. Customers are allowed to partake of succulent fruits and vials of blossom nectar, engage in dalliances or romantic confluxes, and experience the myriad raptures of Muse culture, as they desire. Entertainment is provided by male and female Muses, who use their telempathic powers to project panoramas of color and sound for the benefit of their clientele (and according to their whims).

Profile: *Amarylis*
Muse Esthesian, 18th Level
This beautiful, nymph-like creature with lavender-blue skin and hair is both amorous and exotic, but like all Muses seems somewhat distant and aloof to outsiders. Amarylis speaks fluent Low Talislan, and loves to mimic the voices and accents of others. She is watched over by her two small friends, Mig and Scag, a mated pair of Wood Whisps who constantly cause trouble in the market by stealing small fruits and sips of nectar.

19. The Caravansary
A sprawling tent-complex serving as an inn and tavern, the Caravansary caters to travelers from the desert kingdoms of Djaffa, Carantheum and Kasmir. The atmosphere is casual – customers recline on silken cushions, and are attended to by veiled serving girls bearing trays of honeyed dates, skewers of roasted meat, and palm wine. Silver cucurbits of steaming-hot mochan, a dark and stimulating beverage popular throughout the Desert Kingdoms, are imported directly from Djaffa after each year's harvest.

The tents contain three large common rooms, numerous small suites, and a half dozen baths. Outside are extensive facilities for the stabling of beasts, with additional areas for wagons and drays. Farad merchants enter the Caravansary at their own risk. Prices are slightly above average.

Profile: *Nabu Al Abas*
Dracartan Navigator, 26th Level (retired)
This retired land-barge captain now acts as proprietor of the Caravansary. In his day, he sailed the desert sands of Djaffa and Carantheum, even skirting the borders of the Quan Empire. Like most Dracartans, he is somewhat sedate. Even so, Nabu-al is always eager to hear any news concerning Rajan Assassins or renegade spiritforms, his two private terrors.

20. Subterranean Market
In this underground market-place, run by the Kingdom of Durne, Gnomekin merchants sell mushrooms and fungi, fresh rock urchins, precious stones, low-grade magical crystals, and other commodities. Wagons head to and from the Subterranean City of Durne through the Underground Highway, which has a surface entrance here. Gnomekin fare – roots, koriana tubers, dried Zog and Boro fish, and pungent Whitecap Mushroom ale – is available in the grotto tavern, though moss-lined nooks serve as the only available style of accommodation. Prices are below average in most cases.

Profile: *Ibo Azo*
Gnomekin Crystalomancer, 12th Level
As coordinator of the Subterranean Market, Ibo Azo is charged by the Gnomeking with setting fair prices for all Gnomekin exports. He drives a hard bargain. Because of his duties, Ibo has forced himself to become literate – a rare achievement for a Gnomekin. The ability to read has opened up the world of traditional magic to his study, and he has already mastered several non-crystalomantic spells. Ibo Azo is currently working to construct Talislanta's first crystalline automaton.

21. Site of the Magical Fair
Situated directly above the Subterranean Market, this area serves as a public park during all but two weeks out of the year, when Cymril's famous Magical Fair is held here. The Fair offers an incredible variety of attractions: pageants, exhibitions of magical virtuosity, windship races, and many other challenges, oddities and amusements. Especially popular are the numerous small booths and stalls, which offer for sale all manner of magical and alchemical appurtenances – potions, powders, phylacteries, philtres, medicants, tonics, dusts, and exotic fragrances. Small magical boats sail in the moat which surrounds the grounds, and the waters are stocked with colorful fish and mollusks. The Fair is attended by folk from all across the continent, and is an event of paramount importance to the merchants of Cymril.

Profile: *Celene*
Cymrilian Enchantress, 12th Level
Known for her skillful illusions, subtle charms and placid demeanor, the Enchantress Celene serves as the Director of the Magical Fair, responsible for the coordination of all events and attractions. Permits for booths may be obtained from her clerks at a cost of 100 gold lumens per day, subject to Celene's final approval. Rumors hint at a romantic liason between the enchantress and the Wizard King.

22. Museum of Antiquities

A monolithic structure over four centuries old, the Museum of Antiquities contains rare artifacts, many of which date back to the Forgotten Age. Included are exhibits on the ancient civilizations of Elande, Pompados, Sharna, Phandril, Xambria, and others. There are rumors that a collection of Quaranian artifacts is kept behind formidable magical wards and locks. Of special interest to scholars and antiquarians is an exhibit featuring relics of unknown origin and usage.

Profile: *Modan*
Sindaran Collector, 27th Level
An aged Sindaran serves as Curator of the Museum of Antiquities. He is sometimes available to appraise newly-unearthed artifacts, and may be convinced to arrange financing for archaeological expeditions organized by qualified individuals. Initial fears that the Sindaran curator would be unable to resist "borrowing" from the Museum to improve his personal collection of artifacts pertaining to the Labyrinths of Sharna seem to have been foolish.

23. The Arcanum Society

This is a private club open only to members of the Arcanum Society, who include many of the instructors at the Lyceum Arcanum, as well as other scholars of the arcane arts, and a number of prominent wizards and archimages of various races and nationalities. Admission to the Society (as a member or guest) is by invitation only. The club is said to maintain an excellent library of magical and alchemical writings, plus a collection of rare and potent magical artifacts. The structure is warded against thieves and intruders to such an extent that mere proximity to the building can be dangerous. The Society also sponsors an annual awards ceremony that is the talk of the Seven Kingdoms.

Profile: *Azradamus*
Cymrilian Archimage, 43rd Level
Azradamus, the Chief Administrator of the Lyceum Arcanum, also serves as head of the Arcanum Society. Over 200 years old, his powers may finally be on the wane, yet he remains a magician of great personal force. Azradamus interviews all prospective members, and testily insists that only Phaedran (the dead language of a fallen empire) should be spoken within the Society's halls.

24. The Lyceum Arcanum

This labyrinthine structure houses what is perhaps Talislanta's foremost institute for the study of magic and alchemy (the Academy of Thaumaturgy in Carantheum is also highly rated, but its curriculum is less varied). Courses are available at Apprentice, Initiate, Adept and Master levels, with classes offered in such esoteric fields as magical scripts, alchemical procedures (basic and advanced), rituals of summoning, metaphysical doctrines, the concoction of magical mixtures, interdimensional travel, the creation of homonculi, and many more.

Tuition is 1,000 gold lumens per septemester (seven weeks), or 100 gold lumens for Cymrilian citizens. Application and placement exams are required prior to acceptance to the Lyceum. Failure to meet accepted standards is considered cause for suspension from advanced courses or, at the dean's option, expulsion from the school. The Lyceum faculty presently consists of the following individuals:

Azradamus
Cymrilian Archimage, 46th Level
Chief Administrator, head of the Board of Directors, Professor Emeritus of Arcane Lore and Metaphysical Doctrines

Talmaj the Green
Cymrilian Magician, 30th Level
Assistant Director, Lyceum Treasurer, member of the Board of Directors, Professor of Occult Sciences and Extra-Dimensional Studies

Nymandre
Tanasian Wizard, 35th Level
Dean of Adepts, member of the Board of Directors, Professor of Extra-Dimensional Studies

Ebonarde
Tanasian Wizard, 33rd Level
Dean of Initiates, member of the Board of Directors, Professor of Metaphysics

Pandaran
Cymrilian Magician, 32nd Level
Dean of Apprentices, member of the Board of Directors, head of the Alchemy Department, Professor of Alchemy and Mysticism

Abascar
Dracartan Thaumaturge, 36th Level
Head of the Thaumaturgy Department

Alb of Elwan
Aamanian Archimage (expatriate), 34th Level
Associate Professor of Theosophy and Ethics

Califax
Cymrilian Cryptomancer, 18th Level
Associate Professor of Cryptomancy and Linguistics

Cirelle
Thaecian Enchantress, 30th Level
Associate Professor of Enchantment

Merdigan the Miraculous
Zandir Wizard, 15th Level
Associate Professor of Illusions and Conjuration

Naryx of the Gloved Hand
Tanasian Necromancer, 23rd Level
Associate Professor of Primitive Magic and Necromantic Studies

Nostros
Pharesian Sage, 32nd Level
Professor of Arcane Lore and Talislantan Culture

Omir of Kasir
Kasmir Wizard, 25th Level
Associate Professor of Constructs, Security Advisor to the Lyceum

Pharian
Cymrilian Magician, 21st Level
Director of the Apprentice and Initiate Undergraduate Programs, Professor of Magical Academe

Qual the Phantasian
Phantasian Astromancer, 21st Level
Associate Professor of Astromancy

Skree Cha K'Ya
Green Ardua Botanomancer, 24th Level
Associate Professor of Botanomancy

Torann
Sindaran Alchemist, 26th Level
Archivist Emeritus, Associate Professor of Alchemy and Antiquarian Lore

Zariste
Dhuna Warlock, 17th Level
Associate Professor of Magic and Witchcraft

25. The Library at Cymril

This venerable institution is an adjunct of the Lyceum Arcanum. The library contains over 20,000 tablets, scrolls and volumes, many quite rare or even unique. The sections on magic, alchemy, ancient history, geography, and languages are especially well-regarded. It is not permissible to borrow research materials except by special arrangement with the Lyceum Arcanum.

Profile: **Sophistes**
Callidian Cryptomancer, 24th Level
The Head Archivist at the Library at Cymril is not particularly sociable, but he is efficient and highly competent despite his handicap – his tongue was removed by a vengeful Gnorl Rhadomancer as punishment for revealing a stolen secret. The Cryptomancer communicates with patrons by scribbling with glitterchalk on a slate he wears slung around his neck. Sophistes keeps a keen eye on all who enter the Library, and is especially alert for thieves and vandals – it is said that he keeps a captive Shaitan in a brass bottle hidden beneath the folds of his cloak.

26. Cymril Magical Supply

Like the library, this establishment is an adjunct of the Lyceum Arcanum. All sorts of magical and alchemical supplies and paraphernalia are available here, including alchemical apparatus, powdered plants and animals, crushed minerals, crystal containers of various shapes and sizes, magical inks and pigments, several varieties of parchment, and a host of related materials. The more common types of magical and alchemical mixtures, many concocted by students at the Lyceum, can also be obtained here. This shop buys raw ingredients and magical apparatus only from licensed dealers – ever since the scandal concerning tainted Euphorica (a mood enhancer and intoxicant) and the plague of inebriated Harbinger Imps two years ago. Prices for goods tend to be rather high due to the large local demand.

Profile: **Dabn Nada**
Kasmir Merchant, 5th Level
Dabn Nada runs this establishment for the Lyceum. She receives a small percentage on everything that is sold here, and has no patience for haggling, since it cuts into her commissions. Dabn is often the target of pranks and mischiefs from the Lyceum's apprentices – Mung berries in her mochan, cantrips that cause her ledgers to explode with silver-sparkle when opened, and on one occasion, a baby draconid that was ensorceled into following her wherever she went. Her patience is growing thin.

27. The Alchemist's Wares

This small establishment offers powders, potions and mixtures of various sorts at close to average rates. The proprietors purchase raw materials from independent sellers, provided the quality of such wares is up to their standards. Unknown mixtures are analyzed at a cost of ten gold lumens. This is a very reputable establishment, known for fair prices, honest dealing, and quality merchandise. It is also the informal gathering place for the Sindaran alchemists who dwell in Cymril.

Profile: **Zured**
Sindaran Alchemist, 15th Level
Zured is one of three brothers, the other two being Zohrn and Zagrib. All are proficient alchemists, and are respected by the diverse members of Cymril's magical and alchemical communities for their efforts to expose the practitioners of dark magic.

28. The Magic Sigil

One of the most colorful shops in the city, the Magic Sigil is owned by a Rahastran wizard named Merdan. The shelves lining the walls of this shop are laden with all manner of strange objects: books, phials, curios, scrolls, statuary, sarcophagi, urns, old clothing, jars filled with various anatomical parts preserved in amber-colored fluids, crystals, maps, chests, and a thousand other oddities. Merdan makes no effort to catalogue his wares, nor does he care to spend much time bargaining with customers. Pay the asking price, and the object is yours: no guarantees or refunds. Merdan is equally renowned as a buyer – no questions asked, take his offer or leave it.

Profile: **Merdan**
Rahastran Wizard, 27th Level
Known for his stories, some of which verge upon the fantastic, Merdan claims to be no less than 411 years old, the seventh son of the seventh son of the mad wizard Rodinn. His cadaverous appearance and archaic style of dress would seem to lend credence to the first claim. He owns a Zodar deck but refuses to use it, claiming that the cards have turned on him. Merdan loves to wager on Trivarian, and has vowed to learn how to play it someday.

29. The Sanctum

Ostensibly a shop dealing in rare books and magical writings, the Sanctum bears a shadowy reputation as an establishment owned, operated, and frequented by black magicians. It is widely believed that contraband substances and stolen goods are bought and sold here.

*Profile: **Nocturnus***
Farad Necromancer, 17th Level
An individual of dark and saturnine moods, not prone to idle chatter, Nocturnus is the topic of much speculation among his fellow shopkeepers. Some claim that he is a dealer in the narcotic K'tallah, an agent of the sinister Rajans, or that he has secret connections with the Witchmen of Chana. Few dare to make such claims in his presence, however. The Wizard King's investigators have charged the Farad on several occasions with the felonious importation of forbidden substances, but have never been able to prove their case in court. Nocturnus is reputed to own an ancient Sardonicus named Quaz, whom he reportedly keeps in a sealed iron vault.

30. The Four Winds Travel & Supply Co.

This run-down complex of buildings is owned by two partners, a Cymrilian magician and a Phantasian dream merchant. One structure houses facilities for the construction and maintenance of windships; another is a warehouse for the storage of various ship's components. There are several docks, including one reserved for windships coming in from the mines on the Sea of Glass. An old watchtower, dating back to the time of the Beast Wars, houses a small, dingy office. The Four Winds Travel and Supply Company offers the following services:

• Windship Leasing	2,000-12,000 gold lumens per month
• Docking	50 gold lumens per week
• Install levitationals	1,000+ gold lumens
• Windship Repair	10-40 gold lumens per day
• Passage to –	
Dracarta	5,100 gold lumens
Hadj	3,400 gold lumens
The Sea of Glass	3,500 gold lumens
Thaecia	4,300 gold lumens
Zanth	2,400 gold lumens

Ships depart monthly, though schedules tend to be erratic at best. Accommodations vary in quality; when available, first-class fares are generally double the standard rate. Passage to other locales must be arranged privately – the standard rate is 10 gold lumens per mile, plus a departure fee and retainer of at least 500 gold lumens.

*Profile: **Corolian***
Phantasian Dream Merchant, 9th Level (retired)
A middle-aged Phantasian with a scruff of white hair, spindly legs, and a bit of a paunch, Corolian got into the windship business several years ago. Since her Cymrilian partner was reported missing following a crash, she has been somewhat depressed and has taken to drink.

31. Cymril Glass Co.

Situated adjacent to the Four Winds Travel and Supply Company, this facility stores, cuts, polishes, and ships green crystal mined and imported from the Sea of Glass. The Glass Workers' guildhall is located on the premises, and includes an interesting exhibit of items found entombed within cut blocks of glass – presumably trapped since the formation of the Sea of Glass. Mining ships arrive and depart monthly, off-loading and taking on cargo at the Four Winds' docks. The owners are reluctant to hire mercenaries to protect their ships, saying that they'd rather lose a cargo than be bled white by over-priced warriors.

*Profile: **Malnar***
Cymrilian Artisan, 4th Level
The owner of the Cymril Glass Company, which he inherited from his father, Malnar is in his forties, heavy-set, with a gruff temperament. He employs a work force of 40 Cymrilian glassworkers, 10 Monad servitors, and two dozen experienced Cymrilian Air Men to crew his two large cargo-carrying windships. His quarters are decorated with green-glass statuettes, all depicting the same sword-wielding female warrior – Malnar claims to have sculpted the figures himself. If asked, he says the woman is only imaginary, a figment from recurring dreams the Cymrilian has experienced since childhood.

32. The Four Winds Tavern

This tavern and inn caters primarily to Cymrilian Windpilots and Air Men, though shipcrafters and glassworkers sometimes come here as well. Not surprisingly, their talk is largely of windships, atmospheric conditions, and goings-on in foreign lands. The establishment offers good food and drink at nominal prices, overnight accommodations of adequate quality, and private lounges where individuals with a surfeit of wealth can enjoy a phial of Phantasian dream essence in repose. It is sometimes possible to obtain the services of a qualified windpilot or levitational engineer by inquiring on the premises.

*Profile: **Arcturian***
Phantasian Astromancer, 7th Level
The proprietor of the Four Winds Tavern is an Astromancer of some renown in Western Talislanta – at one time, he served as an advisor to the Sultan of Zandu, and the Hierophant of Aaman is said to have put a price on his head. Arcturian has traveled across the length and breadth of the continent, and loves to regale customers with tales of his travels, such as the time he smuggled a chest of gold out of the Khadun's Tower in Rajanistan, or the night he spent with an alluring Dhuna witch as a covert witness to the Rites of Zar. Though somewhat past his prime, he remains an avid ladies' man.

33. Artisans' District

Here are found numerous small shops, featuring gemsmiths, ambersmiths, metalsmiths, weaponers, tanners, glassblowers, makers of green dyes, jewelers, furniture builders, potters, weavers, and so forth. The wares are reasonably priced, and the merchandise is of good quality.

*Profile: **Melisanthe***
Sawila Artificer, 16th Level
Just one of the many artists who work in this part of the city, Melisanthe is a weaver of gossamer tapestries – delicate creations which often sell for over 1,000 gold lumens apiece. Her works are said to have an unusual charm, and children are especially enraptured by the scenes she weaves. Young and attractive, she has many suitors, including the Zandir painter Rochalle, the Cymrilian sculptor Quast, and Kadath the Tanasian (who constantly sends Bodor Musicians to serenade her).

34. Seraglio's

An establishment dealing in exotic costumes of all types and origins, Seraglio's is owned by a Zandir clothier of the same name. Elaborate and fanciful costumes are for sale or rental here, and custom-made apparel is available by arrangement. Prices are high, but the quality of Seraglio's work is unmatched in the Seven Kingdoms.

*Profile: **Seraglio***
Zandir Artificer (clothier), 18th Level
A foppish Zandir, Seraglio is about 40 years old and a bit out of shape. He dresses in the most extravagant costumes, and affects a somewhat snobbish attitude. Seraglio is always in step with the latest fashions, no matter how outrageous. He has no idea that among the relics in his shop are several articles of clothing with dire sorcerous properties, and the Zandir would be shocked to the core if he were aware of the actions he takes nightly in his sleep.

35. The Key and Lock

This establishment specializes in the design, repair, installation, removal, and maintenance of intricate trapmechanisms. Also available here: keys made to order (10 gold lumens), custom locks (20 gold lumens and up), a lockopening service (25 gold lumens on site, 100+ if travel is required), plus such unusual items as shackles and cages. Prices are exorbitant, even for goods of such high quality.

*Profile: **Azin al Din***
Kasmir Wizard, 22nd Level
The accomplished wizard and trapsmith is much in demand among the wealthier magicians of Cymril, for whom he provides such security measures as are required to safeguard their homes and possessions. Azin al Din is said to hoard a veritable fortune in gold and gemstones, supposedly in a vault hidden in the basement of his tower-shop. His only child, Ibda al Din, has the talents of her father but not his self-control – only by large, well-placed bribes has the Trapsmith kept her from serving a sentence in the glass mines of the Sea of Glass.

36. Wilderlands Outfitter

This immense warehouse and stable complex offers almost anything which an aspiring traveler or caravan-master could desire: trained beasts of many types, wagons, drays, rope, tents, weaponry, armor, clothing, and even small punts and skiffs. Prices are within reason; quality is good and sometimes excellent.

*Profile: **Muharabi***
Djaffir Merchant, 16th Level
Muharabi abandoned the nomadic lifestyle of his people and settled in Cymril some years ago. He is regarded as a crafty businessman, fair but firm in all his dealings. Muharabi continues to be on good terms with his tribesmen, who supply him with the finest quality of merchandise. He is said to keep a harem of no less than eleven wives, all of different nations and exotic customs.

37. Talislantan Imports

This subsidiary of the Wilderlands Outfitter (see above) deals in a wide variety of goods imported from across the continent. Many types of commodities may be available at any given time, depending upon supply and demand, and might include: furnishings, fabrics, exotic hardwoods, spices, scintilla, amber, gourmet delicacies, liquors, and curios of various sorts. Yitek nomads come here to sell items unearthed from the numerous ruins which litter the Wilderlands of Zaran. Prices are high (at least double standard rates), and quality varies considerably.

*Profile: **Wanibi***
Yitek Spiritsinger, 11th Level
The chief wife of Muharabi, who owns the Wilderlands Outfitter, Wanibi serves as both the head of his household and the mistress of his harem, as well as the proprietress of Talislantan Imports. The other wives are said to fear her.

38. Tower of Coins

A windowless stone structure resembling a small fortress serves as the office of the Kasmir money-lender Abn Qua. Here one can exchange foreign currencies (for a 10% surcharge), deposit money or valuables for safekeeping (5% fee per month), or apply for a loan (30% minimum interest).

*Profile: **Abn Qua***
Kasmir Auditor, 10th Level
This Kasmir is fair in his dealings, but he has little patience for those who do not make good on their loans. Abn Qua is suspected of having hired the services of Arimite Revenants and Jaka Manhunters to persuade debtors to pay up promptly and in full.

39. Technomancer

This stall is run by a family of Technomancers which designs, repairs, and maintains all sorts of mechanisms, devices and conveyances. The quality of workmanship is superior; fees begin at 10 gold lumens per hour, plus materials.

*Profile: **Kwadinn***
Yassan Technomancer, 15th Level
Kwadinn leaves the business in the hands of his spouse, spending most of his time ruling Cymril's small Tek (clan) of Yassan Technomancers. Hard-working and industrious, he has gained favor with the Wizard King, whom he hopes to persuade to grant lands for the settlement of his Displaced race. All five of Kwadinn's daughters work for him and bear his name.

40. Temple of the Ten Thousand
Located opposite the Temple of Aa, this is not actually a temple, but a lively tavern and brothel frequented by traveling Paradoxists (chiefly from Zandu). Wine and spicy Zandir dishes are available at fair prices. Entertainment is provided by Bodor musicians, Thiasian dancers, and Zandir Charlatans.

Profile: *Xanique*
Zandir Courtesan, 11th Level
An aging courtesan manages this colorful tavern and brothel. Once lovely beyond compare, Xanique's fading beauty is now necessarily enhanced by the use of magic. She believes in living for the here and now, and is a great favorite of the many folk who patronize the Temple of the Ten Thousand. Few realize she was once the pampered companion of a now-deceased Exarch of Arim, nor that she knows secrets of the hidden passages of the palace in Ahrazahd.

41. Temple of Aa
An edifice dedicated to Aa the Omniscient, the stern patron deity of Aaman, this structure is frequented mainly by members of the Orthodoxist cult on pilgrimages to the East. Aa has few followers in the Seven Kingdoms.

Profile: *Aalm*
Aamanian Archimage, 15th Level
A stern-faced Aamanian of middle years, Aalm's assignment to Cymril brings him no joy – it is his belief that he is surrounded by infidels, and that Cymril is a city of sin. Still, he obeys the dictates of the Hierophant unfailingly and without question. Aalm is served by an Aamanian Warrior-Priest named Aaslan (13th Level), who bears a shadowy reputation amongst the local citizenry as a witch hunter.

42. Temple of the Creator
The beneficent deity known as the Creator has a wide and varied following, including many Cymrilians, Ardua and Sindarans. Services are held only twice per year, on special holy days.

Profile: *Bahal*
Cymrilian Priest, 12th Level
Tall, reserved, and introspective, aside from his priestly duties Bahal is an avid scholar of metaphysics, and owns a considerable collection of manuscripts on the subject.

43. Temple of Terra
This underground temple is dedicated to the Gnomekin's patron deity, Terra the Earth Mother.

Profile: *Abo Surabia*
Gnomekin Priestess, 10th Level
The High Priestess of the Temple of Terra is compassionate to the needs of all beings, and never turns away a person in need, regardless of the individual's religious beliefs.

44. The Living Tapestry
The most intricate and colorful tattoos may be obtained here at a cost of approximately 5 gold lumens per square inch.

Profile: *Dran*
Thrall Warrior, 16th Level
This scarred, one-eyed Thrall specializes in the art of tattooing. He can reproduce any design, and is an expert in the tattoo art of the Thrall race. At a glance, Dran can decipher the meaning and import of any Thrall tattoo. Though somewhat infirm, the old soldier can still wield a sword or club at need – as many a drunken and unruly Air Man has learned to his dismay.

45. Hireswords Exchange
The owners of this establishment act as agents for mercenaries and others for hire, arranging to lease them to interested parties on a temporary basis. Available in their current portfolio are Arimite knife-fighters (100 gold lumens per week), Za mercenaries (75 per week), Jhangaran scouts (50 per week), Saurud and Ahazu bodyguards (1,000 per month; six-month minimum), Vajra engineers (300 per week), Sunra mariners (200 per week), and such unusual hirelings as Green Men symbiotes (250 per month), Mandalan savants (500 per month), and Batrean concubines (1,200 per week, 200 per night). Mercenaries and tradesmen of all sorts visit here regularly, looking for work. Privately, there are those who claim that the proprietors also sell slave contracts, a practice forbidden throughout the Seven Kingdoms.

Profile: *Matheus*
Farad Procurer, 11th Level
This tall and imposing figure serves as the chief administrator of the Hireswords Exchange. Matheus is impatient and demanding – individuals who fail to meet his expectations are summarily dismissed. He is neither well-liked nor greatly trusted by those in his employ. This establishment is believed to be owned by Mendar, the Monopolist of Sard Island and one of the wealthiest of all the Farad.

46. Cymril Mausoleum
A gigantic edifice of dark-green crystal, the mausoleum is the final resting place of many Cymrilians. As was the fashion among their Phandre ancestors, the Cymrilians inter their dead in glass. Green crystal is the least expensive and most popular material (2,000 gold lumens per sarcophagus, the lighter and more translucent shades costing quite a bit more), while amberglass is favored only by the very wealthy (20,000 gold lumens). Encased in solid crystal, the departed are perfectly preserved, and may be viewed by untold future generations of admirers and descendants.

Profile: *Dismar*
Cymrilian Mortician, 13th Level
A gaunt man with pale-green skin and ice-cold hands, Dismar serves as the mausoleum's chief mortician. When extending his sympathies to the bereaved, he wears a mournful expression and attires himself in sombre black garments. When not on duty, Dismar can be found at the Temple of the Ten Thousand, pouring back glasses of green wine and ogling the young courtesans.

The Kingdom of Astar

Astar is a land of sylvan glades, lakes and streams, interspersed with fields of bright meadow blossoms. Here dwell the last of an ancient and enchanting race of beings known as the Muses.

The Muses

Nymph-like creatures believed to be of magical origin, the Muses are the most beautiful of the man-like races. Their bodies are slender and lithe, their features delicate and exquisitely fashioned. They dress in translucent gowns, shaded in hues complementing the colors of their skin, hair and butterfly-like wings: pastel blue, turquoise, violet and rose, to name just a few.

Customs

The Muses of Astar are by nature flighty and irresponsible. Most seem content to lay about, dreaming secret dreams, sipping the nectar of flowers, or gazing at butterflies, birds, and Muses of the opposite sex.

In actuality, Muses are natural telempaths, able to communicate by means of thoughts and images. All Muses possess this unusual ability, the range and scope of which increase with practice. They can sense the strong emotions of others, broadcast and receive thoughts, project mental images, sense the presence of living beings, and even influence others' emotions. As a consequence of their ability to mind speak, Muses have come to regard common speech as rude and unaesthetic.

The Muses live in small villages, seldom larger than a half dozen elaborately-woven huts, scattered throughout the length and breadth of their Enchanted Grove. They possess a natural talent for all artistic pursuits, but create only when struck by inspiration. Though some few of a curious bent become adventurers, most Muses are quite content to spend their entire lives in Astar.

They don't seem to have a government, at least not in the sense that other societies do — the Muses draw straws once each month to determine who represents their nation at the Council of Kings in Cymril. The holder of the short straw is crowned king or queen, as the situation dictates. The national color of Astar is azure, probably for no good reason, but possibly in honor of nearby Lake Zephyr.

The Whisps

The other, sometimes forgotten residents of Astar are the Wood Whisps. Diminutive creatures of elemental power, they dwell with the Muses in the En-

Muse enchantress and Wood Whisp guardian

chanted Grove. Their magical powers, shrewd natural cunning, and ability to fly keep them safe from harm. They know all the secrets of the woods in which they live, but seldom reveal their wisdom to outsiders.

Mischievous and tormentive to others, the Whisps actually serve as friends and guardians to the much larger Muses — their "Big Friends." Each Muse commune is associated with a Whisp clan, and whenever a Muse leaves the safety of Astar to venture into the world, one or more Whisps accompany him.

Lake Zephyr

This scenic body of water is a favorite trysting place of the Muses. Diaphanous-winged crystal moths, Water Whisps, and many colorful species of avian and aquatic creatures are common to the region, as are less benign creatures such as skalanx.

On the far eastern banks of Lake Zephyr is a docking facility, comprised of a number of ornate wooden barges tethered together and moored to the shore. Here, Dracartan merchants come to trade sweet crystalline powders and Thaecian nectar to the Muses. In return, they are allowed to take drinking water. Thaumaturgists transmute the liquid into solid form, load the ten-foot-square blocks onto their wagons, then begin the long trip by caravan and land barge to the Red Desert and Carantheum.

The Kingdom of Durne

Durne is a land of grassy knolls, gently rising hills, and sparse woodlands. There are no rivers, and few lakes. The only visible "settlements" are the timber watchtowers of the Seven Kingdoms' Grand Army, and a rude military encampment on the banks of the Axis River.

The Forest of Ironwood occupies the western portion of the kingdom. The steel-grey ironwood trees are much favored for use in heavy construction, since the wood is nearly as tough and resistant to damage as black iron. Only the presence of malathrope and shathane above ground, and giant land kra in the subterranean ways beneath, deter those who would exploit this resource.

Given the lack of any sign of habitation, the casual traveler might be surprised to discover that this land does not lie unclaimed — rather, its possessors merely dwell below ground.

The Gnomekin

A race of diminutive man-like beings, the Gnomekin average just over three feet in height. They have nut-brown complexions, muscular bodies, and wide-eyed, cherubic features. Both the males and females have a crest of soft black fur running from the center of the forehead to the small of the back. Despite their small size, the Gnomekin of Durne are quite strong, and are as agile and sure-footed as mountain goats. Their language sounds much like the purring of cats.

Customs

Gnomekin are a warm and friendly folk, possessed of an almost childlike innocence. Their families are close-knit, and often quite large; it is not uncommon for a Gnomekin couple to have a dozen or more offspring.

The earth goddess Terra is revered by the Gnomekin as their benefactor. They are not much for dogmas and formal ceremonies. Simple worship and prayer services are conducted in sacred caverns by the female priestesses of the Great Mother.

Durne is ruled by a hereditary monarch known as the Gnomeking. He is responsible for seeing that fair prices are received for the goods produced by his people, which are delivered on the Underground Highway to Cymril once each month. Additionally, the Gnomeking is commander-in-chief of the country's small but feisty army, the Fellowship. The cooperative nature of the Gnomekin keeps political strife to a minimum. The national color of Durne is brown, the favored color of Terra.

Gnomekin Crystalomancer

The Subterranean City of Durne

Capital of Durne of the Seven Kingdoms, the Subterranean City of Durne lies some 200 feet below ground. The settlement consists of numerous moss-lined cave dwellings (called nooks), connected by a complex network of tunnels and underground lakes and streams. Large caverns are used for the growing of mushrooms and tubers, while the lakes serve as hatcheries for several species of subterranean fish and mollusks. The Gnomekin also grow crystals, which are useful in the making of scrying devices and Cymrilian amberglass.

Tunnelrock

The only entrance to the Subterranean City is through a craggy mound of stone known as Tunnelrock, honeycombed with winding passageways and tunnels. The Gnomekin fashioned the elaborate network of passages, an unknown number of which lead to their underground city 50 miles to the southwest. The rest terminate in deadfalls, bottomless shafts and cul-de-sacs. The purpose of the maze is to baffle unwanted intruders seeking access to the Gnomekin capital. Without the benefit of a map or Gnomekin guide, it is practically impossible for outsiders to find their way through Tunnelrock.

The Kingdom of Kasmir

An arid region, Kasmir is bordered to the south by the Jaspar Mountains and to the east by the Wilderlands of Zaran. It is a harsh land, uninhabited save for a few hardy species of reptilians, desert palms, and the folk who dwell here.

The Kasmir

Short and lean, the Kasmir have odd-looking, shriveled features, and skin the color of weathered mahogany. They dress in hooded cloaks, loose robes and sandals, and exhibit a suspicious attitude toward outsiders.

The Kasmir are a wealthy people, though how they acquired their fortune is unknown; some say they were once partners of the Djaffir. Whatever their history, the Kasmir are renowned throughout the continent as misers, and as crafty negotiators.

Customs

Money-lending is the business of the kingdom. Kasmir money-lenders and auditors are unexcelled in their craft. They finance caravans, deal in large quantities of trade goods, and lend money to fund ventures of many different sorts (typically at somewhat high rates).

The Kasmir are also known for their wizards, who turn their arcane skills toward the construction of the most ingenious and elaborate locks and security devices.

The society of the desert dwellers revolves around the Old Families. Each clan is led by a Patriarch, who coordinates the activities of his extended family through strict control of the clan's purse strings.

The ruler of the Kasmir, known simply as the King of Kasmir, holds his job only as long as the Patriarchs feel he effectively represents their best interests. Should he fail to live up to their expectations, the King is beheaded and a new ruler chosen. For this reason, the position of king is one which few Kasmir aspire to, despite the high pay and numerous perquisites. The national color of Kasmir is purple, an elegant hue popular among all the people of this land.

The money-lenders do not condescend to perform manual labor, preferring to hire foreign laborers for such tasks. Maruk, free Monads and Arimites are the chief immigrants, but individuals from almost every land are drawn here to seek work. The other foreigners commonly seen in the kingdom are the Thrall mercenaries who comprise Kasmir's army.

Kasmir Trapsmith

The City of Kasmir

The capital of Kasmir is the City of Kasmir, an important center for commercial and financial ventures of all sorts. The Kasmir work and live in windowless stone towers, intended to safeguard their considerable stores of wealth. Their servants live in shacks outside the city.

Built on the ruins of a forgotten citystate, the City of Kasmir long ago outgrew its ancient walls. but the Patriarchs refuse to spend money to erect new, larger fortifications. Instead, the Kasmir crowd themselves ever more tightly within the same space. The streets are little more than alleys, running in every direction and at every angle.

Kasir

West of the capital lies the wealthy Kasmir settlement of Kasir, notable for its wizards, who are considered unsurpassed in skill. They are no doubt aware of their reputation as trapsmiths, which is evidenced by the exorbitant fees which the mages charge for their services (a minimum of 100 gold lumens per day, plus expenses).

Kasir is also a regular stopping point for caravans traveling the Seven Roads.

The Kingdom of Sindar

This is a land of towering mesas, suspended arches, and other strange configurations of time-worn stone, bordered to the east by the barren canyons of the Dead River. Sindar is rich in minerals — including copper, tin and silver, plus an abundance of quartz crystal, marble, basalt, and certain semi-precious stones. Underwater springs and geysers provide a plentiful supply of water for the beings which inhabit this land: hostile satada, land kra, and the strange race known as the Sindarans.

The Sindarans

A race of dual-encephalons (*meaning:* double-brained) of unknown origin, the Sindarans bear little resemblance to any other man-like species native to the continent. They stand over seven feet in height, emaciated in build, with wrinkled, sandy-colored skin. All Sindarans have a row of horn-like nodules running from the crown of the head to the back of the neck, and a curved spur of cartilage protruding from beneath the chin.

Customs

The people of Sindar are renowned as collectors, antiquities being especially favored by these folk. To finance their collections, Sindarans concoct various types of alchemical mixtures, which they export for sale in Cymril. The rationale for the Sindarans' interest in collecting is not known, though some suspect that by doing so they hope to solve some mystery, or perhaps to unearth lost secrets of the Forgotten Age.

When not preoccupied with their collections, Sindarans enjoy playing Trivarian, a complex game which the single-brained races find incomprehensible. The game is something of a national obsession, second only to collecting. The drinking of Skoryx, a potent liquor of ever-shifting taste sensations, is also a favored Sindaran pastime.

The Sindarans live in mesa-top communes composed of elegant tiered structures, each built around a structure of carved stone blocks and hardwoods imported from Vardune and Taz. Gossamer curtains, dyed various shades of orange and burnt umber, serve as the walls of the Sindarans' pavilions. Blowing gracefully in the warm breezes, the curtains provide a measure of privacy while retaining a feeling of wide-open spaces.

Communication between Sindaran communes is possible by means of large reflective crystals, mounted on tripods and used to flash coded messages from one outpost to the next. At night, giant lanterns provide light to signal by.

Sindaran Collector

The ruler of Sindar, called the Nadir Absolute, is the country's most skilled Trivarian player. Every third year, a five-day Tournament is held to determine the best player in the land, who also assumes the rulership of the kingdom upon receiving his championship. The national color is orange.

The Cities

The largest Sindaran settlement, Nankar is the capital of Sindar. The city extends for two and a half miles across the flat crown of Nankar Mesa, and is a magnet attracting merchants and scholars with an interest in alchemy. Nearby stands the ancient Nankar Bridge, spanning the Dead River chasm but seemingly leading nowhere except the wastes of the Wilderlands.

The second major city of Sindar is Nadir, home of the kingdom's foremost Trivarian players (known as "nadirs"). Built atop a mound of stone 200 feet in height, the settlement is favored for its cool breezes and splendid view. A natural geyser provides abundant water.

Sahar is little more than an outpost, famed only for the moonstones found in the nearby canyons. Unfortunately, chasm vipers, satada and the fearsome opteryx also dwell among the ravines.

The Kingdom of Taz

Taz is a land of thick jungle, bordered to the south by the low ranges of the Cinnabar Mountains. Virulent species of plants and animals — such as mantrap, alatus, aramatus and bog devils — haunt this region.

The kingdom's western border is the Axis River, a very wide but shallow river which can be safely navigated only by flat-bottomed skiffs, barges and the like. The sluggish waters can be difficult in spots, due to the presence of sandbars, snags, and — less commonly — giant river kra.

The Thralls

A hybrid race created long ago by the sorcerers of some ancient and forgotten kingdom, the Thralls of Taz were once required to serve as an army of slave warriors. The entire race is tall and muscular, hairless and devoid of pigmentation. Thralls are distinguishable only by gender; otherwise, they all look exactly alike.

Customs

In defiance of their racial similarity, Thralls decorate their bodies from head to toe with elaborate tattoos, thereby attaining some degree of individuality.

Bred for combat, most Thralls desire no other life than that of a soldier. Many serve as protectors of the Seven Kingdoms, serving in the Grand Army or the various individual kingdom armies; other Thralls work as sentinels, caravan guards, and bodyguards.

The basic unit of Thrall society is the tribe, led by a chieftain and various officers of war. Each village is a fortified camp, with log palisades, warehouses for supplies, and communal barracks. Narrow trails link the villages — the only paved road in the kingdom is the highway leading to Cymril.

The Thralls are ruled by an individual known as the Warrior King (or Queen, as the case may be). The position is open to challenge by duel once every year during the Tournament of Challenges, the winner of the fierce competition becoming the next ruler of Taz. The national color of the kingdom is a blood-red shade of crimson.

The Fortress of Tor

A fortified communal complex, Tor serves as the capital of Taz. Situated in the midst of the jungle, the city consists of a number of squat, rectangular structures built of stone blocks, surrounded by two thick walls and a defensive network of interconnected towers. Mangonel lizards, greymanes and marsh striders are maintained in stables for military use.

Thrall Warrior

Targ Swamp

A sodden marshland overgrown with mosses and trailing vines, Targ Swamp is located in the southern jungles of Taz. The bog is a favorite hunting ground for Thralls of the nearby settlements, who come here to sharpen their combat skills against bog devils, swamp demons and batranc, all of which are found here in large numbers. Individuals less enamored of such forms of "sport" tend to avoid Targ Swamp.

The Thrall community of Targ lies on the western fringes of the swamp. Like most Tazian settlements, the city comprises a number of simple stone dwellings set within a walled enclosure. The local Thralls bear tattoos which are predominantly yellow and green in color.

Trang

Located in the eastern jungles on the border with Astar, the city of Trang is built on a hilltop which contains a rare entrance to the Underground Highway. Individuals hailing from this city generally bear tattoos which favor the colors of red and blue.

The Kingdom of Vardune

A densely forested region bordered by the Axis River to the west, Vardune is divided into two great woodlands.

Northwood is home to the Blue Ardua, as well as to herds of wild greymanes, solitary malathrope, and dreaded forest grues. Giant viridia plants grow wild here, along with violet creepers, tanglewood, sorcerer trees and ironwood.

Southwood is the residence of the Green Ardua. Here, countless exotic species of plants, shrubs and trees are found, including viridia, yellow stickler, green lotus, shrinking violet, tinsel tree, dryad bush, and many more. Exomorphs and bog devils stalk these woods.

The Ardua

Formerly a race of sky-roving hunters and gatherers, the Ardua are a race in the process of devolving from an avian to a ground-dwelling state. Their vestigial wings, once used for flying, have atrophied from disuse. For many Ardua, these appendages are more decorative than functional.

There are two sub-species of Ardua: Green Ardua, who seldom exceed five feet in height; and the taller and more aggressive Blue Ardua. Both species are slender and frail in stature, with skin which glistens with a metallic sheen. A crested cox-comb of feathers adds to the distinctive appearance of these beings. By contrast, their manner of dress is simple and austere, typically featuring a short tunic and a cape of plain viridian linen.

Customs

The race of Ardua became refugees when their ancestral homeland was annexed by the forces of the (now defunct) Phaedran Empire. The survivors settled in the Forest of Vardune, building a number of small settlements along the eastern banks of the Axis River.

The Green Ardua adapted well to their new home. Determined never to flee before another invader, they refined the art of Botanomancy so that they could groom the forest itself to defend them. They also learned to read and write in Talislantan script (as well as the Arduan bark-rune alphabet) in order to obtain wisdom from books. However, the Green Ardua have pledged to never abuse this knowledge (as they believe the ancient Phaedrans did).

The Blue Ardua, governed primarily by instinct, continue to retain certain of the barbarous ways of their ancestors. They are larger and stronger than the

Blue and Green Ardua

Green Ardua, and better gliders. Many of them serve as mercenaries within the Grand Army of the Seven Kingdoms.

The ruler of Vardune is the River King, who may be either a Blue or Green Ardua. He (or she) is elected by the Great Council of the Ardua, which is composed of representatives from each of the Ardua clans. The national color is aqua-blue.

The River Capital

Vashay is the capital of Vardune, and is renowned as a source for useful herbs and plants. Situated on the banks of the Axis River, the settlement consists of numerous tiered dwellings constructed of woven vines within the trees themselves. Vashay's most important crop is a giant species of pod-bearing viridia. Boats made of dried viridia pods ply the river alongside the larger barge-forts of the Blue Ardua. The Vashay Bridge spans the Axis River and leads to the Western Lands.

Valanis

A fortified river port situated in Northwood, Valanis is the largest Blue Ardua settlement. Here are docking facilities for the dozens of Arduan barge-forts which patrol the Axis River. Scouts and trackers sometimes come to Valanis to hunt grues - hostile quasi-elementals which pose a considerable danger to the viridia crop. There is a bounty of 500 gold lumens for every grue killed or captured withinthe territorial boundaries of Vardune.

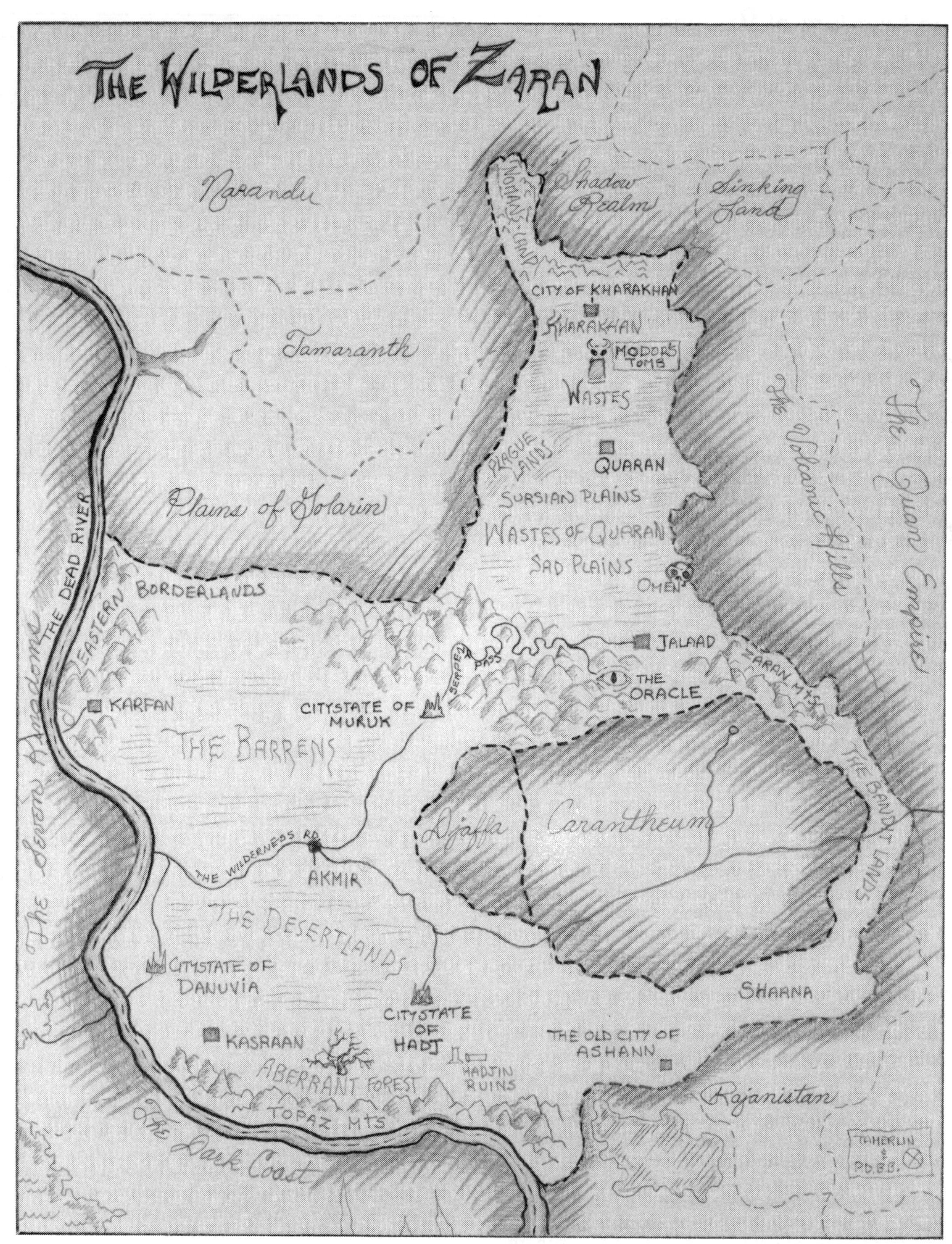

Scale: 1" = 95 miles.

THE WILDERLANDS OF ZARAN

From the borders of the Seven Kingdoms to the Volcanic Hills, the vast territories of the Wilderlands of Zaran occupy much of the central portion of Talislanta. Here, amidst shadow-haunted wastelands, lie the ruins of the long-dead civilizations of the Forgotten Age: Elande, Zaran, Sharna, Xambria, Ashann, and others too old to recall.

Much of the devastation caused by the Great Disaster took place within this region, and the Wilderlands have remained largely uncivilized ever since that time.

The Wilderlands Road

An ancient thoroughfare runs through the Wilderlands, called — appropriately enough — the Wilderlands Road. The road was originally paved with hexagonal stones, many of which have long since been worn away by the elements or scavenged. In some places, the route now consists of little more than a hard-packed dirt trail.

In the spring, heavy rains render sections of the road useless for weeks on end. During other times of the year, the highway is heavily traveled — by Aamanian pilgrims, merchant caravans from the Seven Kingdoms, Zandir traders and others — all enroute to Carantheum.

Regardless of the time of year, the presence of bandit gangs and predatory beasts makes passage through this region in anything less than a large, well-armed group a foolhardy, and possibly suicidal, endeavor.

The Dead River

Once the greatest waterway on the continent, the Dead River flowed from the North Sea (now known as the Lost Sea) south and east to the borders of Faradun. When the sea inexplicably dried up, so did all of its outlets.

The Dead River is now a winding chasm, and forms the western frontier of the Wilderlands. It is difficult to cross due to its depth, which ranges from a mere 40 feet (in the vicinity of Urag) to as much as a 120 feet (especially along its southern extremities).

It is less difficult to traverse the Dead River lengthwise. The river bed forms a natural trail extending from north to south across much of the continent. Djaffir merchants, Orgovian traders, and Farad merchant caravans sometimes follow this route to Nankar or Kasmir. So, alas, do a variety of hostile creatures, including behemoths, malathrope, chasm vipers, satada, and Za bandits.

The Topaz Mountains

Bordering the Wilderlands on the southwest, the Topaz Mountains run for hundreds of miles in a wavering line of cliffs and precipitous peaks. Covered in thick jungle along the lower altitudes, the mountains are home to numerous strange creatures and beings, including batranc, manrak, chasm vipers, satada, and Nagra spirit trackers. Topaz crystals weighing up to 20 pounds have been found in these mountains.

Other Regions

Although the Wilderlands is populated mainly by wild beasts and savages, a few bastions of civilization exist in isolation. Known collectively as the Independent Citystates, these minor principalities wield little political or economic influence beyond their city walls, but serve a useful purpose as safe havens for travelers.

Hadj, the richest of the municipalities, claims both of the other citystates as debtors. Danuvia is a city of warrior women, and its stalwart soldiers have kept the citystates safe from invasion time and time again. Maruk is the weakest of the cities, but no one wishes to seize it from its possessors — the site is quite evidently cursed.

Other regions stand out for their terrain, the savages who dwell there, or the ruins which stud their surface. The Desertlands, for instance, is the largest expanse of sandy waste outside of the Red Desert itself. The Barrens are likewise...well, barren — little grows on the salt flats. And the Aberrant Forest is a lush woodland which defies logic by prospering in the midst of the wastes.

The Banditlands, in the distant east, is named after the Za bandits who lair there — the same folk whose ancestors (the Zaran) gave this entire land its name. Likewise, the Kharakhan Wastes are named both for the Kharakhan Giants who dwell there, and for the ruins of the ancient city of the same name.

Sharna and Ashann are wastelands distinguished only by the ruins of those lost kingdoms. Similarly, an entire territory is known as the Wastes of Quaran, after one of the most infamous of the ancient lands.

The Aberrant Forest

Pinched between the Desertlands and the Topaz Mountains is the Aberrant Forest, a weird and grotesque woodland the origins of which are often attributed to a magical mishap of unparalleled proportions.

All manner of rare and exotic vegetation can be found in this place, though nothing that grows or lives here is as nature intended it to be. The plants and trees appear heedless of natural law, growing to immense proportions or becoming gnarled and twisted in form.

From the underbrush, animate tendrils of tanglewood reach out to ensnare the incautious traveler. Hedgerows of thornwood make swift passage through the woodland an implausible stratagem. Less easily identifiable types of flora and fauna make their presence known by biting, tripping, speaking in mysterious tongues, or through even more unusual methods.

Among the reports of talking Mang trees, giant species of slugs and scavenger slimes, and strange insect-reptile hybrids, are interesting tales of contacts with intelligent plant-creatures. Most scholars, however, consider the descriptions of gangly plant-beings living in a lake village and devouring sunlight for food as merely entertaining stories.

At times, the very laws of the Omniverse seem to be contravened here. Murky streams flow uphill, stagnant ponds move slowly across the land, and the ground itself seems at times to pulse as if it were alive.

Because many varieties of rare and costly herbs grow throughout the Aberrant Forest, visitors to this macabre woodland are not unknown. Botanomancers, alchemists, and other individuals with an interest in naturalism sometimes come here, drawn by the region's seemingly endless variety of strange and exotic lifeforms.

The Legend of the Mad Wizard

The profusion of oddities which populates this region might seem to lend credence to an ancient legend. The tale claims that the Aberrant Forest and its unusual residents are the creations of the Mad Wizard Rodinn, a rather obscure magician believed to have lived during the latter part of what is now known as the Forgotten Age.

A benign if somewhat erratic sort of fellow, Rodinn was forced to flee his native land of Pompados after committing a series of indiscretions, purportedly involving the wife and seven daughters of the Emperor of Pompados. Seeking refuge in the Wilderlands of Zaran, Rodinn constructed a manse deep within a secluded and scenic woodland area.

Here, the wizard continued the magical experiments for which he is known to history. During this time, legend claims that Rodinn chanced upon the discovery of quintessence, a substance capable of transmuting the very nature of matter. An accident led to the untimely release of a great quantity of this material, which wreaked havoc upon the surrounding environs.

Some apologists theorize that Rodinn's swift intervention prevented an even greater and more widespread catastrophe; others pinpoint Rodinn's mishap as the catalyst which spawned the Great Disaster, ending the most glorious age of Talislantan civilization.

In any case, Rodinn and his manse both reportedly survived the ordeal (if legends can be believed), though the Mad Wizard has never been heard from in the centuries since.

A village of the legendary plant-men

The Banditlands

Bordered to the west by the Red Desert and to the east by the Volcanic Hills, this region is known as the Banditlands. The land of arid hills and scorched dust-flats is the bane of merchants and travelers alike, who must suffer the depredations of desert kra, manrak and opteryx – in addition to marauding bandits – in order to proceed east along the Wilderlands Road to Hadran, the gateway to the Quan Empire.

The rugged peaks of the Zaran Mountains are the final refuge of bandits who lay low in these parts to elude inquisitive patrols of Dracartan desert scouts. The region is rich in black-iron ore and certain types of semi-precious stones, but vasps and manrak from the Volcanic Hills plague the heights. The marauders are said to have numerous hide-outs in the mountains, where they temporarily stash excess loot and inconvenient slaves.

The Za

These badlands are the domain of the Za – a clannish and barbaric race which claims descent from the original inhabitants of the lost kingdom of Zaran. Contending that the Wilderlands region rightfully belongs to them, the bandits rationalize robbing and murdering any who trespass in "their" territory.

Nomadic bandits who range far and wide throughout much of the Wilderlands, the Za are lean and muscular, most standing at or just under six feet in height. Their skin is a pallid yellow in hue, leathery in texture and lined with creases and wrinkles.

Customs

The Za shave their skulls, and forgo all but the most abbreviated attire. Necklaces of hammered black-iron disks are favored, as are bands of reptile-hide worn on the head and upper arms. Males generally wear long, braided mustaches; females, two long braids, one above either ear.

The tribesmen wield jagged-edged broadswords, and fire barbed arrows with their bows. Greymanes, with their long manes and tails done in tight braids, serve as steeds for the bandit clans.

Though the Za sometimes take prisoners for sale as slaves, they usually put their victims to death by the sword, this being thought of as fitting punishment for trespassers. Exceptionally valorous foes are accorded the dubious honor of being taken alive, so that they may later be slain in ritual fashion. The Za drink the blood of these vanquished enemies from skull-cups, believing that this gives them the strength of their foes.

Za Bandit mounted on equs

There is little sense of unity among the bandits, who often engage in violent clashes over the rights to the best raiding territories. It is all the more surprising, then, that the Za claim to have a single ruler, known as the Tirshata.

According to tradition, the identity of the Tirshata must remain unknown until the time comes for the Za to reclaim their lost homeland. At the designated hour, say the bandits, "the Tirshata shall be revealed, and the Za will rise up and smite all their enemies, until they alone rule the lands from east to west." Talislantan scholars, who by and large consider the Za to be on an intellectual par with the Wildmen of Yrmania, lend little credence to this folk tale.

The Ruins of Jalaad

The crumbling ruins of the ancient city of Jalaad are located north of the Zaran Mountains. Though long since stripped of most of its hidden treasures by many generations of Yitek tomb-robbers and Za bandits, the ruins still shelter a relatively intact Library. The scriptorium was preserved due to the efforts of a cabal of Callidian Cryptomancers, which has endeavored to protect the facility's store of iron tablets since the time of the Great Disaster. Individuals who wish to explore the library may do so only under the watchful eye of the Callidians, who deal sternly with looters and vandals.

The Barrens

Westernmost of the Wilderlands territories is the Barrens, a region of rocky hills, salt flats, and wide stretches of scrub plains. Herds of land lizards, valued throughout Talislanta as pack and burden beasts, roam the sparse plains in great numbers. Mangonel lizards, a combative species of reptile employed as war-steeds by the Thralls of Taz, can also be found here.

The Enim

The hills of this region are inhabited by the Enim, a race of giant cannibalistic devils which hails from the lower plane of Oblivion. The devils have skin the color of brass, curved horns, and tusk-like fangs. Standing up to 14 feet in height, Enim are a fearsome sight to behold. They weld huge stone clubs carved with the visages of leering devils, and wear necklaces of skulls collected as mementos of their grisly conquests.

Customs

The Enim are solitary creatures who dwell in caves located deep below the surface, emerging in order to hunt for food. Like all devils, they are the mortal foes of demonkind, and have a special dislike for Earth Demons. Enim are fond of Men, however, whom they regard as fine eating.

When not motivated by hunger, Enim sometimes entertain themselves by attempting to crush other creatures with large rocks, which they are able to hurl considerable distances. In the rare instances when two or more Enim meet above ground, they almost always engage in some game of chance, wagering on the outcome. Individuals who have a penchant for high-stakes gambling should be wary of gambling with the devils — most Enim know something of magic, and they are not averse to cheating if given the opportunity.

The Eastern Borderlands

The Seven Kingdoms lies adjacent to much of the Wilderlands, and the Seven Kings have a healthy interest in what happens in this largely unsettled and dangerous region. Several Seven Kingdoms military outposts are located in the Wilderlands, including the fortresses of Akmir and Karfan. Their mission is to safeguard the caravan routes, particularly in the case of goods bound to or from the Seven Kingdoms. The outposts are run by Thrall commanders, and are manned by the Legion of the Borderlands — a body of hard-bitten mercenaries, outcasts and criminals from many lands.

The region adjacent to Karfan is known as the Eastern Borderlands, and is considered the Seven Kingdoms' first line of defense in the event of another invasion by the Beastmen of Golarin.

Akmir

Easternmost of the Seven Kingdoms' outposts, Akmir stands at a crossroads between the citystates of Maruk and Hadj. The fortress serves as a way-station for travelers in need of shelter, and is regularly frequented by Djaffir merchant tribes and Orgovian traders.

The archaic, walled fortress is regarded by professional men-at-arms as the most dismal of assignments. Situated far from civilization, Akmir is beset by harsh weather, wild beasts (such as omnivrax and malathrope), and marauding bandits. Consequently, the fortress is manned by the dregs of Talislantan society: Jhangaran exiles, Arimite knife-fighters, renegade Ur clansmen, devious half-men, and so forth.

Karfan

A small, walled fortress constructed by the Seven Kingdoms, Karfan has woefully limited facilities for travelers. Since the outpost is considerably off the beaten path, traders visit here most infrequently.

Dicing with Devils

The Citystate of Danuvia

A great stone citadel, the Citystate of Danuvia was established on the site of a ruined city by refugees who fled the Phaedran Empire during the Cult Wars.

The municipality is a sovereign state, ruled by a royal Gynecocracy — a government run exclusively by females, under the ultimate authority of the Queen of Danuvia. The citystate is also notable for its mercenary army, which is composed solely of female archers, swordswomen and lancers (mounted on aht-ra bought from Djaffa).

The Danuvians

The Danuvians are a bronze-skinned race with strong features. The males are uniformly feeble, lazy, and addle-brained — therefore, the society is dominated by females, who serve in all positions of authority.

The warrior-women of Danuvia — known as Viragos — decorate their faces with colored pigments, and ride greymanes into battle. Equipped with black-iron corselets and parrying bracers, they are considered among the most skilled fighters on the continent.

Customs

Rather than accept their own, pathetic mates as companions, Danuvian females also seek male partners from other lands.

Each year, the Queen of Danuvia holds a great pageant in the city, called the Conjugal Feast. The purpose of the festival is to find suitable mates for the Queen, and men of all nationalities are invited to compete for her affections. The top three contestants are rewarded by being appointed to the royal harem of male consorts. Lower-ranking Danuvians stake claims to other desirable males, according to their rank.

The Bridge at Danuvia

Two caravan routes lead away from Danuvia. The most heavily traveled is the trail leading north to the Wilderlands Road and thence to Kasmir. The lesser used path heads southward across the fertile Danuvian plains toward Astar and the Dracartan installation on Lake Zephyr. Water caravans bound for Carantheum enter Danuvia by wagon, then depart for the Desertlands where land-barges await to load the precious transmuted cargo.

Crossing the great gorge, the Dead River Span consists of two black-iron suspension bridges stretching from each bank to a central rock spire. A ramp provides access to and from the river bed below.

Danuvian Swordswoman, known as a "Virago"

The Desertlands

This stretch of parched terrain, located to the southeast of the Citystate of Danuvia, is one of the most desolate regions on the continent. Nothing grows here, for there is no water. The only creatures which can tolerate these environs are horned devil-men and sand demons, neither of which require moisture to survive. Both require sustenance, however, and so hunt each other relentlessly. Scattered across the landscape are the remnants of several ancient civilizations, along with the skeletal remains of unlucky travelers and their beasts.

The Ruins of Kasraan

The Kasraan ruins lie deep within the Desertlands. Though the city itself has been reduced to a shambles by the ravages of wind and time, the catacombs located below ground remain largely intact. These subterranean haunts contain the petrified remains of the kings and queens of ancient Kasraan, sealed within crypts of solid stone. Gaining entrance to these vaults is said to be a formidable task: the Kasraanians, early ancestors of the Kasmir, took pains to safekeep the bodies of their monarchs from tomb-robbers and other entrepreneurial types. The Yitek, in fact, consider the effort required to gain access to the Kasraanian crypts to be barely worth the reward.

The Citystate of Hadj

A walled city, Hadj stands at the end of a narrow strip of arable ground, in the middle of an arid plain which stretches for miles in all directions. The modern settlement was erected near the ruins of a much older city — Phandril, capital of Hadjistan, the original homeland of the Phandre sub-race of Men.

The masters of this place are an aristocratic and fabulously wealthy people known as the Hadjin, descendants of the ancient Phandre. Virtually impoverished when they fled the collapse of the Phaedran Empire during the Cult Wars, the refugees discovered an incredibly vast store of wealth when they settled here among the ruins of the city of their ancestors. The Hadjin used this fortune to buy vast tracts of real estate across the continent, now managed by their servants and administrators.

The Hadjin

A tall and slender folk of noble bearing. the Hadjin daub their complexions with colored powders, dress in layered robes, and wear upward-sweeping caps and long velveteen gloves.

Customs

A people of highly refined tastes and lofty airs, the Hadjin wave themselves with scented fans when in the presence of outsiders, who are deemed offensive in terms of appearance and odor. The Hadjin possess no useful skills to speak of, and delegate all of the real work of the city to a lower class of administrators (the Hajann) and hired servants.

Both the city and their lifestyle proclaim their devotion to idle pursuits. The Hadjin are the ultimate materialists, and spend great sums to import precious and exotic goods from the far corners of the continent.

The Consortium controls everything that goes on in the citystate, guided by a central principle — to always see that the Hadjin increase in wealth. One member from each of the Forty Families sits on the council. The presiding officer of the Consortium is known as the Grandeloquence, who holds the office for life or until he chooses to retire.

The Hadjin Ruins

The source of the great wealth of the Hadjin is a series of giant obelisk-like structures, located within sight of the city walls. Most of the megaliths remain standing, though some have fallen or lurch precipitously at odd angles.

Among the ruins are crypts which contain untold thousands of mummified corpses from ancient Phandril, each interred with the deceased's most prized possessions. The bodies were preserved alchemically, then placed in sarcophagi carved from great blocks of colored crystal.

The ruins are closely watched by the Hadjin, who employ mercenaries and guard-beasts to ward the grounds. Visitors to Hadj can arrange for a guided tour of the tombs, which costs upward of 200 gold lumens, depending upon the choice of conveyance. Those who crave adventure first-hand can obtain a permit allowing exploration of the ruins, at a cost of 1,000 gold lumens per person, per day. Under the terms of the standard agreement, the Hadjin retain the rights to all treasure recovered, including any and all sarcophagi that may be discovered. The Consortium then sells the treasures, rewarding the discoverers with an amount equal to half the appraised value of the plundered items.

Unfortunately for explorers, the Phandre protected their crypts with traps and deadfalls, as well as magical and alchemical safeguards. Extra-dimensional entities are also known to wander the mausoleum.

Hadjin Noble

The Citystate of Maruk

Maruk is also a walled city, though it is considerably less prosperous than Hadj. Built upon the ruins of an unknown civilization, the city was a place of notable splendor when first rebuilt.

Its citizens, magical craftsmen who were forced to flee the Phaedran Empire during the Cult Wars, renamed themselves the Maruk in honor of the valley in which they had taken up residence. Here, they made a good living as sellers of produce.

Soon after construction of the city was completed, a series of misfortunes — occurring at intervals of 13 months — beset the Maruk. Crops failed, animals died, the city was plagued by infestations of vermin, and the ruling class was slaughtered when the dead rose from their graves one night.

Attempts were made to remedy the problem, which was diagnosed variously as being the result of an ancient curse, malicious spiritforms, ill-aspected stars, sunspots, and a host of less probable causes. Time and again, each of the proposed solutions met with failure.

Much to the chagrin of the Maruk, the Curse has persisted with regularity to the present day. The city has slowly fallen into ruin, all attempts at effecting much-needed repairs and renovations having long since been deemed unprofitable.

The ruling council of the citystate, itself the victim of numerous mishaps and misfortunes, continues to seek a solution to the city's woes. Though the government has technically been bankrupt for decades, a reward of 100,000 gold lumens is offered to anyone who can lift the Curse. The reward draws a few optimistic mystics, charismatic savants, and reputed miracle-workers, though not nearly so many as in years past.

Customs

Reduced to selling ogront dung in order to make ends meet, the people of Maruk have become morose and gloomy. They dress in unflattering garments made of sack cloth, and walk about with their eyes downcast. Wan and unhealthy in appearance, the Maruk are considered harbingers of doom in many lands, and are shunned as if they carry the plague.

The Maruk Mountains

The wind-worn peaks of the Maruk Mountains, lying to the north of the Citystate of Maruk, are believed to be rich in precious stones such as black opal. However, local folk are reluctant to approach the

Maruk Talismancer

heights, saying that the peaks are the haunts of manrak, Kharakhan Giants and bandits.

Serpent Pass is a narrow gulch which weaves its way through the southernmost reaches of the mountain range. The pass offers shelter from sand and dust storms (common throughout the Wilderlands), and so is frequented by Orgovian traders, Aamanian Orthodoxists making the pilgrimage to the Well of Saints, and a few intrepid Maruk dung merchants. Consequently, this route also has its admirers among certain tribes of Djaffir bandits, beastmen and Kharakhan Giants.

The Oracle

A sheer pinnacle of blue and violet porphyry which overlooks Serpent Pass, the Oracle is said to be the abode of an ancient mystic who lives upon the summit — a peak constantly obscured by a bank of clouds. According to legend, the great sage knows the answers to all questions: past, present, and future.

Three trails lead to the top of the mount, each affording climbers with its own distinct set of hazards and disadvantages — an aerial approach, while most direct, is considered ill-advised due to the presence of wind demons.

The Kharakhan Wastes

A region despoiled by firestorms and other unnatural phenomena during the Great Disaster, the Wastes of Kharakhan contain burnt and blackened ruins that stand like tombstones, dismal monuments of a bygone era. Where once flowed mighty rivers, winding chasms now cut across the plains. Giant land dragons graze on dry grasses, heedless of crag spiders and other noxious predators.

Many towering structures of the City of Kharakhan still stand, and oversized artifacts and curios are said to litter the subterranean levels. Of particular interest are the silver coins once employed by the ancient inhabitants, which measure three to four inches in diameter and weigh up to one pound apiece. Even the most miserly collectors seldom offer less than 100 gold lumens for these unique items.

The Kharakhan Giants

A race of giants whose ancestors hail back to the Forgotten Age, the Kharakhan Giants reverted to a primitive and savage existence following the Great Disaster. The race is all but extinct — only a few hundred Giants remain on the continent.

The survivors are nomads, traversing the Wilderlands in warrior clans. They carry their belongings on huge war wagons drawn by teams of ogriphants or land lizards.

The Giants stand 15 feet in height, weigh over half a ton, and are incredibly strong. They speak an ancient and obscure dialect of Low Talislan, and are the only individuals able to decipher the ages-old inscriptions in the Kharakhan ruins. The Farad covet the Giants as slaves, and pay well for captured specimens.

The Araq

A hybrid of Men and Saurans, the origins of the Araq have been long since forgotten. The purpose of the experiment seems to have been to create a race of warriors adapted to harsh climes. The scaly brown hide of the Araq protects them from the glare of the twin suns, and their dorsal membranes masterfully regulate their body temperature. They require little food or water to sustain themselves, and can subsist on almost any type of organic material, including briars and even waste products. Unfortunately, the Araq are as prone to violence as the Saurans, and inherited numerous vices from Men as well: greed, lust, dishonesty and cruelty.

The Araq prowl the Kharakhan Wastes in large numbers, mounted on two-headed reptilian creatures known as duadir. They are skilled in the use of spears and bone war-axes, but will fight with fang and claw if necessary. Their primary source of food is the land dragon, from which they derive material to craft boots, loincloths, shields and weapons. Araq prey upon anything that lives, including crag spiders, vermin, and travelers who venture too near their domains. Their wars with the Saurans of the Volcanic Hills serve the useful purpose of keeping the population of both races in check.

Noman's Land

This narrow strip of wasteland separates Tamaranth from the Shadow Realm. It is believed to be haunted by fantasms — pseudo-demons from the Nightmare Dimension, a place ruled by the entity known as Noman. Practitioners of black magic come to Noman's Land to search for Mordante's Gate, a magical portal said to provide entrance to the lower planes.

Modor's Tomb

According to the Ariane, the Kharakhan Giant named Modor was buried in this inert volcano, along with his store of stolen riches (said to exceed 100,000 gold lumens). A 200-foot vertical shaft reportedly leads to seven doorways, only one of which leads to the actual tomb. Touching the treasure will supposedly bring the deceased Giant back to life.

Araq mounted on duadir.

Sharna

The southern Wilderlands contains several maze-like structures of certifiable antiquity. Some scholars attribute these ruins to the Sharna, a long-dead race of whom little is known. The purpose of the structures remains unclear — artifacts unearthed from the ruins range from costumes, utensils and odd furnishings to weapons, crystals, magical paraphernalia, and articles of no apparent utility whatsoever. Few of the labyrinths have been explored thoroughly, being considered unsafe due to their extreme age.

Artifacts from the labyrinths are highly valued as curios and collectibles, if for no discernible reason other than their avowed scarcity. In truth, the Sharna appear to have had an uncommon talent for creating items of the most tasteless and unaesthetic sort. Nevertheless, the demand for these unattractive objects continues to be high, a behavioral anomaly which has heartened many a generation of antique and curio dealers.

Contributing to the rarity of Sharna artifacts is the presence in this region of nightstalkers — weird creatures which hail from the astral plane, and are attracted to the material dimension by the dreams of sleeping beasts and men.

The Ferrans

The areas about the Sharna ruins are populated by Ferrans — rodent-faced, man-like beings of short stature, whose bodies are covered with a coat of dirty brown fur. They live in underground tunnel complexes, coming forth in groups to scrounge for food or to rob unwary travelers of their possessions. Ferrans steal anything that they can carry off and drag into their lairs. They are shrewd and cunning, and have been known to employ exotic weapons and gear pilfered from others in their raids.

Ashann

The territory known as Ashann is similar to Sharna, in that both regions are named for the ancient kingdoms said to have once existed there. Aside from crumbling ruins, there is little in either place to testify of past grandeur.

The shattered ruins of the Old City of Ashann consist of seven concentric rings, the outermost of which encompasses an area approximately two miles in diameter. At one time, these ancient stone structures may have measured nearly 100 feet in width, and over 40 feet in height.

Desert scouts from the kingdom of Carantheum claim that the region is uninhabited save for sand demons, satada, and the mysterious beings known only as the Wanderers of Ashann.

The Wanderers of Ashann

These mysterious individuals are among the most peculiar inhabitants of the Wilderlands. Known only as the Wanderers of Ashann, they stand nearly eight feet in height, and dress in long, billowing robes which hang loosely upon their angular frames. Their features are entirely concealed beneath elaborate headdresses, and each carries a staff of white oak inscribed with a curious symbol: a staring orb, set in the center of a silver pentacle. Some believe that the Wanderers are without eyes and can only see by means of these devices, which are supposed to be magical in nature.

The Wanderers may be the last of the Shan, survivors of the Kingdom of Ashann which was destroyed by the Great Disaster. According to this theory, when the Shan beheld their cities and lands reduced to desert, they forever rejected civilization in favor of a nomadic life.

To the present day, the Wanderers of Ashann refuse to settle in any one area, preferring instead to wander. They are sometimes encountered walking among the ruins of the Old City of Ashann, seemingly lost in thought.

Wanderer of Ashann, with Ferran

Wastes of Quaran

Peering down the corridor of time like a spectre that refuses to be buried, the Citystate of Quaran continues to stir the minds of men despite the fact that its cabal of sorcerers fell from power eons ago. This entire region of the Wilderlands resounds with the curse of having been associated with such a reprehensible memory.

The Ruins of Quaran

Despite the combined effects of time, the elements, and the cataclysmic upheavals resulting from the Great Disaster, the ruins of the Citystate of Quaran still stand as grim reminders of that dark and nearly forgotten age. Here, amidst stark stone towers and nightmarish effigies, once flourished the capital of the most sinister empire in the annals of Talislantan history.

Generations of occultists, black magicians and tomb-robbers have come to the ruins to sift through the debris in search of clues to the Quaranians' dark and macabre secrets. Many articles have been retrieved from the ruins, often to the great regret of those who have found them: cursed tomes, diabolical artifacts, instruments of torture and death, and things too terrible to describe. Countless other items remain buried in tombs, vaults and underground pits, awaiting discovery by those who covet infernal knowledge above all other considerations.

The Plaguelands

North of the ruined citystate, this cracked and barren plain was laid waste centuries ago by some unknown catastrophe, possibly in conjunction with the Great Disaster. It is a widely-held belief that any living thing which passes through the Plaguelands will be changed or transformed in some unpredictable manner. Consequently, few intelligent creatures willingly venture into this region.

The Sursian Plains

West of Old Quaran is the Sursian Plains, an arid grassland pockmarked with holes and craters. Here can be found the remnants of the once-mighty Kingdom of Sursia: the twisted and charred hulks of terrible siege engines, the ruins of blasted stone towers, and shards of fused metal and glass.

Packs of Ferran bandits live in tunnels beneath the plains, inhabiting a network which links the region's largest craters and crevasses. Gigantic ogronts mindlessly graze on the dry grasses, while azoryl glide across the sky. If not for the presence of such creatures as these, the area would resemble a ghostland.

The Sad Plains

These barren plains, south of the dead citystate, are lined with rows of aged and pitted stone statues, each portraying one of the Necromancer-Kings of ancient Quaran.

On this site the nation of Xambria once stood, its cities shining brightly in the light of the twin Talislantan suns. Now nothing remains, all trace of this once-prosperous civilization having been obliterated from the face of the continent by the merciless armies of Quaran.

Since that time, the plains have been inhabited only by ogront, land dragons and malathrope. Marauding bands of Araq and Kharakhan Giants sometimes sweep through the Sad Plains, but they seldom linger in this strange and mournful place.

Omen

This cursed place is avoided by most Talislantans. In ancient times, the Necromancer-Kings of Quaran erected at Omen a mountain of skulls nearly 1,000 feet in height, representing untold millions of victims. The mountain stands to the present day, and is sometimes visited by descendants of the victims, who seek to commune with their ancestors.

Omen

The Displaced Peoples

A number of different races traverse the territories of the Wilderlands without inhabiting any specific lands. Most are descended from refugees whose homelands were destroyed in the Great Disaster, their lands now long abandoned and fallen into ruin. Some are driven by modern oppressors, such as the Quan Empire; others are members of dying races.

The Bodor

An amber-skinned people of uncertain origin, the Bodor are round faced, portly of build, and eccentric in their choice of costume. Modest and unassuming by nature, Bodor are content so long as they have work. They are consummate musicians, proficient with such instruments as gossamer harps, glass flutes, crystal bells, a device known as the intricate spiral-horn, and four-man bellows-pipes. Traveling troupes of Bodor musicians are common throughout the citystates of the Wilderlands, and may be found in such lands as Zandu, Faradun, the Seven Kingdoms, Carantheum, and the Quan Empire.

The Nagra

A primitive, man-like race, the Nagra have mottled grey-green skin, black fangs, peaked skulls, and eyes like tiny ebony specks. They dress in rude garments made from the furry hides of winged apes, and carry blowguns and long knives made of bone.

The Nagra are spirit trackers, possessing the ability to follow any track or trail, regardless of its age or origin. They once lived in the East, but were driven into the Wilderlands by the Kang, who hunted them like animals. Some who survived made a new home for themselves in the jungles of the Topaz Mountains, while others settled in the Jade Mountains to the east of Rajanistan.

The Rahastrans

This race of itinerant wizards and mountebanks travels throughout the Wilderlands of Zaran and beyond. Tall and dark-skinned, Rahastrans wear cloaks, gloves and long coats of blue fustian, and pendants of carved amethyst.

These wizards are skilled in the art of the Zodar, an archaic game which utilizes cards, each of which is marked with a different arcane symbol. While Zodar is often thought of as a game of chance, the cards may also be used to divine the future, or to reveal a person's deepest thoughts and desires. As a result, Rahastran wizards are regarded with mixed emotions by other Talislantans, who are fascinated with the Zodar, yet fearful of the secrets which the cards may reveal.

The Sauruds

Immense, man-like reptilians believed by some scholars to have been the progenitors of the Sauran race, the Sauruds wander throughout the Eastern Borderlands and the Volcanic Hills. They stand eight feet in height and are massively built, with rough, scaly brown hide. Their features are not unlike a land lizard's in appearance, though their eyes are smaller and more deep-set, and their fangs somewhat less obtrusive.

Sauruds favor abbreviated attire, loinclouts and bands of strider or dragon hide usually sufficing to suit their needs. In battle, they wield huge spiked clubs; partly as a matter of preference, but also because the giants lack the manual dexterity required to utilize more sophisticated weaponry.

Their tiny reptilian brain is incapable of grasping any but the least intricate of ideas. Sauruds are sometimes employed as bodyguards and sentinels, positions for which the ferocious brutes are well-suited. The race seems on the verge of extinction, and there are perhaps only a few hundred Sauruds left on the entire continent.

The Xambrians

These folk are descended from the citizens of ancient Xambria, a kingdom destroyed before the Great Disaster. Few in number, they are a grim and moody lot, regarded with suspicion by most Talislantans. The Xambrians blame the demise of their kingdom on the sorcerers of ancient Quaran, and distrust all spell-casters. Many Xambrians are mercenary wizard-hunters by trade.

Xambrians resemble the Ariane in stature, but have bone-white skin and long, raven-black hair. Their customary mode of dress includes a cape, high boots, a vest, and tight breeches of black strider hide, with gauntlets of fine silver mesh.

The Yitek

A nomadic people, the Yitek are brown-skinned, built along lean and narrow proportions. They dress in veiled headdresses, capes, and loose-fitting garments made of woven gauze, usually grey with the dust of crypts and barrows.

The Yitek are tomb-robbers by profession. They scour the Wilderlands, ranging from the Labyrinths of Sharna to the Kharakhan Wastes, searching for valuable treasures and artifacts. They are frequent visitors to the Citystate of Hadj, and are friendly with the Djaffir. Known for their morbid sense of humor, the Yitek are avoided by many folk, who find their line of work distasteful.

Scale: 1" = 105 miles.

AAMAN

Aamanians: Warrior-Priest, Monitor, and Archimage

Aaman is a land of low hills and wooded glens, bordered to the east by the Axis River, and to the west by the Sea of Sorrow. Once part of the Phaedran Empire, Aaman became an independent state upon the conclusion of the long and bloody Cult Wars, which pitted the Orthodoxists against the Paradoxists of neighboring Zandu.

The Aamanians

A stern folk, the Aamanians are tall and straight of bearing. They have skin the color of cinnabar, with sculpted features and deep green eyes.

As required by the arch-conservative tenets of Orthodoxism, Aamanians refrain from individualistic behavior. Only the most modest attire is deemed permissible – colorless smocks, robes designed to conceal the figure, and caps of starched linen. In order to promote the Orthodoxist ideal of "oneness in body and spirit," Aamanians use an extract of the bald nettle plant to remove all facial and body hair, thus achieving a sameness of appearance.

The Orthodoxist Cult

The doctrines of Orthodoxy center around the Aamanians' patron deity, Aa (also known as "Aa the Omnipotent," "Aa the Omnificent," and so forth).

The tenets of the cult are recorded in a series of iron-bound volumes, collectively known as the Omnival. The first volume contains the revelations which Aa supposedly granted to the founders of the cult, and the subsequent tomes were written over the course of many generations by the ruling theocrats. The Omnival purports to reveal the secret knowledge of Aa; the answers to all questions and mysteries; the correct manner of achieving ordered thought; and 100 proscriptions against infidels, heretics and witches. According to the Aamanians, "What the Omnival does not teach, the true Orthodoxist need not know."

Customs

Strict adherence to the inflexible tenets of Orthodoxism strangulates life in Aaman. Conditioned from childhood to conform to acceptable patterns of speech and behavior, Aamanians converse mainly in cliches and axioms. Disagreement with Orthodoxist doctrine is considered tantamount to heresy, and results in most unpleasant consequences. Intoxicants and public merriment are considered the domain of infidels, and are expressly forbidden.

The Aamanians have a rigid caste system based upon the acquisition and accumulation of spiritual purity, which they measure in terms of mana.

At the head of the theocracy is the Hierophant, the celibate high priest of the realm, who possesses unlimited mana. The Hierophant is entrusted with sole curatorship of the Omnival, and thus wields absolute power. At his decree, the book of scripture may be expanded to include such strictures and observances as he sees fit to impose upon the populace.

Serving the Hierophant are the Monitors, each of whom serves as the ruling prelate of an assigned district. The Monitors are responsible for awarding mana to those worthy of advancement in status, and to withdraw it from individuals judged to be unworthy. Only Aamanians who have earned a minimum of 1,000 aalms (points) of mana can aspire to the lofty position of a Monitor .

Next in status come the Aspirants. These individuals are divided into ten orders, separated by 100-aalm increments. (Thus, an Aspirant of the First Order must possess a minimum of 100 aalms of mana, an Aspirant of the Second Order must have at least 200 aalms, and so on.) Aspirants of the Tenth Order vie for promotion to the status of Monitor, though few can attain such an exalted position.

Individuals who have no mana are considered Pariahs, with a status comparable to that of an infidel. Slaves are Pariahs as well, and have even fewer rights – they are the property of the state.

Advancement in status is a preoccupation of the Aamanians, who believe that their position in the Orthodoxist hierarchy at the time of their death determines how they will fare in the afterlife. Accordingly, the attainment of mana is considered to be of primary importance.

The most reliable method of gaining mana, provided one can pay the high cost of tuition, is to enter the priesthood and study to become an Archimage or Warrior-Priest. Temples and monasteries offering instruction can be found in any city in Aaman.

A less costly means of attaining enlightenment is to enlist in the combat ranks of the Theocratic Order, the militant arm of the Orthodoxist Cult. Attired in shining white armor (actually, black-iron plate-mail covered with glossy white lacquer), Knights of the Theocratic Order serve as protectors of the realm, under the direct command of the Hierophant. They are employed as officers in all branches of the regular army and navy. Other members of the Order serve as specialists: Witch Hunters hunt down and persecute "enemies of the faith" (witches, warlocks, and other so-called heretics who do not share the Cult's narrow-minded views). Inquisitors preside over rituals designed to purge unorthodox desires from penitents' hearts – methods that resemble what others might call torture.

Some members of the cult find it easier to simply purchase mana, by making donations to one of the many Temples of Aa found in Aaman. The going rate for this form of enlightenment is 100 gold lumens per aalm of mana – a not-insubstantial price, even considering the purported benefits to the soul.

Because few Aamanians can afford to acquire mana by such convenient means, the most popular way to achieve elevated status is to undertake a pilgrimage to one of the cult's officially sanctioned holy places. In order of esteem, these are: the Well of Saints, which lies within the Volcanic Hills; the Watchstone, situated amidst the Plains of Golarin; the Red Desert of Carantheum; and Faradun's Sea of Glass. Returning with some item or substance native to the holy place is required in order to gain the recognition of the Monitors, who must verify all such claims.

The Great Barrier Wall

Stretching the entire length of the Aaman-Zandu border is perhaps the most bizarre and spectacular structure in the region: the Great Barrier Wall, an immense stone structure 60 feet in height and half as wide at its base. It was built as the culmination of the Cult Wars, the series of religious conflicts that pitted the Orthodoxist Cult against their rivals, the Paradoxists.

The Great Barrier Wall is open to travelers of all races and nationalities, though a toll is charged at each of its three gates (one gold lumen per person, animal, or conveyance). Proprietorship of the wall and its toll facilities are determined on a yearly basis during the annual event known as the Clash of Champions.

The Clash of Champions

This yearly contest of skill pits two great champions against one another: one representing Aaman, and the other representing Zandu. Both the Aamanians and the Zandir expend a considerable amount of effort searching for a suitable champion for the annual match, the outcome of which is worth a small fortune in revenues. There are a few minor restrictions: quadrupeds are barred from competing in the event, as are demons of any sort. The Aamanians insist that their champion be male, and a Believer. Otherwise, practically anything goes.

The contest is held atop the Great Barrier Wall, with spectators on both sides applauding their country's champion. People from many lands come to see the Clash of Champions, bringing a substantial amount of business to the innkeepers, shopowners and vendors of both lands. Betting is always brisk, and pick-pockets from neighboring regions regard the event with an almost religious reverence.

The Capital City of Ammahd

The capital of Aaman, Ammahd is the center of all Aamanian trade, commerce and culture. The Hierophant lives here in a mighty tower of ivory-colored stone, attended by his most trusted advisors.

Far below, thousands of low-ranking Aspirants and infidels toil, loading wagons and canal barges with ore and precious stones from Arim. The cargo is conveyed wherever the Hierophant dictates. Profits are tallied by the Monitors, and stored for safe-keeping in the Hierophant's Tower — heavily guarded by the Knights of the Theocratic Order.

The cities of Ammahd and Zanth were both built upon the ruins of Badijan, the former capital of the ancient Phaedran Empire, reduced to rubble in the later stages of the Cult Wars. Aside from their close proximity on the map, the two cities have practically nothing in common.

The City of Andurin

The site of Aaman's largest military installations, Andurin is also an important staging area for trade with the Seven Kingdoms. The city is the home of several monasteries for infantry and cavalry knights, maintained by the Theocratic Order. Orthodoxist pilgrims often stop here to visit the Abbey of Andurin, where acolytes are trained in the tenets of Orthodoxist dogma.

The Monastic Hills

This ancient region of gently sloping hills was once a Phaedran forest preserve, where countless exotic species of birds and beasts were allowed to roam freely. Following the winding down of the Cult Wars, the Aamanians cleared much of the woodland for fuel and timber, and planted acres of provender plant — a type of tuber from which is derived a bland but nutritious wafer, the staple food of Aaman.

The Port City of Arat

This large port city served as an Aamanian naval installation during the Cult Wars. The facilities are now crowded with Aamanian merchant vessels, which sail along the coast from the Aaman Canal (leading through Ammahd all the way to the Axis River) in the north, to the settlement of Alm in the south. Aamanian sailors will not normally venture beyond these areas, fearing that to do so will invoke the disfavor of Aa the Omnipotent.

The Sea of Sorrow

Once known as the Phaedran Gulf, the Sea of Sorrow was renamed following a disastrous sea battle between the navies of Aaman and Zandu, during which thousands perished. Ships from many lands now ply these waters, headed to and from port cities in Zandu and Aaman. Salvagers scour the sea-bottom for sunken treasure and other valuable items of lost cargo.

The Ironworks at Aabaal

A settlement located in the forested highlands of western Aaman, Aabaal is renowned primarily for its ironworks. Here Orthodoxist cult relics are made, fashioned from black iron by a cloistered order of artisan-priests. The craftsmen of Aabaal are forbidden to deviate from the traditional designs and forms approved by the Hierophant, and are noted for their reclusive habits.

The Flagellants of Alm

Alm is a small village situated in the forested highlands along the southwestern coast of Aaman. An especially fanatical order of Orthodoxists, known as the Flagellants, founded this settlement. They can sometimes be seen wandering the roads of Aaman, beating themselves with ritual flails and chanting Orthodoxist slogans.

The Phandril Forest

The dreaded monsters known as shathane prowl this woodland, which perhaps explains the reluctance of the Aamanians to visit this region. The last of Aaman's truly wild woods — the others having been leveled for fuel, timber or farmland — the Phandril Forest is also a source of revenue for the Orthodoxy.

In the pre-Phaedran era, the first refugees from Phandril buried their dead in these woods, beginning a tradition that lasted for centuries. The old cemeteries, now overgrown, still litter the interior. These tombs are occasionally sought out by Orthodoxist plunderers seeking relics, and the local Monitor sometimes sells high-priced exploration permits to foreign adventurers.

City of Ammahd

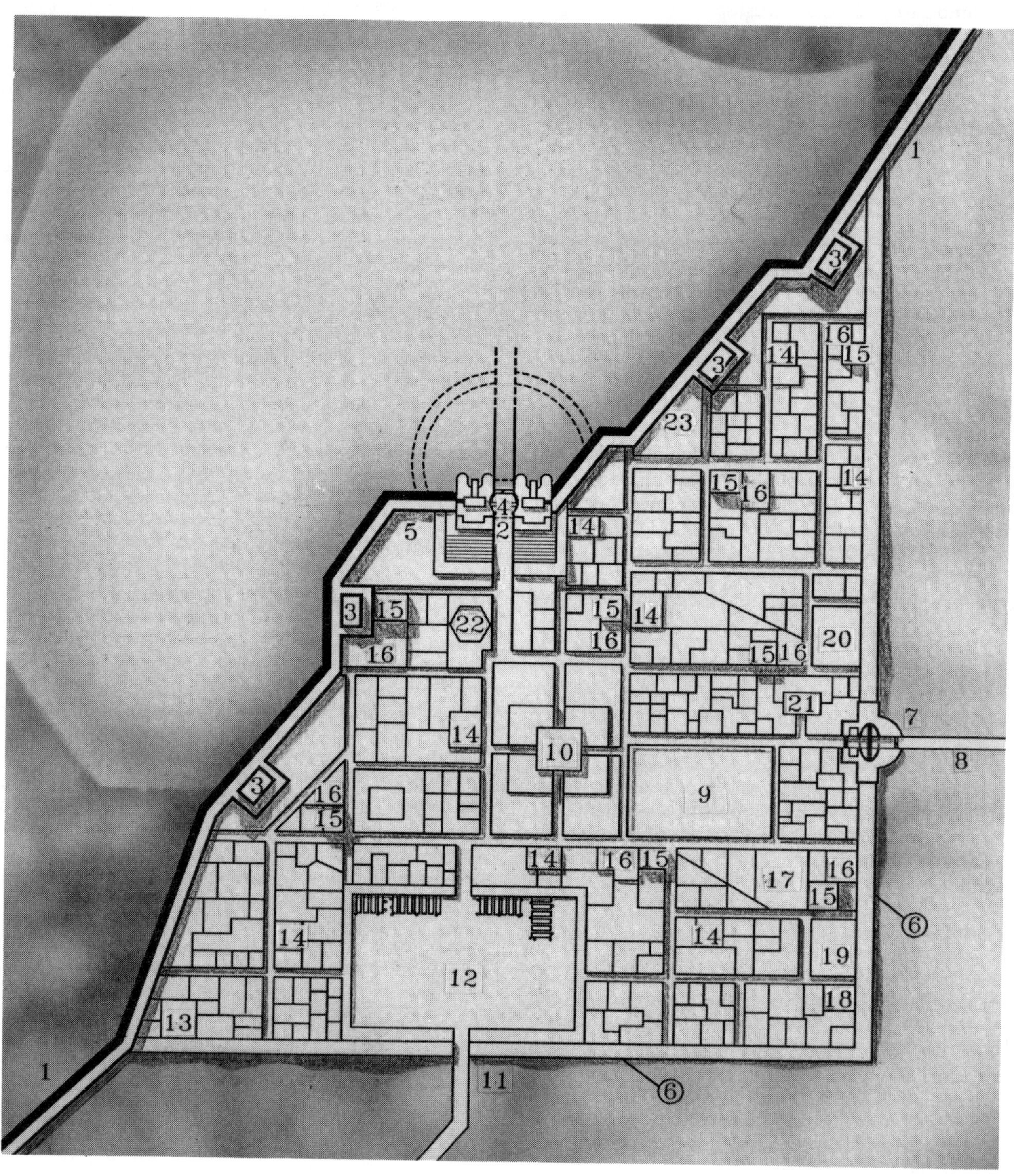

The City of Ammahd

The capital of Aaman, Ammahd is easily the most monotonous city on the continent. The buildings are constructed of white brick and stone, white-washed and roofed over with Arimite slate – they all look much the same. All houses except the Temples of Aa are composed of rooms whose dimensions can be measured in increments of ten feet. The architecture consists of a bland compilation of squares set in a grid pattern, reflecting the unimaginative nature of its architects, the Orthodoxists of Aaman.

As is true throughout the country, the influence of the Orthodoxist Cult is evident everywhere in the city. Individuality has been thoroughly suppressed: all Aamanians dress alike, they converse in tired cliches, and effect identical manners and behaviorisms. Travelers from other lands stand out like beacons against this colorless backdrop, and are generally treated as inferiors, tolerated only if their presence is of some advantage to the state.

Aamanian laws are unenlightened. Individuals who commit even the slightest transgression against cult doctrines are dragged away to the Halls of Penance. At the discretion of the Inquisitors, non-believers may be forcibly converted to an Orthodoxist point of view. Or they may simply "disappear." Accordingly, the city and the surrounding environs remain a low priority for visitors from other lands.

1. The Great Barrier Wall

Sixty feet in height, the Great Barrier Wall runs from the mountainous border of Arim to the Sea of Sorrow. It is built of stone hauled from the Onyx Mountains. The Exarch of Arim supplied laborers and much of the raw material for the project, and profited greatly from the endeavor.

2. Toll Gates

The three gatehouses, like the wall itself, are considered neutral territory. The country whose representative wins the annual Clash of Champions is awarded proprietorship of the wall for the year, including the right to collect all toll revenues. By mutual agreement, the toll may not exceed one gold lumen per person, animal and conveyance. Both sides take pains to avoid losing revenue when proprietorship of the wall is theirs, posting armed sentinels at regular intervals along the length of the structure.

3. The Watchtowers

Aaman maintains a number of these structures, each of which measures 70 feet in height and is constructed of black iron painted with white lacquers. Each tower is manned by ten sentinels, whose duty it is to keep a constant watch on the Zandir side of the border. Gongs placed within the towers are to be used in the event of an enemy attack (none have been rung since the wall was completed). The sentinels posted in these watchtowers are armed with crossbows, which they use freely upon unauthorized individuals seeking to scale the wall.

4. Site of the Clash of Champions

This elevated, 20-foot-square platform serves as the arena for the annual Clash of Champions. The opponent who falls or is forced off the platform loses the match; if not already dead, the loser usually perishes as a result of the ensuing fall. It is considered a particular coup to cause a vanquished foe to fall amongst his (or her) own supporters.

5. Stadia

These immense structures were built to afford seating for spectators viewing the Clash of Champions. Canopied pavilions are available to individuals of importance or position in their respective governments. Vendors hawking food, drink, spyglasses and souvenirs circulate freely amongst the crowds during such events, as do pick-pockets, cutpurses, and other ne'er-do-wells. The stadia go unused throughout the rest of the year.

6. City Walls

The white stone walls around the rest of Ammahd stand nearly 30 feet in height. Aamanian sentinels outfitted in white plate-mail patrol the walls in groups of ten. Their demeanor is typically unfriendly, particularly as regards infidels – a term equivalent, in Aaman, to foreigner, non-believer, evil magician, and so on.

7. Gatehouse

The gates to the city are guarded by a platoon of Aamanian Border Knights, commanded by a Warrior-Priest. Travelers are required to register their names and state their reasons for entering Ammahd. If enroute to Zandu, they must continue on to Zanth without stopping, regardless of prevailing weather conditions or other considerations. Zandir citizens may be turned away or escorted to the border (most avoid possible difficulties by traveling through Arim, avoiding Aaman entirely).

*Profile: **Archimage Gortovane***
Aamanian Warrior-Priest, 9th Level
Paranoia is considered a prerequisite for command of a Border Knight unit, and Gortovane certainly fits the bill. When he isn't making a merchant unload "suspicious" wagons, or forcing travelers to submit to tests that supposedly demonstrate their spiritual purity, the Archimage is dreaming of schemes to entrap Heterodoxist agents.

8. The Phaedran Causeway

This ancient highway dates back to the time of the Phaedran Empire. Poorly maintained, the roadway is marginally serviceable at best. At the worst spots, loose stones, unstable shoulders, and flooded sections of road can cause extensive delays in travel.

9. Cemetery of Aa's Effulgence

Here are buried the untold thousands of Orthodoxists who died during the Cult Wars.

10. The Hierophant's Tower

An imposing structure standing nearly 100 feet in height, this tower serves as the dwelling place of the Hierophant, the ruler and high-priest of Aaman. The tower's functions are multi-fold. Ten heavily guarded vaults contain the country's vast stores of gold and precious artifacts, as well as treasures (magical, cultural and artistic) confiscated from individuals accused of heresy. Four levels are devoted to the scriptorium, which boasts a collection of some 30,000 books and folios. The upper five levels are for the Hierophant – the two uppermost for his personal use, the two lowest for his bodyguards and attendants, and the mid-level for his advisors. The grounds surrounding the tower are obsessively patrolled by Knights of the Theocratic Order:

Profile: **Omniturge the Blessed**
Aamanian Archimage, 24th Level
The scion of a long dynasty of powerful Monitors, Omniturge is the first of his lineage to achieve the exalted position of Hierophant. His official concerns have been the traditional ones: expansion of political and commercial influence abroad, subversion of the Paradoxist regime in Zandu, and the safeguarding of the sacred relics. One paramount concern is the Hierophant's wand of office – the Aamonicle, consisting of a sphere of black ivory mounted within a lunar crescent atop a hardwood staff – which has suddenly and mysteriously begun to pit and corrode.

11. The Aaman Canal

This man-made channel is fed by a tributary of the Axis River, and courses through the city of Ammahd to the Sea of Sorrow. The ancient Phaedrans built the canal some six centuries ago. The Aamanians, concerned more with spiritual purity than physical realities, have allowed the facility to deteriorate, particularly the intricate system of locks designed to modulate the flow of water. The canal is now used primarily by Arimite ore-barges and Aamanian patrol vessels bound for the Axis River.

12. Docks

Lowly Aspirants and infidels are found here, unloading shipments of black-iron ore from Arim. Caravans laden with ore and precious stones load up and leave for points elsewhere in Aaman on a weekly basis.

13. Laborers' District

This blandly unattractive area is occupied mainly by lower-class laborers and slaves. The latter are kept in walled labor camps, which are little better than prisons.

14. Temples

These edifices are dedicated to Aa the Omniscient, the patron deity of the Orthodoxist Cult. Each is run by an Archirnage, who wields control over a retinue of underpriests, acolytes and devotees. The temples compete for upper-level Aspirants, whom they hope to lure into their congregation in order to solicit greater contributions to the temple fund. The most powerful temples strike alliances with factions within the Theocratic Order, thereby attaining an even greater degree of influence.

Profile: **Archimage Tortomal**
Aamanian Archimage, 17th Level
The Temple of Munificent Aa is one of the most splendid of the sanctuaries in the capital, and its Archimage is endowed with the influence and respect accorded to a senior cleric. Tortomal is a tall man of sepulchral appearance, and his speaking voice is deep and resonant. His arresting sermons on the rewards of the afterlife are well-attended, though jealous priests have accused him of dabbling in Ariane heresies. Tortomal avidly collects memorabilia concerning the Holy Founders of the Orthodoxist Cult.

15. Towers of the Monitors

These 50-foot stone towers serve as the dwelling places of Ammahd's Monitors, each of whom holds the position of ruling prelate in his assigned district. Individuals hoping to verify increases in mana must file a claim with the Monitor assigned to their district. Adjudicators serving each Monitor process the petitions, posting the results beside the tower gates at sunsdown.

The number and wealth of a district's temples, the prestige of its archimages, and the extent of its influence with the Theocratic Order are all factors contributing to a Monitor's prestige and status, and competition between them is fierce. These administrators are also under the constant scrutinization of the Hierophant, through his agents in the Theocratic Order.

Profile: **Monitor Oslid**
Aamanian Knight, 16th Level
Oslid gained his status the hard way – he fought his way to the holy places and back scores of times, sheepherding with him flocks of the Faithful. The one-eyed former Knight is an energetic administrator, intolerant of sin and the faults of his subordinates. Oslid hates the Beastmen of Golarin for ravaging one of his pilgrimages.

16. Monasteries

Sequestered within these fortified structures are the various factions of the Theocratic Order. Each is a military enclave, specializing in a single military function: marine operations, cavalry, infantry, border patrol, or guarding the temples. The facilities available vary in type and quality, according to the degree of influence wielded by their Master-Archimage within the Order. Though all members of the Theocratic Order are sworn to obey the dictates of the Hierophant, various factions typically vie with one another for the best recruits, and for contributions from temples seeking to gain a monastery's allegiance.

Profile: **Master-Archimage Tranto**
Aamanian Warrior-Priest, 13th Level
This Orthodoxist cleric is responsible for the monastery which provides Aaman's naval patrols on the Axis River. Tranto commands from a great wargalley, whenever he can free himself from the boundless paperwork required of him by the Theocratic Order. He hates the Ardua, and believes that Aa will someday allow the Faithful to drive the avians out of the Forest of Vardune.

17. Reliquary

This museum houses artifacts purported to have great significance to the god Aa: the soiled garments of an Orthodoxist seer, the personal effects of martyrs to the cult, the bones of Aamanian saints, and so forth. Many other sanctified items were dredged from ancient ruins and holy sites by pilgrims of the faith. A donation of ten gold lumens is charged for admittance.

Profile: Knight Sevesto
Aamanian Knight, 21st Level

It is one thing to adhere to the dogmas of the faith, and another to serve Aa as faithfully as the god requires. So thinks Sevesto, and the Hierophant must think likewise, or the old Knight would not hold the post that he does. Sevesto will make whatever deals are required to obtain the artifacts which he covets, and he has the full cooperation of the Theocratic Order. He speaks several languages fluently, and often travels in disguise as one of the non-believers.

18. Depilator

This is a facility where cultists come for the ritual removal of facial and body hair, a process accomplished through immersion in vats filled with the foul-smelling juice of the bald-nettle plant. This is the first of many ritual observances which new converts to Orthodoxism must undergo. The depiliators (usually male and over the age of 70) customarily wear blindfolds while engaged in their work. A donation of five gold lumens is required.

19. Halls of Penance

Here, newly-depiliated converts and individuals accused of impropriety are absolved of their sins. The methods employed vary greatly, and include dunking (in deep wells), flogging, beating with wooden staves, and more unusual forms of physical and psychological punishment. The Inquisitors assigned to the Halls of Penance are quite creative, particularly as regards the extraction of confessions from tight-lipped sinners and heretics. A dungeon is housed in the lower levels, for the benefit of those recalcitrants who are deemed to require a more prolonged form of absolution.

Profile: Inquisitor Maxyr
Aamanian Inquisitor, 12th Level

Extracting confessions is the speciality of this Inquisitor. Maxyr is one of the rare converts to Orthodoxism, and originally hails from Rajanistan. His great size and strength — he is gigantic in stature, like all of the Shadinn — serve him well in his trade, and his success rate is his best answer to those who would condemn him for his infidel origin.

20. Pilgrimage Supply

This immense establishment — owned by the Orthodoxist Cult, and administered by the Hierophant's agents — offers all that an individual undertaking a pilgrimage or crusade could possibly desire: cult-approved travelers' raiment, maps, wagons, burden beasts, dray beasts, slave bearers, rations, Orthodoxist holy items, and a host of sundries and assorted goods. A trio of Archimages supervises the operation. Costs are twice average.

Profile: Archimage Zadoz
Aamanian Archimage, 8th Level

One of three clerics who operate a mammoth emporium known as Pilgrim Supply, Zadoz knows nothing about commerce. This does not stop him from performing his job — he sells with religious fervor, and becomes offended if asked to bargain, since the prices are set "according to the precepts of Orthodoxism." He is worried for his niece and shop assistant, Doxa, since her desire to travel is not apparently allied with a passion to visit the holy sites.

21. The Pilgrim's Rest

This inn caters to pilgrims of the Orthodoxist Cult, many of whom come to visit Ammahd and tour the locations made famous by the struggles of the Cult Wars. The inn's fare is notably devoid of flavor or spice. Alcoholic beverages and musical entertainment are prohibited, and costs are somewhat above average.

Profile: Adjudicator Kosxa
Aamanian Witch Hunter, 18th Level

Retired from active service with the Theocratic Order after four decades spent traveling the north — Werewood, Arim and Urag — Kosxa gives the semblance of being little more than a strict but kindly innkeeper. However, his fervor rises to the fore when he gets wind of any degree of heresy. Kosxa especially hates Dhuna witchery, and has many devices designed to detect spell-casting and its practitioners.

22. Hall of Meditation

The devout among the members of the Orthodoxist Cult gather here with their peers to meditate, discuss the doctrines of Orthodoxism, or learn of the latest decrees of the Hierophant. Archimages are on hand to assist the faithful in committing to memory cherished phrases from the Omnival.

23. Mercantilers' District

This section of the city includes many small shops and mercantile establishments, such as limners (selling white lacquers), clothiers (cult vestments only), tanners, millers, masons, carpenters, potters, and so forth. None dare sell their wares unless the designs and materials have been approved by the Orthodoxist Cult.

ARIM

Arimite Knife-Fighters on night watch at the Citadel of Akbar.

Arim is a land of rough and irregular hills, interspersed with grassy steppes and thickets of stunted oak and briar. To the north lie the dark peaks of the Onyx Mountains; to the east is Lake Venda, source of the great Axis River, fed by countless mountain streams and brooks. West lie the forbidding forests of Werewood; along the northeastern frontier, the towering Cliffs of Bahahd fall away into the Darklands of Urag.

The Arimites

The people who live in this grey and windy realm, known as the Arimites, are a dour and moody lot. They are swarthy of complexion, with long black hair and dark, deep-set eyes. The men tend to be gaunt and wiry, with hatchet-like features; the women, heavy-set and lacking in charm. The customary mode of dress in this region consists of sackcloth garments, animal-hide boots, and bulky fur vests, accented with wristbands, ear-rings and knives made of black iron.

Customs

The Arimites are a humorless people, most of whom live hard lives as miners of the country's considerable mineral wealth. They have no love of song or dance, but favor chakos, a fiery liquor brewed in black-iron kegs. Abuse of this potent intoxicant is widespread in Arim, especially among the overworked miners, who seek escape from the tedium of their existence.

Even discounting the influence of chakos, various forms of pathological deviant behavior seem to be ingrained traits among these folk. Accordingly, the Arimites have a reputation in other lands as cutthroats, an assessment which experts say is not without merit.

The Revenant Cult

A secret society that specializes in a wide range of covert and often deadly activities, the Revenant Cult may be hired to carry out almost any act of vengeance, including arson, theft, muggings, extortion, and even slander. Murder-for-hire is probably the cult's most lucrative line of business.

Anyone who can afford their fees — which range from as little as ten silver pieces to over 100,000 gold lumens — can obtain the services of the cult. This is done by the simple method of posting a notice in some public place. The prevalence of the cult is such that a Revenant, attired in customary night-grey cloak and veil, will perform the desired service by the following day.

Government officials, common laborers, merchants, and even jealous lovers and irate housewives have all been known to employ the services of the Revenants to settle disputes or avenge affronts. The popularity of this impersonal means of seeking redress is such that, in most parts of Arim, the mere shaking or brandishing of a change purse is considered suggestive of a threat to hire the Revenants.

An example of this unusual custom is provided in the story of the hillman and the chakos merchant, a popular Arimite folk tale. As the story goes, the hillman returned from hunting to find that his wife, in his absence, had come into possession of a full cask of chakos. Having left his mate with funds insufficient to purchase such a quantity of liquor, the hillman became suspicious of the local chakos merchant, whom he believed might be seeking to gain the affections of his wife by plying her with valuable gifts.

Accordingly, the hillman paid the Revenants ten silver pieces to perform a mischief upon the merchant. The chakos dealer awakened on the following day to find his wagon bereft of its wheels, with an anonymous note warning against further indiscretions. Outraged, the merchant guessed the identity of his enemy, and paid the Revenants 20 silver pieces to poison the hillman's favorite steed. This so upset the hillman that he at once gave over 50 gold lumens to the Revenants with instructions to have the merchant thrashed. On the next day, the chakos merchant made similar arrangements for the benefit of his hated rival.

This was the final straw for the hillman, who realized that only the death of his enemy would now suffice to bring their feud to a conclusion. While in town posting a notice for the Revenants, the hillman chanced to meet the merchant, who was there for the same purpose. The two antagonists, too bruised and weary to fight, and nearly bankrupt of funds, decided to strike a compromise: each contributed half the fee necessary to have the hillman's wife assassinated, thus removing the source of their differences. Relieved to have put an end to their dispute, the two men parted friends.

Unfortunately, neither ever saw the other alive again. Unbeknownst to either man, the hillman's wife was a member of the Revenant Cult, whose followers are strictly forbidden to do harm to one of their own kind.

The Forbidden City of Ahrazahd

The Forbidden City of Ahrazahd is home to the ruler of Arim, a recluse known as the Exarch. Here in this lofty mountain retreat, the Arimite lord lives in seclusion, surrounded by a retinue of bodyguards, concubines and royal wizards. Shipments of gold, gemstones and provisions are brought here by caravan once each month. Aside from this, the capital city is closed to outsiders – the Exarch governs the country through his subordinates in Shattra and Akbar. The monarch does not dare to set foot outside of Ahrazahd, for fear of being assassinated by Revenants.

The Citadel of Akbar

A formidable military outpost which stands at the mouth of a deep gorge, Akbar bars incursions by the clans of Urag into the land of Arim. Its walls are over 40 feet in height, and are studded with 50-foot towers mounted with fire-throwers. No less than 10,000 Arimite soldiers, archers, scouts and artillerists man this massive installation. The fortress also serves as a center for trade, and is occasionally visited by Jaka hunters, Djaffir merchants, and Farad slave-mongers.

The Trading Post of Shattra

The mining and trade center of Shattra is located on the banks of the Axis River. It is a filthy place, crowded with ramshackle wooden tenements and covered in a perpetual haze of smoke and soot. Raw black-iron ore is brought here to be smelted down into ingots and shipped by barge or caravan to Aaman, Zandu, the Seven Kingdoms, and beyond.

Shattra is visited primarily by miners and ore traders, though grey-skinned mongers from Faradun do a brisk trade in slave girls, courtesans and concubines – women of grace and beauty are a rare commodity in Arim. The secretive Revenant Cult is believed to have its base of operations here.

The Onyx Mountains

Rich in black-iron and silver – as well as emeralds, garnets, sards, carnelians, and beryls of passable quality – the Onyx Mountains are dotted with caves known to contain moonstones of immense size and impeccable color. Cliff-dwelling Stryx, bands of Darklings from nearby Urag, and the fearsome Nocturnal Strangler haunt these environs, dulling the enthusiasm of many would-be prospectors. The highlands are also home to exomorphs, yaksha and herds of equs.

The Cliffs of Bahahd

In the eastern Onyx Mountains, these precipitous cliffs have long protected Arim from invasion by the Ur clans to the east. They rise over 300 feet in height, and are nearly impossible to scale. Bands of Stryx once lived in caves here, but were smoked out by the Arimites.

The Druhks

The wooded hills and mountains of central Arim are the domain of the fierce Druhk tribes — bestial sub-men of violent temperament. Similar in stature to the Arimites, the tribesmen dress in the skins of wild beasts, stain their hair and bodies with the purple juice of wild mountain berries, and wield stone war clubs and jagged-edged bone daggers.

Customs

Druhks are decidedly unfriendly, finding great enjoyment in skinning alive individuals who trespass into their lands. Among these folk, mercy is considered a sign of weakness, and compassion is virtually unknown. Their Songs of Fear and Death are said to strike madness in those who hear them.

The tribes range in size from a few dozen individuals to several hundred. Druhks build no permanent dwellings of any kind, ranging instead as nomads throughout the central portion of Arim. Their warriors (both male and female) ride wild greymanes also dyed purple with berry juice — a most unusual sight.

Lake Venda

Source of the Axis River, Lake Venda lies at the foot of the Onyx Mountains in Arim. Fed by numerous small streams and brooks, its waters are cold and clear.

Despite its seemingly peaceful appearance, the lake is avoided by the Arimites, who say it is accursed. According to legend, Lake Venda is inhabited by nine great Shaitans. They supposedly live in the ruins of an ancient sunken city, and prey upon unwary sailors and fishermen. Each is said to possess a fabulous treasure — one of the Nine Keys of Knowledge, or one of the Devil Rings of Orlax, depending upon which of the many conflicting accounts one wishes to believe.

The Druhk tribes which inhabit the surrounding hills claim to give the legend little credence, but nevertheless, the tribesmen shun the wide and watery expanses of Lake Venda in favor of the shallows around the shore.

A Druhk war party on the attack.

SILVANUS

Sarista "culture"

Silvanus is a woodland region located to the west of the Necros River and the forests of Werewood. It is also bordered by the deep-blue expanse of the Azure Ocean, which is traversed by fishing vessels of many nations — Zandu, Gao-Din, Imria, Parthene, and Faradun — as well as the ships of Orthodoxist Witch Hunters pursuing heretics. Sea dragons are not unknown in coastal waters, and storm demons may be encountered during the fierce storms of the spring and fall.

Unlike the dreary and fell territories of its eastern neighbor, Silvanus and its wooded glens are scenic and relatively tranquil. Fields of meadow grass offer respite from the forests, and cool streams converge amidst thickets of silver-beech, carpets of moss, and quiet ponds.

The Sarista

Among the few folk known to frequent this region are the Sarista, a nomadic race of indistinct origin. The gypsies are built along slender proportions, and have skin the color of rich topaz, dark eyes, and jet-black hair.

They are partial to ear bangles, facial tattooing, and all types of gaudy raiment. The men sport capes, berets, tight-fitting hose, sashes, and high boots, while the women prefer all manner of sultry and seductive attire.

Customs

The Sarista are a people of diverse qualities. Some are loners who make their living as peddlers, mercenaries or vagabonds. Others, notable for their skill at witchcraft, live in secluded wilderness regions. The majority of these folk are gregarious, fond of traveling in gypsy caravans, carrying all that they own in wagons or on the backs of burden beasts.

Sarista roam the Western Lands and beyond, stopping in cities and villages along the way to raise money by their performances. In such places, the gypsies are renowned for their talents as folk healers, animal trainers, fortune tellers, acrobats, dancers, puppeteers and thespians...or as mountebanks, thieves and tricksters, depending upon one's point of view.

The discrepancy of opinion regarding the Sarista may be attributed to their mysterious customs, traditions and history. The Sarista have their own language, a version of the common Talislan tongue which allows the speaker to convey hidden meanings by the use of subtle gestures and inflections.

The tribes do not keep written records of any sort, but rely upon the elder Sarista to raise their offspring and teach them the secret lore of their people. These studies consist primarily of minor folk magics, herb lore, and "Sarista culture" — a euphemism held to be roughly equivalent to the less-flattering term, "thievery." By age seven, a Sarista child knows every woodland trail in Silvanus by heart, and has a comprehensive understanding of so-called Sarista culture.

Sarista religion revolves around two obscure demigods: Fortuna, the lovely but fickle goddess of luck, and the grim entity known as Death. They revere Fortuna but mock Death, whom they strive to cheat at every opportunity.

The history of the Sarista consists of a baffling collection of anecdotes, fables and bawdy ballads. Some scholars believe them to be a people displaced during the time of the Great Disaster. Others claim they are descended from the numerous bandits who roamed these woods before the rise of the Phaedran Empire.

Flora and Fauna

The woods of Silvanus are rife with wood whisps and colorful insects such as the crystal moth. Roots and herbs known for magical or healing properties are common. Two plants of particular note are found here: whisperweed (which often tells the most astonishing secrets) and needleleaf (an obnoxious, needle-throwing succulent).

The Necros River

These sluggish black waters run from the mountainous borders of Khazad southward, finally emptying into Zantium Bay. Issuing from some underground source, the Necros smells vile and is believed to be tainted by black magic. So much as a single sip is said to bring on terrifying nightmares.

The Valley of Forgetfulness

The Necros River runs through this densely-forested vale, which falls partly in both Werewood and Silvanus. Late in the evening, silver-grey mists rise upward from the river and hang over the valley. Individuals who breathe these vapors purportedly suffer partial or even total memory loss, the duration of which may last from one to ten days. Werebeasts and banes prowl the slopes of the valley, where the bodies of convicted felons were interred in the time of the Phaedran Empire.

The Dire Woods

This dark and dreary region occupies eastern Silvanus, and is overgrown with thornwood and hangman's tree, all hung with strands of grey-black spidermoss. The woods receive their name from their awful inhabitants, which include ghasts, malathrope and necrophages, to name but a few. Legends of hidden treasure, supposedly buried here by an extinct race of seafaring marauders, go largely unheeded.

Castabulan

A rocky isle located off the western coast of Silvanus, Castabulan is fringed with copses of tanglewood and stunted gall oak. A cabal of blue-robed astromancers resides on the island, and has erected an eccentric "observatory" constructed of rough-hewn timbers and stone.

Descendants of a group of Phantasians whose windship crash-landed on the isle in the year 447, the Astromancers of Castabulan have developed a close affinity to the forces of nature, which they have had occasion to experience first-hand since being marooned so long ago. They monitor changes in the weather, and claim to be able to predict storms, droughts, tides, and other meteorological phenomena. It is customary for Zandir captains sailing to or from the port of Zantium to send a messenger to Castabulan, seeking the astromancers' advice and augery .

Talisandre

Another small island which lies off the coast of Silvanus, Talisandre is a virtual paradise, populated by a plethora of wild flora and fauna. A race of xenophobic Men, known as the Azir, lives in this idyllic setting. They know nothing of the civilized world, a condition which they have adopted by choice — visitors from the outside world are greeted with fusilades of stones, and told in no uncertain terms to depart the Azir's island refuge.

The Gulf of Silvanus

This narrow and winding inlet between Silvanus and Khazad is considered unnavigable, due to the presence of maelstroms and unpredictable cross-currents. Ancient sea dragons are believed to sleep in the depths, another reason why Talislantan sailors prefer to steer clear of these waters.

WEREWOOD

A Werebeast on the prowl (foreground); Bane, Mandragore, and Weirdling (background).

Werewood is a dark and tangled forest region situated to the north of Zandu. By day, it is an eerie place — tendrils of grey moss hang from its gnarled and misshapen trees, suspended above thick swards of bracken, toadstools and molds. Were-rooks, perched on the limbs of rotting spider-oak trees, assail travelers with pointed remarks and morbid prophecies. Strange shadow-forms prowl the undergrowth, their presence felt more than seen. Other creatures, less withdrawn, wait for victims to approach within reach of talon, claw, or fang.

It is in the evening hours, however, that the true nature of Werewood is fully revealed. Clouds of mist rise, cold and dank, from the forest floor. From the darkening woods, mournful howls issue forth: the baleful cries of Werebeasts on the hunt.

Although Werewood is a perilous place, it is not without redeeming qualities. Many useful herb and plant species thrive here, including such rarities as the prophet tree, shrinking violet, tantalus, contrary vine, and cleric's cowl. Quaga — a large species of fresh-water mollusk — dwell in brackish ponds, and are sought after for the rare, violet-colored pearls which they produce.

Werebeasts

Huge and horrid in appearance, these creatures are nocturnal by habit, and seldom venture from their caves during the daylight hours. By night, Werebeasts can no longer control their hunger, and must feed. Only minimally intelligent, they hunt in small packs, and generally attack anything that moves. They are noted for their cruelty, and often torture their prey.

Banes

More sinister than Werebeasts, Banes are black as polished obsidian, and are nocturnal by nature. These vile man-like beings have pointed fangs and eyes that glow in the dark like burning embers.

Banes are vampiric, and feed on warm-blooded prey of all sorts. They possess the uncanny ability to mimic sounds of any kind: they can produce animal calls, imitate voices, and even repeat magical spells and incantations. The deadly creatures are exceedingly swift, but are capable of moving with great stealth. Their intelligence borders on the diabolical. It is fortunate that they are few in number.

Mandragores

Perhaps the most unusual denizens of Werewood are the plant creatures known as Mandragores. About three feet in height and vaguely man-like in form, mandragores stand rooted and immobile throughout the day. During this time they resemble common woodland plants, though it is said that individuals skilled in Botanomancy or herb lore can detect otherwise.

When darkness falls, Mandragores uproot themselves and set out to hunt for prey, which they capture with nets of vines and grasses. Their luckless victims are bound and then buried alive. In time, the decomposing bodies fertilize the soil, thereby providing nourishment for the Mandragore population.

Weirdlings

Also found in various parts of Werewood are the diminutive creatures known alternately as Weirdlings or Wish-Gnorls. Bent and gnarled in form, these shrivel-faced, man-like beings are both odd and eccentric. They are known to amass great fortunes, which they horde in garishly-decorated underground burrows.

According to legend, if a Weirdling is caught, he must give over his treasure or grant his captor a wish (hence their nickname, Wish-Gnorls). To demand both treasure and wish, or to cause harm to a Weirdling, is said to invalidate the contract.

Fortune-hunters have long searched Werewood for Weirdlings. The beings sometimes roam about at night, stealing other creatures' valuables and scavenging for lost or buried treasure. Despite their rumpled, almost comical appearance, the creatures are nimble and elusive — even banes cannot catch them if they have room to maneuver.

Locating a Wish-Gnorl's burrow is said to be a much more efficient way of capturing these strange little creatures, as their lairs seldom have more than a single entrance. Those who seek Weirdling lairs are advised to be wary: the creatures jealously guard their treasures and wishes, and often ward their burrows with dangerous tricks and traps.

Castlerock

A high promontory of jagged basalt overlooking the Straits of Khazad, Castlerock is situated on the northern coast of Werewood. The mount is a natural stone fortification, and may in fact have been utilized for such purposes during the Forgotten Age. It is thought to be a roosting place for wind demons, and is avoided by sensible beings.

The Dread Forest

This dense and tangled region lies adjacent to the Necros River. It is a favorite haunt of ghasts, necrophages and the like, and so is generally avoided, except by certain varieties of pseudo-demon — most notably, fiends, who seem in some unknown manner to be drawn to the ancient ruins which lie scattered throughout this region

Gnorlwood

The Forest of Gnorlwood is located in the south central region of Werewood, adjacent to the Zandir border. It is one of the oldest woodlands in Talislanta, its once-tall trees now stooped and withered with age. The softly sloping hillocks are home to the Gnorls, an ancient race of smallish, gnarled man-like beings whom some believe to be related to Gnomekin and Weirdlings.

The Gnorls

Gnorls live in underground nooks, typically situated in woodlands. They are skilled in an ancient form of witchcraft known as rhabdomancy, the "art of divin-

A Gnorl Rhabdomancer in her nook.

ing secrets." Gnorls collect secrets, which they gather by various means, including communing with spiritforms. Some earn a living by selling, buying and trading secrets; others as healers who offer their services in exchange for secret knowledge. The Gnorls of Gnorlwood are generally reclusive by nature - a reasonable attitude, as the surrounding woods abound with banes, mandragore, and giant, shaggy-haired humanoids known as shathane.

Mordante's Deep

This forested region derives its name from the legendary black magician, Mordante, who is believed to have lived here for a time after fleeing Faradun. (Legend has it that he was pursued by Xambrian Wizard Hunters.) Supposedly, his castle still stands — covered by vines and creepers, and haunted by ghasts and wind demons.

The Mushroom Forest

Located in northern Werewood, the Mushroom Forest is a murky region rife with giant fungi, toadstools and molds. It is inhabited by numerous hostile organisms as well, including grues, pseudomorphs and scavenger slimes. Despite this, Dhuna and Gnorls sometimes come here to gather certain rare varieties of fungi. The Mushroom Forest is an especially eerie place by night, when the entire region is suffused in a weird, phosphorescent glow.

Green Lagoon

A swirling quagmire, the Green Lagoon is a sinkhole into which the waters of the eastern Sascasm are slowly and irresistibly drawn. Many creatures visit to drink from the Lagoon, including banes, werebeasts, malathrope, ravengers, and shathane. More than a few fall prey to skalanx, aquatic demonoids which lurk below the surface, anchored by their tails to the roots of massive swamp trees.

The Sardonyx Mountains

Stretching from east to west, these mountains form a natural border between Yrmania and Werewood. The lower-lying regions up to the timberline are thick with grey baobab and tanglewood. Kitewinged batranc soar above the clouds, safe from the depredations of yaksha, exomorphs and tundra beasts. Rumors persist that deposits of gold can be found in the easternmost regions.

The Sascasm River

Originating in northern Werewood, the Sascasm River divides into two channels. The western Sascasm runs through Zandu before emptying into the Azure Ocean, and the eastern Sascasm is drawn into the Green Lagoon. Skalanx and river kra live in these waters, which are also infested with metal-scaled fish, called chang.

The Phaedran Tombs

At one time, it was the fashion among the wizards of ancient Phaedra to be buried along the banks of the Sascasm. According to the style of the day, the magicians (whose modern descendants are the Koresian and Tanasian mages of Cymril, in the Seven Kingdoms) made arrangements to be interred in odd mausoleum-like structures. The interior decor of these edifices was often made to resemble an elaborate sitting room, dining hall or bedroom, according to the wizard's preference in leisure-time activities.

The mummified body of the late wizard, dressed in lavish garb and propped-up in some appropriate pose, added the finishing touch to the burial chamber. Though grave robbers have stripped many of the tombs of their wares, it is probable that a number of these crypts remain undiscovered, overgrown with weeds, vines and mosses.

The Weeping River

The upper stretch of the Sascasm River, before it branches into eastern and western channels, is known as the Weeping River amd originates near Mordante's Deep in northern Werewood. Giant river kra lurk in these waters, which are difficult to navigate due to tangled vegetation and accumulations of silt and mud.

Witchwood

This woodland region, located in the eastern portion of Werewood, is home to the Dhuna — practitioners of witchcraft, who fled here to avoid persecution by the Aamanians following the Cult Wars. Hidden deep in these woods, the Dhuna discovered a number of sacred groves, each containing a circular ring of 10-foot-tall runestones. The witches settled near one of these groves, where they remain to the present day.

The Dhuna practice an ancient form of folk magic, and are said to possess certain extraordinary attributes, not the least of which is the reputed ability of witchwomen to capture a man's heart with but a single kiss. The Dhuna live in communal groups, called covens. There are seven known covens, each aligned with one of the Talislantan moons.

ZANDU

The City of Zanth

Zandu is a land of gentle hills and sparse woodlands, shifting to deep forests along its northern borders. To the east lie the southern stretches of the Onyx Mountains of Arim; to the south, the rocky shores of the Sea of Sorrow.

In the interior, groves of blue pomegranates and quince flourish, fed by numerous small tributaries of the Sascasm River. The undeveloped northern and coastal areas are dotted with ancient stonework towers of varying design, built prior to the fall of the ancient empire of Phaedra. These fortresses once served as wilderness outposts or sanctuaries for traveling merchants, but most are now in ruin. Some are known to be occupied by solitary spell-casters, who find isolation most suitable to their peculiar needs.

The Zandir

The people of Zandu bear a marked physical resemblance to the Aamanians, both being descended from copper-skinned Phaedran ancestors. Unlike their Orthodoxist neighbors, however, the Zandir are a colorful folk renowned for their lack of inhibition.

Customs

The Zandir are fond of music, dance and all manner of stimulating pastimes. They enhance their features with vividly colored pigments, adorn their hair with silver bands, and dress in flamboyant apparel — velvet blouses and trousers, capes of silken brocade, curl-toed boots or slippers, and so forth. The womenfolk practice the quaint custom of hiding their faces behind decorative fans, giving the impression that they are shy and demure. This is hardly the case, as male visitors to Zandu often discover. Zandir men are even less subtle, and in other lands are widely regarded as lechers and philanderers. The people of this land regard romance as a fabulous game, to be played constantly.

The Zandir have retained the unique and diverse ethnicity of their forebears, the Phaedran imperials. The populace includes numerous minority groups and factions, including the Causidians, formerly a class of law-makers, now employed as legal advisors, diplomats and scribes; the Certaments, a class of professional duelists; the Zann, who effect a deliberate contrariness regarding any issue; and the Serparians, who are professional beggars.

Zandir culture is complex and many-faceted. The best musicians and artists are rewarded with appointments to the Sultan's retinue, and wizards are also esteemed — particularly Zandu's Charlatans, the seers of the Paradoxist faith, though many who claim sorcerous powers are actually scoundrels.

The Sultan

Zandu's ruler wields absolute, unquestioned power over all his subjects. All citizens are theoretically equal, and therefore equally subject to the whims and moods of the Sultan of Zandu, which sometimes run to the extreme. Unlike the Hierophant of Aaman, the Sultan is far from celibate. Zandir custom allows men to take as many wives as they can afford, and the ruler of Zandu is a very wealthy man.

Zandir laws are generally lax. A popular local saying notes that "what no one sees, no one knows." So long as thieves exercise a certain amount of discretion, the authorities usually "look the other way." Accordingly, petty theft is rampant, particularly in the larger cities, such as the capital of Zanth.

On the other hand, criminals who make the mistake of attracting too much attention can expect to be dealt with severely. Convicted thieves may be tortured, chained to a pillory and placed on public display, or banished into the depths of Werewood. The worst crimes are punishable by any of a wide variety of gruesome and slow deaths, inflicted by the legendarily creative Zandir executioners.

The Sultan personally judges cases during the morning hours, and determines the appropriate verdict for each as the mood suits him. On a good day, he may allow offenders to go free after a brief lecture on morality; on a bad day, the Zandir executioners have their hands full. Imprisonment in the wretched dungeons of Zanth suffices as punishment in the rare instances when the Sultan can come up with no more creative form of punitive action.

Prisoners may spend days or even weeks awaiting an audience with the Sultan, who is often lax in the completion of his duties. Individuals accused of committing a crime are allowed to hire Causidians to represent their interests. Arrangements must be made through the jailors, who customarily charge a healthy "finder's fee" for their services.

The Cult of Paradoxy

The Zandir are Paradoxists, professing to be mystified by the nature of their own existence. The tenets of the Zandir "religion" are perhaps best explained in the Paradoxist text, *The Book of Mysteries*, a lengthy tome filled with 100,000 questions — and no answers.

The Clash of Champions

Of great interest in Zanth is the annual Clash of Champions, held atop the Great Barrier Wall between Zandu and Aaman. Each year the Sultan sends out dozens of his wizardly advisors to scour neighboring lands in search of suitable candidates. The eventual champion, chosen by tournament, is treated like royalty until the day of the match. It is customary for the Sultan to shower a victorious champion with riches, fame and glory. There is no reward for losing — fortunately, the vanquished rarely survive.

The Night of Fools

Of especial importance to the Zandir is the festival known as the "Night of Fools." Held once each year, on this evening virtually all of Zandu's laws are temporarily rescinded. From sunsdown to sunsrise, the capital is transformed into a veritable madhouse. Dressed in ludicrous costumes, and reeling from the effects of opiated wine (provided free of charge by the Sultan), the Zandir spend the evening in revelry, debauchery and mayhem. On the following day, order is restored.

Trade and Relations

Zandu is diametrically opposed to Aaman in nearly all respects. For many centuries the two countries waged ceaseless war against each other, until the establishment of the Great Barrier Wall Treaty. Modern relations between the former antagonists, while overtly peaceful, are still far from cordial. The differences between their cultures remain extreme, and there is no love lost between the two peoples.

Zandu has strong trade ties with Arim, a major supplier of black iron, copper and precious stones. Exports from the Paradoxist nation include utensils of copper and brass, exotic fragrances, spices, narcotic herbs, fine wines, and opals. Blades made by Zandir craftsmen are held in high regard throughout the continent, and are popular trade items.

The Capital City

The capital of Zandu, Zanth is a beautiful city of copper spires, minarets and arched causeways. Like Ammahd, the capital of Aaman, Zanth is built upon the ruins of the ancient Phaedran city of Badijan. At the conclusion of the Cult Wars, the Great Barrier Wall was built through the center of the rubble, and the two nations each built new capitals on their portion of the ruins.

The Sultan lives in Zanth, in a fabulous palace thinly layered with silver and gold. A second, adjacent palace houses the Sultan's wives, which some claim exceed 4,000 in number.

The Phaedran Causeway

Constructed during the reign of the Phaedran emperors, this roadway stretches across Zandu from Zir to the Aamanian border at Zanth. The causeway is indifferently patrolled and is often in need of repair.

The Citadel of Zadian

This fortress is situated amid the central coastal region of Zandu. A sizable contingent of Zandir troops is stationed here, including units of ontra-mounted lancers and archers, swordsmen and women, and border scouts. The citadel stands atop a hill overlooking the rich estates, vineyards and groves of Zadian's wealthy aristocracy, who live much in the manner of feudal lords.

The Sea Ports

A small Zandir coastal settlement, Zantil is built on a peninsula jutting into the Sea of Sorrow. There is a lighthouse here which serves as an aid to ships navigating the rocky waters. In addition, a red beacon — produced by torchlight reflected through a ruby crystal — warns vessels of the presence of giant sea scorpions, which occasionally enter the area via the Phaedran Straits; by day, bellows-horns sound the alert as well.

The port of Zir is where Zandir warships were constructed during the Cult Wars. The shipyards now primarily turn out merchant vessels, and Zir has become a haven for Zandir freetraders. Ships head from here to such exotic locales as Thaecia, Batre and Faradun — some take on passengers or cargo here, while others await repair.

The narrow waterway adjacent to Zir is known as the Phaedran Straits, and is utilized by ships bound to the Sea of Sorrow from the open sea. This was the site of many a terrible battle during the Cult Wars, and not a few Aamanian and Zandir vessels lie on the bottom. Jagged rocks along the coast render the passage hazardous, particularly in foul weather.

Westernmost of Zandu's seaports, the walled settlement of Zantium lies near the terminus of the Sascasm River, on Zantium Bay. Timber, costly perfumes, and exotic plants and beasts from the Zandir Moors are the chief exports. Trackers come to the trading post to sell hides and captured animals.

Located on the western coast of Zandu, Zann is notable primarily for its stubborn and contrary citizens. The Zann rarely agree with others, and are rude and highly opinionated by nature. Most are fishermen, boatmen, or woodland guides. Local streams are thought to be tainted by the Necros River, which may go far to explain the curious behavior of the Zann.

Korak's Mountain

In ancient times, the great sorcerer Korak had constructed on this mount a fabulous manse of eleven amberglass towers, in which he kept his collection of wonders, curiosities and amazements. Harassed by throngs of curious sightseers, the sorcerer finally retired to another dimension, taking all he owned. A quirk of fate caused his manse to become trapped in a temporal rift, with the result that Korak's abode occasionally reappears for several hours at a time on the mountain which now bears the sorcerer's name.

Conjuror's Point

This rocky peninsula is named for the legendary magician, Cascal, who kept a small cottage here in ancient times. A homonculus, left untended in one of Cascal's vats, supposedly escaped when the magician was away and laid waste to his home. The inhabitants of nearby Zantium claim that this creature still lives on Conjuror's Point, and blame the homonculus for almost any occurrence for which there is no ready explanation, including incidents of missing persons, lost articles, and acts of violence.

The Zandir Moors

This area of verdant knolls, flatlands and bogs is notable for its numerous exotic varieties of wildflower, from which are derived costly scents, essences and enchanted philtres. The rare everblue starfire is valued at over 1,000 gold lumens. Aspiring botanists and fortune-seekers are advised to beware of malathrope and bog devils.

The Woodlands of Zandu

This forested area was razed by torch-wielding Orthodoxists during the Cult Wars. The Paradoxists restored the area after the war, according to their own eccentric designs — they created a forest preserve. resplendent with groves of quince, blue pomegranate, incense tree, and succulent barb-berry. Man-made streams and ponds dot the mossy terrain, interspersed with copses of spice tree and giant fern. Acreage has been reserved for the pleasure of the Sultan of Zandu, who is said to be an avid avirwatcher. A troupe of Zandir swordsmen always accompanies the Sultan's entourage, conferring protection from the woodland's exomorphs, malathrope, and poisonous, metallic-scaled vipers.

The fortified border outpost of Zandre houses a contingent of Zandir scouts, and is adjacent to an old stone bridge which spans the Sascasm River. It is frequented by hunters and traders, as well as the fishermen of Zann, who sail their small skiffs up the Sascasm in order to sell their wares at the outpost.

City of Zanth

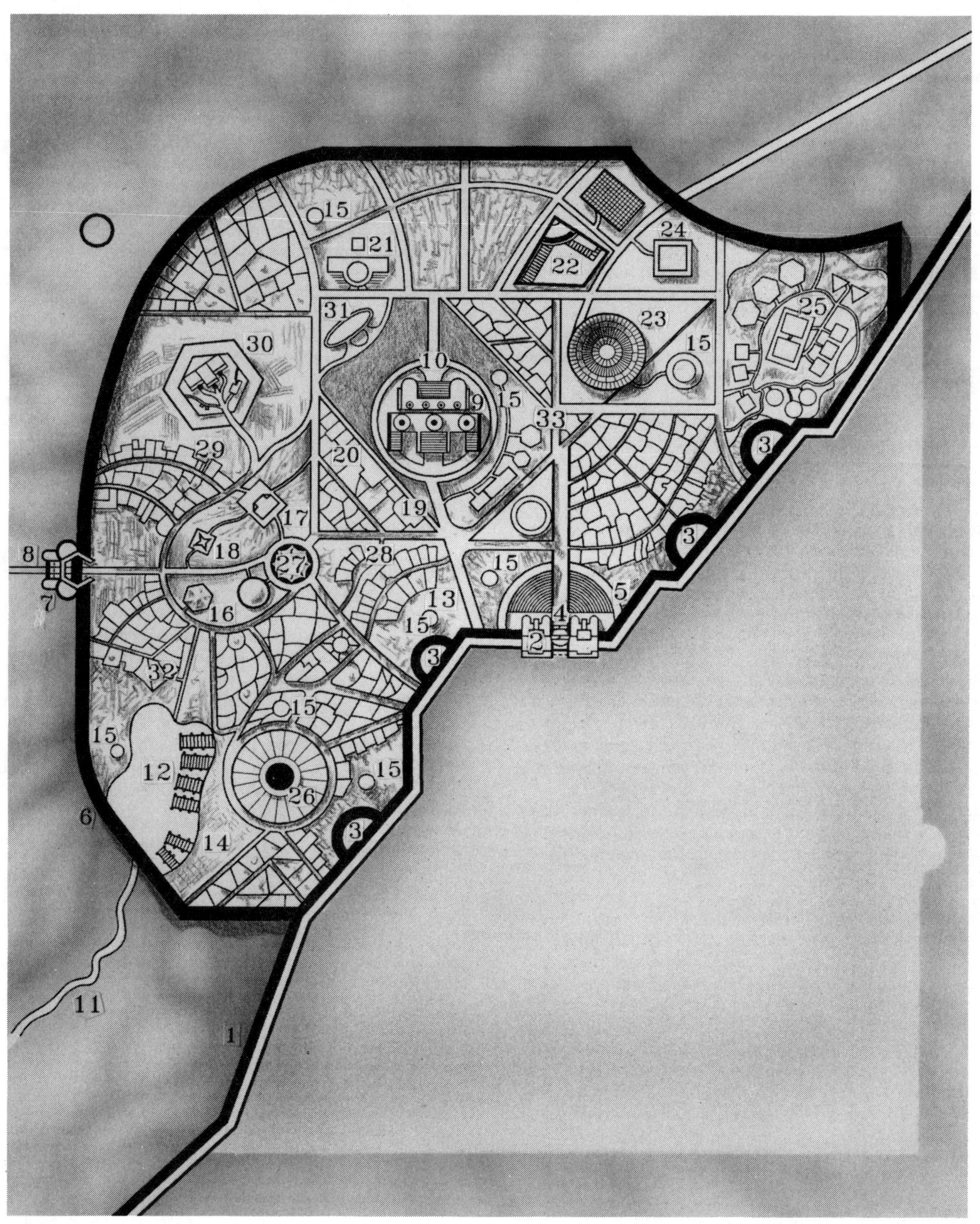

The City of Zanth

Zanth is the capital of Zandu, and is one of the most colorful and exotic cities in Talislanta. From the shining palaces and minarets of the central sector to the slums of the Beggars' District and the Sarista ghetto, Zanth is a study in contrasts. The crowded streets and marketplaces teem with a conglomeration of races and professions: bands of street urchins, Jaka manhunters, Paradoxist seers dressed in brightly colored cassocks, Jhangaran mercenaries, drab Kasmir merchants, blue-robed Causidians, charlatans, fakirs, and many others.

The city, like the rest of Zandu, is notable for unusual local laws and customs, certain of which seem to fly in the face of any standard concept of logic. For example, there are no restrictions in Zanth against insobriety, the bearing of arms, or acting in a lewd manner. Boisterous or reckless behavior, fighting, and insulting a woman, on the other hand, are offenses punishable by imprisonment in the wretched dungeons of Zanth. Dueling is considered acceptable so long as formal arrangements have been made, and is a common practice throughout the land.

1. The Great Barrier Wall
Sixty feet in height, the Great Barrier Wall runs from the mountainous border of Arim to the Sea of Sorrow. It is built of stone hauled from the Onyx Mountains. The Exarch of Arim supplied laborers and much of the raw material for the project, and profited greatly from the endeavor.

2. Toll Gates
The three gatehouses, like the wall itself, are considered neutral territory. The country whose representative wins the annual Clash of Champions is awarded proprietorship of the wall for the year, including the right to collect all toll revenues. By mutual agreement, the toll may not exceed one gold lumen per person, animal and conveyance. Both Aaman and Zandu take pains to avoid losing revenue when proprietorship of the wall is theirs, posting armed sentinels at regular intervals along the length of the structure.

3. The Watchtowers
Zandu maintains a number of these structures, each of which measures at least 65 feet in height and is constructed of black iron. Otherwise, the towers have nothing in common with each other, the designs being unique and often fanciful. Each is manned by ten sentinels, whose duty it is to keep a constant watch on the Aamanian side of the border. Horns placed within the towers are to be sounded in the event of an enemy attack. The sentinels posted in these watchtowers are armed with bows, which they use freely upon unauthorized individuals seeking to scale the wall.

4. Site of the Clash of Champions
This elevated, 20-foot-square platform serves as the arena for the annual Clash of Champions. The opponent who falls or is forced off the platform loses the match; if not already dead, the loser usually perishes as a result of the ensuing fall. It is considered a particular coup to cause a vanquished foe to fall amongst his (or her) own supporters.

5. Stadia
These immense structures were built to afford seating for spectators viewing the Clash of Champions. Canopied pavilions are available to individuals of importance or position in their respective governments. Vendors hawking food, drink, spyglasses and various inexpensive sorts of souvenirs circulate freely amongst the crowds during such events, as do pick-pockets and cut-purses. The stadia go unused throughout the rest of the year.

6. City Walls
The black stone walls of Zanth stand about 30 feet in height. Zandir sentinels, outfitted in black-iron chain-mail, patrol the walls in platoons of ten to twelve individuals (both males and females serve in the Zandir military). Most are friendly, some perhaps overtly so; the Zandir are prone to excess, and notably lacking in restraint as pertains to relations with members of the opposite sex.

7. Gatehouse
Contingents of 20 sentinels guard the gates to the city. Spot checks of suspicious-looking individuals and cargos occur from time to time. In return for the rough treatment accorded Zandir citizens at the border of Aaman, Aamanians who attempt to pass this way are routinely turned away.

8. The Phaedran Causeway
This is the western extension of the ancient roadway. The road forks to the north, leading west toward Zadian and northward into Arim. The northern branch is well-maintained (thanks to the Arimites), though still not entirely free of difficulties: ice and snow in the winter months, fierce Druhk war-parties, and predatory beasts, to name a few.

9. The Sultan's Palace
A fabulous structure thinly layered with silver and gold, the palace is reminiscent of the storied architecture of ancient Badijan. The grounds are decorated with canopied terraces, fountains, walkways, and topiary gardens. The interior boasts lavish aviaries, solariums, spiral stairways, and a vast collection of paintings, sculptures, plush carpets, cushioned divans, and tapestries. Here, the Sultan of Zandu dwells amidst great splendor, attended by his viziers and servitors, the astromancers who advise him, and his personal corps of elite swordsmen.

Profile: **The Sultan of Zandu**
Zandir Swordsman, 28th Level
The Sultan — it is forbidden to call him by his given name — is a man of mercurial moods and passions. He is a slender, handsome man in his early forties, with a decided taste for opiates, women and revelry. His health is on the decline.

10. Palace of the Sultan's Harem
Situated adjacent to the Sultan's own palace, this marvelous structure houses the grand potentate's 4,000 wives, plus half again as many eunuchs, hand maidens and servants. Several hundred of the Sultan's offspring are tended to in a connecting nursery.

*Profile: **Cilia Aquatine***
Batrean Concubine, 14th Level
The Sultan's newest wife and current infatuation, Cilia effects an aquatic look, dressing entirely in seashells and braided seaweed, and having her green-dyed hair magically coiffed so that it seems to be moving in a current. The Sultan has no idea that Cilia was once an Arimite's paramour, or that Revenant agents are seeking for her.

11. The Zandu Canal
This man-made channel runs south to the Sea of Sorrow. Built long ago by the ancient Phaedrans, it has been stagnant since the Aamanians blocked off its access to the waters of the Axis River. Only magical intervention has kept the channel from drying up entirely.

12. Docks
Zandir freetraders arrive and depart from this point, carrying shipments of spices, copper and brass articles, fine Zandir blades, and other goods to such places as the Thaecian Isles, Jhangara, Faradun, and the Zandir cities of Zadian and Zir.

*Profile: **Captain Zirago Vey***
Zandir Swordsman, 14th Level
When in port, Captain Vey is one of the more colorful figures in the dockyard. His brass arm, an enchanted relic of ancient origin, is adept at flinging knives and slapping barmaid's bottoms – Zirago says it has a mind of its own. His ship, the Fountain of Dust, regularly risks the voyage to the Dark Coast, returning with rare goods of many kinds.

13. The Marketplace
This colorful bazaar is frequented by buyers and sellers from many lands: Gnomekin crystal merchants, Ardua horticulturists, Kasmir trapsmiths, Cymrilian potion-dealers, Farad slave mongers and procurers, Sarista fortune-tellers, Jaka trappers, Zandir spice traders, Arimite ore-dealers, and others. The shops and stalls, ablaze with torchlight, are busy late into the night.

*Profile: **Brandia***
Zandir Swordwoman, 14th Level
Recklessly ambitious, Brandia has risen fast in the world of Zandir spice traders. Her next aim is to acquire a cask of cinnilla, the fabulously rare flavoring distilled from the syrup with which manrak feed their young. With her statuesque figure, Brandia has little trouble enticing the brawny men-at-arms she prefers, but her possessiveness is obsessive.

14. Beggars' District
This run-down section of the city is inhabited by the lower echelons of Zandir society, the majority of whom earn a living as beggars - an honest, if not particularly estimable, profession in Zandu. Though many of the inhabitants of the Beggars' District are thieves, cut-throats or outright frauds, the Zandir are fond of their beggars, and expect others to be equally open-minded.

It is the custom of the Zandir to scatter handfuls of copper coins about when accosted by beggars, both as a sign of generosity and to keep from being further harassed. Individuals who fail to adhere to this custom, whether through ignorance or miserliness, may expect to be subjected to public scorn and ridicule.

*Profile: **Toj Sillanu***
Serparian Beggar, 15th Level
The elected Sultan of Beggars, Toj belongs to that class of impoverished charlatans known as the Perjors. With the aid of the right unguents and potions, he can assume the disfigurements associated with the most bizarre and unappealing ailments. This lord of the slums has the final say in all question of admission, expulsion, and punishment within Serparian ranks. He has a rude but lively sense of humor.

15. Sentinel Towers
These three-story structures are manned by 20-soldier platoons, each swordsman outfitted in fine black-iron chainmail. The reliability of these units, given the Zandir penchant for romantic pursuits, is suspect. Their skill, however, is not – only a fool would cross swords with these highly-trained fighters.

16. The Zandu Baths
An exotic establishment popular with many of the folk of Zanth, the baths offer refreshment (Zandir wine and sweetmeats), lavation, and stimulating conversation. Private baths, with or without an accompanying masseuse, are also available. Prices are average; quality of services is exemplary.

*Profile: **Mazilda***
Zandir Charlatan, 9th Level
Cursed with an obsession about personal cleanliness as a result of losing a duel arcane, Mazilda eventually became the proprietess of the Zandu Baths. She can most often be found in the public baths or steam chambers, eagerly seeking tales of the world which her constant washings and scrubbings deny her. Mazilda has a motherly regard for visitors of the adventurous type who are new to the city.

17. Manse of the Sublime Mysteries
A splendid inn and tavern, this manse is decorated in the eccentric style of the ancient Phaedrans, who were enamored of colorful pavilions, diaphanous curtains, and velvet furnishings. All who enter this place must wear a mask of one sort or another, a curious custom which adds an air of mystery and suspense to the proceedings. Entertainment is provided by troupes of Bodor musicians, actors, jongleurs or daredevils, according to the schedule. Prices are well above average, though not excessive given the unique nature of the experience.

18. The House of Chance

This lavish establishment caters to individuals with a penchant for gambling. Here one can find individuals willing to lay odds on just about any game or activity imaginable.

19. Costumer

This shop specializes in masks, elaborate costumes and other fanciful apparel. Made-to-order outfits are available at double the usual prices, which are not cheap. Body-painting is available at costs ranging from 20 to 200 gold lumens.

20. The Bladesmith's

The largest and most prestigious weaponer's shop in Zandu, the Bladesmith's has been owned and operated by the same family of Zandir craftsmen for many generations. Over a hundred bladesmiths work here, filling orders from across the continent. Prices are double standard rates (triple for custom orders), but the quality is beyond compare.

21. Zandu School of Swordsmanship

The most renowned martial institute in the country, the Zandu School offers private instruction in the famed Zandir sword-fighting style. Courses are available at all levels, from beginner to master. Tuition is 200 gold lumens per septemester (half for Zandir citizens). Individuals who wish to serve in any branch of the Zandir military must first earn a degree from this unique school.

22. The Citadel at Zanth

This fortress serves as the base of operations for the six branches of the Zandu military: greymane cavalry, sea patrol, border scouts, city sentinels, heavy infantry, and elite guardsmen. Each branch has its own barracks, center of operations, and armory. The Zandir military is essentially mercenary – only trained swordsmen are accepted, with qualified individuals hired on a contract basis. The starting pay is good: 100 gold lumens per week.

23. Arena of Champions

This large arena hosts weekly battles between armed contestants, and a process of elimination decides who will represent Zandu at the annual Clash of Champions. The competition is open to warriors of any race, creed or nationality, and offers a chance for gold and glory: each weekly victory in the arena is worth 1,000 gold lumens, and the champion is accorded status commensurate with a prince of the realm by the Sultan himself. Seats are available to spectators at costs of 1, 10, and 100 gold lumens.

24. The Dungeons of Zanth

An archaic facility which dates back to the Phaedran Empire, the Dungeons of Zanth serve as a place of incarceration, torture and execution. The structure stands only three stories in height, but extends some seven stories below the ground. Rumors regarding the dungeons are numerous: Some say the structure is riddled with narrow tunnels created by prisoners attempting to dig their way to freedom. Others claim that the lowest levels were sealed off centuries ago; that unspeakable acts were performed therein; and that there are tombs in the subterranean depths.

25. The Zandu Menagerie

This zoo and park is open to the general public. Wild beasts of many sorts are kept here, including a number of rare and nearly extinct species; admission is one silver piece. Of special interest is a cage holding the only known pair of Mendaxites, a species of smallish man-like beings physiologically incapable of telling the truth.

26. Sarista Ghetto

Formerly a public park, this area has been taken over by wandering Sarista gypsies from the woodlands of Silvanus. Wagons are scattered throughout the area, the numbers alternately shrinking or growing with the arrival and departure of new clans. The Zandir government grudgingly tolerates the presence of the Sarista, who are quite popular among the citizens of Zanth. Many Zandir come here to have their fortunes told, or to consort with the uninhibited gypsies.

*Profile: **Sarissimi***
Sarista Rogue, 14th Level
This gypsy spends every winter in the Zanth ghetto, working with the animals she performs with during her summer tour. The highlight of the act is a trained urhound, which bounds from the back of one ogront to another through a ring of fire. Her mascot is a sassy Wererook named Octar.

27. Institute of Paradoxy

Erstwhile center for the study of Paradoxy, the Institute is actually a school for magicians, charlatans and self-styled seers. The curriculum and faculty are hopelessly disorganized, with the result that individuals graduating from the Institute may or may not actually have attained any appreciable magical abilities. Tuition is 100 gold lumens per septemester (seven weeks); halved for Zandir citizens.

*Profile: **Wyleth***
Zandir Charlatan, 19th Level
A young man of pallid complexion and weak constitution, Wyleth is the Institute's Dean of Enticement. It is said that he can, for a price, manipulate the heart of the most aloof or remote person. Oddly enough, he is believed to live alone in a hilltop manse, and has no known romantic entanglements.

28. The Mystic Circle

This shop specializes in magical paraphernalia, alchemical ingredients, and Paradoxist literature (including copies of the curious cult manifesto, the *Book of Mysteries*.) Prices vary, as does the quality of merchandise offered here.

*Profile: **Scilla***
Zandir Charlatan, 27th Level
An aging crone with reputed psychic powers, Scilla owns the Mystic Circle. She receives regular shipments of herbs and animal ingredients from a Dhuna warlock, who purportedly makes his home in the depths of Werewood.

29. Zandu Properties

A wealthy Zandir merchant owns this establishment, which sells parcels of land, refurbished manses, and abandoned tower keeps. Most of these properties are situated along the northern border or the ocean coast — not exactly preferred locations, though the relatively low prices (5,000 to 50,000 gold lumens) are not unappealing, particularly to individuals on a limited budget.

30. Robalo's Winery

One of the country's most respected wineries, Robalo's offers excellent, vintage wines at reasonable cost. Weekly tours of the vineyards, costing one silver piece per person, are a popular attraction, and contribute greatly to the general lack of sobriety exhibited by people in these parts.

31. Crematorium/Mausoleum

Here, interred in brass urns, are the ashes of untold thousands of Paradoxists who died during the Cult Wars between Zandu and Aaman. Another section is set aside for modern interments.

32. The Werewood Tavern

This inn and tavern is frequented by a truly diverse clientele: Arimite knife-fighters, Jaka manhunters, and Zandir of all sorts — chiefly charlatans and thieves, with a few swordsmen thrown in. The fare is plain but hardy, and reasonably priced. In the large common room are held such entertaining spectacles as knife-throwing contests, exhibitions of magic, and tests of strength and skill. The private booths are quite popular with certain of the tavern's more disreputable customers, who are said to use the facilities for the sale and distribution of contraband, stolen merchandise and various illicit wares. All in all, there is seldom a dull moment at this night-spot.

*Profile: **Armotas the Chespian***
Zandir Charlatan, 14th Level
One of the regulars here, Armotas can usually be found in a corner booth, consorting with a coterie of wizards and supposed scholars. She proclaims herself to be a Chespian, a specialist in the lost arts of the kingdom that once ruled the Lost Sea. Actually, Armotas is addled — the locals know better than to listen to her schemes to obtain ancient riches.

33. Causidians' Guild

This hall is a meeting place and guildhouse for Zanth's considerable population of Causidians, whose services may be obtained for a price of 50 gold lumens per day — more, if the Causidian has garnered even the slightest reputation.

*Profile: **Joyila Orto***
Zandir Causidian, 26th Level
This begemmed and necklaced older Causidian, pudgy with the rewards of a successful legal practice, now dedicates his time to serving the poorer classes at minimal charges — in fact, he almost forces himself upon his clients. His obsession to fairness outweighs his loyalty to those he defends, as he has been known to remind judges of pertinent but inadvantageous facts, or to "accidentally" betray convicting confidences.

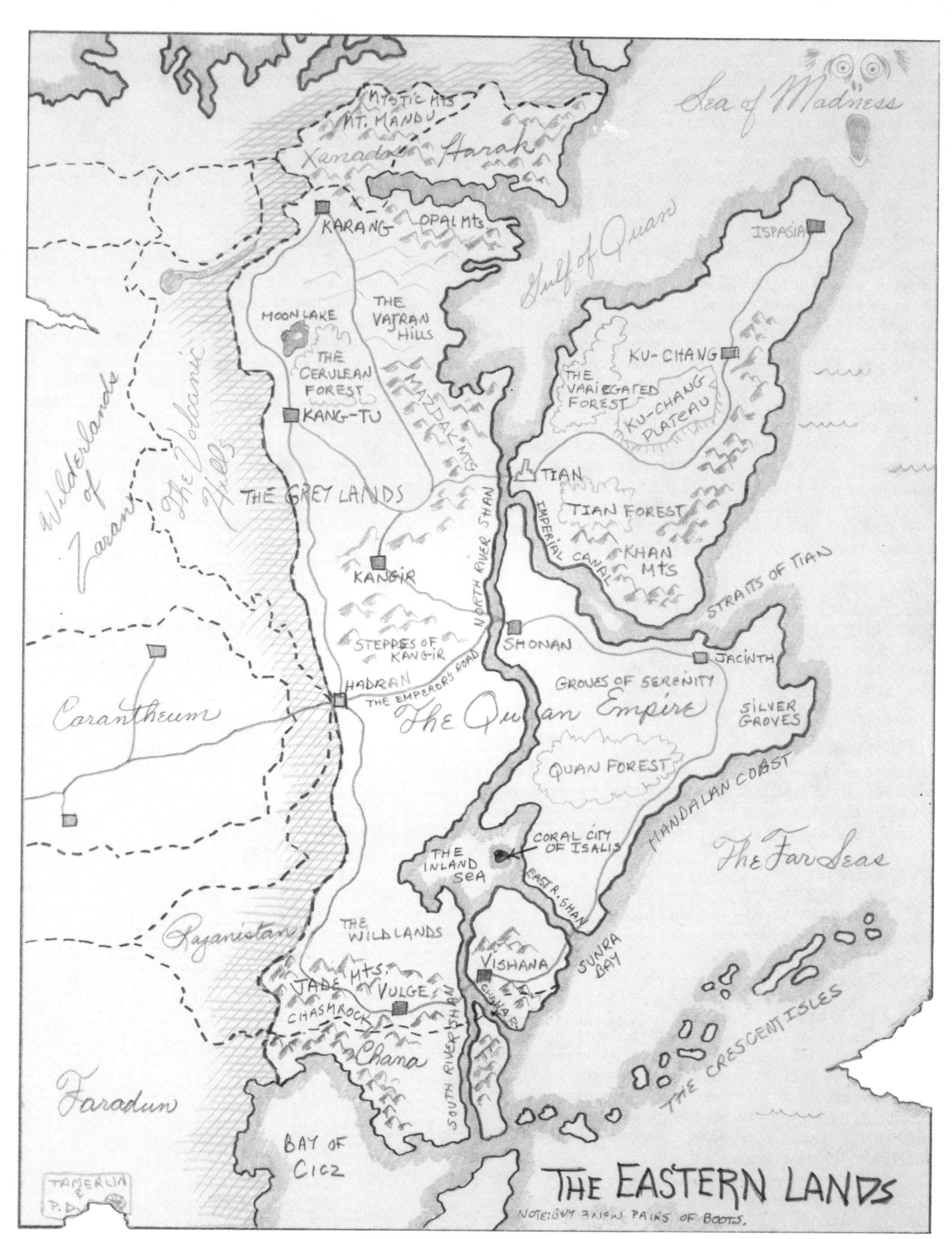

Scale: 1" = 125 miles.

CHANA

Chana Witchwoman and Witchman

The Jungles of Chana occupy part of the southeastern coast of Talislanta, from Faradun in the west to the Mandalan region of the Quan Empire. The solid jungles of the coasts meld into rain-forests as the land rises upward into the Jade Mountains.

Chana's jungles are known to harbor an abundance of riches, including costly herbs, precious stones and exotic animals. Magical herbs and necromantic paraphernalia are additional lures to raiders — such as the Imrians, who sometimes venture ashore here. Not surprisingly, more than a few of the local savages bear the shrunken and scaly-skinned heads of such souvenir hunters on their belts.

The climate in this region is hot, wet and unbearably humid — ideal conditions for Chana's many varieties of tropical plants and trees, which can literally spring up overnight after a drenching rain. Virulent species of animals and insects likewise find the jungles to their liking, making travel in this region a dismal proposition.

Worse still are the fierce tribes of savages which dwell here: the Witchmen, dwelling along the southern coast of Chana and in the eastern jungles; the Manra, in the remotest parts of the central highlands; and the Nagra, in the western jungles.

The Witchmen

A people of dark and sinister repute, the Witchmen are known to have tastes for such pastimes as head-hunting and cannibalism, which have endeared them to few other races. A reliance upon various narcotic herbs (primarily kesh, which is derived from the jabutu plant) contributes heavily to the unhealthy appearance of these folk, who are tall and cadaverous in stature, with bilious green skin.

Customs

The Witchmen do their utmost to appear fearsome: filing their teeth to sharpened points, decorating their glowering visages with occult glyphs and symbols (as yet indecipherable, even to the savants of Cymril's Lyceum Arcanum), and wearing the shrunken heads of their adversaries on cords slung about the neck. It is customary for these folk to wear their hair in a single topknot, lacquered and braided with leather thongs or sinew.

Witchmen tribes are warlike in the extreme, and fight among each other constantly, each vying for control of the other's jabutu-growing territories. The savages employ throwing sticks, blow-guns and spears in combat, and generally disdain frontal assaults in favor of ambushes and traps. In addition to their usual depredations, bands of Witchmen occasionally cross the border into the Quan Empire, wreaking havoc on the plantations there.

The tribes lack all of the civilized virtues, but possess certain undeniable (though gruesome) talents. Witchmen shamans are skilled in the concocting of strange and unique substances, such as devilroot and kesh. The former is an herbal poison which can be made to varying degrees of toxicity, and may be prepared in powdered or resinous form. Kesh is a pungent liquid derived from the root of the jabutu, a plant found only in the Jade Mountains. This drug is notable for its profound narcotic and magical properties, and is used extensively in the black magic rituals of the Witchmen.

The Witchmen have also learned how to charm the poisonous serpents known as Death's Head Vipers. The natives call these foot-long snakes, "wrist vipers," and wear them like deadly, living bracelets. The serpents are trained to attack on command, and have other practical uses as well.

Perhaps the most infamous of the Witchmen's talents is their reputed ability to steal souls, which the shamans are said to imprison in enchanted stones. These "soulstones" are supposedly used to create jujus — mindless zombies, controlled through the use of a graven image. Shrunken head fetishes, purportedly used by the shamans to communicate with the lower spirit realms, are also said to be popular. The process by which jujus and shrunken head fetishes are made is sufficiently revolting to warrant omission from this text, however.

The Manra

These savages resemble the Witchmen in physical stature, but exhibit none of the frightful or unhealthy characteristics associated with those hostile people. Manra possess the unique ability to assume the forms of other living things, such as wild beasts and even plants. A derivative of the jabutu plant, prepared in some secret manner, is believed to be the source of the Manra's shape-changing abilities.

Customs

The Manra are nature worshipers, whose primary concern is the protection of the rain-forests which they call home. They live in small villages composed of thatched huts, and tend to keep to themselves.

The tribes are generally peaceful in nature, though deviant Manra clans are believed to exist. All of the shape-changers bear considerable resentment for the Witchmen, their rivals for the region's limited supply of the jabutu plant.

The Jade Mountains

Sweeping northwestward in an arc, the Jade Mountains run from Chana to the Volcanic Hills. The deep-green peaks of these ancient mountains are swathed in thick vegetation, and inhabited by such predators as batranc and ravengers, and numerous species of tropical avir, poisonous serpents and giant insects. The Jade Mountains are also rich in such natural resources as black diamonds, moonstones, k'tallah, lotus, devilroot, and a tropical variety of cleric's cowl.

Hidden amid the ravines and rain-forests of these mountains are the majority of the surviving Nagra, a people once persecuted by the Kang of the Quan Empire. Fierce, aggressive and violent, these tribesmen are renowned for their ability to *spirit track* — to perceive and trace the faint trails left by a creature's spirit essence.

The River Chana

A fork of the South River Shan, the River Chana's murky waters are infested with aramatus, skalanx and grey ikshada...which explains, perhaps, the Chana Witchmen's extreme reluctance to cross almost any body of water.

Many varieties of rare plants and herbs grow along the banks of the Chana River. Imrian slavers occasionally venture upriver in order to obtain stores of fresh provisions — primarily, slugs and giant waterbugs, which the amphibians regard as delicacies.

The Bay of Cicz

Adjacent to the eastern coast of Faradun and the western coast of Chana, the Bay of Cicz is populated by sea demons, giant sea scorpions, and the marauding vessels of Mangar Corsairs — to the dismay of Farad merchant vessels and Imrian slave coracles, which also traverse these waters.

The Imrians raid the coastal regions of Chana on a regular basis, taking Witchmen slaves. There is a market for the primitive shamans in Faradun, where the savages are sold for use in the narcotics and contraband trades.

HARAK

Harakin, mounted on dractyl

Harak is a bleak and desolate land, hemmed in on all sides by mountains and swept by frigid winds from the north. The landscape of this northern land is nightmarish: jagged spires of rock jut upward from the cracked and barren earth, and scattered shards of black iron litter the ground. Here, in this most inhospitable of regions, dwell the fierce warriors known as the Harakin.

The Harakin

A gray-skinned sub-race of Men, the Harakin are lean and rugged of build, averaging over six feet in height. They dress in loincloths, cowls, high boots and heavy gloves, all of which are usually made of reptile hide. Both the males and females paint the areas around their eyes with black pigments, giving them a fearsome aspect.

Customs

A hard-hearted people, the Harakin are utterly devoid of mercy or compassion. Ultimate survivalists, they view all other living creatures as prey. Forced by the circumstances of their existence to endure great hardships, the folk of Harak have no concept of morality or religion, and are by nature fatalistic and grim. They take what they want, raiding both rival clans and neighboring lands.

The clans of Harak are nomadic, traveling from place to place in search of food and water — both precious commodities in this region. When their hunts and raids prove fruitless, the Harakin subsist on scorpions, spiders, and bits of lichen and mosses.

All Harakin consider themselves to be warriors. Skills and trades not related to warfare are regarded as useless. Each clan member learns to make his or her own weapons, which are hammered and honed from the fragments of black iron found almost everywhere throughout this region.

The tribesmen employ several unique types of weapons, including the *tarak* (a four-bladed iron axe), the *khu* (a double-bladed dagger), the *krin* (a heavy crossbow that fires iron spikes) and the *jang* (a thrown weapon resembling an edged scythe). All other survival skills — such as hunting, dressing game, finding water, and so forth — are considered warriors' skills. In fact, the Harakin word for "survival" and "fight" are one and the same.

The Dractyl Riders

Although the Harakin show few other traces of civilized behavior, they have domesticated the dractyl, a species of winged reptile native to the sheer cliffs of Harak's coastal regions. Large and ungainly, dractyl have gray-green scaly hides and great membranous wings.

Their beaks are lined with rows of pointed teeth, and their hands and feet are clawed. The rheumy, yellow-eyed stare of these creatures is somewhat unnerving, a fact from which dractyl seem to derive a certain strange pleasure.

In the wild, dractyl live on the ledges of cliffs and chasms, usually in small groups. They have a language of sorts, but are among the most dour and rancorous of creatures in Talislanta.

The dractyl's diet normally consists of vermin, scorpions and spiders, though they will eat almost anything that can be obtained without great exertion. Mean and untrustworthy, dractyl will abandon a weak or indecisive master if not closely monitored. The creatures are also known to bicker among themselves, particularly during the dractyl's month-long mating season.

The Harakin use trained dractyl for transport and in battle. However, the avians have little love of combat, and obey their masters primarily to avoid being eaten at the next meal. Even so, these reptilians are capable of delivering a nasty bite, and can use their front and rear claws to some effect if and when the need arises.

Dractyl require little food and are themselves somewhat edible, factors which hold a certain appeal for their masters. The avians are only fair as fliers, however, and cannot or will not fly at altitudes in excess of 100 feet. As a result, the Harakin must ride them on foot when attempting passage through mountainous regions.

In spite of the shortcomings of their beasts, the warrior clans of Harak are known to range as far as the Quan Empire and the Volcanic Hills in their depredations. Able to survive the rigors of their own land, the Harakin have little difficulty tolerating the colder climates of Xanadas or L'Haan, or the volcanic terrain of the Volcanic Hills — these lands all seem pleasant by comparison with Harak.

However, the Harakin attack L'Haan less frequently than they do the other neighboring countries, generally considering the grueling passage through the towering peaks of the Mystic Mountains to be a profitless endeavor. The powerful and efficient Mirin military is also a deterrent against Harakin raids.

Dealings with Outsiders

An unusual tale regarding the Harakin is told within the Quan Empire. There, it is said, a group of Mandalan scholars once ventured forth on a mission to Harak. It was their contention that the Harakin were not evil beings, but were simply the products of the harsh and cruel environment of their homeland. As such, the savants intended to convince a few of the Harakin to accompany them on the return trip to Quan, where their scholarly theories might be put to the test.

Upon sighting a small band of the nomads, the wise men threw up their hands and raised their voices in greeting. When the Harakin approached, the scholars gave them gifts of gold, fragrant oils and precious stones.

These the savages examined, and then discarded. Without apparent enmity they slew the scholars, divested them of their fur cloaks and boots, and fed their remains to the clan's dractyl. The Harakin then slew and quartered the Mandalans' mounts, loaded the meat on their winged steeds, and continued on their way across the bleak terrain of Harak.

The Sea of Madness

A turbulent body of water which lies between Harak and the Quan peninsula, the Sea of Madness is regarded as the limit beyond which most sailors of the East will not trespass. The waters are said to be subject to strange and inexplicable phenomena, such as fierce maelstroms, spiraling columns of water, sudden outbursts of noxious gases, and raging storms of black lightning.

Since ancient times it has been rumored that terrible sea monsters haunt these waters. The largest of these is the legendary Gargantua, which scholars of past ages believed could attain lengths in excess of two or three miles.

All of this, plus the unwelcoming sheer cliffs along the coasts of Harak, keeps this desolate land unvisited by maritime voyagers.

THE QUAN EMPIRE

Quan noble and Ispasian advisor

The territories of the Quan Empire extend from the southern jungles bordering Chana to the northern reaches of the Opal Mountains. Once home to numerous rival warrior clans, the East came under the dominance of a single tribe of barbarians around the beginning of the New Age. By various means, these warriors eliminated their rivals, retaining only those peoples who could be coerced or bribed into serving them. These diverse elements have since been incorporated into an empire, governed by the subrace of Men known as the Quan.

The Quan

A pale-skinned folk of average height and build, the Quan were once a barbaric people, but now exhibit the lofty airs and delicate sensibilities normally associated with royalty. They are an unexceptional race, and possess little in the way of creativity, being just sufficiently aggressive and cunning to rule an empire. The Quan have no religious affiliations, the concept of worship being without interest to these folk, who consider themselves akin to gods.

Customs

The Quan do no work, but simply oversee the various peoples that their ancestors conquered, who together supply them with all their needs. From birth, the imperials are attended hand and foot by slaves, who feed them, bathe them, and carry them about on cushioned palanquins. Jewelry of the most ostentatious sort is considered a mark of distinction and elegance by the Quan, and obesity a sign of wealth and success. Even the lowest members of the ruling caste dress in costly silk garments, and the elite of their kind are notable for the most extravagant and garish costumes: elaborate headdresses festooned with baubles, capes of such length that they must be carried by attendants, and so forth.

Imperial society is governed by a rigidly enforced caste system which divides the populace into distinct classes. By careful manipulation of this system, the ruling Quan maintain control of the population, rewarding those of their servants who are most loyal to the regime.

In descending order, the castes within the Quan Empire are:

- Grand Elite   the Emperor and his family
- High Elite   Quan of favored status
- Elite   all other Quan
- Honorary Elite   non-Quan granted special status
- Luminaries   the seven lower classes

The Empire

Despite an outward appearance of civility, the Quan rule their empire without mercy. Most criminal offenses are punishable by death, a variety of cruel methods being employed to achieve the desired result. Individuals accused of breaking the law are typically hauled before a magistrate and sentenced without trial.

As it is impossible for individuals to bring charges of any sort against a person of higher rank or social status, injustice is rife among the less privileged classes. Those seeking to elude imperial justice are hunted down by Kang trackers and their beasts, which are both efficient and cruel.

Although they tend to be distrustful of strangers from the West, the Quan are not entirely averse to doing business with foreigners. No outsider may travel across the Empire without first obtaining an official permit, however. Issued in the form of a lead tablet stamped with the Emperor's seal, these devices are available at Hadran and Jacinth, and cost upwards of 1,000 gold lumens apiece.

The Golden City

Tian is the capital of the Quan Empire. Situated on an island within a man-made lake, the metropolis can only be reached by boat or windship. The city was designed by Mandalan architects at the command of the Emperor of Quan, who demanded that the new capital surpass in beauty all of the cities of the Empire — even that of the Mandalan city of Jacinth.

Tian is considered by many to be the most splendid city on the continent. The gilded spires and domes of the Palace of a Thousand Fountains, wherein the Emperor resides, are especially noteworthy.

The Imperial Canal

This man-made waterway links the River Shan to the Gulf of Tian, and was built to allow access to the lake that surrounds Tian. It was constructed in twelve years by vast crews of Vajra slave laborers, at a terrible cost in lives.

A system of locks and channels allows traffic on the canal to be strictly monitored. Quan pleasure barg-

es, Sunra fishing vessels, and other boats utilize the Imperial Canal, but the waterway is of an insufficient size to accommodate the dragon barques of the Sunra — an oversight attributed to the Quan rulers, who rigidly insisted that the canal be constructed as quickly as possible.

Tian Forest

Just east of the capital, the Forest of Tian is as odd a place as one may find in Talislanta — a man-made woodland, comprised of orderly groves of silver deodars and shade trees, separated by neatly mowed grass trails lined with arrangements of colorful shrubs and flowers.

The Quan aristocracy had the forest "built" for the pleasure of the Emperor, so that he might come here to hunt "wild" game as did his ancestors. Mandalan savants fabricated the forest, under the strict supervision of the Kang.

The woodland is continually re-stocked with selected types of creatures, all rendered harmless by declawing, de-fanging, and the administration of sedative elixirs. The Emperor — borne aloft in a sumptuous palanquin, and escorted by a vast retinue of guards, trackers, servitors, and aides — rarely does more than watch others hunt.

The Emperor's Road

This highway spans the length and breadth of the Quan Empire, from Hadran to Ispasia, and from Karang to Vishana. Without a doubt, it is the best-maintained roadway on the continent, showing signs of neglect only in the most dangerous jungle regions of the south.

A minimum toll of five gold lumens is charged at all bridges and city gates, the alleged purpose of these somewhat exorbitant fees being to keep the roads clear of riffraff. Heavily-armed Kang sentinels patrol the Emperor's Road at regular intervals.

WESTERN QUAN

Stretching from the River Shan to the frontier with the Volcanic Hills, Western Quan consists of two districts: the barren wastes known as the *Greylands*, and the rocky hills and grassy plateaus of the *Steppes of Kangir*. The Greylands were once the domain of wild sub-men tribes, the scattered descendants of which are rumored to survive in secluded areas. The Kang deny these claims, insisting that the only creatures inhabiting these lands are wild tarkus, striders, durge, winged azoryls, and perhaps a handful of crested dragons. Kang scouts patrol the western borders, alert for signs of Sauran invaders.

The Steppes are the traditional hunting grounds of the Kang, who ranged throughout this area prior to being absorbed by the Quan Empire. Kang still come here to visit the land of their ancestors, and to hunt wild tarkus, striders, azoryls and megalodonts.

The Kang

A tall and fierce people, the Kang have fiery red skins, white pupil-less eyes, and almost reptilian features. They wear their long black hair pulled straight back in a single queue. Iron collars and armbands are the fashion among their warriors. The Kang have a long tradition of hostility and aggression — they seethe with wild passions. Counteracting this is the intense military training which all Kang undergo from birth, instilling in them a deep-seated respect for authority.

Tribal leaders govern by force of arms. The chief ruler of the Kang is the Overlord, a figure subservient only to the Emperor himself. This warlord commands the Empire's vast military resources, and is responsible for keeping the populace under control. For serving the Quan Empire, the Kang are paid in gold, and are accorded a position of status second only to the Quan themselves.

The Citadel of Hadran

The largest military installation in the Quan Empire, Hadran houses thousands of Kang troops, along with their striders and support personnel. The fortress is also the headquarters of the Overlord of the Kang. Built of marbled green-and-black stone from the Jade Mountains, Hadran overlooks a yawning 600-foot-deep chasm which runs for a hundred miles along the western frontier. A massive bridge allows access to the West, and a toll of 100 gold lumens is charged to all visitors of foreign extraction.

The Fortress City of Shonan

An impregnable fortress which has withstood countless attacks by the Sauran tribes which dwell

Kang Warlord

to the west, Shonan is built of dull grey stone from the Volcanic Hills. The citadel is surrounded by a 40-foot-high wall lined with rows of black-iron spikes. Hundreds of Kang are stationed here, along with Vajra artillerists and engineers, all charged with guarding the Empire against Sauran raids from the Volcanic Hills.

Primarily a military installation, Shonan serves as a center of trade only because it is located at a nexus of the River Shan and the Emperor's Road. Goods of many sorts pass through here: precious metals, gemstones and cerulean dye from Karang; foodstuffs and moonfish transported upriver from Isalis; rare herbs and hardwoods from Vishana; and Mandalan silkcloth from Jacinth. A bridge spans the river, and a toll of five gold lumens is charged to all who cross.

Kangir

A fortified outpost at the edge of the Greylands, Kangir is a supply facility where siege-engines are built, maintained and refurbished. A large garrison of Kang strider cavalry is stationed here, along with a contingent of Vajra engineers and artillerists. Merchants and traders from across the Empire often stop here, enroute to or from Karang, Hadran or Tian.

SOUTHERN QUAN

The placid waters of Sunra Bay serve as an entrance to the waters of the East River Shan, and beyond, the Inland Sea. Dragon barques patrol this waterway, which is off-limits to foreign vessels. Sunra fishing vessels can be seen along the coast, trolling for rare moonfish, the egg-sacs of rainbow kra, and pearl-bearing mollusks. Water raknids, skalanx and adolescent sea dragons are also attracted by this delectable prey, and are ignored by sailors at their own peril. Upriver lies the formidable expanse of the Inland Sea, whose jade-green waters sustain nar-eels (sought for their ivory horns), spiny-shelled echino-morphs, moonfish, and giant lake-kra.

Further south are the hostile jungles of the Wildlands, home to kaliya, winged apes, malathrope and alatus. Many rare herbs and plants grow here, such as tantalus, red and black lotus, narcolesian, and devilroot. These resources go largely untapped, due to the hostile nature of the environs.

The Sunra

Semi-aquatic man-like beings who live in the fabulous Coral City of Isalis, the Sunra are elegant creatures — graceful in stature, with silvery-scaled skin and deep-blue eyes. They are known for their love of the Inland Sea, which they reverently refer to as the "Mother of Life." Their ancestors once ranged the Far Seas in glittering dragon barques, hunting sea dragons and trading with far-distant lands, before the Quan conquest. The sea people greatly resent their imperial masters, and long for freedom.

The Sunra are the finest sailors and astromancers in the known world, and use intricate astrolabes to navigate according to the position of Talislanta's twin suns and seven moons, and "read" the currents and tides for aid. They have been compelled to put their fleet of powerful dragon barques at the service of the Quan Empire.

The Coral City of Isalis

Beside being home to the Sunra, the Coral City of Isalis hosts the Empire's vast flotilla of dragon barques, merchant skiffs and fishing boats. A reef serves as the foundation for the city, which is fashioned of pink, blue, red and green varieties of coral. Its "streets" are narrow waterways which course among the elegant coral structures. A garrison of Kang troops maintains order and discipline.

Sunra sea-farmers ply the shallows around the city, harvesting kelp, algae, edible mollusks, and other aquatic foodstuffs. Moonfish — rare creatures reserved by law for eating by the Quan only — are caught and shipped to Tian in water-filled spheres.

Sunra Mariner

The Jungle Outposts

Located in the hot and humid jungles of the far south, *Vishana* is a military outpost situated on the River Shan. Soldiers from here are sent to patrol the Emperor's Road, though the task is made difficult by wild beasts and marauding Witchmen. The Kang trackers and cavalry which patrol the Empire's southern borders have a particular loathing for duty here. To instill enthusiasm among the troops, the fort commanders offer a bounty of 100 gold lumens for each Witchmen head taken on jungle patrols.

A second, more isolated fortress, set in the Jade Mountains, *Vulge* is manned by a contingent of Kang trackers and their beasts. The occupants live in constant fear of Manra raiders. Nagra spirit trackers, kaliya, and winged vipers are likewise native to this hostile area.

Chasmrock

A great canyon located in the Jade Mountains of southern Quan, Chasmrock is flanked on both sides by rows of twisting stone spires. Nagra spirit-trackers come here to hunt manrak, the heads of which bring a sizable bounty in Faradun, the Quan Empire, and other lands. Black diamonds are also found in this forbidding region, where civilized men rarely go.

CENTRAL QUAN

The wooded coasts of Mandala stretch on for several hundred miles, from Sunra Bay in the south to the Silver Groves. Valuable hardwoods, incense trees, and various sorts of magical herbs grow here in plentiful supply, as do many cultivated crops, planted in areas cleared by order of the Kang. Mandalan slaves tend these plantations, which provide grains, fruits, and vegetables for a large portion of the Empire. The farms are very productive, though malathrope, winged vipers and kaliya pose a constant threat to workers in the fields and their taskmasters.

In the west, the great River Shan runs north from the Inland Sea to the Gulf of Quan. Fishing vessels, merchant skiffs and Quan pleasure barges ply the waters of the Shan, which teem with edible fish, crustaceans and mollusks. Echinomorphs, chang and other hostile creatures likewise inhabit the river. The Shan is wide and slow in the south, becoming narrow, swift and treacherous farther north.

The Mandalans

A golden-skinned folk, the Mandalans are slender of build, with almond-shaped eyes and pleasant features. Theirs is an advanced and enlightened culture, centered amidst the pastel spires, arches and promenades of the coastal city of Jacinth. Practitioners of an ancient mystical discipline, Mandalans abhor violence, considering militarism to be the domain of unsophisticated and primitive peoples. Their interests include the study of mysticism, meditation, and various scholarly pursuits.

Skilled Mandalans serve the Quan as artisans, scholars, historians, personal servants, gardeners, and menial laborers. Some believe that the passive Mandalans are not as submissive as they seem, but that they oppose the Quan through means too subtle for their masters to detect.

The City of Jacinth

Once the center of Mandalan culture, the coastal city of Jacinth is now a resort area enjoyed by the wealthiest of the Quan ruling class. A large number of Mandalans still live here, serving as slaves of the Empire. In Jacinth are found ancient collections of scrolls and books, and gardens of crystal dendrons, mosses and prismatic blossoms. Elite units of Kang guard the city from attack by land, and Sunra dragon barques patrol the harbor where Quan pleasure barges drift.

The Groves of Serenity

Just beyond the city walls, the beautiful moss gardens, topiary mazes and shaded arbors of the

Mandalan mystic

Groves of Serenity are the product of untold generations of Mandalan savants, who created these patiently-crafted settings for use as places of relaxation and meditation. The areas are still tended by the Mandalans, though they are seldom used now due to the Quan, who have outlawed the mystical meditative practices.

The Silver Groves

This scenic forest rings the northernmost promontory of the Mandalan Coast, terminating just to the east of the City of Jacinth. Here, stately silver deodars tower high above the forest floor, where rainbow lotus, tantalus, shrinking violet, and other exotic herbs grow wild.

Though splendid to behold, the Silver Groves are not as placid as they appear. Giant shathane make their home in this place, as do exomorphs, mandragores, and the occasional plant grue.

The Quan Forest

This expansive woodland region is inhabited by ogriphants, malathrope, shathane, and the voracious insectoids known as chigs. The insects are so destructive that Kang trackers and trained ibik are regularly sent to hunt and destroy the chig colonies.

NORTHEASTERN QUAN

The Quan Peninsula is easily divided into three regions: In the north is Ispasia, a cool but pleasant land. The Ku-Chang Plateau dominates the central peninsula, and in the south are the wooded slopes of the Khan Mountains.

Ispasia

Tucked away in the far-northern corner of the peninsula, the Citystate of Ispasia is a mercantile center through which foreign trade is transacted. The city was annexed by the Quan in the early days of the Empire. Although a Kang garrison is stationed in the city, the local citizens are permitted to govern themselves, albeit within the limits of Quan law.

The Ispasians are a folk of slender physique, lemon-yellow skin and expressionless features, who always dress in robes of fine silkcloth. They bear a well-deserved reputation as ruthless and calculating businessmen, attracted to high-stakes ventures. The Ispasians serve the Empire by administrating trade and transport across the length and breadth of Quan. In return, the imperials allow Ispasia a degree of autonomy equaled only by the Kang.

The Variegated Forest

Named for its wildly colorful flora and fauna, Ispasia's Variegated Forest is home to plants and animals which sport the most exotic and vibrant hues — avir with six-colored plumage, lime-green malathrope, groves of purple tanglewood, yellow shathane, even pink monitor imps. There is a considerable market in Tian and elsewhere for these plants and creatures, which are wondrous curiosities.

Ku-Chang

This rugged, rocky region is valuable due to its deposits of gold, silver and copper. Crag spiders, cave bats and other dangerous creatures occupy the caves and gullies of the plateau. Kang patrols comb the heights by day, searching for signs of intruders, but do not dare to venture forth at night.

The *Outpost of Ku-Chang* is a mining installation where crews of Vajra slave laborers exhume gold and silver, crystals, cinnabar, antimony, and a half-dozen varieties of precious stones. A garrison of Kang warriors and trackers keeps the Vajra in line, and protects the vital installation from murderous raiding parties.

The Khan Mountains

The sheer peaks of the Khan Mountains extend across the southern end of the peninsula. The

Mondre Khan

mountains remain a largely untapped source of minerals and precious stones, due to omnivrax, shriekers, lopers, yaksha, muskronts, tarkus, giant shathane...and the fierce tribes of half-men known as the Mondre Khan.

The wooded hills and mountains are the domain of the Khan, who are the last indigenous people to resist subjugation by the forces of the Empire. A nomadic folk, the Mondre Khan have proved to be a resourceful and dangerous enemy.

Holed up in their mountain retreats, the tribes have waged a successful campaign against numerically superior Kang forces for over four centuries — launching surprise attacks against merchant caravans, stealing military supply wagons, and repeatedly raiding the mining settlement of Ku-Chang. The Kang consider the Mondre Khan to be akin to animals, and hunt them down like beasts.

The Mondre Khan resemble a cross between Men and beasts, and exhibit the ferocity and cunning of wild animals. Some scholars theorize that their race is devolving back to an animalistic origin with each passing generation. The Khan are intelligent enough to make metal weapons and armor, however, and are experts in the art of covert warfare.

NORTHWESTERN QUAN

The traditional territories of the Vajra, the Vajran Hills are rich in minerals, timber and other natural resources. After the Quan annexed this part of their Empire, the Vajra were deported from their subterranean homes and taken to slave camps near the Opal Mountains. The underground settlements were sealed, and have never been reopened.

The Vajra

A subterranean race native to the regions beneath the hills of northern Quan, the Vajra are short and squat, with barrel-like torsos and heavy limbs. Their bodies are covered with overlapping orange-brown plates, which form an effective natural armor.

The Vajra are an industrious and peaceful folk, known for their ability to withstand great hardship without complaint. Like the Gnomekin of Durne, they worship a manifestation of the earth goddess, Terra, though such practices are officially outlawed by the Quan.

Forced to serve the Empire as miners, engineers, stone workers, and infantry, the Vajra live in underground labor camps, where they excavate for precious stones and metals. The gold and gems from the mines have made the Quan fabulously wealthy.

Vajra engineer

The Citadel of Karang

Located to the north, Karang is a walled citadel built by Vajra slaves under the orders of the Emperor, to safeguard against incursions of barbaric Harakin from beyond the Opal Mountains. Most of the Vajra live in the sub-levels of this ponderous structure, which is crisscrossed with catacombs and tunnels after the Vajran style. Precious stones and metals from several mines are stored here until they can be shipped by caravan to Shonan. Kang trackers patrol the outskirts with deadly hunting beasts.

The Cerulean Forest

This forest is named for its vegetation, all of which is resplendent in various shades of blue. Costly cerulean dyes, rare herbs, and beasts (such as muskronts, yaksha and omnivrax) are found in the Cerulean Forest. Individuals who traverse these parts regularly know to string nets above their campsites to ward against attacks by metal-plumed shriekers.

The placid waters of Moon Lake, located in the western forest, are home to a freshwater species of moonfish much favored as pets by the Quan. The woods surrounding the lake are populated by grues (demonic entities which hail from the lower plane of Cthonia) and giant shathane.

The Fortress of Kang-Tu

Adjacent to the Cerulean Forest, at the furthest northern reaches of the Greylands, Kang-Tu is a base for Kang trackers, who regularly patrol the borderlands. There is some trade here with merchants from Kangir and Karang, but not much — Kang-Tu has long been a favorite target of the Saurans, who periodically storm the installation from their bases in the Volcanic Hills.

The Mountains

The *Opal Mountains* extend from the western border of Harak to the Sinking Land, circling the Quan Empire from the north. The peaks are among the tallest on the continent, averaging 20,000 feet in height. Black-iron ore, silver, gold, and precious stones are found here, particularly in the south. The inhabitants of the region include winged dractyl, omnivrax and frost demons.

Former haunts of the barbaric Mazdak tribes, the *Mazdak Mountains* lie to the southeast, along the Gulf of Quan. The Kang insist the region is inhabited only by tarkus, wild striders, and a few crested dragons, but rumors persist that a handful of rebels have established a base in the region.

XANADAS

An isolated region located high amidst the towering peaks of the Opal Mountains, Xanadas is covered year-round with deep layers of snow and ice. Here is the tallest mountain in the known world — Mount Mandu, rising over 30,000 feet in height. At its summit stands the Temple of the Seven Moons, where the Savants of Xanadas gaze into enchanted seeing stones, observing and recording all manner of events and phenomena.

Scattered along the difficult trail which leads to the mountain's summit are the frozen remains of explorers and adventurers who sought in vain to find the Temple. Aside from frost demons and ice dragons, few living things can survive for long in the frigid upper altitudes of Mount Mandu. Here, where even the dreaded Ice Giants will not go, dwell the fabled Savants.

The Savants of Xanadas

Believed to be old beyond reckoning, the Savants are said to extend their lifespans by adherence to certain secret regimens and practices. They dress in long robes of silver and black, and wear elaborate headdresses inscribed with arcane runes, symbols and sigils.

Customs

The Xanadasian Savants are mystics and scholars of unrivaled ability. Self-appointed chroniclers of Talislantan history, they observe and record phenomena of all sorts: the positions of the stars and planets, the delicate fluxes of time and space, the emergence and disappearance of plant and animal species, and so forth. Seated on pedestals of lavender stone, they gaze into crystals of polished blue diamond, monitoring and noting the activities of the continent's peoples. Every event of note is recorded in massive leather-bound tomes. When filled with information, these books are stored in great underground vaults.

Members of a secret mystic order, the Savants and their predecessors have chronicled the history of Talislanta for many centuries. The origin of the current occupants of the Temple of the Seven Moons remains a mystery. Some believe that the sages are Mandalans who long ago fled from the Quan Empire; others claim that they are survivors of a past age.

The Savants of Xanadas are said to welcome visitors, whom they question at length in order to supplement or verify their observations. They are a curious lot, and seem to want to know everything. It is their practice to allow any who come here to study, and

The Temple of the Seven Moons

on occasion, some do. Passage to the mountain retreat of the Savants is difficult, however, and fraught with peril.

The Legend of Xanadas

Some scholars connect the activities of the Savants of the Temple of the Seven Moons to the obscure *Legend of Xanadas*. According to the ancient tale, many years ago a great mystic named Xanadas was summoned by Death to meet his inevitable end. As his pupils and associates grieved upon hearing of their master's imminent doom, the sage bade them not to worry; he would visit with the gods for a time, after which he pledged to return to the material plane and relate the secrets of the afterlife to all who waited for him.

Those who accept this legend as fact believe that the Xanadasian Savants are the last of the great mystic's followers. They say that the Savants record important events, believing that their master will wish to know all that has transpired in his absence.

Though many scholars think the legend to be somewhat far fetched, others point out that the tale is supported by certain odd traditions observed among the Savants. These include the leaving of a light in each of the Temple's windows by night, the custom of setting one extra place at all meals, and a few other minor eccentricities. When asked the significance of such observances, the Savants merely shrug and cast their eyes heavenward.

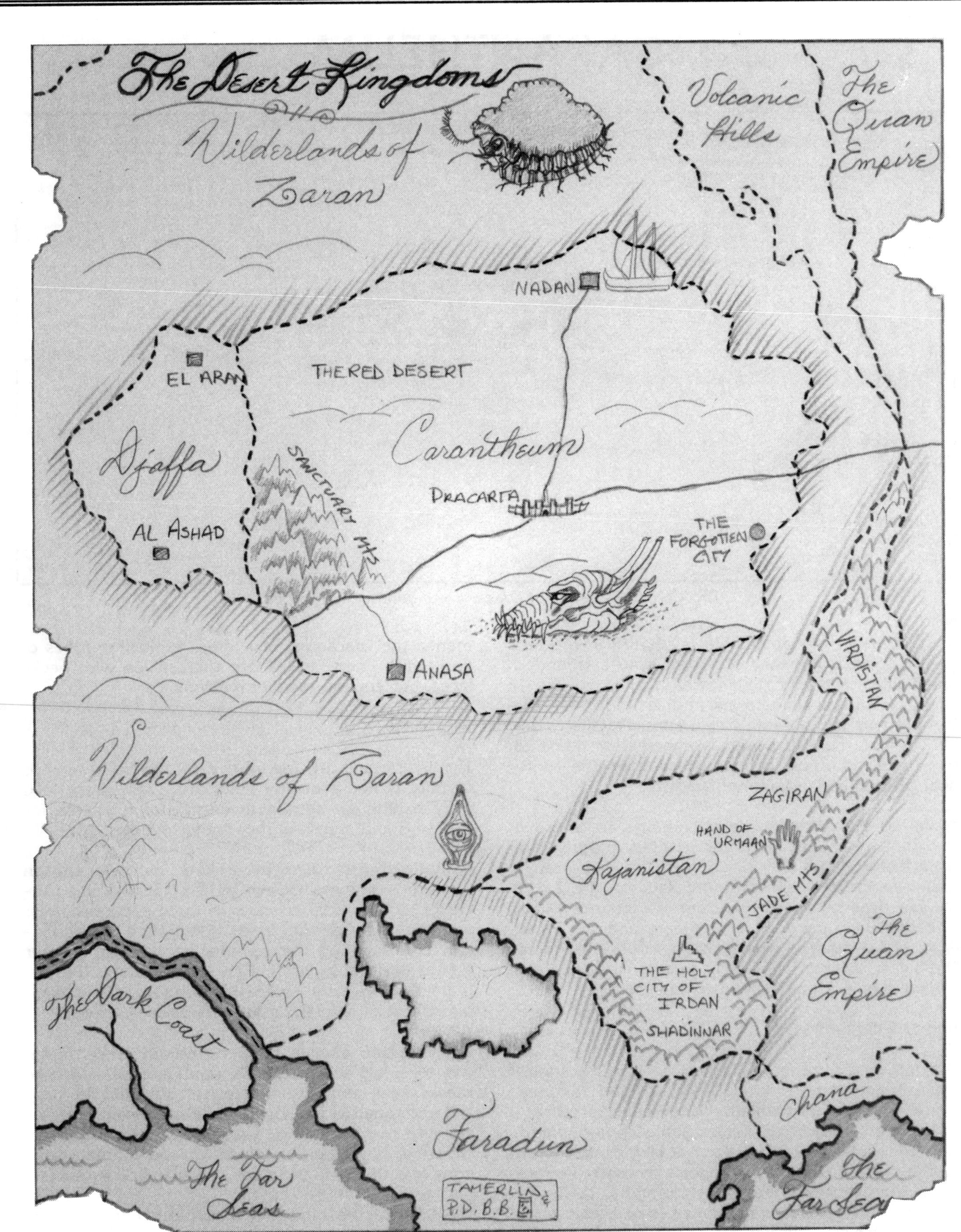

Scale: 1" = 65 miles.

CARANTHEUM

The Crimson Citadel of Dracarta – capital of Carantheum

The Kingdom of Carantheum is located in the Red Desert, a great expanse of scarlet sand surrounded on all sides by the Wilderlands of Zaran. It is a harsh land, swept by sandstorms and scorched by the burning rays of Talislanta's twin suns. Practically devoid of life, the Red Desert is nonetheless home to one of the foremost centers of trade on the continent: the Crimson Citadel of Dracarta.

Travel to Carantheum, despite efforts to improve conditions, remains a rather perilous proposition. From the East, the only practical routes lead through territories claimed either by the Saurans, the Za, or the fanatical Rajans. The ancient Wilderlands Road, sole causeway between Carantheum and the West, is beset by bandits, wild beasts and other dangers. The safest means of traveling to this land is in the company of a large, well-armed caravan.

The Dracartans

The folk of Carantheum, known as the Dracartans, are tall and jade-skinned, with chiseled features. Formerly a tribe of nomadic wanderers, these hardy folk settled in the Red Desert some centuries ago. With the discovery of the secret of how to create red iron (a metal superior in all aspects to common black iron), the Dracartans became rich, and Carantheum soon became an important center of trade and commerce. Once able to afford only the meanest of garments, the Dracartans now dress in flowing robes of fine white linen, and adorn themselves with necklaces, bracers and torcs of red iron.

Customs

The Dracartans are friendly, if somewhat reserved; frivolity is not a quality associated with these folk. They exhibit an admirable degree of tolerance for the ways and beliefs of most other peoples.

Carantheum is ruled by a king, who is chosen through a process known as the "Test of the Ancients." This ordeal consists of three separate parts: a journey through the desert, the scaling of a mountain of glass, and the retrieval of a magic scepter from a vault deep inside a crystal mountain. The test is held once every twelve years, unless the premature death of a reigning king requires otherwise.

A committee of nine elder statesmen meets in secret to select three suitable candidates. The first to successfully complete the test is ordained as king, and enthroned in the royal palace at Dracarta. The remaining two applicants, assuming they survive, are crowned as princes of the realm and granted positions of authority in the cities of Nadan and Anasa.

The laws of the Kingdom of Carantheum are strict, but fair. Individuals convicted of minor offenses are sentenced to a period of hard labor, typically entailing some sort of civic duty (such as cleaning municipal sewage receptacles). Banishing criminals to the Wilderlands is also a popular punishment.

Merchant caravans from many lands come to Dracarta, bearing goods of all varieties: amberglass from Cymril, woven goods and hardwoods from Vardune, scintilla and amber from Jhangara, metal and precious stones from Arim, beasts from Djaffa, and many other items.

The desert people are especially in need of those materials scarce in their own land: herbs and spices, burden beasts, timber, fabric, and foodstuffs. From Astar, the Dracartans obtain much-needed stores of water — thaumaturgically solidified, cut into massive blocks, then transported in wagons and sand-sailing land barges.

The Dracartans count as their friends the Djaffir, going all the way back to the time of both peoples' nomadic ancestors; the various states of the Seven Kingdoms are also their allies. Carantheum's enemies are somewhat more numerous: The Necromancers of Rajanistan covet the Red Desert's riches, and have launched several attacks against the Dracartans in the past. The Quan Emperors are also believed to have an overly acute interest in this desert region, and the mercantile nation of Faradun is obviously jealous of wealthy Carantheum.

The Cult of Jamba

The folk of Carantheum revere Jamba, the mysterious god of their nomadic ancestors. Dracartans build pyramid-shaped shrines in honor of their patron, whose ways are said to be beyond the understanding of mere mortals. The priests and priestesses of Jamba do not profess to comprehend the ways of their arcane deity — most walk about with puzzled looks on their faces a good deal of the time.

According to legend, it was Jamba who guided the Dracartans into the Red Desert and aided them in discovering the lost art of thaumaturgy. Although the deity has been somewhat lax in the working of miracles since then, he is still well thought of by his desert followers.

Thaumaturgy

Carantheum is famed for its thaumaturges, who are greatly esteemed for the wondrous products which they create. Not the least of these is the elusive substance known as *quintessence*, a crystalline powder derived by a secret alchemical process.

By skillful utilization of the magical properties of quintessence, Dracartan thaumaturges are able to transmute the very nature of substance. Thus, they are able to solidify water, liquify stone or metal, turn sand into glassine stone, or place elemental forces in suspension. The symbols of Dracartan thaumaturgy are the *star of four triangles* (representing the relationship of the four elements to the three states of matter) and the *caduceus*, or thaumaturgic wand.

The power of the thaumaturges makes possible one of the more unusual sights in this region: the Dracartan duneships and land barges. These vessels skim across the desert on red-iron runners, braving the hazards posed by sandstorms, hostile bandits, and the scorching suns.

Sails provide some impetus, but the real motion is provided by thaumaturgically-energized wind machines. Resembling coils of metal tubing, these arcane devices are powered by crystals of Elemental Wind, captured and solidified by the Dracartan Thaumaturges.

Citadels of the Desert

Anasa is a Dracartan citadel which stands at the southern edge of the Red Desert. Primarily a military outpost, it has its own fleet of duneships and a garrison of desert scouts. Some trading is done here, mainly with the Djaffir.

Nadan is a fortified settlement located at the northern edge of the Red Desert. It is notable for its duneship construction yards, and for its large population of Yassan. This dispossessed people are skilled at the art of technomancy, and are able to repair, assemble or modify just about anything that has working parts.

The Sanctuary Mountains

These imposing peaks served as a safe haven for the early ancestors of many of the desert peoples, when they were driven from their homelands following the Great Disaster. The old stone forts are now occupied by Dracartan desert scouts, who use the crumbling facilities as watchposts. Predatory satada, land dragons and winged azoryl are also found in this region, as are abandoned gold and silver mines.

The Forgotten City

The name of this ruined metropolis has long since faded from the memory of Talislantan scholars. Even so, the majestic spires and domes conjure up visions of the grandeur of a bygone age, and continue to attract explorers intent upon unearthing their ancient treasures. The proximity of war bands from Rajanistan poses some danger to would-be archaeologists, as does the presence of sand demons and predatory satada.

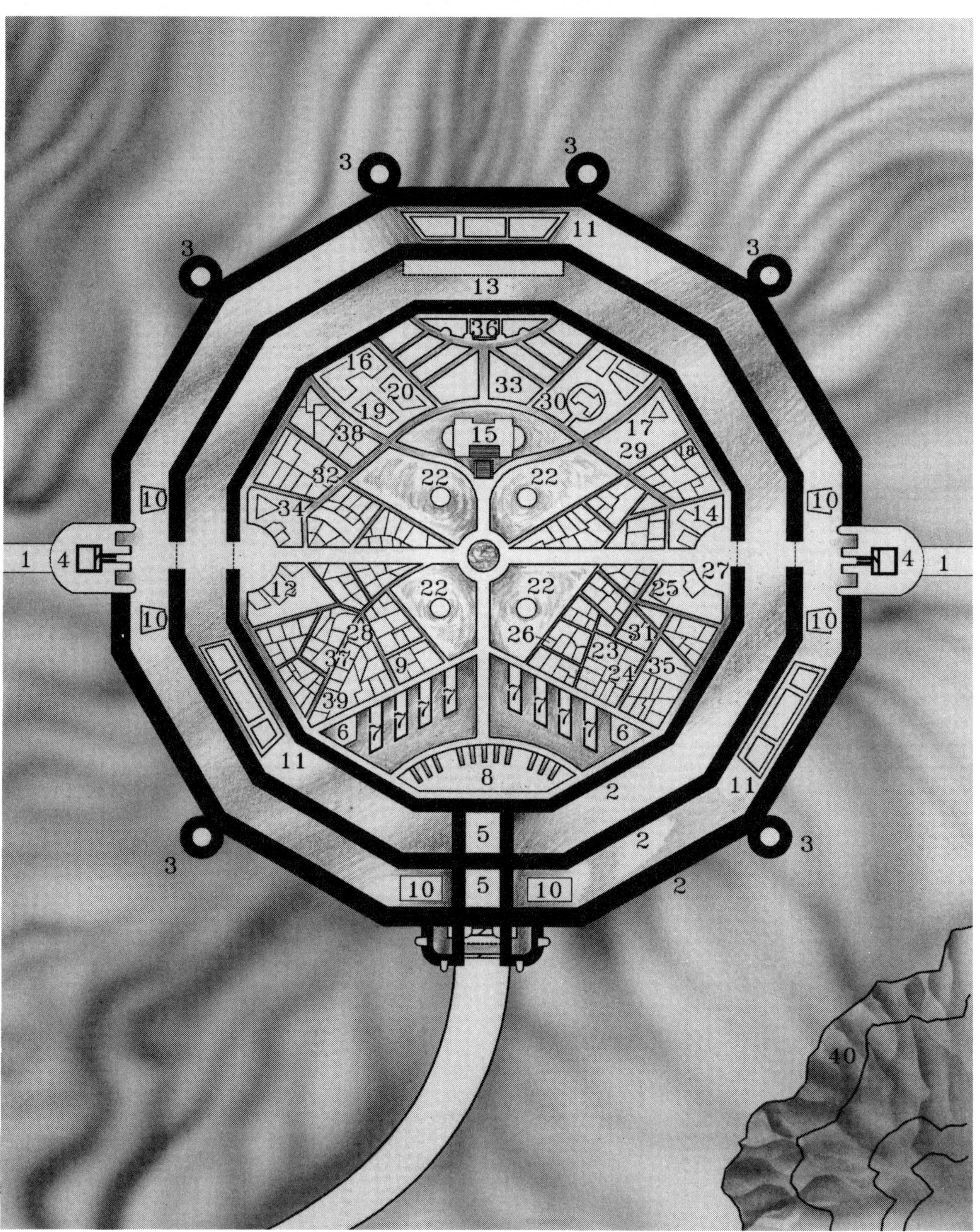
3
3
11
3
3
13
36
16
33
20
30
19
15
17
38
29
8
32
22
22
10
10
34
14
1
4
27
4
1
12
22
22
25
26
10
10
28
31
37
9
23
35
24
39
7
7
6
7
7
7
7
6
11
8
2
11
5
2
3
3
5
2
10
5
10
2
40

The City of Dracarta

The capital of Carantheum, Dracarta is one of the most important trade centers on the continent. It is striking to behold, with triple walls and towers plated with red iron, and roads paved with white stone.

1. The Wilderlands Road
The Desert Scouts carefully maintain these hexagonal cobblestones, since this highway is vital for purposes of trade. Duneships parallel this road, crossing it only where drawbridges expose a sand channel to allow sandships to pass.

2. City Walls
The three walls of Dracarta stand over 40 feet high, and are plated with red iron. A system of conduits built into the walls allows quantities of red menace (liquefied fire) to be rained from various strategic points upon would-be attackers.

3. Towers
Each of these four-story structures is equipped with a large roof-mounted siege-hurlant, and a mechanism to disperse the thaumaturgical product known as red menace through ports in the outer walls. A crew of eight artillerists operates each hurlant, and teams of a thaumaturge and two apprentices are employed to handle the fire mechanisms.

4. City Gates
The gates to the city are made of solid red-iron, and flanked by twin gatehouses. A platoon of 20 Desert Scouts is assigned to each, and 10-soldier squads patrol the walls, completing one full circuit in about an hour. It is customary for the guards to perform cursory inspections of incoming cargos, assisted by functionaries of the Ministry of Customs and Commerce.

5. Sand Channels
The walled entranceways are used by arriving and departing duneships and land barges. A network of drawbridges controls access and egress.

6. Ministry of Customs and Commerce
The clerks of these offices are responsible to monitor and register all incoming goods. Agents of the Ministry are empowered to seize suspicious cargos or contraband, and to make arrests as warranted.

*Profile: **Sedrik Nomos II***
Dracartan Administrator, 6th Level
The friendly official in charge of morning inspections, Sedrik is bumbling and inefficient – if not for his connections at court (his sister is scribe to the Queen), he would have been demoted long ago. The Dracartan has been known to accidentally break delicate valuables, misplace or exchange shipments, and to mistake contraband for legitimate goods (and vice versa). When caught in an error, Sedrik is always sincere in his well-meaning but clumsy attempts to right the wrong and make redress.

7. Warehouses
Merchants store goods here while awaiting sale or until the departure of the next caravan. Goods confiscated by the Ministry of Customs and Commerce are also stored here, in rented facilities.

8. Desert Harbor
This is a docking area for duneships and land barges. Facilities for maintenance and repair are nearby.

9. The Dunesailors' Inn
This inn and tavern is frequented by the crews of duneships and land barges in port. Recent news from the Dracartan citadels of Anasa and Nadan can be had here, though casual visitors are best advised to steer clear of this drinking establishment – the clientele is generally rowdy. Prices are average, comparable in most instances to the quality of the services afforded.

*Profile: **Pegro Samstna***
Dracartan Dunesailor; 25th Level (retired)
A veteran of four decades of service with the West Dune (army) of Carantheum, Pegro comes to the Dunesailors' Inn nightly to enjoy the rough company and remind himself of hard times. He especially seeks out younger soldiers, whom he lectures with a rugged cheerfulness. His unfulfilled dream is to someday return to Djaffa and, reunited with a Yitek tomb-robber named Ojo, solve the mystery of the lost treasure trove of the bandits he helped to pursue and slay two decades ago. Pegro is one of the few Dracartans who can tolerate the presence of the Yitek – Ojo was his special partner in the bandit pursuit, and saved him from being devoured by a giant desert kra.

10. Barracks
Each of these structures houses a contingent of 40 Desert Scouts, 20 artillerists, and 10 engineers. Yassan technomancers are assigned to the maintenance and repair of the citadel's fortifications and siege engines.

11. Military Bases
These fortified structures serve as training centers and bases of operations for the Dracartan military. Over 2,000 Desert Scouts and their support personnel are stationed at each, including armorers, engineers and thaumaturges. Stables capable of housing up to a thousand aht-ra are maintained in adjacent facilities.

12. The Hurlant
This tavern is frequented mainly by members of the Dracartan military, and is usually avoided by the general public. Patrols fresh from tours of the Red Desert often come here to unwind, with fairly predictable results. Entertainment is occasionally provided by down-and-out Bodor musicians (few performers will take work in this establishment unless nothing else is available).

Profile: **Gurio Mock Ta**
Dracartan Desert Scout, 18th Level
A Guide (platoon commander) in the Dracartan military, Gurio is assigned to the Reserve Dune in the capital, where his duties are supposedly ceremonial. In reality, this officer is a special agent of the King of Carantheum, and his men are all hand-picked for courage and survival skills. He comes to the Hurlant after particularly rough missions – to unwind, blow off steam, and get spectacularly drunk.

13. Stables
This large public facility is regularly utilized by merchant caravans and travelers. Costs are average.

14. The Red Desert Inn
This inn and tavern is frequented by diverse sorts: Djaffir traders, Yitek tomb robbers, Maruk dung merchants, Danuvian swordswomen, wandering Rahastran wizards, and (less commonly) even despised Farad mongers and procurers. Dancing girls, jugglers and musicians provide entertainment and lend a festive air to the proceedings. The prices are reasonable, and the accommodations approach excellence in most regards. Especially recommended is the mochan, an invigorating Djaffir beverage served steaming hot from brass samovars.

Profile: **Samahd Moritar**
Djaffir Merchant, 24th Level
Samahd, the owner of the Red Desert Inn, is a retired Djaffir who has traveled much of the continent. He is known as a storyteller of seemingly endless capacity, and most of his tales involve escapades of brigandry and robbery. Samahd claims to have earned his modest fortune as an astute trader, but others think he had a less legitimate career.

15. The Crimson Place
Dwelling place of the King of Carantheum and the royal family, the Crimson Palace is a magnificent structure built of sandstone blocks plated with red iron. In the great hall, the King meets daily with the Council of Elders, a group which includes representatives from the Dracartan army, the Ministry of Customs and Commerce, the Academy of Thaumaturgy, the Halls of Justice, and others. A hundred Dracartan Sentinels guard the palace and grounds.

Profile: **King Romedis**
Dracartan Thaumaturge, 39th Level
The sovereign of Carantheum is an energetic man of middle years, enormously talented at the thaumaturgical arts. A devout believer in Jamba, Romedis seeks a way to obtain further wisdom from the elusive Dracartan deity, and is especially interested in rumors that further thaumaturgical principles can be discovered by the study of ancient texts.

16. The Archives
This cavernous structure houses an uncountable number of books, scrolls and tablets, and serves as a library and hall of records for the Dracartan people. Much of the material contained within is accessible to the public, through arrangement with any of the 70-odd archivists employed here.

17. The Academy of Thaumaturgy
One of the most renowned institutes of magic in Talislanta, the Academy of Thaumaturgy is a vast pyramidal structure over 140 feet in height. The curriculum features courses in alchemy, metaphysics, and the secrets of the art of thaumaturgy: the distillation of elemental essences, the transmutation of substance, and the concocting of the marvelous substance known as quintessence. Only citizens of Carantheum are accepted in the Academy's seven-year program, though certain lectures and symposiums are available to visitors from other lands. Tuition is 700 gold lumens per year; a nominal fee of 10 lumens is charged for extracurricular lectures.

Profile: **Nomoscar**
Dracartan Thaumaturge, 18th Level
The younger brother of Abascar, the Dracartan thaumaturge on the faculty of Cymril's Lyceum Arcanum, Nomoscar is an innovator whose proposed experiments are often too daring for the Academy of Thaumaturgy to accept. He is a Professor of Aerial Essences, with a qualification in distillation sciences, and is available for consultation.

18. The Thaumaturge's Crucible
This tavern caters to students and faculty of the Academy of Thaumaturgy, and discourse on subjects relating to the Academy and its curriculum is commonplace, occasionally enlightened by a heated debate or disagreement of some sort. Otherwise, the atmosphere is a bit too low-key for most peoples' tastes. The prices are high for the quality of services available, though the private booths are not without certain practical purposes.

Profile: **Saranto Pied Xa**
Dracartan Thaumaturge, 20th Level
The keeper of the Crucible is a strange man, given to sudden spasms and coughing fits. Saranto is fanatic about preserving the secrets of thaumaturgy, steering unwanted visitors out of the shop as quickly as he can, and reminding students to be careful where and what they speak.

19. The Halls of Justice
The Council of Elders, Dracarta's esteemed legislative body, holds sway here, handing down rulings on all matters pertaining to the laws of the land. They also serve as advisers to the king, and administrate Dracarta's police force, the Sentinels. Individuals accused of wrongdoing are tried in these halls: if found guilty, offenders may face a period of enforced labor, banishment to the Wilderlands, or – for truly heinous offenses – a sentence of *retribution* (immersion in red iron). The Council is empowered to remove a reigning king, should he fail to meet acceptable standards of behavior and ethics.

20. Hall of Infamy
Here are arrayed the worst and most despicable criminals in Dracartan history – the statue-like forms standing as a warning to future offenders, preserved by immersion in liquefied red iron. Among the most notable: *Thados*, the second Khadun of Rajanistan, who led an unwarranted attack

against Carantheum in the year 445; the dreaded *Sados*, reincarnated torturer-king of ancient Quaran; and *Xargn*, a renegade thaumaturge punished for his unconscionable crimes against the Dracartan people. A popular tourist attraction, the Hall of Infamy is open daily to the general public. An admission fee of one silver piece is charged, the proceeds being used for maintenance of the hall.

21. The Traders' Market

This open-air marketplace is patronized by merchants and traders from across the continent. Some of the more common wares include land lizards, all three species of aht-ra (from the desert kingdom of Djaffa), red-iron ingots and blades, land-dragon hide, cloth, timber, mochan, dried dates, duneship and land-barge accessories, and antique artifacts from the Wilderlands. Prices vary considerably.

Profile: **Huevomar The Monger**
Dracartan Merchant, 25th Level
Rich and wise, Huevomar has traveled the continent, and is a most atypical Dracartan – class distinctions mean nothing to him, and he is rather jocular. In fact, the merchant feels more than a little out of place among his countrymen, and prefers the company of foreigners – especially Muse females (he once had a romance with a Muse dancer named Dewdrop, but she refused to follow him into the desert). He has valuable connections with the Kang Overlord at Hadran.

22. Wells

Dracarta's water supply is stored in underground cisterns, accessible by means of closely-guarded conduits and aqueducts. Water is a precious commodity in Dracarta, and wasteful use of this resource is a criminal offense. Deep wells provide part of the populace's needs, augmented by shipments of thaumaturgically-solidified water conveyed in large blocks from Lake Zephyr, in the Kingdom of Astar of the Seven Kingdoms.

23. Red Iron Plating Co.

This sizable establishment utilizes advanced thaumaturgic techniques to work metals of many sorts. Specialties include custom-designing of jewelry, the crafting and inscription of red-iron blades, and red-iron plating of every sort – all at the best prices.

24. The Forges of Dracarta

This extensive installation, owned and operated by the Kingdom of Carantheum, is where the Dracartan thaumaturges turn sand to stone, and extract red-iron ore from Red Desert sand. The thaumaturgical sandstone is rendered into many practical shapes, including columns, blocks, spheres and arches. For convenience, the ore is smelted into 10-, 20- and 50-pound ingots. Land barges loaded with the red-iron ingots depart for the West on a weekly basis.

25. Caravan Supply

This establishment features all manner of new and used equipment for the caravan trade, including burden beasts, wagons, tents and, occasionally, refurbished land barges and duneships. It is sometimes possible to arrange for passage with caravans heading to Hadj, Danuvia, Maruk, or the West through the auspices of this establishment.

Profile: **Eomar Rannt**
Dracartan Desert Scout, 9th Level
A retired soldier, Eomar now owns Caravan Supply. He accepts secondhand and bartered goods in exchange for his wares, no questions asked – or answered.

26. Central Talislanta Map Company

This small shop specializes in maps of the Wilderlands of Zaran, the Volcanic Hills, the Sinking Land, and the Red Desert. Prices range from as low as five gold lumens (for a common map) to over 10,000 gold lumens (for especially rare or unusual charts).

Profile: **Regia Aereonautus**
Dracartan Savant, 23rd Level
The owner of the Central Talislanta Map Company, Regia is an aged Dracartan scholar who claims to have studied for a time with the Savants of Xanadas. He can be hired to authenticate obscure maps and schematics at a cost ranging from 20 to 200 gold lumens, depending upon the amount of research required.

27. The Red Sands Inn

This inn caters to the caravan trade, and the decor is appropriate: the rooms are decorated to look like tents, the floor is covered with sand, and the large common room is ringed with potted palms. It is often possible to find caravan masters, draymen, mercenary guards, and drivers looking for work here, or to hire on with a caravan of one sort or another. The quality of the inn's services is adequate at best, hardly sufficient to justify the somewhat steep prices.

Profile: **Krepass**
Kasmir Money-Lender; 9th Level
The owner of the Red Sands Inn, alas, is a miserly Kasmir exiled by her family for poor financial management – she was once an insatiable gambler. Krepass is determined to restore her fortunes, here and now, whatever it takes. The Kasmir knows that if she could only get her hands on a breeding pair of aht-ra, she could break the Djaffir monopoly, make a fortune, and redeem herself in the eyes of her family – all at the same time! However, the Caliph of Djaffa would not stand idly by while such animals were stolen...

28. Four Winds Travel Co.

Little more than an expanse of sand and a single, small building, this is the local outpost of the famous Cymril-based travel company. It is supposedly possible to arrange passage via windship through this often-abandoned establishment, which is operated by a pair of eccentric Orgovians from the Seven Kingdoms.

29. The Caduceus

A small shop specializing in thaumaturgical paraphernalia, alchemical apparatus, and magical mixtures, the Caduceus' prices are within reason, and the owner often buys and sells used goods as well as new (and more expensive) items.

30. Thaumaturges' Guild

This guildhouse also serves as a hostel for Dracartan thaumaturges. The guild's registry service lists all dues-paying thaumaturges, their current status (whether employed or not), and special fields of interest. Thaumaturgical components are sold here at a one-quarter discount to guild members, who may also use these facilities – including a library, workrooms, and private cells – at a cost of just ten gold lumens per day. A membership costs 500 gold lumens per year, and is available to practicing thaumaturges only.

31. Red Blades of Carantheum

A family of Dracartan ironsmiths owns this shop, which specializes in red-iron weapons and armor. They offer red-iron armor and weaponry in a wide variety of styles and types – and for only double the normal price, will custom-make any piece to order. The quality of their work is unsurpassed in the region, and their prices are within reason.

32. Desert Clothier

This reputable establishment offers apparel suitable for arid and desert climes. Styles include Dracartan, Djaffir, Hadjin, Kasmir, Farad, and Yitek. Custom work is available at double the usual prices...which, to be frank, are already a little above average.

33. Memorial Park

This oasis, decorated with statues, commemorates the Dracartans' nomadic ancestors, who founded the Kingdom of Carantheum. Swaying palms and shaded dunes lend a peaceful and serene ambience to the park, which is frequented by individuals from many parts of the kingdom.

34. Temple of Jamba

This great pyramidal structure is dedicated to Jamba, the mysterious god of the Dracartans. It is customary for Priests of Jamba and visiting worshipers to maintain respectful silence while within the temple, lest some utterance of Jamba go unnoticed.

35. Carantheum Imports

This odd establishment bears an uncanny resemblance to an indoor junkyard. The owner is justly renowned as a collector of oddities, trinkets, gewgaws, and bric-a-brac (most seemingly bereft of any redeeming virtues). Occasionally, one uncovers a find of some sort amongst the bizarre items which litter this shop, but not often. Still, hope springs eternal in the hearts of the many would-be collectors who visit this shop, many of whom are drawn by the fact that no item in the place is ever priced above ten gold lumens.

36. Amphitheater

This large arena seats up to 20,000 spectators, and exhibitions of skill are held here once each week. Some of the more popular events include: contests pitting warriors against dangerous beasts, team wrestling atop a raised platform, battles between armored land-barges, exhibitions of thaumaturgic skill, non-fatal duels fought for prize money, and – a particular favorite – *retributions*, ingenious contests pitting condemned felons against hazards appropriate to the crime which they committed. Admittance is one gold lumen for adults; one silver piece for children.

37. Surcease From Care

The deceased are prepared for burial in this facility. As is the custom in Carantheum, the bodies of the dead are thaumaturgically treated to prevent decomposition, then placed in enchanted sarcophagi and interred in the desert. Costs range, primarily depending on the type of sarcophagus desired. The embalmer traditionally handles all arrangements, including purchase of the sarcophagus.

38. Office of Taxation

Like death, the demands of this institution are also inevitable. The kingdom collects a tithe of one-tenth of each citizen's annual income.

39. The Catacombs

This gloomy inn and tavern is popular among the Yitek, whether they be tomb robbers, grave diggers, embalmers, or members of the Dracartan army's "corpse squad" (mercenaries who clear battlefields in return for exclusive scavenging rights). The common room of the inn and its private chambers are located below ground, amidst a morbid, mausoleum-like setting. Prices and quality are average.

40. The Mountain of Glass

This is the site of the legendary "Test of the Ancients," where prospective applicants for the position of King of Carantheum are put to the test. Secret passageways, traps and other features are updated as needed, so that no two Tests are ever alike.

DJAFFA

A Djaffir merchant, or bandit — the distinction is said to be essentially one of semantics.

Nearly surrounded by the Wilderlands of Zaran, Djaffa consists primarily of scrub plains and desert. With the exception of the vegetation at a few scattered oases, practically nothing grows in this arid region. This desert is home to the nomadic people known as the Djaffir, who are divided into two types of tribes: merchants and bandits.

The Djaffir

Uniformly slender and wiry of build, the Djaffir are dark skinned and of average height. Flowing headdresses, robes and cloaks of beige or white linen are worn, along with boots of soft animal hide.

Customs

It is the peculiar custom of all Djaffir to wear leather masks, which are made to cover the entire face. They will not remove these masks except in the privacy of their tents, believing that "the face mirrors the soul," and that their masks protect them from hostile magics. Fashioned by Djaffir wizards, these devices do indeed seem to confer some protection from magical influences, and certainly are of practical use during sandstorms (common in Djaffa). Indi-

viduals of a more skeptical nature claim that the Djaffir wear masks simply to conceal their identities from those who, by one means or another, they eventually intend to relieve of their money.

Beasts of the Djaffir

The desert folk produce few marketable wares, though they make lances, daggers and short bows of good quality for their own use. The Djaffir have some talent for herding and animal husbandry, however, and have managed over time to foster the development of a unique burden beast.

The aht-ra is a variety of beast similar in some respects to the equs, but having a heavier torso, longer legs, spiraling horns, and a serpentine tail. The Beasthandlers of the Djaffa claim to have created the species centuries ago, by the accidental crossbreeding of various riding and burden beasts; no one knows for certain the exact composition which contributed to the existence of these eminently useful hybrids.

Though the normally placid nature of these beasts can sometimes make motivation a difficult task, they are among the most useful of Talislantan creatures. They usually sell for 200 to 800 gold lumens apiece, regardless of type — age and overall condition being the most important factors affecting cost. Young aht-ra are seldom available except through the auspices of Djaffir merchants, who sell only gelded males in order to maintain their countrymen's monopoly on this valuable commodity.

Despite their ungainly appearance, aht-ra are surprisingly swift and agile afoot. More impressive is the endurance of these creatures, which is unmatched in the animal kingdom. With their characteristic long and loping stride, aht-ra can travel for days without stopping for rest. By retaining fluids in their hump-like sacs, aht-ra can go without water for long periods of time (one month per hump is thought to be an accurate estimate). The creature's scaly hide renders the beast immune to the effects of the rays of Talislanta's twin suns, and translucent membranes shield its eyes from sun and sand.

There are three varieties of aht-ra, each possessed of its own individual virtues: Swiftest is the one-humped *ontra*, bred mainly for speed. The two-humped *batra* is somewhat slower and can carry 800 pounds of weight (compared to only 400 pounds for the ontra). The three-humped *tatra* can carry 1,200 pounds of cargo, but is the slowest of the three, and will not run at full speed unless constantly goaded with a prod or riding crop.

Plans for a four-humped variety of aht-ra were proposed by Djaffa Beasthandlers at one point, but were subsequently discarded as being impractical, and possibly absurd.

Other animals herded by the Djaffir include land lizards, greymanes, and the fierce war-beasts known as mangonel lizards.

Of Merchants and Bandits

By far the most numerous of the two types of tribes, Djaffir merchants tribes carry goods to and from the civilized countries of Talislanta, from as far west as Zandu to the eastern lands of the Quan Empire and even the Volcanic Hills. Their chieftains are generally regarded as the shrewdest and most skillful traders on the continent.

It is said that Djaffir merchants will travel anywhere, regardless of the dangers, as long as there is a profit to be made. In truth, the only trails found in certain remote regions are those established over the years by the trade caravans of these nomadic merchants.

The bandit tribes, though fewer in number, are nearly as persistent as their mercantile counterparts. Primarily known as caravan robbers, Djaffir bandits are relentless in their pursuit of prey. The larger tribes have been known to raid small villages, taking women, slaves, and anything else of value that can be carried off.

Though they will kill in order to get what they desire, Djaffir bandits are not known to engage in wanton or senseless violence. Neither are they known to attack the caravans of Djaffir merchants, a fact which has led many observers to suspect collusion between the sheiks of the two tribal groups. Some Talislantans go so far as to claim that the distinction between Djaffir merchants and bandits is one of semantics only.

Whatever the relation between the two tribes, it is certain that both have much in common. Generally speaking, the Djaffir bandits prefer the faster one- and two-humped aht-ra, while the merchant traders mainly employ the three-humped tatra.

Settlements

As the folk of Djaffa are nomads at heart, they have no true cities. However, two extensive tent settlements exist, growing or contracting in size according to the comings and goings of the various merchant and bandit tribes. Both cities are located at oases, and are comprised entirely of tents and pavilions, allowing them to be moved at need.

Al Ashad is the southern tent settlement. The wells are heavily guarded, for water is a precious commodity in this region. It is said that the Djaffir merchant tribes prefer this settlement due to its close proximity to the Wilderlands Road.

The northern oasis-settlement, *El Aran,* is identical in most respects to Al Ashad. Djaffir bandit tribes reportedly prefer this place, due to its isolated location in the desertlands. Sand demons proliferate in this region.

It is said that the Caliph of Djaffa, whom both merchants and bandits regard as their spiritual leader, is always to be found at one of these two settlements. Aside from his duties as arbiter of all tribal disputes, the ruler performs no other known function. Even so, it is said that at a single word from the Caliph, all the tribes of Djaffa would unite to do his bidding.

RAJANISTAN

Shadinn executioner and Rajan necromancer

Far to the east, between the scorching sands of the Red Desert and the green swirl of the Sea of Glass, lies the warlike nation of Rajanistan. Known as "the Scourge of the Desert," it is the most populous of the desert kingdoms.

This is a harsh and arid land, made hospitable only by numerous small springs found scattered across its far-ranging territories. The Jade Mountains ring it on nearly all sides; elsewhere the terrain is monotonous in form, a sprawling expanse of yellow sand interrupted only by sparse patches of date palm, nettle and briarbush.

The mountains and deserts are rife with dangerous beasts, including yaksha and sand demons, and rare crested dragons are not unknown in these parts. During the spring, water from thawing ice caps cascades down the southern mountains, carrying with it many small bits and chunks of gold. Adventurers with a flair for the melodramatic sometimes attempt to steal into the mountains, hoping to escape the desert natives, harvest the gold and become rich.

The Rajans

A fierce, dark-skinned folk, the masters of Rajanistan are tall and wiry of build, with blood-red eyes, and horn-like protrusions jutting forth from their chins and foreheads. They dress in dark grey capes, veiled headdresses, and loose-fitting garments bound with cords at the wrists, ankles and waist. These same cords are used for many practical purposes by the Rajans, including the strangling of enemies. It is the unfriendly custom of both the males and females of this people to carry concealed weapons on their persons, curved daggers being considered especially elegant.

Customs

The Rajans are a race of fanatics, utterly devoted to the dread entity known as Death — and his minion the Khadun, absolute ruler of Rajanistan and Necromancer-Priest of the Black Mystic Cult. The cultists believe that the Khadun is the earthly manifestation of Death, and revere him as a demi-god.

Only by dying can they become one in spirit with their mystic deity, or so the Rajans have been taught from birth by the Necromancer-Priests; therefore, they are eager to sacrifice their lives for any cause that the prophet of Death endorses.

Under the iron rule of the Khadun, Rajanistan is among the most repressive states of Talislanta. The punishment for most crimes is the removal of an appropriate body part: liars have their tongues cut off, thieves lose a hand, and voyeurs (those who attempt to peek beneath a woman's veil) lose an eye. The penalty for adultery is especially grim. Individuals accused of treason or heresy are imprisoned in the Tower of Irdan, where torturers practice their arts.

Rajanistan marks Carantheum and Djaffa as hated foes, and bears no love for the Seven Kingdoms. The fortress of Hadran intervenes between the desert nation and the Quan Empire — given the Quan's history of expansion and conquest, Rajanistan may also have some reason for concern in this direction.

The Rajans covet the ore-rich sands of the Red Desert, but attempts to conquer the Dracartans have failed. Defeat has not swayed the tribes from this cause, and the Khadun has sworn to crush Carantheum, if every man, woman and child in Rajanistan must die in the attempt. As his generals are unfortunately known more for fanatical obedience than their tactical abilities, observers speculate that such a result is within the realm of possibilities.

Rajanistan has political ties with no other nation except Faradun, a vital trade partner. The Rajans are an impediment to east-west trade as long as they continue to plunder caravans on the Wilderlands Road — a situation favorable to the Farad, whose trade routes do not pass through the Red Desert.

The Black Mystic Cult

The Rajan tribe is ruled by the Black Mystic Cult, just as the Rajans are the masters of the other inhabitants of Rajanistan. The necromancers of the cult wear dark vestments and skull-like iron masks. Mages of greatest power are reportedly capable of manifesting a third eye in the center of their foreheads, of use in detecting invisible or spirit presences.

The Rajans believe that by killing non-believers, they make converts for their morbid deity. They have been taught this by the Necromancer-Priests, the Death-mages who also train the elite corps of religious assassins known as the Torquar. Under the command of the Khadun, the Cult exports terrorism to many lands. The Torquar are known for magic, and for their skill with the *da-khar* (a leather gauntlet equipped with retractable metal claws).

The Temple of Death in Irdan is the sanctum of the Black Mystic Cult. Here, the Necromancer-Priests of are said to consort with the spirits of the deceased, hoping to exhume lost magical secrets of the Forgotten Age.

The Holy City of Irdan

A warlike and violent people, the Rajans long ago conquered and subjugated the other tribes of this region, then employed them as slaves to build Irdan, a dark fortress located on the lower slopes of the Jade Mountains. The massive citadel is the only major settlement in Rajanistan, and serves as the country's capital.

Aside from an occasional visit by Farad merchants, the city is closed to foreigners. Gold, mined in great quantities from the Jade Mountains, is smelted into ingots in Irdan, then used to purchase weapons and k'tallah. The Khadun resides within the Temple of Death, protected by necromancers, elite Torquar and giant Shadinn warriors.

The Other Tribes

Though the masters of this country are the Rajans, four other nomadic tribes make their homes here. All are related in some manner to the Rajans: the warrior Aramut, the mountain-dwelling Zagir, the giant Shadinn, and the despised "mongrel" Virds.

The *Aramut* and *Zagir* tribesmen closely resemble the Rajans, but are shorter in stature and favor less elaborate attire. Their homeland, the arid mountains of Zagiran, was conquered by the Rajans toward the end of the third century. Satada, earth demons, azoryl, and land dragons are all found in this rugged, mountainous area.

The *Virds*, a people of mixed ancestry, are devoid of any single set of definable characteristics. The Rajans consider them expendable, and send them to carry out suicidal attacks against enemies.

Virdistan was conquered by the Rajans in the early part of the fourth century. The nomadic Virds tend herds of land lizards, durge, and other creatures. Sand demons, wild duadir, and the much-feared opteryx are common to this arid land, and Araq raid from the north.

The *Shadinn* resemble the Rajans, but are giants, averaging seven feet in height. They live in tent settlements scattered across the southern desert, which is also inhabited by sand demons, satada and desert kra. Shadinnar was conquered by the Rajans at the beginning of the fourth century.

The Hand of Urmaan

This 150-foot-tall stone spire, located in the Jade Mountains, resembles a massive grasping hand. According to the Rajans, this oddity was created by Urmaan, the first Necromancer of Rajanistan. Some say that the hand wards Urmaan's lost sanctum, the secret entrance to which may be hidden somewhere in the vicinity.

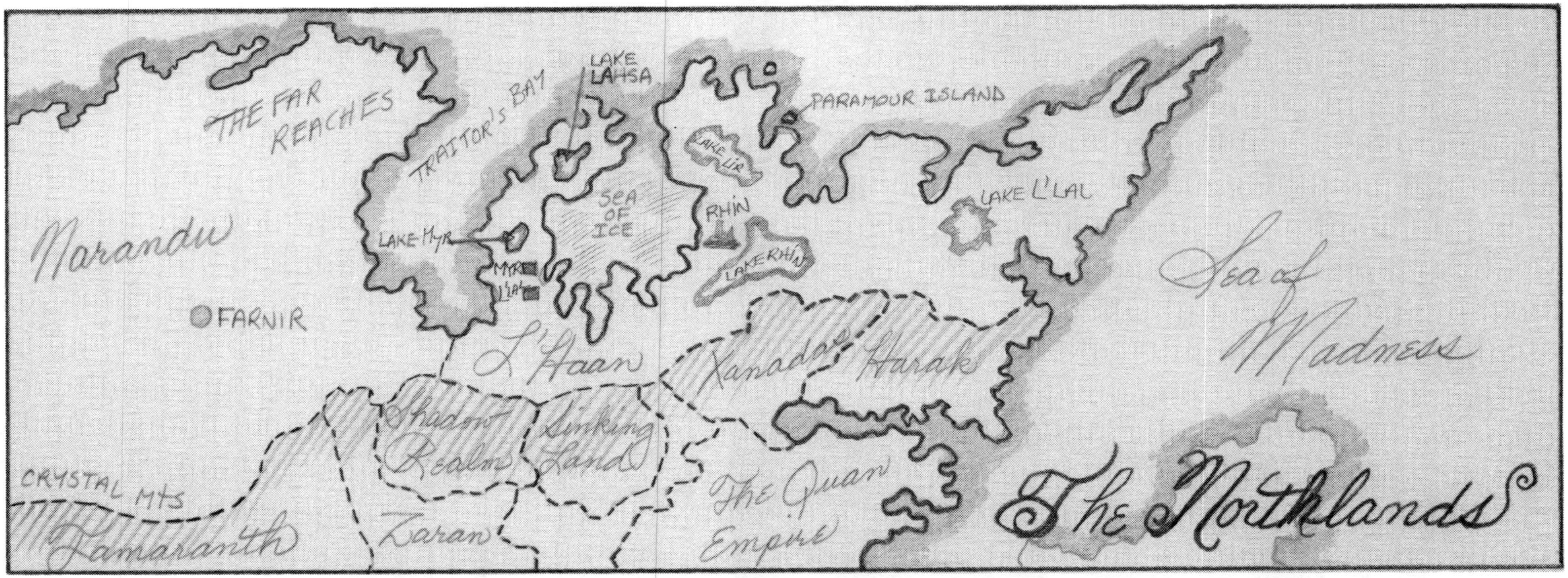

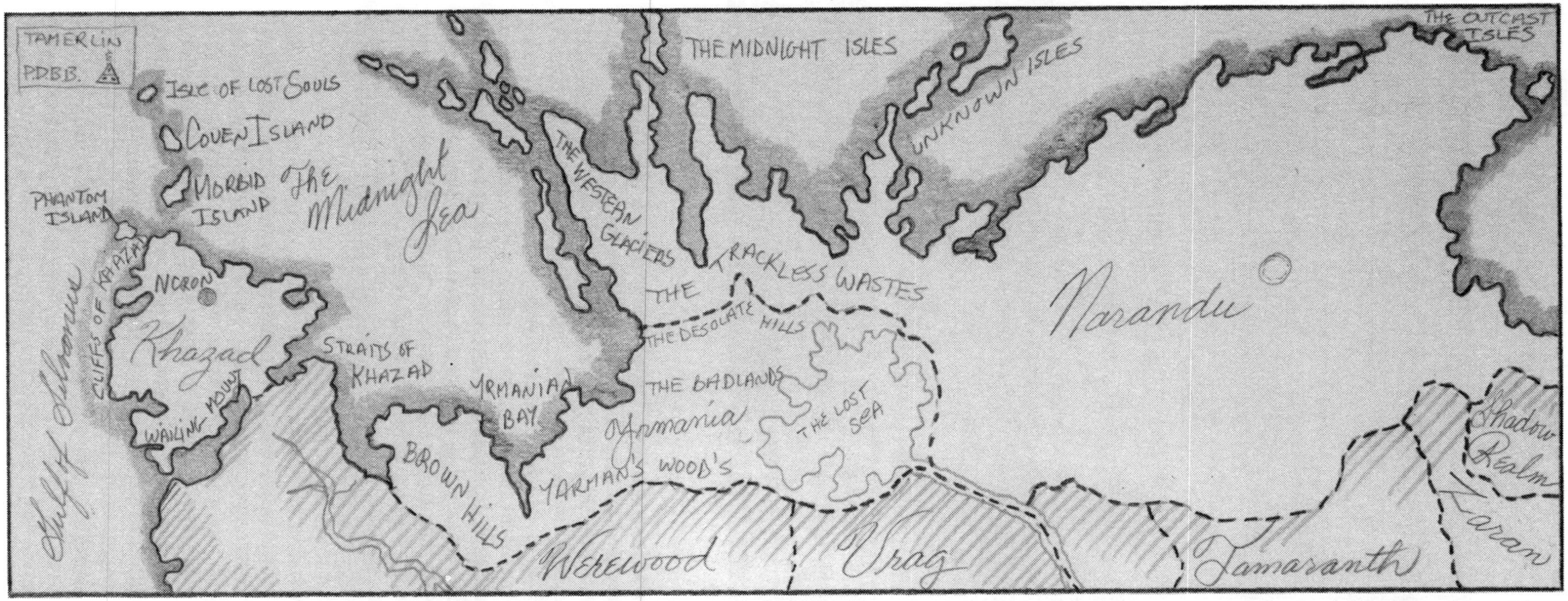

The Northlands

Sea of Madness

Lake L'Lal
Paramour Island
Lake Rhia
Rhia
Lake Lir
Sea of Ice
Lake Lahsa
Traitor's Bay
The Far Reaches
Lake Myr
Morandu
Farnir
Crystal Mts
Tamaranth
Zaran
Ramador Hauk
L'Haan
The Quan Empire
Phantom Sinking Island
Shadow Realms

The Outcast Isles
Shadru Realm
Zaran
Tamaranth
Morandu
Unknown Isles
The Midnight Isles
Trackless Wastes
The Desolate Hills
Armonia
The Lost Sea
The Badlands
Yarmand's Woods
Urag
Weirwood
The Western Glaciers
Brown Hills
Armania Bay
Straits of Khazad
Khazad
The Morbid Midnight Sea
Isle of Lost Souls
Cover Island
Phantom Island
Cliffs of Khazad
Negro

Tamerlin PDBB A

Scale: 1" = 135 miles.

KHAZAD

The Cliffs of Khazad

A strange and largely unknown realm, Khazad is located at the furthest northwestern reaches of Talislanta. Practically inaccessible to all but the most determined travelers, its terrain is foreboding: A line of precipitous cliffs runs the length of its western coast, and a ridge of mountains extends along its eastern borders. To the north lie fields of ice and snow; beyond this is the Midnight Sea, where sailors fear to go. The waters of the Gulf of Silvanus, rock-strewn and perilous, deny easy access from the south.

As a result of these impediments to travel, much of what is known of Khazad is based upon the rare accounts of wandering Sarista gypsies and the few hardy adventurers who have survived journeys to this isolated area. According to their accounts, the interior of Khazad is less than inviting. Patches of bleached and barren gall oak stand like skeletons, silhouetted against a dreary purple-and-grey sky. Broken and irregular lines of hills dot the landscape, interspersed with moors, quagmires and stagnant ponds. The air is heavy with the stench of moldering vegetation, and exudes an unsettling, ancient quality.

The Lost Kingdom

Scattered throughout the region known as Khazad are the ruins of a long-forgotten civilization. Far to the north are vast burial grounds, denoted by row upon row of age-worn stone markers. Less frequently encountered are mausoleums of pitted stone, engraved with arcane symbols of obscure origin. Though some sites have been plundered of their hidden secrets, most are unexplored.

The remains of a man-like race, entombed in massive sarcophagi of strange design, have been found in some of the ancient crypts. Some individuals — apparently those of importance — were buried wearing gold funerary masks of frightening aspect. In the less elaborate tombs and graves, similar masks of silver, copper, tin, and lead have been unearthed. Though the purpose of these artifacts is unclear, scholars at Cymril's Lyceum Arcanum believe the masks were intended to ward demons or evil spirits from the bodies of the deceased. The value of the metal used in the making of these masks is believed to have been a measure of the wearer's social status or cult ranking.

The brass urns found in the tombs of this region are especially popular with collectors. Sealed with paraffin, these artifacts sometimes were used in ancient times to imprison bottle-imps or to safekeep the corpse-dust of departed wizards. Prized by curio collectors and necromancers alike, these relics bring high prices.

Unfortunately for those who would explore the tombs of Khazad, necrophages haunt the region, craving fresh corpses in preference to the dry bones of the long dead. Malathrope prowl the moors, as do omnivrax from the Serpentine Mountains. Wind Demons, though far from common, are sometimes known to leave their larvae in the hollows of dead gall oaks in this area.

The City of the Dead

There is a legend to the effect that a vast complex of ruins lies in far-northern Khazad. Referred to as Necron on several ancient maps, the ruins are called the "City of the Dead" by the Sarista. Here, or so the gypsy legend goes, an entire city and all its inhabitants lie buried beneath the ground; the former residents of the metropolis all supposedly having been mummified and interred in stone sarcophagi.

Very little reliable information is available regarding this archaic necropolis or its people. Some scholars postulate that they were the seafaring race whose ships are known to have plied the waters of the Midnight Sea in bygone times. Some of those who support this theory cite the legend of an underground waterway which leads to Necron from some point along the northern coast of Khazad.

The Serpentine Mountains

These peaks stand like shadowy sentinels along the southern border of Khazad. The uppermost heights are haunted by yaksha; the lower, by ghasts, banes and grues.

Where the mountains reach the western sea, sheer 200-foot cliffs ring the coastline of Khazad. Of interest to scholars of the occult are the giant diabolical visages carved into the cliff-sides along portions of the coast, which some believe represent various members of the Shaitan hierarchy. A particularly odious clan of horned devil-men makes its home in the mouths and eye-sockets of these immense stone effigies, complicating attempts to study the cliffs at close range.

Further south lies *Wailing Mountain,* a high, twisting spiral of grey basalt. The peak derives its name from the dismal groaning sounds which seem to originate from its uppermost reaches. Most scholars attribute these noises to wind and the mountain's unusual configuration. A few cite an ancient Phaedran legend, which states that the great archimage, Soliman, imprisoned a treacherous Shaitan somewhere within a northern mountain. Those who lend credence to this tale say that the awful wailing noises are the sounds made by the giant chained devil, lamenting its fate.

Two waterways penetrate the mountains from east and west, so that Khazad has only the smallest of borders with the southern region of Werewood. The western waterway is the Gulf of Silvanus; the eastern and most treacherous body of water is known as the Straits of Khazad.

Perilous, rock-strewn, and supposedly infested by sea monsters, the straits are considered unnavigable except in the late fall, when ice-going craft can be employed to skim across the frozen waters. The dark vessels of the Nefaratans sometimes frequent the region, though for what reason, few care to hazard a guess.

The Northern Islands

A chain of four bleak and frozen islands leads northward from the northern coast of Khazad. In order from south to north, these are: Phantom Island, Morbid Isle (of which nothing is known except for its name, as recorded on ancient charts), Coven Island, and the Isle of Lost Souls.

Phantom Island, forlorn and deserted, is rumored to be haunted by shadow wights (or perhaps shadow wizards). No one knows for certain, nor do many scholars seem eager to resolve this minor mystery. Ships from Nefaratus have also been reported in the waters off the island — another excellent reason to avoid the place, as far as most folks are concerned.

Bleak and deserted in appearance, *Coven Island* is a little more than a mound of stone riddled with caves, crevasses and tunnels. According to some historians, the isle once served as a hiding place for Dhuna witches and other mages seeking to avoid persecution by the Orthodoxists of Aaman and their Witch Hunters. It is not known if the island is currently inhabited.

The frozen *Isle of Lost Souls* is purportedly inhabited by the night demon Thanus and a number of his followers. It is said that the demon has a penchant for collecting souls, which his assistants gather by night and bring back to his island lair. Thanus then stores the "lost souls" in enchanted amberglass vials, which he keeps for his amusement on a shelf .

L'HAAN

A Mirin Ice Schooner. Off in the distance: the City of L'Lal.

L'Haan is a land of vast snow fields, glittering ice peaks, and frozen lakes. Located in the nethermost reaches of eastern Talislanta, the region is predominantly wilderness, populated by tundra beasts and great herds of snowmanes and woolly ogriphants. Along the shores of the Sea of Ice live the only civilized folk native to L'Haan: the blue-skinned race known as the Mirin.

The Mirin

A people of noble appearance, tall and statuesque, the Mirin live in crystalline ice castles, and are skilled in the arts of enchantment, alchemy and elemental magic. Renowned throughout Talislanta as artificers of the highest order, the Mirin fashion superior weapons and implements from adamant, an alloy of blue diamond — the fabled "permanent ice" of legend.

Customs

The Mirin are an enlightened and peace-loving people, who shun the use of violence except in defense of their land and its cities. A deeply religious peo-ple, the Mirin revere Borean, the God of the cold North Wind. The white witches and warlocks of Borean do not build temples in his name, but do erect altars on the snowy steppes around frozen lakes such as L'Lal and Rhin. It is only in such open and natural surroundings, the Mirin say, that one can truly feel the presence of the God of the North Wind.

It is the custom among these folk to undertake a "bonding of spirits" with a chosen mate or friend. The procedure, known as melding, creates a psychic link between the two individuals. While melded individuals cannot actually communicate via this ability, each instinctively knows if the other is in danger or great distress.

The Mirin seldom venture beyond their own borders, as they dislike any but the coldest climes. Druas from the Maze-City of Altan sometimes come here, as does at least one tribe of hardy and extremely determined Djaffir merchants. Despite generous offers from other lands, the Mirin refuse to trade any but the smallest quantities of blue diamonds or adamant, substances which they consider vital to the defense of their land.

The Sea of Ice

An expanse of shimmering, perpetually-frozen water, the Sea of Ice is traversed by Mirin ice schooners. These majestic sail-driven vessels glide across the ice on runners made of gleaming adamant as they journey from L'Lal to Rhin, bearing cargos of adamant, blue diamonds and alchemical mixtures. Ice dragons, spawned in the frigid depths of the Midnight Sea, pose a hazard to ships, as do the razor-sharp edges of partially-submerged glaciers.

Three major Mirin settlements ring the Sea of Ice: Rhin, L'Lal, and Myr. On the eastern shore is the walled city of *Rhin*, the capital of this far-northern land. The Snow Queen — a figure of some mystery, said to be a white witch of surpassing ability — is the ruler of L'Haan, and lives in a fabulous ice palace in this city. Rhin is renowned for its alchemists, who are skilled in the art of magically forging adamant.

L'Lal, likewise a city of shining ice castles, stands on the western shore of the Sea of Ice. Closest of the Mirin cities to the territories of the evil Ice Giants, L'Lal is surrounded by walls over 40 feet in height. The greater part of L'Haan's formidable military force is stationed at this ice fortress, warding against possible invasion by the Ice Giants of Narandu. Equipped with light chain mail, swords, shields and spears all of adamant, the Mirin present a formidable challenge to intruders venturing into their realm. Mirin war sleds, drawn by teams of snowmanes, allow swift response to threats from all across the territory.

Myr also stands on the western lakeshore, opposite Rhin. This city is famed for its shipyards, where graceful ice schooners and smaller ice skiffs are constructed. The walled city is also the foremost supplier of blue diamonds on the continent.

The Ice Lakes

The five fresh-water lakes of L'Haan lie in the snowy reaches of L'Haan's interior. The Mirin sail the frozen waters in double-bladed ice skiffs, hunting for frostweres, tundra beasts and ice dragons. Icefishing is also a popular pastime in this region, though one enjoyed almost exclusively by Mirin icedivers, whose uncanny metabolism enables them to survive in the freezing-cold waters below the surface of the frozen lakes. The crystal eggs of ice dragons, shimmering blue pearls of the northern Quaga, and various species of edible aquatic creatures are harvested by Mirin divers.

Lake Rhin is the largest of the lakes, and is something of a fashionable resort among the Mirin, The northern folk like to vacation here in ice lodges built along the shores.

Travelers should be cautious near *Lake Lir*, which is known to be the domain of frost demons.

The Mystic Mountains

These mountains separate the land of L'Haan from its southern neighbors, Xanadas and Harak. The peaks are so named for their unusual configuration — some say the range resembles a line of towering stone figures, dressed in the voluminous robes of sages or mystics.

The Mystic Mountains serve as an impediment to the hostile Harakin clans, who therefore rarely raid the icy wastes. The heights are also believed to be a source of blue diamonds, but the Mirin refuse to confirm this belief. Bitter cold, the precipitous terrain, and the local concentration of frostweres have together discouraged concerted efforts to take advantage of the region's natural resources.

Northern Waters

Several areas of interest lie along the frigid north coast of L'Haan. The icy stretch of water known as *Traitor's Bay* is named for the infamous Rasmirin, a cult of anarchists and black witches which once schemed to usurp the rule of the Snow Queen. The traitorous Mirin launched an assault on L'Haan's fleet of ice schooners in the year 403 N.A. and were defeated, then banished to dwell forever on the Outcast Isles at the mouth of the bay. Sunken ships from the battle, laden with treasures plundered from the City of L'Lal, still lie somewhere at the bottom of the bay.

The frigid and rock-strewn *Outcast Islands* serve as home to the exiled cult to the present day. The Rasmirin dwell in rude ice fortresses, ever plotting new schemes to overthrow the ruler of L'Haan.

Further east lie two neighboring islands of very different history. The ice island of *Warlock's Keep* protrudes upward from the Midnight Sea, and resembles a jagged crystal tower. According to Mirin legend, this place is home to an ancient warlock named Nobius — a master of Grey Witchcraft, and a figure of unpredictable temperament. Lending credence to the legend are reports from Mirin tundra scouts, who claim to have spotted matrices of colored light hovering above the island.

Paramour Island also has its place in folklore. The Snow Queen of L'Haan had a fabulous ice castle built upon this island for the many suitors who desired her hand in marriage. The situation became untenable when the rivals began to plot against each other, causing great mischief. The facility was abandoned, and remains deserted to the present day. Now, only frost demons inhabit the island.

NARANDU

An immense and frozen wasteland, Narandu stretches across much of the far-northern regions of Talislanta. Here, jagged mountains of ice pierce the bleak tundra, and frigid winds howl through chasms ringed with hoarfrost. Only the hardiest creatures can survive in this tortuous region, which is home to the monstrous beings known as the Ice Giants.

Aside from its Giant population, Narandu is home to man-eating frostweres and the fearsome creatures known as Frost Demons. Both subsist on warm-blooded prey, and in fact are not unalike in appearance. The harsh climate of Narandu allows few plants to prosper in its territories. The exception is the silver-white snow lily; a plant which, when prepared in an elixir or potion, has the virtue of conferring resistance to cold.

North of Narandu lies a dark and ominous body of water known as the Midnight Sea. Icebergs and frozen straits pose hazards to vessels attempting to ply these waters, which are believed to be haunted by night demons, ancient sea dragons, and phantom ships from the long-dead kingdom of Khazad.

The Ice Giants

These creatures are aptly named, for their bodies are composed entirely of solid ice. The Ice Giants are frightening to behold, standing well over ten feet in height, and weighing as much as a ton. Spiky protrusions of ice cover their bodies, and their hands and feet are clawed. Although they are bestial and lack great intelligence, the Giants are formidable foes. Their very bodies emanate a piercing cold, so much so that the presence of large groups of Ice Giants can lower temperatures in a wide area.

Customs

By advancing further south each year, the Ice Giants are slowly extending their territories, converting temperate lands to bleak tundras. The Gryphs of Tamaranth have long warned of these intrusions, though generally to little avail. Even scholars who acknowledge the Gryph claims contend that the Giants' southern progress is so gradual as to warrant little concern; most estimate the overall rate of advance at less than one-half foot per year. Despite the fact that the Ice Giants advance along more than a 1,000-mile front, scholars claim that the annual loss of land is so minimal as to be insignificant.

The Ice Giants are ruled by a mysterious being known only as the Ice King. Unlike his brutish subjects, who know nothing of magic, the Ice King is

An Ice Giant warrior

believed to be a powerful warlock. His sworn enemy is the Snow Queen of L'Haan, who has long opposed the Ice King's plans of conquest. Fierce battles, pitting the Ice King's legions against the Snow Queen's Mirin armies, have raged across the borders of L'Haan for many centuries.

The Giants erect no structures more permanent than tunnels and caverns carved in glaciers or mountains of ice. In such places, they store plunder obtained in battle with the Mirin, the frozen carcasses of creatures such as tundra beasts and woolly ogriphants (the Ice Giants cannot obtain nourishment from anything that is not frozen solid), and precious blue diamonds. The Ice King is said to dwell in a massive complex of similar design carved within an ice mountain, but its location remains unknown.

The land of Narandu is rich in deposits of blue diamond, the magical substance which is also known as "permanent ice." The Giants lack the knowledge to utilize the magical properties of these gemstones, but mine them nonetheless for use in making crude weapons. They use war clubs embedded with uncut blue diamonds, to some effect.

Eastern Narandu

One of the more unusual features of this portion of Narandu is the great chasm known as the *Black Pit of Narandu*. Located north of Tamaranth, this supposedly bottomless fissure is the source of many colorful legends. Some scholars claim the Black Pit leads to the demon-haunted dimension of Cthonia. Others believe the Pit to be the entrance to an extensive system of tunnels which winds its way as far south as the Wilderlands of Zaran. Certain scholars, noting the clouds of steam which issue from the Pit's mouth, theorize that the Black Pit exits into a vast underground sea.

Deep in the frigid interior of Narandu lie the ruins of *Farnir*, a city frozen under layers of crystalline ice. Before the coming of the Ice Giants, Farnir reputedly was the site of an enlightened civilization, steeped in the arts of magic and alchemy. No less a personage than the great sorcerer Korak claimed to have visited here, and the ancient mage was reportedly impressed by the talents of the Farnir mages.

Apparently, their talents did not extend into the realm of military defense, since Farnir was overrun by advancing Ice Giant hordes several centuries ago. The Mirin claim that some of the Farnir magicians still live, frozen in stasis by the extreme cold.

In the far north are the mountain lands known as the *Far Reaches*, a region inhabited mainly by frostweres and ice dragons. Scholars theorize that parts of the area were once underwater, in order to explain the reports of shipwrecked vessels found frozen here within solid blocks of ice.

Central Narandu

The northern coast of central Narandu is dominated by the *Ice Peaks*, jagged shards of ice said to be haunted by frost demons. As far as anyone knows, the demons are the only creatures who possess any desire to venture into this region. Even the Mirin consider the Ice Peaks to be impassable.

Stretching south is a vast expanse of frozen tundra known as the *Plain of Blue Frost*. It derives its unique coloration from the pollen of snow lilies which, carried upon the winds, settles across the terrain for hundreds of miles.

Muskronts, lopers and other beasts come here to graze on the lilies, and to lap up the plants' nutritious blue pollen. This in turn draws a variety of predatory species, including frostweres and packs of two-headed tundra beast.

The icy peaks of the *Crystal Mountains* form the southern border of central Narandu, extending from the Lost Sea to the borders of Tamaranth. Impassable except by means of a handful of little-known trails, the mountains are reputed to contain deposits of blue diamonds. Avalanches – as well as ice dragons, frostweres and other hostile entities – pose significant dangers to would-be prospectors.

Western Narandu

The *Trackless Wastes* stretch north of the Lost Sea and are rumored to be uninhabited, save for a possibly mythical being known as the Crystal Kaliya. Naturalists have offered rewards (up to 50,000 gold lumens, in at least one instance) for anyone able to capture this elusive creature.

Further west, a stretch of bleak, icy terrain is inhabited mainly by herds of lopers, tundra beasts, frostweres, and Ice Giants. These are the *Western Glaciers*, where blue diamonds and snow lilies can be found by entrepreneurs willing to risk exploring this bleak domain.

The Northern Isles

In addition to the sites already described, three chains of islands spread out northward from the mainland coast of western Narandu, proceeding into the Midnight Sea like victims irresistibly drawn toward their doom.

The *Unknown Isles* form the easternmost chain, and are the most mysterious to Talislantan cartographers. Though these frozen islands appear on ancient sea charts (dating back to the Forgotten Age), no one is known to have mapped or explored the isles in the modern age.

Next to the west are the *Midnight Isles* which, according to legend, are the abode of night demons and other terrors of the darkness. More than a few Talislantan seamen believe that the end of the world lies but a few miles north of these isles; thus, there is little enthusiasm for the area in general.

The westernmost chain, reportedly obscured constantly by clouds of ghostly grey mist, are the justly-named *Spectral Isles*. As far as anyone knows, none of these islands has ever been explored, possibly due to the belief that monstrous ice dragons dwell in this isolated area.

YRMANIA

Yrmanian Wildman and Jaka Manhunter

An untamed wilderness region, Yrmania lies to the west of the barren ice fields of Narandu. Hemmed in by mountains along its frigid southern borders, this land features a widely divergent mixture of terrain: rocky hills, stretches of coniferous forest, solitary peaks, tundra, and the treacherous badlands, studded with cliffs, ravines and sinkholes. In eastern Yrmania, the flat plain of the Lost Sea stretches for miles on end.

The Jaka

Native to the Brown Hills of western Yrmania, the Jaka are a race of intelligent man-like beings, with features resembling a cross between Man, wolf and panther. They are a striking people, with sleek black fur, a silvery-gray mane, and blazing green eyes. Most stand about six feet in height, a certain lithe muscularity being a common trait of all members of this race.

Jaka Customs

The Jaka are solitary beings, sullen and introspective in nature. Hunters of predatory beasts by trade, they prey primarily upon werebeasts and yaksha, selling the hides and fangs to traders.

Though considered barbaric by most Talislantans, the Jaka are actually a complex and cunning folk. They are canny traders, and as mercenaries are much in demand as scouts, hunters and guides. A few also possess some talent for the taming of wild beasts, an ability which in ancient times led to the ancestors of the Jaka being known as "the Beast-masters of the Northern Woods."

While the Jaka are loners at heart, they are said to make steadfast companions when they do choose to work with a partner. They are equally famous for turning on those who seek to cross them, and are quite capable of cold-blooded murder if the situation warrants.

The Wildmen of Yrmania

The sparsely-wooded badlands of central Yrmania are home to the strange folk known as the Wildmen. Bestial in appearance, they have sharp fangs, nostrils like slits, and dark, deep-set eyes. The savages wear their shaggy hair in braids and dreadlocks, daubed with various colored pigments. For clothes, the Wildmen employ rude loincloths, as well as arm- and leg-wrappings made from strips of hide from the animals they prey upon.

Wildmen Customs

As travelers into their territories have found, the Wildmen (and Wildwomen) of Yrmania are aptly named. They are as vicious as mad demons, and prone to fits of seemingly mindless behavior — in the heat of battle, Wildmen have been known to suicidally leap off cliffs or rock ledges, turn upon each other, or simply attack anything in their path (including trees, bushes and other inanimate objects). The savages have been known to attack large, well-armed parties without the slightest hesitation or provocation. The shamans — few of whom seem to possess any actual magical abilities — are said to be even more unstable than the common tribesmen.

In combat, the Wildmen weld the *r'ruh*, a sharpened stone blade affixed to a long leather thong. Swung over the head at great speed, r'ruh emit a "singing" sound which is intended to strike fear in the hearts of the Wildmen's foes.

As far as anyone knows, the savages have no settlements, but simply travel about from place to place, stopping temporarily when they become tired or bored. Rival clans often fight each other, a situation which has proved useful in keeping the otherwise prolific Wildmen and their growing population within reasonable limits. None of the tribes will enter the Sardonyx Mountains which lie to the south, since it is their superstition that the jagged peaks are the teeth of a gigantic earth-monster which the Wildmen call Yrman.

The sub-men sometimes launch raids into the Brown Hills, though seldom to any great profit. The Jaka, mounted on swift steeds, generally keep their distance and harry the Wildmen with their short bows until the invaders tire of the futile exercise.

The Cult of the Mad God

The Wildmen of Yrmania revere Manik, a mysterious entity referred to in certain scholarly texts as "the Mad God." Little is known of their religion other than fanciful speculation, such as reports that Wildmen shamans (both male and female) mate with the hideous creatures known as yaksha — a claim which is obviously the height of absurdity.

More acceptable are reports of the Wildmen's use of skullcap, a bone-white variety of parasitic mushroom. A lethal toxin when ingested by most Talislantan races, the mushroom does not seem to harm the Wildmen, who have evidently developed an immunity to the substance's deadly effects. Under the influence of this drug, the savages are totally without fear and even seem to be immune to pain, and continue to attack with savage bloodlust though riddled with scores of wounds.

Geographical Highlights

The *Desolate Hills*, in far-northern Yrmania, are largely uninhabited save for yaksha, tundra beasts, and the ungainly creatures known as lopers. Semiprecious stones can reportedly be found in low depressions throughout the hills, a factor which occasionally draws would-be prospectors to this region.

This sparsely-wooded *Badlands* of eastern Yrmania are home to the Wildmen. Yaksha, muskronts and tundra beasts inhabit the rugged hills, ravines and tanglewood groves of this wilderness.

Yrman's Woods range throughout the rolling hills, irregular bluffs, and deep gullies of central Yrmania. The trees are old, gnarled and stunted specimens of spider-oak, withergall and tanglewood, of little value as timber. Some claim that veins of silver and black iron run through the wooded hills. So too, do packs of two-headed tundra beasts, mated pairs of yaksha, and herds of vile darkmanes.

The open expanse of *Yrmanian Bay*, which penetrates between Yrman's Woods and the Brown Hills, is seldom frequented by ships for the reason that there would be little purpose in doing so — the Yrmanian Wildmen are notable for their insane and unpredictable behavior, and Night Demons from the nearby Midnight Isles are reputed to infest the area in numbers.

The *Brown Hills* of western Yrmania are home to the Jaka. The sepia-tinged forests teem with wild beasts of many types, including muskronts, wild greymanes, yaksha, werebeasts, nighthawks, and omnivrax. Jaka hunters do a brisk business trading hides, horns and wild beasts with merchants from Arim and Zandu.

The Lost Sea

Along the eastern borders of Yrmania lies the flat wasteland known as the Lost Sea. By all accounts, this area does indeed appear to be a dry seabed, as it is littered with the ancient skeletons of sea dragons and other aquatic monsters. Some claim that half-sunken sea vessels of unknown origin can be found in isolated places, many purportedly containing fabulous artifacts and treasures from a lost age.

As Wildmen bands, Darkling hordes, and Ur war parties sometimes traverse the Lost Sea, explorers and entrepreneurs should exercise caution when traveling in these lonely parts. The fearsome nocturnal strangler is reputed to be found here also, which is as good a reason as should be needed for not dallying in this region.

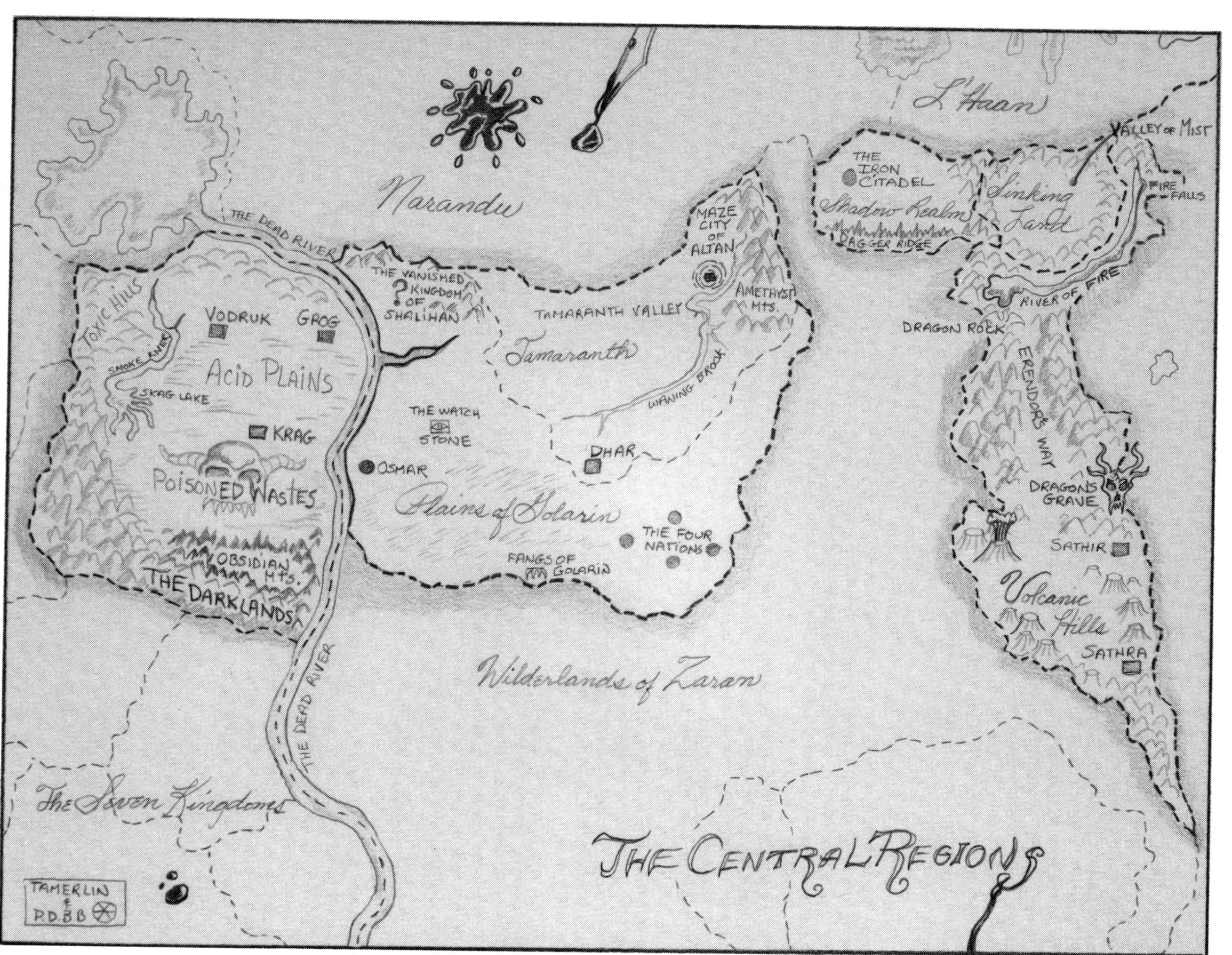

Scale: 1" = 95 miles.

THE PLAINS OF GOLARIN

A Beastman reigns-in his darkmane mount.

Northward beyond the Wilderlands of Zaran lie the grassy steppes of the Plains of Golarin. This is a place of some mystery — the crumbling ruins of an unknown number of ancient civilizations litter parts of the interior, long abandoned by their makers and overgrown with weeds and creepers.

Where once mighty armies clashed on ancient fields of battle, now roam ogriphants, great herds of greymane, and giant, six-legged megalodonts. What lost secrets lie hidden here remain largely a matter of speculation, this due in great part to the aggressive nature of Golarin's current occupants: the predatory Beastmen.

The Beastmen

Savage beings, the Beastmen of Golarin are ignorant and primitive, yet possessed of a certain animalistic cunning. A coat of bristling fur, usually dirty brown or grey in color, covers their muscular frames. Though man-like in form, Beastmen have many features which are more reminiscent of wild beasts — slavering fangs, deep-set eyes, pointed ears, and protruding jaws typify the vast majority of this folk.

Customs

The Beastmen exhibit few civilized traits. They are able to employ the fierce steeds known as darkmanes, and the more intelligent members of their species sometimes set crude traps to disable their prey. Having no noticeable talent as craftsmen, the barbarians are limited in their weapons and other equipment to such gear as they can scavenge or pillage. They have only the crudest of languages, which consists mainly of growls, howls and barking.

The savage Beastmen range the length and breadth of Golarin in mounted bands of up to 40 individuals, often stopping to rest or make camp in the ruined cities which lie scattered across the plains. They are quite unparticular with regard to their eating habits, having an equal fondness for herd beasts, carrion or luckless travelers. Beastmen sometimes hunt intelligent prey purely for sport, but they indulge themselves in this way only when food is plentiful.

On the hunt, a band of Beastmen behaves much like a pack of wild hunting beasts. They pursue their prey relentlessly, driving their darkmane steeds on, harrying their prey until the victims become too weak from exhaustion to continue. The savages are superior trackers, who will never quit a blood trail.

Though fierce when encountered in numbers, the Beastmen have seldom been known for individual displays of courage — just as most pack animals lose their bravery when separated from their group.

The Vanished Kingdom

In ancient times, on a site believed to lie in the northern Golarin plains, stood the fabled Kingdom of Shalihan — a land renowned for its formidable magicians, who were masters of illusion. (The legendary illusionist, Cascal, may have hailed from Shalihan, or so some scholars believe.)

Where Shalihan is now, no one knows; apparently, the entire kingdom simply vanished into thin air sometime after the onset of The Great Disaster. Individuals who aspire to search for the Vanished Kingdom must contend with the region's present residents, which include Beastmen, malathropes, and herds of vicious darkmane.

The Watchstone

On the north-central plains stands the Watchstone, an immense pillar of grey basalt several miles in height. An age-worn stairway, carved into the face of the Watchstone, winds upward in a slow, twisting spiral. Climbing to the summit, an endeavor requiring the better part of a day to complete, allows one to see clear across Golarin.

The Watchstone is considered a holy place by the Orthodoxists of Aaman, who claim that from this lofty height one may glimpse the gates of paradise. Ravengers favor the high elevations as well, primarily for purposes of preying on groups of rapturous and incautious Aamanian pilgrims.

While the origins of the Watchstone remain uncertain, recent discoveries indicate that this immense structure may have been created by the Drakken — a race of giant, intelligent reptilians who ruled the continent of Talislanta before the Archaen Age.

Ancient Osmar

The wind-worn towers of Osmar stand like silent sentinels on the western plains, their occupants long since gone and forgotten. The artifacts which they created — blades of blue-black iron, fine ceramic vases, ornate helms and suits of archaic armor, enchanted amulets and bracers — can still be found buried among the ruins.

Unfortunately for those who would explore or plunder the site, the ruined city is the occasional domain of no less than six different Beastmen clans, each of which stakes a claim to a different sector of the ruins. Beastmen who hail from the Osmar ruins are often well-armed with relics of a lost age, and their pack-leaders are occasionally dressed in full battle armor and bear enchanted weaponry.

The Fangs of Golarin

These twin spires of rock are located along the southern border of Golarin. Standing over 100 feet in height, the Fangs are a favored roosting place for ravengers while the predators scan the surrounding environs for food. Scholars are divided as to whether the rock structure is natural or the product of a lost civilization.

The Four Nations

The crumbling ruins of these four once-mighty city-states, which lie within a 100-mile region of the eastern plains, offer mute testimony to the madness of their former rulers, each of whom coveted the lands of his neighbors. The resulting "War of Four Nations" solved nothing, and in fact led to the destruction of all four of the participating countries. Barbaric hordes from Quaran rode in to finish off the survivors, and to steal as much as they could carry on their war-beasts.

The four nations faded quickly into obscurity; no one living even remembers the names of these archaic places. According to the reports of the Phaedran scholar Erastes, these ruins hold such treasures as:

"...the gilded tomb of Irkhan, the mysterious Elixirs of Immortality, the soulstones of the four blind savants of ancient Elande, a great crystal golem named Satur, the Nine Books of Knowledge, the treasure-horde of Minra the Miser, and the mummified body of the great dragon, Orrix."

As Erastes makes no mention of where these purported treasures are to be found (or even definitions of what some of them are), many modern scholars have branded him a sensationalist; the term "fraud" has also been applied. Still, fortune hunters continue to come to Golarin, though none of Erastes' treasures have ever been found.

THE SHADOW REALM

The Iron Citadel

At the northernmost edge of the Wilderlands lies an eerie and deserted wasteland, a region said to be haunted by the ghosts of a dozen vanished civilizations. The landscape is correspondingly unpleasant, and consists largely of broken hills, outcroppings of wind-blasted rock, and thickets of stunted tanglewood and thornwood. Shattered ruins, worn beyond recognition by the centuries, are found throughout the district. The Ariane of Tamaranth call this place *Oranthus:* literally, "The Shadow Realm."

Decimated by the forces unleashed during the Great Disaster, the Shadow Realm is incapable of supporting any natural species of plant life. Normal animal and insect species are likewise practically unknown here, though various horrid forms of abominations can occasionally be seen wandering across the bleak terrain.

The few brave souls who dare to venture into this region generally come here to obtain Sardonicus (also known as "bottle imps"), which can sometimes be found lurking about the ruins. Much favored by spell casters, who find them to be useful familiars and companions, Sardonicus can command prices of more than 1,000 gold lumens apiece. Demons of all sorts consider them especially tasty, a fact which prospective bottle-imp trappers would do well to keep in mind.

Various other strange and unnatural creatures roam the Shadow Realm, including the gaunt, horned pseudo-demons known as fiends, and the diminutive variety of devils called monitor imps.

The Shadow Wizards

Among the intelligent and malign beings known to inhabit this forlorn land are the Malum, a cabal of Arch-Spectres from the Nightmare Dimension. Comprised of animate darkness, these spiritforms of deceased magicians resemble man-like shadows, distorted in form. They cloak themselves in hooded vestments, and bear ebony runestaves studded with black diamonds. The Shadow Wizards' eyes burn with a fiery incandescence, and their bodies may change from substantial to insubstantial form at will.

The Malum are skilled in the Black Arts, and are sometimes forced to act as thaumaturges, advisors and subordinates by more powerful beings (such as Noman, the master of the Nightmare Dimension). Conversely, Shadow Wizards occasionally employ lesser entities — such as shadow wights, harbinger imps and fantasms — as their servants.

The Shadow Wizards prefer to dwell in solitude, during which they engage in such pursuits as interest spectral mages — arcane studies, magical experimentation, consultations with other entities from the lower planes, and so forth.

Though it is considered a dangerous practice to contact one of the Malum, there have always been those willing to accept the risks entailed in such operations in order to gain a measure of occult knowledge. Among the secrets said to be known by the arch-spectres are many ancient spells, rituals and arcane formulae, including the lost process of creating obsidian mirrors, and the principles which control the fashioning of certain artificial lifeforms.

The Iron Citadel

After escaping or being exiled from the Nightmare Dimension, the Malum of the Shadow Realm took residence in the deserted ruins now known as the Iron Citadel, a ruined structure of ancient and obscure origin. In the towers are eyes of carved obsidian, which constantly scan the surrounding environs, alert for signs of any intruders who would dare to venture into the realm of the arch-spectres.

From within the dark confines of their sanctum, the Shadow Wizards reputedly consort with creatures from the lower planes, including fantasms, bat mantas and void monsters. It is not known what contacts, if any, the arch-spectres have with Malum elsewhere in the Omniverse and their various masters (including the entity known as Death, and Noman of the Nightmare Dimension).

Kabros' Monograph

Because the Shadow Wizards of this region are reclusive by nature, very little is known of their motives. However, the intrepid sorcerer Kabros claimed to have visited the Shadow Realm on at least one occasion. In volume six of his famous *Guide to the Lower Planes*, there appears a brief monograph on the subject, recounted here in part:

"I approached the Iron Citadel, heedless of the obsidian eyes which stared at me from the castle's black metal towers. Twin portals of solid iron — each engraved with weird runes and sigils, and standing over 20 feet in height — opened slowly as I drew near. A foul wind issued forth, cold and unnatural, as if originating from another world. Summoning the remainder of my resolve, I entered into darkness.

"For a time, I groped about blindly, fearing lest I should stumble into some unseen pit or other obstacle. At last my eyes adjusted to the gloom, and I could discern the vague outlines of a long, winding stairway. I ascended and, after a seemingly interminable period of time, emerged into a vast and eerie chamber.

"Within, a group of shadowy figures stood occupied at various tasks, apparently oblivious to my presence. Some worked at tables piled high with tangles of alchemical equipment and tubing, distilling some sort of dark, viscous liquid; others fed malformed imps to caged bat manta, attended steaming vats, or conversed in hushed whispers with winged fantasms. With a pair of tongs, one of the Shadow Wizards brought forth a small creature from the largest of the vats: a hideous man-thing with a bloated head, covered with barbs, horns and sharp protrusions.

"An icy terror gripped my soul at the sight of this being, freshly fashioned from the stuff of which nightmares are made. My mind reeled: this was Fear itself, given tangible form and substance by the black arts of the Shadow Wizards. I fled, unable to bear the scrutiny of those dark eyes, and anxious only to return to the world of light and reason..."

Dagger Ridge

Explorers wishing to enter the Shadow Realm from points to the south must surmount the obstacle known as Dagger Ridge, a line of knife-like peaks which separates the land of the Malum from the Kharakhan Wastes.

The ridge is considered impassable to all but the most expert climbers. It is wise to keep in mind that satada are expert climbers, and that such creatures are not unknown in these parts.

THE SINKING LAND

Situated in the northeastern reaches of the Wilderlands of Zaran, the Sinking Land lies just north of the Volcanic Hills, and south of the Opal Mountains. The skies above this region are ever dark and grey, while the earth below is a vast quagmire of inert brown sludge. Passage through the Sinking Land is deemed next to impossible, the muddy terrain tending to slowly swallow up creatures or beings who remain stationary for more than a few minutes' time.

A few species of plants and animals have somehow managed to adapt to this bleak environment, including several varieties of giant fungi, the mud-dwelling Snipes, and the flat-rooted barge tree.

An intelligent species of mollusk, the Snipe possesses the ability to move swiftly through the muddy ground of the Sinking Land as easily as fish swim through water. They are insatiably curious creatures, always eager to exchange bits of news and to gossip with other sentient lifeforms.

Adventurers who claim to have explored the Sinking Land cite the barge tree as being a great boon to travelers, who can take their rest in the wide, low-lying branches of this tree in relative security. As these trees are not securely rooted, they do tend to drift about to some extent, but this is said to be only a minor inconvenience. The barge tree also bears a most edible and nutritious fruit, though gatherers should be warned that precautions against ikshada (horrific parasites which sometimes infest the fruit) are necessary. Also found among the leafy canopy may be the ironshrike, a metal-plumed bird which feeds on ikshada.

The City of the Four Winds

No reasonable person would care to enter the Sinking Land were it not for the tales concerning the City of the Four Winds. Known in legend as the capital of the ancient kingdom of Elande, the City of the Four Winds is believed to be the last surviving vestige of an advanced and enlightened civilization. It was built by the greatest magicians of the Forgotten Age, who invested the city with magical properties which allowed it to hover suspended above the ground.

According to several unconfirmed accounts, the City of the Four Winds survived the Great Disaster and still floats generally above the Sinking Land, moving slowly on the winds. The travelers who claim to have caught a glimpse of the fabled city describe it as being most enchanting, its wind-worn towers and archways still capable of conjuring up visions of the halcyon age of Elande.

A pair of curious Snipes

The sorcerer Kabros sought and claimed to have found the Lost City. Of his discovery, he would only say: "The City of the Four Winds must be believed in order to be seen, and seen in order to be believed."

What riches lie within the airborne city can only be surmised. Legends hint at the existence of hidden treasure caches containing arcane scrolls, jeweled amulets and magical talismans. One account claims that the city's artisans created six rare and scintillant colors which never before existed. Another states that Elande's magicians, upon learning that their civilization was doomed to perish in the Great Disaster, imbued a number of soulstones with their life essences and memories. It is believed by certain optimistic individuals that anyone who gains possession of one of these soulstones will acquire all the knowledge of the great magician who created it.

Since it is thought to have been abandoned for untold centuries, scholars speculate that the City of the Four Winds, if it does still exist, may not be entirely devoid of inhabitants. Though it is doubtful that the Elande or their descendants still live within the floating city, other creatures or beings might conceivably be found there. Wind demons, shadow wights and necrophages have all been reported to reside in the lost city, but none of these accounts are considered authoritative or thoroughly reliable.

TAMARANTH

The eldest and most impressive of Talislanta's woodland regions, Tamaranth is dominated around the perimeters by light vegetation and thickets of low-lying trees, progressively becoming more dense as one approaches the deep woods of the interior. Here, giant span-oak and fernwood tower above a forest floor thick with a carpet of moss and trailing vines. Swift-running streams course through the underbrush, and the woods teem with an abundance of plant and animal life.

Travelers delving into the woods of Tamaranth may expect to find a number of unusual plant and animal species. Under no condition should one ignore a sighting of exomorph tracks, which may provide the only advance warning of this chameleon-like predator's presence. Assuming that this creature is possessed of mere animal intelligence is a common, and often fatal, error. Malathrope and shathane also dwell in this region, though the numbers of these predators in the forest is kept in check by hunting parties. The traveler is also advised to avoid nagbirds, whose incessant cackling often draws the unwanted attentions of predators. Beastmen prowl the westernmost outskirts of Tamaranth, but seldom dare to enter the forest itself. Dangerous when encountered in numbers, the savages are less so in small groups.

Given its name, the fact that stranglevine should be avoided is likely to come as no surprise. The second threat from the plant kingdom comes in the evening, when the ambulatory shrubs known as violet creepers begin to shamble about, causing dismay to unwary campers. The adhesive liquid exuded by the yellow stickler is more a nuisance than a threat, except for whisps, imps and similar diminutive beings.

Two intelligent races dwell in the Forest of Tamaranth: the Gryphs, an avian species; and the Ariane, a reclusive and mystical folk.

The Gryphs

An impressive race of winged, man-like beings which has inhabited the Forest of Tamaranth for untold centuries, Gryphs stand up to seven feet tall, with wingspans in excess of 24 feet. Their bodies are covered with a thick feathery down (usually brilliant red or orange in color), and they have hawk-like visages and bright, piercing eyes.

Customs

Like the birds of prey they resemble, Gryphs are hunters by nature. They have exceptionally keen vi-

Gryph and Ariane

sion, which enables them to spot from great altitudes even the slightest movement on the ground. The clans subsist primarily on fresh game, usually large predators and other dangerous beasts. The Gryphs are skilled in the use of the *duar* (a type of two-pronged spear) and the heavy crossbow. They consider themselves to be the protectors of Tamaranth Forest, and groups of the avians regularly patrol the borders of the forestland.

Gryph families live in eyries built in the tops of the tallest span-oaks. Their dwellings resemble great bird's nests, and are constructed of woven vines, roofed with canopies of leafy boughs. Most stand at altitudes of over 100 feet, making access by nonavians a chancy endeavor. A Gryph settlement may consist of as many as 40 eyries, each housing a family of up to eight individuals. The largest settlements often include Council Eyries which span two or more trees in length and breadth.

Situated in the southern portions of Tamaranth Forest, *Dhar* is the largest of all the Gryph settlements, consisting of nearly a hundred communal eyries nestled high in the treetops. Among these is the Great Council Eyrie, where the chieftains of all the clans come to meet each year, during the first week of Jhang. The area around Dhar is regularly patrolled by heavily-armed Gryph scouting parties, who do not take kindly to unauthorized intruders venturing into their territory.

Innumerable species of avian creatures reside in Tamaranth, or migrate to the secluded woodland during the fall months. The Gryphs offer these beings their protection, and in return receive information gathered by their guests from all across the continent of Talislanta.

Although they are territorial by nature, Gryphs sometimes leave their eyries to travel to distant lands. Through the reports of such travels, and their communications with other avian species, the Gryphs are often aware of events which have transpired in even the most far-away places.

Some of the avians occasionally take to adventuring for the sake of profit, accepting mercenary posts as scouts, guides or bounty hunters. The majority of Gryphs, however, consider the prospect of departing their beloved woods to be only slightly more desirable than contracting a case of gange (the dreaded disease of the avians, also known as the "slow death"). An independent and strong-willed race, the Gryphs prize their freedom above all other things — therefore, Gryph mercenaries can be difficult employees. They often quit a job after only a few months of work, typically claiming that they felt they were losing their pride or control of their lives by tying themselves down to a single task and master.

The Ariane

Perhaps the oldest of Talislanta's many races, the Ariane are striking in appearance. They have skin the color of onyx, long snowy-white hair, and grey eyes flecked with sparkling silvery motes. Tall and slender of build, the Ariane exhibit a grace and serenity approximated only by the enchanting folk of Astar or Thaecia. Their mode of dress is simple but elegant: their capes, flowing garments and high boots are all made of spinifax, a silken cloth derived from the flax-bearing pods of the thistledown plant.

Trans–Ascendancy

The ways of the Ariane are difficult for others to comprehend. On the surface, these people seem closed, devoid of emotions, and introspective, as if dreaming or lost in thought. In truth, the Ariane possess an altogether different view of the world than most Talislantans, and are practitioners of the mystic doctrine known as Trans-Ascendancy — a philosophy seemingly incomprehensible to non-Ariane.

To the Ariane, time is "the river upon which all living things flow enroute to their next incarnation." The river's source is the Elemental Plane — the center of the Omniverse, according to the teachings of Trans–Ascendant Mysticism.

Masters of Trans–Ascendancy claim to be able to "read" a person, revealing the past lives of the spiritual essence within the subject. High Masters of the dogma are reportedly able to become fully aware of their past lives, to maintain a constant consciousness throughout any number of their future incarnations, and are even said to be able to determine the nature of their successive future reincarnations.

While the great majority of the Ariane do not possess such impressive talents, the practice of Trans–Ascendancy enables all members of their race to develop other useful abilities. For instance, all possess the ability to commune with nature, enabling them to communicate telepathically with the elemental spirits which reside within such natural entities as plants, stones, the winds, water, and so forth. (Such spirits are normally invisible on the material planes, though they exist in tangible form on the Elemental Plane.) It is not unusual to see an Ariane engrossed in silent communion with an avir, tree or boulder — a disconcerting sight to the uninitiated.

Different results can be gained, depending on what the Ariane is communicating with. Earth and stones are often reluctant to answer questions in haste, preferring instead to ponder for a time before making their reply. Lakes, streams and other bodies of water possess knowledge of events transpiring within their depths, but have a distorted view of occurrences reflected in their surfaces (due to the action of waves and ripples). Carried upon the winds are countless secrets, many from far-distant lands. Even the modest breeze may know a thing or two, though the elemental spirits of the air are unable to discern whether the words they bring are true or false. Plants and trees, having a marked lack of interest in the affairs of the Men, often prove to be limited sources of information, but speaking with beasts may yield productive results.

Sometimes it is possible for the Ariane, by focusing their full powers on their surrounding environment, to discern the subtle emanations of past ages: sights, sounds or visions from another time, telling of events which happened long ago. In general, only the most vivid impressions — such as those pertaining to events of an exceptionally emotional, violent or otherwise significant nature — can be perceived with any degree of clarity.

Customs

The Ariane belief in reincarnation has influenced their culture in many ways. Fearing to do harm to some reincarnating lifeform, the Ariane eat only ripened fruits and vegetables, and their tools and utensils are fashioned from stone or dead wood, never from living trees.

The forest people have no formal laws, but believe firmly in the right of all living things to exist in peace. However, individuals or creatures which engage in violent or disruptive acts are dealt with decisively. While the Ariane are a non-violent people, they are not averse to the use of force when it comes to defending their lives or land, and many are surprisingly proficient with their weapons. Mounted on swift silvermanes, bands of Ariane regularly patrol the heights surrounding their Maze-City of Altan. Unwanted intruders are sternly urged to depart, occasionally encouraged by a fusilade of arrows.

Intruding individuals who commit crimes of a more serious nature are often imprisoned in cages of living wood. The length of interment varies according to the severity of the infraction, the Ariane's somewhat abstract conception of time often tending to add to the duration of such stays. In severe cases, the mystics reserve the right to kill; the Ariane prefer to think of this as just another way of hastening the natural process of reincarnation.

The Seekers

The majority of the Ariane spend their entire lives in the city of Altan, where they strive to master the secrets of Trans-Ascendency. Yet for some, the search for enlightenment requires them to journey beyond the Forest of Tamaranth, perhaps even to distant lands. Such an individual, known as a *Druas* (meaning: "seeker"), may be encountered almost anywhere in Talislanta.

There is a reason for everything a Druas does, usually associated with such esoteric concepts as fate or destiny, and always concerned with the gathering of unique experiences. He forages for what food he needs, makes his own garments and implements, and prefers to sleep in natural surroundings, seated in a meditative position.

The Tamar

The Ariane highly value the experience of existence, and consider knowledge to be the greatest of treasures. The mystics record the collective histories and experiences of their people on *tamar* – orbs of violet stone, magically imbued with the thoughts, feelings and memories of those who create them. For example, it is the custom of the Seekers to return to Altan once every seven years in order to relate what they have seen and learned in their travels. This information is magically inscribed upon the tamar, allowing other Ariane to partake of the Seeker's experiences.

Each of the Trans-Ascendants has his own tamar, within which is contained the sum total of that individual's experiences. By the exchange of tamar, the Ariane are able to communicate their thoughts and feelings in ways which mere words cannot convey.

When an Ariane passes away, the individual's life experiences are transferred to the great obelisk which stands at the center of the Maze-City of Altan. This structure is actually a giant tamar, and has served as a repository for the accumulated knowledge of the Ariane for countless centuries.

The creation of a tamar takes seven days and nights, and requires the individual's complete and total concentration. At the end of this time, the tamar is imbued with a minor enchantment, allowing the stone to receive telepathic impressions from its maker. Thereafter, the tamar's crafter may store his thoughts and memories in the violet stone as they occur, or as desired.

To "read" a tamar, an Ariane need only hold the orb in his hands and concentrate. If the individual is properly attuned to the artifact, he will be able to perceive the information contained within the stone; typically, as a torrent of vivid sights, sounds and images.

Geography of Tamaranth

Three features within Tamaranth are of special interest. In the north-central region of Tamaranth, surrounded on three sides by the purple-hued peaks of the Amethyst Mountains, is a sylvan valley of rare beauty. The woods here exude an ancient magic, as if permeated with the essences of a forgotten age. This is the *Tamaranth Valley*, and at the foot of the mountains lies the Maze-City of Altan, home of the mystical Ariane.

The violet-hued *Amethyst Mountains* surmount the northern forests of Tamaranth, encircling the Tamaranth Valley and the Maze-City of Altan. Gryphs patrol the skies above, and predatory exomorphs, malathrope, and peaceful herds of wild silvermanes roam the wooded lower slopes. There is a single, hidden trail which leads through the Amethyst Mountains into Tamaranth Valley. A rare type of violet stone, used in the making of the Ariane tamar, is found only in this region.

Once a great river which ran from the Amethyst Mountains through the Forest of Tamaranth and beyond, *Waning Brook* has diminished considerably over the course of several centuries, and is currently little more than a wide, swift-flowing stream. The brook's present condition is attributed to the Ice Giants, whose southerly advances have sufficed to freeze many of the old river's former tributaries.

Maze-City of Altan

The Maze-City of Altan

A wondrous and curious place, the Maze-City of Altan was fashioned over centuries of time from a single mound of violet stone. Radiating outward from a central obelisk, each of the city's many unique structures was designed, formed, and polished smooth solely through the use of Trans-Ascendant magics. The complex network of interconnected structures continues to undergo subtle modifications and additions even to the present day. No tools have ever been employed, lest the spiritforms dwelling within the stone be unduly offended.

Altan is a place of magical beauty, its timeworn structures overhung with all manner of fruiting and flowering vines. Along the winding walkways are quiet ponds, gardens filled with exotic vegetation, and bright meadows. At night, the luminous blossoms of hanging lantern plants emit a soft luminescence, bathing the Maze-City in their purple glow.

The Ariane dwellings are enchanting creations comprised of smoothly polished arches, tunnels, domes, and spirals of violet stone. Furnishings of living plants decorate the interior of these structures, no two of which are alike. Water is provided by running streams, which pass through and amongst the Ariane dwellings, gathering in pools and grottos. In all the city, there is not a single door or lock — no Ariane would ever steal from another, and crime is virtually non-existent in Altan.

The Maze-City is situated in a wooded valley surrounded on all sides by the Amethyst Mountains. There is only one trail leading through the mountains to the city, heavily guarded by Ariane cadres mounted on swift silvermanes. Gryphs from the Forest of Tamaranth provide aerial reconnaissance and airborne support, as needed.

Visitors to the Maze-City are few, this being due as much to Altan's isolated location as to the admittedly reclusive nature of the Ariane themselves. Gryphs sometimes come here to obtain medicinal mixtures, or to deliver news from other regions. In return, the Ariane provide the Gryph clans with bolts of fine spinifax, which the avians use to barter for goods from other lands. Travelers in need of food or shelter are never turned away by the mystics, though only those accompanied by a Seeker may remain in the Maze-City for longer than seven suns-sets.

1. Tamaranth Valley

The wooded vales surrounding the Maze-City teem with numerous species of flora and fauna. Herds of silvermanes run wild along the slopes of the valley, feeding on the provender plant which grows here in abundance. As the Gryphs of Tamaranth refrain from hunting in these parts — to please the sensibilities of the Ariane, whose Trans-Ascendant doctrines include a belief in reincarnation — the region is also populated by a variety of predatory species, including exomorphs and malathrope.

2. Trails

This winding path leads through the Amethyst Mountains to Altan. It is regularly patrolled by a cadre of 10-20 Ariane, mounted on silvermanes and armed with bows and maces. Beyond the lone trail, the mountains are considered to be impassable, except to fliers such as the Gryphs.

3. City Walls

The walls of Altan measure over 30 feet in height, and are approximately 20 feet thick. Like the rest of the Maze-City, the barriers are composed of violet stone.

4. Gates of Altan

These two archways allow access to the city. Ariane mystics stand watch here at all times. If need be, the archways can be closed off by means of Trans–Ascendant magics.

5. Streams

The Waning Brook, flowing down from the Amethyst Mountains, passes under the city walls into the settlement. Divided into various minor streamlets, the waters flow through the Maze-City, emptying into ponds and joining with natural springs before outflowing into a mountain crevasse.

6. The Great Obelisk

This ancient stone pillar stands approximately 140 feet in height, and measures 70 feet across at its base. The obelisk is actually an immense tamar, which serves as a repository for the collected knowledge of the Ariane people. By placing a hand upon the surface of the stone, a mystic may partake of the experiences of past generations of Ariane.

7. The Meadow

Surrounding the great obelisk is a field of flowers and grasses, accessible by means of arched passageways fashioned in the ring of stone which circles the meadow. The Ariane elders meet here to meditate and to study the histories of past ages, as recorded in the great obelisk. Druas who have recently returned from the outer world may also be found here, along with any Ariane who wish to record their experiences within the great obelisk.

8. The Grottos

These sylvan retreats serve as places of contemplation and reflection, and are utilized by much of the populace.

9. Enchanted Pools

These pools are reputed to exhibit magical virtues. Some possess healing properties; others confer wisdom, restore lost vitality, or offer other beneficial effects.

10. Ironwood Grove

Creatures detained by the Ariane are incarcerated in prisons of living wood or placed in stasis within solid stone. Despite their crimes, prisoners of the Ariane are always accorded humane treatment.

URAG

Stryx, Ur clansman, and Darkling

Urag is a harsh and wind-swept region of arid plains, winding canyons and sprawling mountain ranges. Once a thriving forestland, the area has slowly been reduced to a near wasteland by centuries of neglect and abuse. Its streams are fouled with offal and refuse, its woods have been felled for timber and fuel, and its hills and mountains have been ravaged and plundered by crude and polluting mining techniques.

Few natural animals are found here, and those that are have generally wandered from elsewhere: herds of graceful silvermanes, which run up and down the Dead River Canyon and sometimes cross into Urag's interior; and giant ogronts, mindless herbivores of incredible strength that browse for food along the borders of Golarin. The fabled smokk, found only in Urag, is an odd-looking bird reputed to have an unerring ability for locating precious stones and metals .

The individuals responsible for defiling this land are known as the Ur, a savage race of sub-men who settled in the region after being driven from southern Narandu by advancing hordes of Ice Giants.

The Ur

Standing between seven and eight feet tall and weighing upward of 500 pounds, the Ur are a vile and brutish race. They are frightening to behold, having leathery hide of a yellow-green color, curved fangs, and facial features of a most unendearing sort: furrowed brows, pointed ears, and deep-set black eyes, the pupils of which gleam either white or red.

Customs

The Ur are members of a warlike race, and rule strictly by force of arms. They ride ogriphants outfitted with crude spiked armor, and build massive siege engines and catapults. Their warriors wield throwing axes, and war clubs made from the mummified claws of yaksha and other predatory species. Necklaces of teeth and bone, pieces of hammered plate armor, and various filthy garments made of fur and hide constitute the typical Ur clansman's wardrobe. Rings of black iron are also favored, and are commonly employed to restrain their hair, which the Ur wear in double or triple topknots.

The Ur profess to have no god, but are known to prostrate themselves before immense stone idols. The nature and origin of these monstrous effigies is unknown, even to the Ur themselves; scholars believe they were fashioned long before the Ur clans settled in Urag. Icons depicting these three-eyed idols are sometimes worn by Ur shamans, and are said to have magical properties. However, the shamans of Urag are generally regarded as charlatans, most seemingly incapable of performing any but the simplest hoodoos and charms.

Since their arrival from the Northlands, the clans of the Ur have succeeded in ravaging much of Urag. They have hunted many animal species into extinction, killing great numbers of creatures in order to indiscriminately harvest the hides, claws and meat. The Ur have felled entire woodlands for timber and firewood, and have ruthlessly stripped the hills and mountains of valuable ores, leaving behind perilous gaping pits and abandoned shafts, and malignant mounds of toxic slag .

Having squandered much of Urag's natural resources, it is supposed that the Ur clans must soon seek to expand into "fresh" territories — perhaps Arim, the Seven Kingdoms, or the Plains of Golarin. To perform such a conquest, the unification of the three Ur clans would be required — an event greatly feared by many of the peoples of Talislanta.

The Onyx and Obsidian mountain ranges have proven effective barriers against the expansionist clans until the present time, as the Ur have found it impossible to transport their massive siege engines across such rugged terrain. The Arimite citadel of Akbar, a towering stone fortress which bars access to Arim via the traversable gorge at Akbar, has long been a favored target of the Ur and their underlings.

Krag, Vodruk and Grod

Each of the three clans of Ur has its own "capital." All of the settlements resemble one another, being surrounded by circular stone barricades topped with iron spikes, and consisting primarily of rude hovels made of packed earth, cracked stone and rough-cut timbers. These places are havens for disease and filth, and contribute much to the pollution of the local environs. Conflicts between the three Ur-kings and their disparate factions are common.

Stationed at each of the three Ur settlements is an Ur-King (commanding a personal retinue of several hundred clansmen), ten or so warlords (each commanding a force of at least a hundred clansmen), a number of Stryx scouts, several batallions of Darkling slaves, and a contingent of beast-drawn and slave-powered siege towers, fire-throwers, battering rams, and scourges.

The Ur-king of Krag, a particularly huge and ugly member of his race, resides in a "palace" in the center of his settlement — a garish structure made of mud and rock, and said to house stolen treasure.

The settlement of Grod is surrounded by a ditch filled with raw sewage and crawling with scavenger slimes, urthrax and other vermin. The Ur-king of Grod considers it great sport to have captives lowered into the moat by means of a rope-and-winch mechanism, where the victims are used as bait to catch whatever predators may be lurking beneath the surface of the water.

Nothing remarkable is known about Vodruk and its Ur-king, but if such facts were available, they would no doubt be as insalubrious as the descriptions of Grod and Krag.

The Stryx

A race of avian man-like beings resembling a cross between vultures and horned devils, the Stryx would stand over six feet tall if they didn't tend to be hunchbacked or stoop-shouldered. Their angular bodies are covered with dark grey or black feathers, and typical specimens have a wingspan in excess of 20 feet. They excel at gliding, and can cover great distances and remain aloft for hours without difficulty. Both their hands and feet are equipped with sharp talons. Stryx have superior night vision, but see poorly in daylight.

The avians typically make their homes in caves dug into the sides of sheer cliffs, though a few clans prefer a nomadic lifestyle. Stryx live in clans which may number as many as 60 adult males, as many or more adult females, and about half as many young. The old and infirm are slain to provide food for the rest.

Tenuous allies of the Ur clans, the Stryx serve the Ur-kings as scouts, spies and messengers. Generally speaking, the Ur regard them as useful, if treacherous and untrustworthy, subordinates. Some say the Stryx associate with the clan armies only because this allows the avians to scavenge battlefields for carrion, which it is their nature to feed upon. The avians are skilled in the use of spears, snaffle-hooks and other pole-arms, but do not possess the manual dexterity required to employ more sophisticated weaponry. Not all of the Stryx enjoy serving the Ur — a few leave Urag to hire out as mercenaries. The hated rivals of the Stryx are their fellow avians, the Gryphs of Tamaranth.

The Stryx revere an entity known as Taryx, the so-called "Scavenger of Souls." Their Necromancer-Priests possess some capacity for the reading of omens and certain black magics, but generally are said to exhibit little facility in the arcane arts.

The Darklings

A wretched race of man-like beings which once controlled the region known as the Darklands, the Darklings are short and wiry of build, rarely exceeding four feet in height, with soot-grey skin, large pointed ears, sharp fangs, and distorted features. They exude a foul odor, are physically weak, and have no great talent for the arcane arts (in fact, most Darklings fear magic greatly). However, Darklings have acute senses, including superb night vision, and the ability to scent intruders up to 100 feet away.

Driven underground by the Great Disaster, this race has become accustomed to living in darkness, and now shuns the light of day. Most dress in rag loincloths, scraps of discarded metal and slag serving as rude ornamentation. They consider art in any form a blight upon the senses, but regard lying as a talent to be perfected through long years of practice. Other skills considered worthy of cultivation include sneak-thievery, hoarding, knife-play, and the torturing and tormenting of lesser creatures for sport. Darklings are forever gibbering, cackling or grumbling over one thing or another. They revere an obscure entity known as Sham the Deceiver (also called the "Master of Lies"), but are not known to have any priests or shamans of note.

The Ur employ Darkling hordes as light (and expendable) infantry, and force them to labor as slaves in mines and timber-cutting operations, at which the Darklings are only minimally effective.

Acid Plains

This stretch of foul-smelling flatland, dotted with pools of bubbling lye, acid and other noxious compounds, sprawls across eastern Urag. The Acid Plains are largely devoid of life, with the exception of abominations, urthrax and other types of vermin.

The Ur are responsible for despoiling this region, which for several centuries has served as a dumping ground for waste products derived from the Ur's massive slag furnaces. Crews of Darkling slave laborers, assigned to dump or retrieve wagonloads of toxic wastes, are generally the only man-like beings who ever enter the Acid Plains.

The Smoke River

The *Toxic Hills*, in northwestern Urag, are the source of the Smoke River. This area was once used for the testing of poisonous alchemical agents, which Ur shamans hoped to develop for use in warfare. The chance discovery of a substance known as *quintoxin* led to the inadvertent contamination of the entire highland. The clans evacuated the area post haste, leaving behind several hundred gallons of quintoxin in large, open cauldrons. The status of this virulent substance remains unknown; Darkling slave crews sent into the area have never returned, and the region is considered completely uninhabitable.

Running south beyond the Toxic Hills, the Smoke River is so polluted that it boils, giving off clouds of noxious steam or smoke. No natural lifeforms can tolerate these waters, though abominations are rumored to dwell in the roiling deeps.

The river empties into *Skag Lake*, which lies like a great, steaming cesspool near the border with Arim. The formidable stench of the lake pollutes the air throughout much of northwestern Urag. A species of horribly mutated lake kra is believed to dwell in the rank waters, which can otherwise be tolerated only by urthrax.

The Darklands

The mountainous southern realms of Urag together comprise the region known as the Darklands — a hostile wilderland, long since stripped of much of its natural resources by the Ur. Above ground, erosion by wind and rain has rendered the land barren of vegetation, and unable to support anything but the most persistent varieties of chokeweed, lichen and briars.

Far beneath the earth, crews of Darkling slave-miners toil ceaselessly in the played-out mines, tunneling in search of a few remaining veins of silver and black-iron ore. A handful of Darkling tribes fortunate enough to have eluded or escaped the Ur make their home in the furthest of the cavernous deeps, fearful to emerge from hiding lest they be captured and put to use as slaves. Giant land kra also dwell in these underground regions.

The glistening black peaks of the *Obsidian Mountains* form a natural barrier between Urag and Durne of the Seven Kingdoms. Yaksha and other hostile predators prowl the mountains in numbers; Stryx nest in the upper altitudes, and Darklings tunnel below the surface. A network of underground trails winds its way through this region, some few of which are utilized by marauding bands of Satada, which sometimes venture here from subterranean haunts in Durne and the Wilderlands.

The *Onyx Mountains* likewise lie between Urag and Arim, and are naturally rich in silver and black iron, as well as precious stones. Having despoiled the regions which lie within their borders, the Ur covet the portions of the range which are claimed by the Arimites. Yaksha, Stryx and Darklings all reside in the mountains, from which they raid Arimite mining camps and prey on travelers.

THE VOLCANIC HILLS

Saurans and Land Dragon in battle regalia

The region known as the Volcanic Hills is one of the most desolate portions of Talislanta. The terrain is tortuous, rising and falling in twisted mounds of pitted pumice-stone, punctuated by angular peaks and deep ravines. Clouds of smoke and ash, by-products of the area's considerable volcanic activity, blot out the suns' light for miles around. Streams of molten lava pose hazards to all but the most adroit and wary travelers, and the air reeks of sulphurous fumes. Few living creatures dwell here, and those that do are of a nature akin to the hostile environment which encompasses them.

The Saurans

The dominant species in this region is a race of man-like reptilians known as the Saurans. Standing up to seven feet in height, they have clawed hands and feet, scaly hide, and powerful jaws lined with rows of sharp teeth.

Customs

A primitive folk of limited intelligence, the Saurans nonetheless have adapted well to their surroundings. Utilizing volcanic mounds as natural forges, they make crude armor and weapons, mostly of low-grade red-iron alloys. The clans have domesticated the massive creatures known as land dragons, which they outfit with plates of hammered metal and ride into battle — though ponderous and slow, the beasts are awesomely strong. The Saurans employ their dragons much in the manner of siege engines, using them to batter down enemy fortifications and to provide cover against opposing missile fire.

The Saurans know little of magic, but do have a religion of sorts. Their patron deity is Satha, a fire-breathing dragon goddess who supposedly gave birth to the Sauran race. The reptilians erect huge cairns of stone in her name, filling them with offerings of firegems — a particularly spectacular variety of ruby common to the Volcanic Hills region. Dragon icons fashioned of beaten metal are also in use among some tribes.

Late at night in certain parts of the Volcanic Hills, the low rumblings of what would seem to be thunder can be heard. According to the Saurans, these sounds issue forth from deep underground, where their dragon goddess lies. The rumbling noises, the reptilians claim, are the sounds of Satha in labor.

A clannish folk, Saurans sometimes war amongst themselves, but most prefer instead to kill Raknids (insectoid beings who also inhabit the Volcanic Hills). Some of the reptilians have an appetite for man-flesh, and occasionally engage in raids against the Quan Empire. The Kang soldiers rely on fortifications and heavy catapults when defending against Sauran war-parties, believing frontal assaults against these foes to be tantamount to mass suicide.

Though noted for their aggressiveness, certain of the Sauran tribes are friendly toward certain of the races of Men. Some trade firegems to Djaffir and Orgovian traders, receiving high-quality metal tools and weapons in return. On occasion, adventuresome Saurans journey throughout Talislanta, often fighting as mercenaries.

Fortresses of the Saurans

The Sauran tribes live in walled stone enclosures of crude design. Two of these are large enough to make note of:

Sathra is a sprawling fortress constructed of a motley assortment of materials: rough-hewn boulders and chunks of volcanic rock, along with blocks and columns of stone pillaged from Wilderlands ruins (Quaran, Jalaad and other sites). Several regiments of troops are stationed here, including dragonriders, land-lizard cavalry, artillerists, and Saurud heavy infantry.

Sathra boasts at least four dozen land dragons, each equipped with an iron battletower and stonethrower. These reptilians have an exclusive trade relationship with one of the Orgovian clans, and slay other merchants who approach them.

Sathir is smaller, housing only half as many land dragons and troops. Both Djaffir and Orgovian traders are welcome here, but other foreigners should be wary.

The Raknids

Hideous insectoids resembling a cross between demonoids and scorpions, Raknids have segmented bodies encased in exoskeletons of tough, iridescent chitin. There are four different types of Raknids: Workers (huge, with eight legs), Warriors (man-like creatures, armed with poisonous stingers), Drones (malignly intelligent breeders), and the giant larval creatures called Queens.

Customs

Raknid society is regimented and inflexible. Workers build and maintain the massive hive complexes which house the colonies. Warriors protect the hives, hunt for food, and exterminate other creatures, thus ensuring the survival of their own species. Drones are driven solely by the urge to mate. Each colony has but a single active Queen, who spawns Raknids of all four types.

It is believed that the evil hive-mentality associated with the Raknids stems from their horrid mistress-rulers, who are sais to exert a powerful mental influence over their subjects.

The River of Fire

An ever-flowing torrent of molten lava, the River of Fire receives its life from the giant volcano, *Dragonrock*. Pyro-demons and earth demons are said to inhabit the depths of the northern volcano, and Saurans believe that the mountain's exhalations are actually the fiery breath of Satha, the patron mother-deity of their race.

Pyro-demons are said to swim in the River of Fire, while Crested Dragons are rumored to drink the liquid fire in order to enhance their fire-breathing capabilities. The northward-flowing river terminates in most dramatic fashion, in an incredible deluge of flame known as the *Firefalls*.

Spectacular when viewed at night, the falls empty into what many claim to be a bottomless chasm. As always, sight-seers should always keep one eye peeled for pyro-demons.

The Valley of Mist

Not far from the Firefalls is the Valley of Mist, which has a foggy atmosphere derived from the Firefalls' close proximity to the snows of nearby Xanadas. In this valley can be found the Well of Saints, the sparkling waters of which are reputed by the Orthodoxists of Aaman to possess miraculous healing properties. Those seeking divine aid should take pains to avoid vorls – insidious creatures of mist, which offer a definite and final cure for all ills.

The Legend of Erendor

A rugged trail, which winds its way through a good portion of the Volcanic Hills, is reportedly the same one which was followed by none other than the legendary Erendor – a wizard of ancient Elande, who is purported to have hidden all of his most precious possessions in a maze of caverns located somewhere in the vicinity.

According to Quan legend, Erendor foresaw in a vision the coming of the Great Disaster and the subsequent destruction of his homeland. Fearing death, he established a hidden retreat where he could reside in safety until the threat subsided. The sorcerer chose a network of caves in the Volcanic Hills as his hideaway, and hastily began to construct a suitable shelter for himself.

Working at night in order to avoid detection, Erendor stocked his underground home with all of his most cherished possessions: ancient librams, priceless scrolls, rare curios, and provisions enough to last him for many years. Finally, he set a number of ingenious traps, designed to keep out unwanted intruders.

This last step proved to be Erendor's undoing, however. In a moment of carelessness, the mage became entangled in one of his own devices. Unable to escape, Erendor met a slow and untimely end.

Neither the wizard, his possessions, nor his cave have ever been found. This is possibly due to the distractions which aspiring treasure-hunters must overcome while attempting such a reconnaissance, which include but are not limited to: land dragons, wild striders, vasps, war parties of Saurans and Raknids, and even raiding Araq from Kharakhan.

Dragons in the Hills

In Sauran legend, the Volcanic Hills are proclaimed to be the birthplace of all Talislantan dragons. While most scholars of the enlightened New Age scoff at this belief, a few naturalists call on them to explain the occasional sightings of young dragons emerging from the mouths of volcanos in this region.

A dead volcano known as *Dragon's Grave,* located somewhere in the heart of the Volcanic Hills, is purportedly the fabled "dragon's graveyard" of many a Rajan and Dracartan folk tale. According to the lore of the desert folk, it is traditional for Crested Dragons to make the long voyage to this mountain when it is their time to die.

The interior of the dead volcano is said to be littered with the remains of untold hundreds or thousands of these great monsters, which popular tales depict as having carried their most treasured possessions with them to their graves.

Treasure hunters and ivory traders have searched for Dragon's Grave for centuries, and a few claim to have found the place and become rich on what they carried away. Others no doubt met an untimely end at the hands of the Saurans and Raknids, vasps, and other threats.

Raknid Warrior, Queen, Drone, and Worker

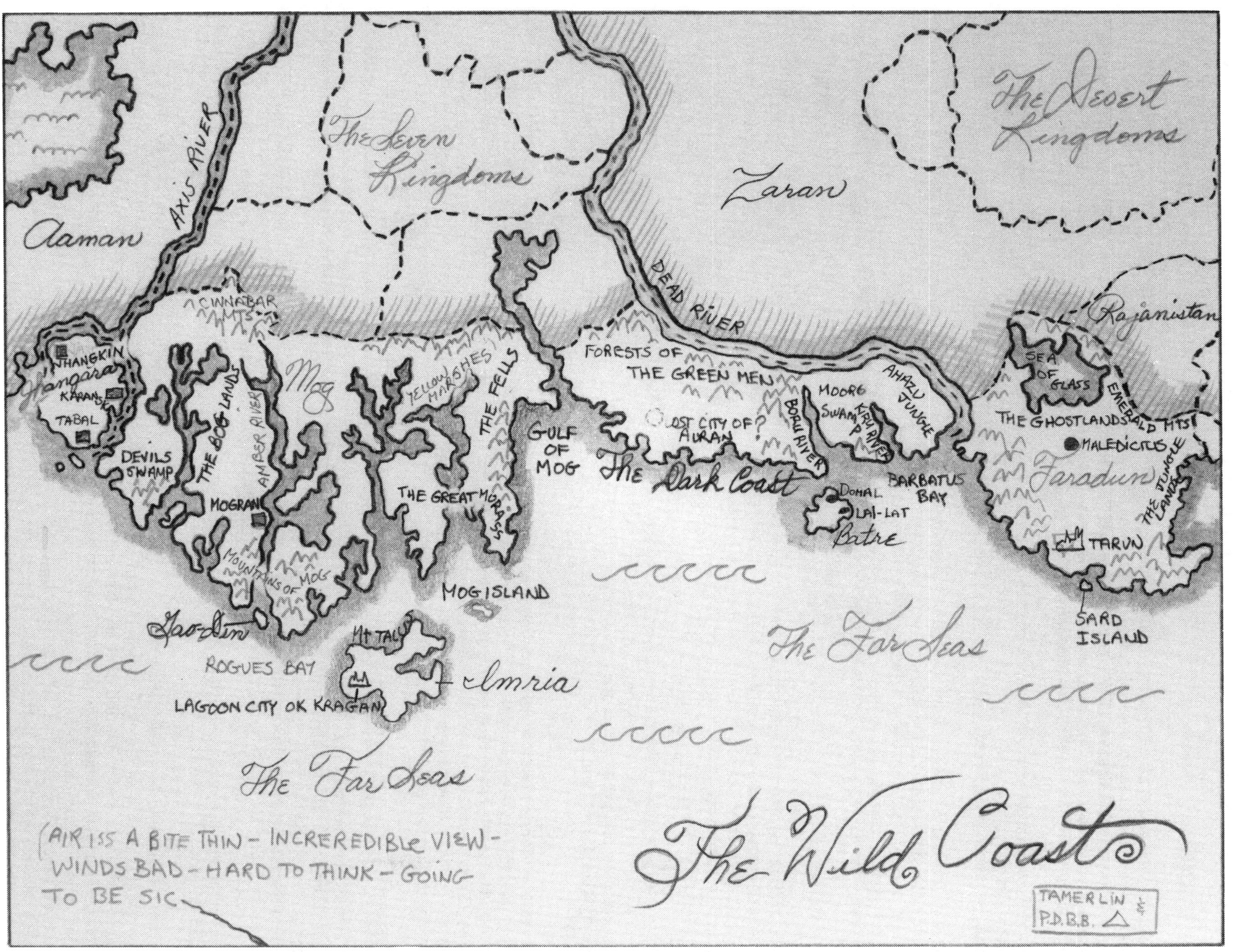

Scale: 1" = 125 miles.

BATRE

A small tropical isle located to the south of the Dark Coast, Batre is a jungled land, abounding with fruiting trees, crystal streams and scenic waterfalls. Dense and forbidding, the interior affords numerous opportunities to meet with disaster, including aramatus (armored leeches), exomorphs, marsh striders and jungle dractyl. Many varieties of rare herbs and plants are also found here, such as green lotus, tantalus and necromantium.

Long a popular stopover point for vessels seeking fresh water and supplies, the island is well known to sailors, who consider it one of the few safe havens in the Azure Ocean. Batre is even more notable, however, for its ivory-skinned inhabitants.

The Batreans

A primitive people, Batreans dress in rude garments of coarse cloth, and dye their hair with indelible blue pigments. Male and female of the race bear so little resemblance to each other that they seem to be from separate species.

The males are huge, slope-shouldered, hairy, and remarkably ugly. Slow and ponderous, they possess the manners of ogronts, and are constantly arguing and fighting among one another.

Batrean females, on the other hand, are engaging creatures, slender and lovely beyond compare. Their movements are graceful, and their manner of speech is charming and at times most eloquent. Batrean males seem unmoved by the beauty of their females, whom they largely ignore – except during the males' brief, week-long mating season.

Customs

It is the peculiar custom of Batrean males to sell their womenfolk for gold, which they hoard in secret underground caches. For many years, entrepreneurial seafarers have risked the perils of ocean travel in order to purchase Batrean females, since the island women bring exorbitant prices as concubines in lands such as Zandu, Arim, Faradun, and the Quan Empire.

As for the Batrean females themselves, few evince any great sadness at being separated from their boorish, slovenly mates. On the contrary, some have even been known to help pay for their release with coins pilfered from the hidden treasure caches of their husbands. None appear to miss the mud-and-thatch hovels which the Batrean males call home, and most seem to adapt to their new surroundings

Batrean concubine and harem guard

with very little difficulty. Once established in their new residences, more than a few Batrean females exhibit an uncanny ability to influence their masters by various subtle and effective means, a talent attributed by some to magic.

The Island Villages

There are only two villages of any significance on the island. *Lat-Lat* consists of a number of mud and thatch hovels inhabited by brutish Batrean males, and two large communal huts utilized by the beautiful females of the species.

A living wall of thornwood surrounds the settlement, providing protection from wild beasts and marauding Imrian slavers. Groups of Batrean males patrol the perimeter.

Domal is similar in most respects to the village of Lal-Lat, but is somewhat smaller, and has only one communal hut for its female inhabitants. The local women make rugs, hammocks and hassocks of woven raffia, pots and vases of sun-baked clay, and wooden utensils. The communal hut is always heavily guarded by male sentinels.

THE DARK COAST

Green Men, Ahazu, and Moorg-Wan

To the north of the isle of Batre lies the uncivilized region known as the Dark Coast. Hemmed in to the north by the low-lying Topaz Mountains, the Coast's terrain consists predominantly of thick and tangled jungle, interspersed with sections of marshland and tropical forest.

The Dark Coast is home to many unusual species of plants and animals. Of these, the winged ape – a vicious predator capable of gliding from tree to tree – is perhaps the most notorious. It is hunted for its single horn, which is reputed to have potent magical properties. Green and scarlet varieties of lotus grow throughout the region, being most common in the central swamplands. Amber wasps also proliferate in this portion of the coast, an indicator that the swamps may well be rich in amber.

The Boru and Kiru Rivers effectively divide the Dark Coast into three territories: the western rainforests, home of the Green Men; the central swamplands, home of the Mud People; and the eastern junglelands, home of the fierce Ahazu. The Kiru River is infested with aramatus and chang, and is wholly unsafe to cross except by means of boats or rope bridges. Mud rays, skalanx, and various types of fresh-water mollusk are common in the waters of the Boru River.

The Green Men

Peaceful beings, the Green Men are small in stature, with skin, hair and eyes all of varying shades of green. Almost imp-like in appearance, they dress in abbreviated garments made of soft, woven mosses, and make their homes in the boles of great, living plants which they call *D'Oko*. Green Men are a communal people, living in groups of up to 80 individuals, each related to the other. The language of these simple folk is pleasant to the ear, being reminiscent of the music of wooden flutes.

Customs

Green Men speak the secret language of the plant world, and possess an uncanny ability to influence all things that grow in the earth. The rain-forest natives have a symbiotic relationship with many types of plants, which they tend with great care and affection. In return, the Green Men derive all that they need to survive in the rain-forests: shelter, clothing, and sustenance.

Gentle and shy, the Green Men avoid contact with most other of the intelligent races, though some are said to have a certain fondness for the Ariane, Muses, and the Gnomekin of Durne. Scholars wish they could study this folk, being fascinated by the process through which they reproduce, which is said to bear a marked resemblance to cross-pollination.

The Green Men are often preyed upon by slavers from Imria, who invade their domains in numbers during the rainy season when the Green Men's young are just beginning to mature (Green Men reach adulthood in about six months' time). As they do not employ weapons of any sort, the forest natives are highly vulnerable to such raids. Their only defenses consist of a variety of ingenious snares and pitfalls, which they excel at making. Many of these devices employ living plants — such as yellow stickler, stranglevine and violet creeper — none of which ever molest the Green Men. When threatened, the natives usually flee deeper into the forest in order to entice pursuers into their cleverly laid traps. The Green Men never engage in hand-to-hand combat, however, and surrender without a struggle if caught or cornered.

Although Imrians find the capture of the forest folk to be no simple matter, the demand for Green Men as slaves — since they are docile in captivity, and make superior servants and gardeners — is deemed high enough for the slavers to warrant the risks involved in their capture. Unscrupulous buyers in Faradun, Rajanistan, the Quan Empire, and (less commonly) the Citystate of Hadj of the Wilderlands deal exclusively in such exotic slave-types. Curiously, the Mud People and Ahazu never harm the Green Men, believing that doing so arouses the wrath of the jungle. The uncommonly mild and sensitive disposition of these benign forest creatures is such that, exposed to unfamiliar surroundings, many Green Men gradually wither and die from sadness.

The Mud People

A brutish folk, the semi-amphibious natives of the central swamplands are squat of build, and covered with thick folds of loose brown skin. The Mud People have four legs, heavy tails and toad-like visages, and are very strong. The semi-amphibians are considerably faster in the water than on land. The language of these creatures consists mainly of grunts and gurgling sounds, said to be almost impossible for man-like beings to replicate.

Customs

The Mud People — or *Moorg-Wan,* as they call themselves — live along the banks of the Boru River, and the sodden territories between the two rivers are their ancestral breeding grounds. Their mud-palace dwellings resemble great, oozing piles of mud and silt, and are connected by networks of above-ground tunnels.

Industrious folk, the Moorg-Wan are constantly engaged in building and excavating, and dredge the riverbanks for amber, as well as sapphires and other semi-precious stones, found here in abundance (so, too, are bog devils, swamp demons, and aramatus). The Mud People consider the lotus plant to be a delicacy, and jealously guard their supplies.

The customs and culture of the Mud People are largely unknown, this due in great part to the unsociable attitude of these folk. The magician Malderon, who was unfortunate (or foolish) enough to have been captured by a tribe of Moorg-Wan, gave an account of the experience in his otherwise mundane treatise on the denizens of the Dark Coast:

"The Mud People, gross though they may appear to us, exhibit certain of the attributes of civilized peoples. They covet riches; particularly sapphires, which they spend an inordinate amount of energy dredging from the muck and mire of their environs. They are religious, as is evidenced by their reverence of Moorg, the giant Mud God (the Mud People, in fact, call themselves the Moorg-Wan, or "Spawn of Moorg"). They raise their offspring from egg to larval newt, then set the young adults to work in the mud mines. Those who find sapphires are rewarded with food; those who do not are slain and served up as their brothers' next meal."

The sworn foes of the Ahazu, the Mud People frequently engage their hated enemies when the yellow warriors enter the swamplands, and sometimes launch reprisal raids into the jungles across the Kiru River. Their favorite weapons are the *bwan* (a heavy club, lined with rows of six-inch long thorns, made from the stump of the thornwood vine) and thorn daggers. At close range, the powerful creatures sometimes drop their weapons and attempt to rend opponents with their webbed claws, or to butt them to the ground and trample them underfoot.

The Mud People fear the Imrians — being somewhat slow and cumbersome, the swamp dwellers are easy prey for the slavers' nets and capture-poles. Despite their aggressive nature, the Swamp People are easily cowed when they are taken into captivity. The prisoners are valued for their strength, the Imrians employing the Mud People as slave-laborers in their Lagoon City of Kragan.

The Ahazu

The natives of the eastern jungles are the fiercest of the Dark Coast's inhabitants. These four-armed, man-like beings may exceed seven feet in height, and are quite imposing to behold. The Ahazu have bright-yellow skin, with fiery red markings lining the face and neck and running down the back of the arms, legs and spine. Though slender of build, they are surprisingly strong and agile. Their features are almost demonic: sloping forehead, forked tongue, thin nostrils, and dark-green, pupil-less eyes vacant of mercy or compassion.

Reptile-hide loincloths and thongs — tied below the shoulder and at the elbows, wrists, knees and ankles — serve as the savages' only clothing. The Ahazu converse in harsh shrieks and yells, frequently punctuated by violent gestures and the brandishing of weapons.

Customs

A warlike and exceptionally hostile race, the Ahazu make no permanent dwellings, preferring instead to sleep in the treetops. Their favored weapons are the *gwanga* (a heavy, three-bladed throwing knife) and the *matsu* (a two-handed warclub, with a rounded stone head and a long, flexible shaft), both of which they employ with great skill. The yellow warriors are also subject in battle to the *shan'ya*, an uncontrollable urge to kill.

The Ahazu have no spell-casters, and consider magic the domain of cowards and weaklings. They are said to revere a secret warrior-deity, whom they believe determines the outcome of all battles.

The yellow warriors attack without hesitation any creatures which enter their territories. They are fearless in battle, but not to the point of recklessness. If outnumbered, the warriors generally retreat, then attempt to ambush or circle back on pursuing enemies. When hunting for food, the Ahazu never venture beyond their own borders. The appearance of a group of the yellow warriors anywhere outside of their junglelands is a certain indicator that the Ahazu are on the warpath, launching a raid, or tracking a fleeing opponent.

The jungles of the Ahazu are also populated by batranc, pseudomorphs and malathrope, and so are generally avoided by most sensible folk. The Imrians never venture here except in heavily-armed groups of 50 or more individuals. The Imrians employ captured bands of Mud People, the dire enemies of the Ahazu, as decoys in order to capture slave-warriors. Once a war party has engaged the hapless pawns, the slavers attack, employing throwing nets and vials of toxic powder. Once captured, an Ahazu will never try to escape, the rigid warrior code of these people prohibiting such a practice. For this reason, Ahazu slaves command high prices, and are greatly valued as bodyguards, gladiators and slave-warriors.

Ancient Pirates

Zandir legends associate the Dark Coast with the Baratus, an ancient, man-like race of seafaring thieves and pirates, which roamed the oceans preying on merchant vessels and terrorizing coastal settlements for two centuries. The Baratus are long since gone, their jungle sanctuaries now the domain of the Mud People and the Ahazu, and their once-splendid sea vessels rotting on the ocean floor. According to legend, the pirates buried countless chests of stolen riches in the coastal jungles. Certain Talislantan historians believe that the greater part of this treasure remains moldering in the ground, awaiting discovery by some fortunate explorer or entrepreneur.

The Baratus may be the former inhabitants of a series of ruins, said to be found within the interior of the forbidding junglelands of the Ahazu. The so-called *Unknown Ruins* have never been explored by civilized beings, at least as far as anyone knows. This is due almost exclusively to the presence of fierce Ahazu wardens, who range far and wide throughout the region. It is the practice of these sentinels to attack intruders on sight, neither granting nor asking any quarter.

Leaper's Ridge

These wavering cliffs stand amidst the eastern jungles of the Dark Coast. A narrow stream drops over the cliff in a 400-foot-long ribbon of water, terminating in a rainbow-hued cloud of mist and vapor. The waterfall is not the region's main attraction, however — at least, as far as the local indigenes are concerned. Rather, Leaper's Ridge is a place where certain Ahazu tribesmen, despondent over having fared poorly in battle, come to hurl themselves to their deaths. Victims of this traditional ritual litter the jungle floor beneath Leaper's Ridge, attracting such scavengers as urthrax and aramatus.

The Lost City of Auran

In Farad legend, Auran is known as the fabled "Lost City of Gold" — a ruined city strewn with golden idols and riches beyond imagining. It can supposedly be found somewhere in the western rain-forest; ostensibly, amidst the territory of the peaceful Green Men. Countless expeditions have been launched by greedy Farad Monopolists, each eager to seize the riches of Auran. Most of these have never returned, falling victim to the hazards of the jungle.

FARADUN

An exotic land located on the southern coast of Talislanta, Faradun is bordered to the north by the rugged peaks of the Topaz Mountains. Also to the north lie two topographical anomalies: the Sea of Glass and Emerald Mountain. Arid and hostile terrain dominates the central region, gradually giving way to patches of jungle and mountains along the coast. Driven by winds from the Far Seas, Faradun's climate is uniformly hot and oppressive.

The Farad

The people who live here, known as the Farad, are a dark and saturnine folk of above average height. They have flint-grey skin, stony visages, and narrow eyes as black as coal. The customary mode of dress for Farad males includes an elaborate headdress, voluminous robes, broad sashes, and velvet boots, all hung with ornate tassels, fringes, and beads of colored glass. Men over the age of 20 wear their beards in twin braids bound with silver fastenings, the length and the degree of ornamentation employed being considered signs of status.

The women of the Farad wear long silken gowns and veils, and adorn themselves with necklaces of silver loops, and rings on each of their fingers. Both the males and females exhibit an air of haughtiness and arrogance that might charitably be described as distant or aloof.

Customs

The social and political hierarchy of Faradun reflects the nation's utter obsession with commerce. The ruler of Faradun, known as the Cral, wields absolute power, and is responsible for determining market prices for all goods which are to be bought or sold in the capital city.

Second in line of authority are the Monopolists, individuals given power by the Cral to determine the availability of various wares. Each is responsible for a single commodity, such as slaves, contraband, gemstones, metals, narcotics, and so forth. Some Monopolists are wizards, who dabble in magic in order to further their business interests.

Next come the Usurers, who lend money at exorbitant rates to finance commercial ventures approved by the Monopolists. Dependent upon the Usurers are the Procurers, who travel far and wide, acquiring merchandise from various sources and establishing new trade contacts. Finally, there are the Mongers: the shopowners, peddlers and hawkers who make up the vast majority of Faradun's citizenry.

A Farad Procurer

Few Farad are employed in any non-mercantile line of work. The country's labor force is composed almost entirely of indentured servants, slaves and convicted felons, while the army and navy are manned by highly-paid foreign mercenaries.

The mercantilists have a religion of sorts, revering the god Avar, deity of material wealth and personal gain. Avar's followers do not erect temples in his name, but prostrate themselves before golden idols purchased in the shops of the capital. Farad merchants pray to Avar that they might obtain more lucrative contracts than their competitors, and that their profits might increase in proportion to their desires. According to the priests of Avar, deception and treachery are astute business tactics, and greed an admirable trait.

Wealthy foreigners and prospective clients may be feted in grand style by the Farad, who can be quite charming when it suits their needs. Conversely, the mercantilists possess a capacity for cold-blooded, emotionless behavior that is matched only by the soulless logic of the barbaric Harakin.

The Port City of Tarun

The sprawling port of Tarun, with its ominous and impregnable defenses, is the capital of Faradun and its center for trade. Through the towering sea-gates pass the ships and merchants of many nations: Imrian slavers, Zandir gem dealers, Aamanian ore traders, and even corsairs from the Mangar Isles and

Gao-Din — the Farad are notable for their singularly unscrupulous business practices, and the mercantilists will buy or sell anything from anyone, with no questions asked.

Although the Farad are involved to some degree in importing and exporting, they much prefer to allow business to come to them. In order to stimulate this type of trade, the mercantilists make every effort to attract merchants and traders to Tarun. Prices for food, drink and lodging are quite reasonable, and tariffs and duties are minimal. Further, any sort of entertainment or diversion imaginable can be arranged through the auspices of the Farad Procurers, who claim to be able to grant their customers' fondest desires...for the right price.

The Sea of Glass

A flat expanse of fused green crystal, the Sea of Glass is believed to have been created during the Great Disaster. Scholars think this might have occurred when Emerald Mountain erupted, spewing forth molten glass which eventually cooled and hardened to a crystalline state.

The Cymrilians operate a mining facility on the western "shore" of the sea, harvesting the green crystal utilized in nearly all Cymrilian construction. The folk of Cymril pay Faradun a handsome price for the privilege of mining the green crystal. There is always work available here for miners, guards, laborers, and caravan drivers, though amenities for such positions are somewhat limited. Windships and wagons laden with glass depart from the area every few weeks, headed for Cymril of the Seven Kingdoms.

Few living things dwell in this region, though miners occasionally stumble upon the sleeping forms of glass dragons, glass imps, and other crystalline oddities; creatures trapped in green glass, and thereby magically preserved and transmuted into crystal. These creatures bring a high price in many lands, where they are regarded as objects of great wonder.

Emerald Mountain

Much to the dismay of the Farad, Emerald Mountain is not truly made of emerald. Neither is it made of green glass, but rather some sort of hard, metallic green ore. The mercantilists considered erecting a mining installation at the base of the mountain, but decided that it was better not to test the veracity of the old legend which describes the cloud-covered summit as being home to the diabolical Shaitan.

Adventurers from faraway lands sometimes attempt to scale the mountain, seeking the favor of the Shaitan. Never numerous, the ranks of these stalwart heroes seem destined to dwindle further still.

The Ghostlands

Beyond the Sea of Glass lies a land so arid and barren that not even snakes and vermin dwell here. Necrophages, shadow wights and unclean spirits, being somewhat less particular with regard to their accommodations, haunt the region in force. Called the Ghostlands, this area has long been used as a place of banishment by the Farad for those convicted of embezzling funds — a crime considered more heinous than murder, in Faradun.

Somewhere in this waste is the shadowy ruined city which the Farad refer to as Maledictus, which means "cursed," or more aptly, "haunted." Precisely who or what it is that haunts the ruins is uncertain. Some claim that a cabal of Shadow Wizards inhabits the city. Others theorize that phasms, ghasts, or the ghost of the legendary warlock Mordante are responsible. Most frightening to the Farad is the idea that Maledictus is haunted by the disembodied spirits of all those who have been cheated or ruined by the unscrupulous merchants and monopolists of Faradun. Whatever the case may be, no Farad would ever dare set foot within the vicinity of these ruins.

The Coastal Jungles

The jungles of Faradun's southeastern coast are best avoided, primarily due to the presence of winged apes, death's head vipers, malathrope, alatus, aramatus, and other unpleasant creatures. The climate is abysmally hot and humid; the terrain alternates between flooded swamp and mountainous jungle.

Costly k'tallah, tantalus and scarlet lotus grow here in substantial quantities, a fact not lost on the Farad Procurers. Oblivious to the dangers inherent in such work, the mercantilists send work crews composed of slaves and convicted felons into the jungles to gather k'tallah (an insidious narcotic which brings high prices on the Black Market in Tarun); the Procurers have determined that the profits realized by harvesting the jungles outweigh the cost in lost slaves by an acceptable margin.

Sard Island

A man-made isle which lies off the southern coast of Faradun, near Tarun, Sard Island is home to several of the wealthiest Monopolists, who live in fortified castles of elaborate design. The island was built by slave laborers, many hundreds of whom died during the ten years which it took to complete the construction of the isle.

GAO-DIN

Gao Sea Rogues

A small and rocky isle, Gao-Din is located some ten miles off the southwestern coast of Mog. It is a dismal place, with treacherous swamps and jungles lining its shore. Inland, limestone cliffs rise above the murky vegetation, culminating in a great central mound of stone. Here, looking out across the Azure Ocean, stands one of the most curious of Talislanta's settlements: the Rogue City of Gao.

Formerly a penal colony of the old Phaedran Empire, Gao was abandoned by both the Orthodoxists and the Paradoxists during the Cult Wars of the middle New Age. The prisoners incarcerated in this heavily fortified installation, mostly thieves, rogue mages and political dissidents, were simply left behind to fend for themselves. Showing a degree of ingenuity born of desperation, the convicts salvaged an derelict Phaedran vessel and embarked upon a career as sea-roving pirates.

Soon thereafter, Gao-Din was declared an independent state, and the Rogue City of Gao was made its capital. Since that time, the Sea-Rogues of Gao have prospered, primarily at the expense of such folk as Imrian slavers, Zandir freetraders, and the Farad.

The Sea Rogues

The citizens of Gao consider themselves to be thieves of the most gallant sort, their swashbuckling antics at the very least setting them apart from the murderous tactics employed by the Mangar Corsairs of the Far Seas. The formal penal colony of Gao-Din has grown into a tiny nation of sorts, the old fortifications of the prison having been expanded upon and modified for purposes of defense. The citystate's current population, composed mostly of thieves, outcasts and freed slaves, is a remarkable admixture of racial and cultural types: defrocked Aamanian priests, Zandir charlatans, Thrall mercenaries, Ahazu warriors, Batrean concubines, and many others.

Customs

Rivals or even deadly enemies under other circumstances, the inhabitants of the Rogue City generally coexist with a minimum of difficulty within Gao. At least part of the reason for this seems due to the city state's unique form of government. The Rogue City of Gao is ruled by an individual known as "the King (or Queen) of Thieves," elected by popular vote once each year.

The king's primary duties are to arbitrate disputes, set fair prices for black market and contraband goods, and enforce the three basic tenets of the "Thieves' Code of Honor." Briefly stated, the three elements of the Thieves' Code are:

1) It is illegal to kill a fellow thief (i.e. any citizen of Gao-Din) while within the city's boundaries.

2) It is illegal to reveal the seven secret passwords of Gao-Din to any non-citizen.

3) It is illegal to steal any item worth more than 20 gold lumens from a fellow thief/citizen, while within the city's boundaries.

In essence, the Code prohibits the citizens of Gao from engaging in acts of violence or thievery against their fellows. All other Talislantans are considered fair game, though as a general rule unwarranted acts of violence within the city are discouraged (and are considered in poor taste).

The punishment for failure to comply with the Code's tenets is variable, based on the king's appraisal of the exact circumstances surrounding the incident in question. In most cases, individuals found guilty of breaking the first or second tenets of the Thieves' Code are bound, gagged and fed to the sea demons.

Those found guilty of breaking the third tenet are given two weeks to reimburse the victim of the theft by an amount equal to three times the worth of the item(s) stolen. Failure or inability to comply with this edict once again brings to the fore the option involving the sea demons.

The Sea-Rogues' system of justice is said to work as well as any other, and bears the distinct advantage of obviating costly facilities for the incarceration of incorrigible felons. Furthermore, the sea demons which live in the waters around the island have become somewhat fond of the citizens of the citystate, and generally refrain from attacking their vessels. When the Sea Rogues are able to feed captured Imrian slavers to the demons, relations between the two species often border on cordiality.

An unfortunate side effect of the citystate's legal system is that, in order to avoid a high incidence of theft, most of the city's black marketeers and shop-owners rarely value any of their wares at less than 21 gold lumens, and they often insist on selling inexpensive items in large lots.

Other strictures governing the citizens of Gao are minimal, most being related to various economic or cultural concerns. The government is allowed a ten percent cut of all booty captured by ships which utilize the city's walled-in harbor facilities, but does not otherwise burden its people with taxes or tariffs. This arrangement has proved satisfactory for the majority of Gao, though unscupulous captains occasionally try to cheat the government of its due by undervaluing the worth of their cargo.

While polygamy is permitted (for both male and female citizens) by Gao-Din law, adultery is frowned upon. Individuals accused of such indiscretions often simply get married, thereby avoiding possible scandal. However, as a result of the city's liberal policies concerning marriage, individuals born in Gao-Din may have any number of legal "fathers" and "mothers," and countless relatives of various races and nationalities.

Restrictions pertaining to religious beliefs are non-existent, and diverse cults and religions proliferate in the Rogue City. This isn't to say that the citizenry doesn't have a few well-known prejudices: slavers are detested, the Orthodoxists of Aaman are despised (for trying to reclaim Gao-Din during the latter part of the Cult Wars), and the Rajan death cultists are ridiculed for their obsession with the afterlife.

Gao-Din citizenship is not easily obtained, though it is technically available to any thief, outcast or scoundrel who seeks it. In order to reduce the chance of spies or informants infiltrating Gao's close-knit society, all individuals applying for citizenship must allow themselves to be subjected to scrutiny by the king's personal advisors, a group traditionally composed of thieves, rogue wizards, astrologers, charlatans, and the like.

Those who pass the test are granted citizenship without further delay, and taught the seven passwords required to gain access to the city. Those who fail are seldom heard from again (unless one happens to be a sea demon, that is).

The citystate of Gao-Din has no formal relations with any other government, religious group, or secret society. Neither has the King of Gao-Din ever ruled out the possibility of associating with other governments or individuals, providing there is a profit to be made by doing so.

IMRIA

An Imrian slaver (foreground); Imrian coracle, drawn by kra (background).

Imria is a large island located off the southern coast of Mog, in the Azure Ocean. Its dense jungles, twisting inlets and underwater grottos teem with such dangerous creatures as kaliya, horned apes, crag spiders, and giant, sightless cave kra. Mount Talus, a large and intermittently active volcano, rises above the jungle to the northwest, and sea demons prowl the coastal waters in force. Perhaps the most dangerous inhabitants of the isle, however, are the amphibious man-like beings known as the Imrians.

The Imrians

Tall and muscular, the Imrians have sloping shoulders, scaly yellow-green skin (typically covered with a light coating of translucent slime), and dark, deep-set eyes. Their hands and feet are webbed, and their powerful jaws are lined with a double row of sharp teeth.

Having both gills and rudimentary lungs, the amphibians are capable of living both on land and under the sea. All Imrians are powerful swimmers — in the water they are surprisingly swift, belying the somewhat slow and awkward movement displayed by Imrians on land.

Customs

The customs and culture of the Imrians are generally unappreciated by the other intelligent races of Talislanta. Most consider the amphibians' taste for slugs, worms and leeches to be disgusting, and find it impossible to enjoy a decent meal in their presence.

Although most of the amphibians are able to speak a crude version of the Talislantan tongue, their slurred and burbling manner of pronunciation does not endear them to foreigners. Imrians prefer instead to converse in the Piscine tongue, the language of fish and other aquatic creatures, when among their own kind.

The light coating of slime which covers the body of a healthy Imrian is likewise unappealing to some —

especially clothiers and launderers, who dread the appearance of an Imrian in their establishments. As Imrians drink only brine, their presence in the port-side taverns of other lands often portends trouble.

The amphibians worship no deity, since any position or level of status possessing greater esteem than that of the King of Imria is beyond their comprehension. Nor do the Imrians have much tolerance for those who worship the various deities of Talislanta — they consider such beliefs and the associated rituals to be primitive and infantile.

The Coral Tablets

The Imrians consider themselves to be superior to the other races of Talislanta. They claim to be the First Race, from whom the "lesser species" (the man-like races) supposedly descended. They cite as evidence certain ancient coral tablets, held in their possession for many generations. Retrieved from a sunken crypt by their early ancestors, the tablets purportedly contain the secret history of the Imrian race, dating back over 20,000 years.

Those Talislantan scholars who acknowledge the existence of the Imrian tablets (there are thought to be several thousand of the coral slabs) believe that they do indeed contain priceless historical information — not relating to the Imrians, but telling of an ancient and advanced civilization which sunk beneath the waves untold ages ago.

The Slave Trade

The amphibians are among the few Talislantans who do not fear to sail into the open sea. Imrians range far and wide in their massive, barge-like coracles, which are constructed from the bones and hide of kra. Smaller vessels of woven reeds, tethered to the coracles until needed, are used for shore raids, to negotiate winding and narrow channels or shallow swamplands, and to transport cargo (often bamboo cages filled with captives) back to the larger ships.

Slavers by trade, Imrians prey upon the primitive tribes which dwell along the southern coasts and isles of the Talislantan continent: the Witchmen of Chana; the Mud People, Ahazu and Green Men of the Dark Coast; the Batreans and Sawila from their respective isles; and the Mogroth of Mog.

In former times, before the founding of the Seven Kingdoms, the slavers ruled a large stretch of Mog and Taz, but the Thralls finally united and cast the intruders back into the sea — to this day, the two races hate one another. Several bloody defeats inflicted by the Grand Army of the Seven Kingdoms have also persuaded the Imrians that slave raids into Astar to capture Muses are no longer profitable.

The slave trade has influenced and shaped nearly every aspect of Imrian culture. For instance, the amphibians employ a number of different weapons, most of which are also used to snare captives: throwing nets, capture-poles, pole hooks, and two especially grisly devices, the *oc* (a type of barbed bola, used to entangle victims) and the *korreg* (a heavy two-man crossbow, used to fire harpoons at swimmers escaping in the water).

A king rules over the Imrians, but he might more accurately be called the chief of the slave-mongers: his primary responsibility is to mastermind Imria's trade in slaves and contraband. For every slave-type, there is a different market: The Quan Empire, Faradun and Zandu vie constantly for concubines and courtesans; Aaman, Zandu and the Quan Empire compete for Green Men from the Dark Coast, whom they employ as gardeners; elsewhere in Talislanta, there is always a slave monger or merchant to bid for Mud People laborers, Mogroth swamp-miners, and warriors from the Ahazu and Witchmen races.

The slavers also traffic in narcotic herbs, exotic beasts, and all manner of contraband, their major customers for these illicit goods being the mercantilists of Faradun.

The City of Kragan

The Imrians have but a single settlement, the City of Kragan. The metropolis is accessible from the sea by several hidden, winding inlets, each heavily guarded by slave warriors, wild beasts and Imrian guards.

Located in the great lagoon situated in the center of the island, the city consists of hundreds of reed and thatch hovels, each plastered with mud and supported on stilt-like poles. The tallest of these structures tower 40 feet or more above the lagoon, and are occupied by the wealthiest Imrians — the King of Imria dwells within the highest. The least prosperous Imrians own hovels which stand just above the water or are partially submerged, depending upon the tide. Slaves awaiting sale — and those kept by the Imrians for use as laborers — are housed in floating pens, moored by heavy lines to the lagoon bottom.

Mount Talus

A large and intermittently active volcano rises above the northwestern jungles of the island of Imria. A trail of acrid vapors constantly issues from the mouth of Mount Talus, within which are believed to reside both earth demons and pyro-demons. The volcano has erupted several times in the past, each time wreaking havoc on the local populace.

JHANGARA

Jhangaran marsh-hunters inadvertently arouse the attentions of a female water raknid.

Bordered to the east and west by twin forks of the Axis River, Jhangara is a hot and humid land, traveled by few civilized people. Its terrain consists of jungle, murky swamp and bog, becoming progressively more dense and inhospitable toward the southern coasts, where untamed marshes predominate. The land is populated by numerous species of unfriendly animals and plants: specifically, kra, stranglevine, violet creeper, and water raknids.

The Jhangarans

The man-like denizens of this land are the Jhangarans – a backward race, odd and ungainly in appearance. The marsh-dwellers have marbled brown-and-sepia-colored skin, elongated limbs, elliptical craniums, and pinched, angular features. Both the males and females are hairless, and may attain heights in excess of six and a half feet.

Customs

The Jhangarans are a sullen and superstitious people, prone to displays of hostile or even violent be-havior. They subsist on sea-slugs and raw meat, do not use fire, and have no knowledge of metal-working or magic. Jhangarans have a great weakness for alcohol, and are particularly fond of Zandir wine and Arimite chakos, both of which drive them mad and make their actions unpredictable.

The Ardua and Zandir tolerate the excesses of the Jhangarans in order to obtain the natives' valuable trade goods, but most other Talislantans believe the marsh dwellers to be thoroughly untrustworthy, and not worth the risk of dealing with. The Farad are a noted exception – lacking scruples themselves, the mercantilists regularly employ the Jhangarans as guards and trackers.

The marsh dwellers live in tribal groups, typically comprised solely of individuals of the same occupation. The Mud Miners and Marsh Hunters generally live in rude settlements, but other clans prefer to move from place to place as circumstances dictate. Rivalries between the various tribes are common, the effects of which may range from prejudicial behavior to all-out warfare. There is no love lost between the Mud Miners and Marsh Hunters, who have resented each other for centuries. As for the Mercenaries, they will fight for anyone who can afford their services, and sometimes attack the other tribes just to keep in training. A number of the tribes own crude river craft, which they use to ply their various trades along the length of the Axis River.

Jhangarans go about barefooted, wearing only loincloths, and bands of coarse cloth wrapped about their arms and legs. The color of the cloth employed denotes the individual's status and occupation: Mud Miners wear grey, Marsh Hunters wear green, black is for the Mercenaries, and red is for Outcasts.

The Outcasts

Strangest of all the Jhangarans are the Outcasts, tribesmen who wander the furthest swamps and jungles. Though few in number, they wield great power. It is the belief of the other Jhangarans that the Outcasts bear with them the "stigma of doom." Being so much as touched by one of the Cursed Ones is enough to immediately brand a person as an Outcast. He or she then has only two choices: to commit suicide, or to join the Outcasts.

In order to avoid being tainted by tribes of Outcasts, the other Jhangarans offer bribes of food, gold or other valuables, always placed at some distance from the supplicants' encampment or settlement. If the Outcasts find the gifts to be sufficient, they depart from the area; if not, they typically threaten to approach the village or camp, bearing with them their accursed stigmas.

There is no simple solution to the plague of Cursed Ones — to kill an Outcast, the Jhangarans believe, brings the curse upon the murderer and his family. The natives sometimes try to persuade or trick foreigners into killing the Outcasts for them, though few knowledgeable visitors will risk undertaking such grim and dangerous work.

The Villages of Jhangara

There are only three settlements of any note within the boggy and humid land of the Jhangarans. Two of these are located along the eastern fork of the Axis River, and the third lies near the mouth of the western fork where it enters the Azure Ocean. All are constructed of rude axe-hewn timbers, and are fortified against attack from Mercenaries, wild beasts, and murderous hordes of water raknids.

The inhabitants of *Karansk* are Mud Miners, and make their living by dredging the riverbanks and swamplands for sapphires, amber and gold. The mud-mines of Karansk are dangerous places — virtual quagmires, teeming with aramatus, urthrax and other vermin. The Mud Miners trade with the Ardua of Vardune, who dwell just 200 miles upriver, receiving in return goods from the Seven Kingdoms.

The denizens of *Tabal* are Marsh Hunters, who trap wild beasts in order to earn their sustenance. The hunters trade captured beasts, hides, feathers, and horn to Zandir freetraders, who travel to this southeastern harbor in their swift vessels, hugging the coast to avoid pirates and the terrors of the ocean.

The Marsh Hunters of Tabal supplement their income by hunting for caches of scintilla — silvery globes several inches in diameter, which emit a sparkling glow. When removed from the translucent casings which bind them together, scintilla produce a long-lasting and pleasant source of illumination. These unique items are valued at up to 100 gold lumens apiece, but are difficult to come by. Scintilla are actually the eggs of water raknids, which infest the marshlands around Tabal in numbers...and bear a distinct hatred for poachers.

Jhangkin is situated on the banks of the western fork of the Axis River, and is a military installation where Jhangaran Mercenaries gather while awaiting their next assignments. The swamps around Jhangkin abound with water raknids, marsh striders, batranc, and bog devils, and are entered only at risk.

Beyond this village lies Jhangkin Bay, an irregularly-formed waterway in which deposits of silt and sediment have accumulated over the course of many thousands of years. The sludge and quicksands render the waters unsafe except for the smallest and lightest of ships. Only the flat-bottomed Arduan barge-forts are able to ply these waters safely, but the appearance of such vessels so far to the south is a rare circumstance.

The Septenarial Concordance

The Jhangaran tribes, despite their differences, are of one mind concerning the subject of the Septenarial Concordance. This peculiar event occurs once in every seven months, when all seven of Talislanta's moons align themselves in the evening sky.

The Concordance remains in alignment for 14 days, during which time no citizen of Jhangara will dare to venture forth into the swamps at night. The marsh dwellers claim that the Horag, a monster of immense proportions, stalks the swamps during the Concordance, searching for man-like victims. Though no native has ever claimed to have seen the Horag, their belief in this legendary creature is quite unshakeable — during such times, tribesmen accidentally caught in the swamps after suns-set have reportedly slit their own throats, rather than face the terror of this fearsome monster.

MOG

A vast swampland, Mog is crisscrossed by countless small tributaries of the Axis River. Travel on foot is impractical, and recommended only to those who possess an unreasoning fondness for wading in knee-deep, murky waters.

The swamps teem with a variety of unusual plants and animals. Morphius, a parasitic plant whose blossoms emit a sleep-inducing fragrance, grows among the branches of certain trees; as does serpentvine, an obnoxious, biting species of vegetation which subsists on small birds and reptiles. Deadman, whose pale white leaves exude a deadly contact poison, is of use in deterring wood whisps and flits, both of which are a great nuisance to travelers. Patches of k'tallah and black lotus, herbs which possess extreme hallucinogenic and mind-altering properties, are highly sought for by dealers in contraband goods.

Cave bats, giant leeches, and lurkers (swamp demons) are all found in the swamplands. By far the most unusual creature to inhabit Mog, however, is the rare and exotic gold beetle. The insect feeds on tiny bits of gold washed down the Axis River. In time, its wings and carapace begin to take on a golden lustre; by adulthood, its entire body has been transmuted to gold of the purest sort. Gold beetles are highly treasured as pets by wealthy Zandir and Quan. Fine specimens bring as much as 2,000 gold lumens each, such is their rare beauty.

The amber wasp, a pestiferous relative of the gold beetle, also inhabits the swamps. As its sting is quite painful, it is sought after with considerably less vigor than its more benign counterpart.

Explorers and entrepreneurs who venture into this realm generally do so in flat-bottomed boats, the gnarled roots of giant bombo trees serving as suitable anchorages for this type of craft. The region's primary asset is amber, which is a lure to freetraders, prospectors and opportunists from Zandu, Arim, and the Seven Kingdoms.

The Mogroth

Of the intelligent species native to this region, the Mogroth are the most common. Huge, sloth-like beings of man-like form, they live in rude huts erected in the branches of large mung-berry trees. Mogroth subsist on the remarkably bitter leaves and fruit of these trees, which are shunned by other creatures; the swamp-dwellers maintain that only those of refined tastes are capable of appreciating the mung tree's distinctive savor.

Mogroth dredging for amber.

Customs

Mogroth are slow-moving creatures of placid temperament. They almost never argue among themselves, and are patient to a fault — Mogroth have been known to sit for days waiting for a single cluster of green mung-berries to ripen, rather than search for other provender.

The swamp dwellers live in communal groups composed of their large extended families: silver-backed elders, mature adults with brown- or buff-colored fur, and tawny-hued offspring. The young cling to their mothers until age two, after which they are too large to carry. Each family has its own tree-hut, and gathers its own food. When too many families congregate in a single area, several wander off to establish a new settlement.

Though Mogroth generally shun the ways of civilized peoples, some have taken to dredging the swamps for bits of gold and amber, which they trade for casks of grog. The most ambitious of these creatures sometimes travel to Jhangara or the Seven Kingdoms, bearing sacks of gold and amber. Slow and somewhat dull-witted by nature, the swamp dwellers seldom strike a hard bargain for their wares, a fact which draws unscrupulous merchants to them like whisps to nectar.

The Amber River

This waterway runs from the Cinnabar Mountains to Rogue's Bay in the Azure Ocean. The river is rich in deposits of costly amber crystal, but its currents are inhabited by skalanx, chang, and other hostile and predatory organisms.

The river has its source in the crimson-peaked *Cinnabar Mountains*, which extend across northern Mog and serve as a natural border between the Seven Kingdoms and the swamplands. Kite-winged batranc can be seen gliding among the upper altitudes. A fleet of six Phantasian windships is thought to have crashed here enroute to Cymril, but the wrecks — along with their precious cargo of dream essence and magical paraphernalia — have never been located.

South of the peaks, the river flows into the *Boglands*, the murky home of bog devils, aramatus and similarly unpleasant entities, and where the Mogroth come to gather mung berries. The Ardua of Vardune claim that a rare variety of lotus grows in this region, the blossoms of which are golden amber in color. Supposedly created by the fabled magician Viridian, the plant is said to have arcane properties, the details of which remain unknown.

The largest of the Mogroth settlements is located here, since the Boglands are rich in amber, rare herbs, and gold washed down from the mountains. Consequently, the site is also coveted by the Imrians and the Farad; to protect themselves, the Mogroth have dredged a moat around the village of *Mogran*, and have lined the riverbanks with triple rows of sharp wooden stakes. These precautions have thus far served to deter invaders, as has the presence of the Tazian fly — an insect whose bite is said to cause swamp fever.

As the Amber River draws to the ocean, it pours through a channel between the *Mountains of Mog*. The heights are draped in jungle, and shrouded in fragrant green mists exuded by giant blossoms known as euphorica. The pollen is a potent intoxicant and mood enhancer, and commonly sells for upward of 75 gold lumens per dram — a single euphorica blossom may contain as much as four drams of pollen.

Individuals hoping to make their fortune sometimes brave these jungles, but the presence of batranc, ravengers, and other noxious predators makes this a difficult undertaking. This is to say nothing of the euphorica itself, which the Mogroth refer to as "mantrap." More than one hunter has been lured to his death by the intoxicating vapors, which draw victims near in order that they may be swallowed whole.

The Swamps

Besides the Boglands, there are four other swamplands of special interest in Mog. To the west, *Devil's Swamp* is rich in amber, quaga, and exotic forms of plant life. Unfortunately, it is also the domain of bog devils, which come here to hunt swamp demons and to search for water-raknid eggs (a delicacy amongst the devils). The Mogroth who live here congregate in settlements near the mountainous southern peninsula, avoiding the lowlands.

The other three swamps are all in eastern Mog. The sallow-hued swamps of the *Yellow Marshes*, deep in the interior, teem with unusual flora and fauna: amber wasps and gold beetles, sulphur trees, topaz-colored winged vipers, yellow marsh-striders, and many others. All blend into the environs, making it difficult to distinguish a hazard at any kind of distance — a situation presenting certain hazards to incautious explorers.

The *Great Morass*, located to the south along the coast, is a wild and treacherous swampland considered by the Mogroth to be utterly impassable. Individuals who attempt to traverse this region on foot sink swiftly below the murky waters; passage by boat is made impossible by the presence of hordes of skalanx; and kite-winged batranc patrol the skies overhead. The reputed presence of an island of solid amber, situated in the midst of the Morass, is not sufficient to lure sensible entrepreneurs here.

The *Fells*, along the easternmost coast, are arguably the most dangerous and foreboding of Mog's swamps, being inhabited by such menacing entities as swamp demons, alatus and giant mantrap. Dealers in contraband sometimes come here to obtain black lotus and euphorica.

The Coastal Waters

The wide body of water which separates the swamplands of Mog from the Dark Coast is known as the *Gulf of Mog*. The waterway is primarily the province of Imrian slaver-ships, and the vessels of Sea Rogues from the island of Gao-Din. Still, skittish Zandir and Farad captains occasionally brave these waters, always preferring to follow the coastline rather than venture into the open sea. Giant zaratan and skalanx are sometimes spotted in the gulf, and sea demons are not uncommon.

A tiny island, draped in steamy jungle, lies between Mog's southern coast and the isle of Imria. *Mog Island* is said to be a plentiful source of rare and costly herbs, including tantalus, scarlet lotus and k'tallah. The isle is also reputedly a breeding ground for bog devils, which come here in droves to mate, usually during the month of Laeolis.

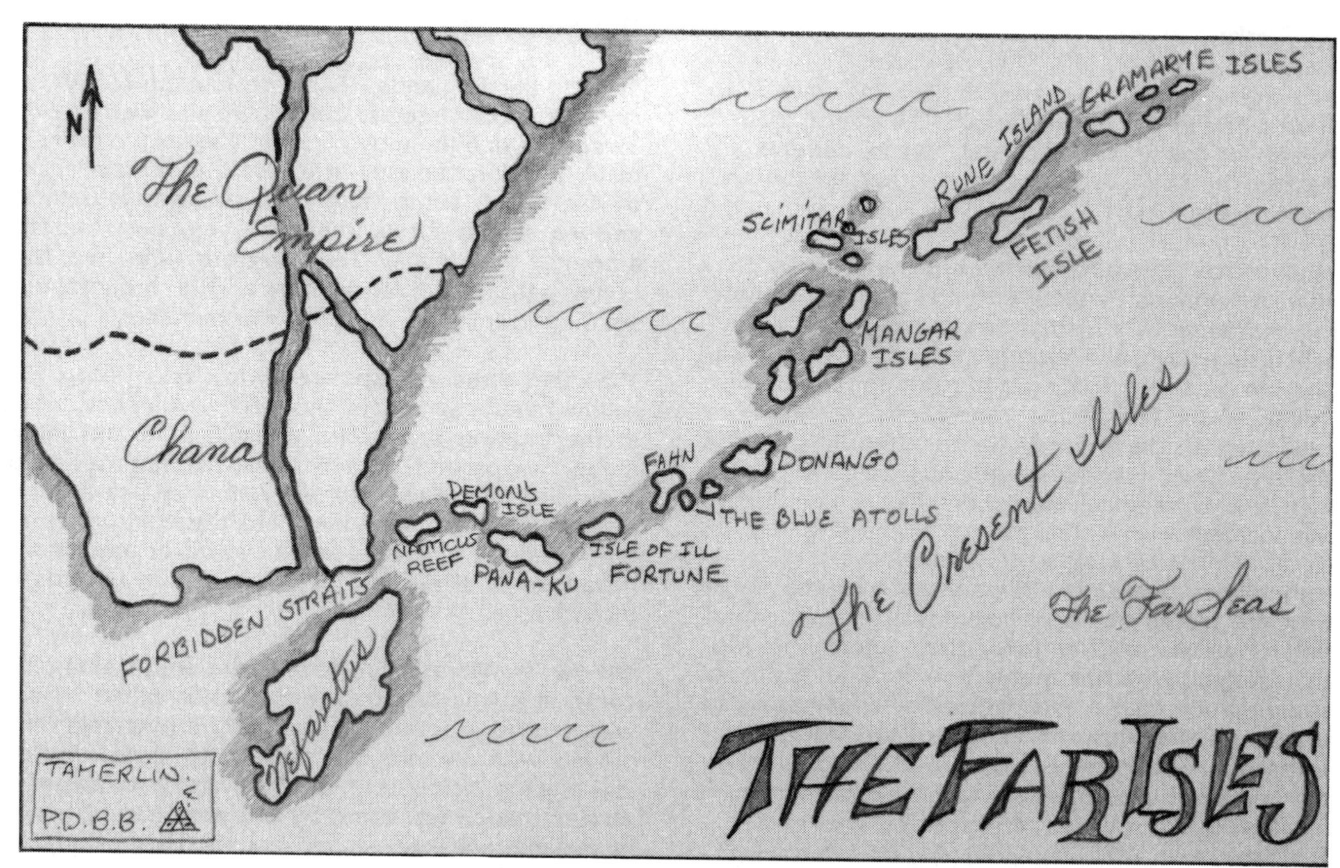

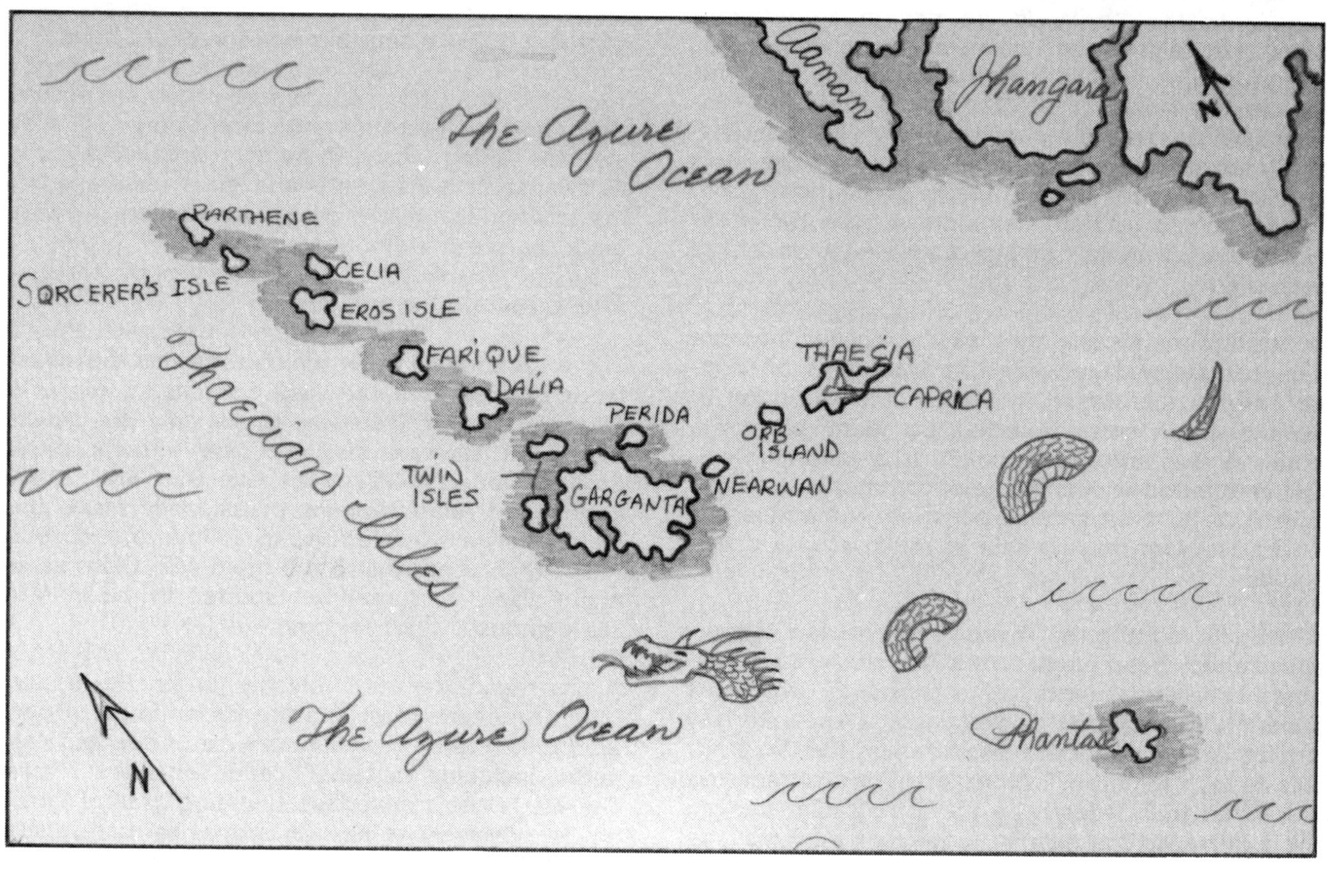

Scale: 1" = 75 miles.

THE CRESCENT ISLES

The stone images of Fetish Isle

The body of water known as the Far Seas stretches across a vast area, from the island of Nefaratus to the northern tip of the Quan peninsula, and from there far to the east. Uncharted at its southern and eastern-most extremes, the Far Seas are often wracked by tropical storms, particularly during the spring months. Giant sea scorpions, sea demons, and other malefic entities are known to infest these waters.

The Crescent Isles are a chain of small islands located in the western reaches of the Far Seas. Small and relatively insignificant atolls, they appear on few maps or sea charts. Some are ages-old coral reefs or mounds of water-worn stone, barely visible above the waves — a hazard to all but the most experienced (or prescient) navigators.

Those islands of note, whether in fact or legend, are (in order from west to east):

Nauticus Reef

This great mass of coral and accumulated detritus was discovered by the ancient mariner Nauticus, whose ship struck the reef while sailing on a cloud-ed, moonless night. Nauticus' vessel went down with its cargo of gold and silver ingots, none of which have ever been recovered. Since that time, Nauticus Reef has claimed an untold number of ships, and the ocean floor around the reef is said to be strewn with sunken treasure. Sea demons and rainbow kra abound in the vicinity, making the re-trieval of such valuables a perilous undertaking.

Pana-Ku

A volcanic isle, Pana-Ku is wreathed in jungle and ringed by a dozen or more reefs and lesser atolls. The isle is home to the Na-Ku, an horrific race of de-monoids — miserable creatures, half-man and half-sea demon.

The Na-Ku are cannibals who feed on the other man-like races. They have indigo-blue skin, yellowish eyes, and gaunt, skull-like visages. Both the males and females are fanged, and have clawed hands, hunched torsos, and serpentine tails. They revere Aberon, whom they believe to be the ruler of all of the demons of Talislanta, and erect massive stone effigies in his honor.

Armed with poison arrows made from the branches of the venomwood tree, the Na-Ku nightly prowl the waters surrounding the Crescent Isles. They prey on man-like beings of all sorts, whom they capture alive to be the main course at grisly feasts held at the base of their isle's largest volcano.

These gory banquets are presided over by the King of the Na-Ku — a giant demonoid, fattened on the living prey fed to him by his vile subjects. It is said that the King sits upon a throne studded with rare black diamonds, though confirmation of this tale would seem an endeavor best suited to those whose thirst for adventure is exceeded only by an utter lack of concern for their personal well-being.

Isle of Ill Fortune

This rock-bound island is believed to be uninhabited. Sailors have long considered the isle to be cursed, though none recall precisely why this should be so. The fact that the waters surrounding the Isle of Ill Fortune are the traditional mating grounds of giant sea scorpions may have something to do with this age-old superstition.

Fahn

A beautiful island, Fahn is considered a veritable paradise by those who have visited here. It is populated by a frail, albino sub-race of Men known as the Sawila. The natives dwell in huts cleverly made of woven vines which, suspended from tall trees, sway gently in the wind. A primitive and peaceful folk, the Sawila wear elaborate costumes of colorful feathers, designed to protect their fair skin from the rays of Talislanta's twin suns. Song, dance and procreation are integral facets of their tranquil culture, which forbids the use of violence for any reason.

The Sawila are preyed upon by the cannibals of Pana-Ku and by slavers from the Isle of Imria. The lovely female albinoids are highly valued as courtesans, and bring as much as 2,000 gold lumens apiece in some lands. The only defenses which the Sawila employ against such threats are their enchanting songs, which possess the ability to effect changes in the weather, tides, wind and — some claim — to have the power to influence various sea creatures. Most scholars consider these songs to be a peculiar and primitive form of elemental magic.

The Demonic King of the Pana-Ku enjoys a grisly feast.

The Blue Atolls

These small islands are composed entirely of a brilliant variety of royal-blue coral. Rainbow kra secure their egg sacs to the numerous small inlets and outcroppings of the atolls, so that their young might find safety from predators until they can mature.

Donango

This seemingly peaceful isle is similar in appearance to Fahn, and in fact, less-than-expert navigators have been known to mistake Donango for its placid counterpart. As the island fairly seethes with hordes of sea demons, such errors seldom go unnoticed for any great length of time. The sea demons of Donango are said to scavenge treasure from the sunken hulks of ancient ships, and to keep the plunder hidden in island caves. Certain adventurous types (most of them lacking in what is commonly referred to as "intelligence") have sometimes been known to come here in the hope of making their fortune.

The Mangar Isles

A cluster of four small islands located in close proximity to one another, the jungled Mangar Isles possess many hidden lagoons and grottos, which are home to numerous small pirate bands, known collectively as the Mangar Corsairs.

Justly renowned as murderers and cut-throats, the Corsairs are the bane of ships that traverse the waters of the Far Seas. There are a number of different pirate bands, all rivals of one another. In lean times they prey on each other, even fighting over potential plunder. The make-up of these bands is quite diverse: Captives freed from Imrian vessels, shanghaied sailors, exiles from foreign lands, and even Chana Witchmen have been found amongst the crews of the dark-skinned, shaven-headed Mangar. Their sleek-hulled carracks are arguably among the swiftest of Talislantan ships.

Like most sensible seafarers, the Corsairs steer clear of Nefaratus, and give the Black Savants' eerie vessels a wide berth. They mark the cannibals of Pana-Ku as enemies, and regard the Sea Rogues of Gao-Din as hated rivals. When not on the hunt, the Mangar favor *ska-wae*, a dangerous game played with curved daggers and dice.

Scimitar Isles

These four small atolls, situated near the perilous Mangar Islands, are thought by most experts to be inhabited only by a few exotic species of wild beasts — including the rare silver draconid, prized by naturalists and collectors, and valued at over 5,000 gold lumens or more.

The Mangar tell tales of a colony of Sunra renegades living in hiding on one of these isles. According to the Corsairs, the Sunra escaped from the Quan Empire in a dragon barque, and now hunt sea dragons as their ancestors did before being conquered by the Quan. Scholars speculate that this story might only be a ruse by the Mangar to divert Quan warships here (away from their regular stations, protecting the sea lanes).

Rune Island

A barren and precipitous mound of volcanic stone, Rune Island is notable primarily for the countless runes and hieroglyphs etched across the entire surface of the rocky isle. Talislantan scholars have long argued over a variety of subjects concerning the isle: the meaning of these cryptic runes, the identity of the individuals or creatures which created them, and their purpose of such beings in undertaking so vast and time-consuming a project.

A thorough study of Rune Island has never been completed, owing to such factors as time, the requisite cost (in labor and materials), and a natural aversion to the less-than-hospitable inhabitants: giant sea scorpions and echinomorphs.

Fetish Island

Scholars of many lands are likewise intrigued by Fetish Island, named for the hundreds of stone images and totems which can purportedly be found in the jungles of its interior region. Most of these artifacts are one or two feet in height, and weigh up to 30 pounds. The cannibalistic Na-Ku of Pana-Ku claim that these stone fetishes have magical properties (specifically, that the totems are "alive," and can speak in all languages), and favor them greatly.

Unfortunately for the future of academic research, the isle is infested with several virulent predatory and parasitic species, including grey ikshada, urthrax and alatus.

Gramarye Isles

These four tiny islands, together constituting the easternmost element of the Crescent Isles chain, are swathed in crimson jungle. Primitive cultists known as the Orad are thought to have once made their home here. The seers and diviners are believed to have been hunted to extinction by a colony of sea scorpions, the only traces of their former existence being the strange paintings found in numerous caves scattered throughout the isles.

NEFARATUS

A Black Savant summons a minor fantasm.

Rising ominously above the waters of the Far Seas is the Isle of Nefaratus, a shadowy mound of black stone rimmed with jungle. Bleak towers of stone dot the isle, each a hundred feet in height and decorated with the graven images of leering devils. Within, the inhabitants of Nefaratus gaze into mirrors of polished obsidian, and work their dire enchantments and divinations. These are the Black Savants, members of a secret magical order that may date back as far as the Forgotten Age.

The Black Savants

Alien in appearance and outward demeanor, the Savants of Nefaratus stand nearly seven feet in height, and are stoop-shouldered and gaunt in appearance — though accurate appraisal of their physical characteristics is difficult, this due to their style of dress.

The true nature of the Black Savants remains unknown. Some Talislantans claim that, beneath their black robes, the Nefaratans are repellant creatures, deathly pale and gnarled in form. The Jaka of Yrmania state emphatically that the Black Savants are not alive, at least not in the same manner as other living creatures. The fabled mystic Hotan claimed to have witnessed what he believed to be the death of a Black Savant:

"The creature, or man, or whatever it was, suddenly reeled backwards; uttering not so much as a whisper, it collapsed, falling soundlessly to the ground. The form within the black robes seemed to wither rapidly, diminishing in size. I approached, to find naught but a pile of smoking, black garments."

The traditional costume of the Black Savants includes high boots, gloves, a cloak, and loose-fitting robes, all of black and satiny cloth, and hooded and veiled so as to obscure their features. Only their dark eyes are normally visible: cold, unfeeling orbs like twin shards of onyx.

The Nefaratans carry staves and blades made of black adamant, a rare alloy which Talislantan alchemists believe to be a union of black diamond and silver. Only the Black Savants know how to make this arcane metal, which reportedly has potent magical properties.

Customs

The Savants are said to claim to be no more than scholars of the occult, with interests which extend to all aspects of the lower planes. Most Talislantan experts, however, believe the sinister race to be diabolists, receiving advice and consul from the race of giant devils known as the Shaitan. Aamanian theologians, on the other hand, believe the Savants to actually be a species of devil.

Korak, the greatest sorcerer of ancient times, wrote of the Black Savants in Volume Nine of his renowned *Guide to the Lower Planes*:

"The Black Savants of Nefaratus are adept in the lore of the dark dimensions, and possess certain knowledge of these regions, particularly the Lower Plane of Oblivion. They employ enchanted devices known as obsidian mirrors, which function as viewports into the nether realms."

Kabros, the self-proclaimed scion of Korak, claimed to have first-hand knowledge of the Black Savants. He wrote a brief monograph on the subject, an excerpt from which follows:

"The Black Savants are survivors of an ancient race whose homeland was ravaged during the Great Disaster. The Nefaratans credit the source of the catastrophe, not to the Mad Wizard Rodinn (as is commonly supposed), but to forces which they believe originated on the lower planes. The Savants claim to monitor activities in these regions as a precautionary practice, but are reluctant to reveal the exact nature of their methodology.

"As to other peculiarities associated with the Savants: the two who came to my home readily admitted to keeping demons as slaves, and expressed a decided preference for the company of devils. Does this in and of itself justify categorizing the Black Savants as an evil race? Perhaps, and perhaps not. Are not each of us, after all, obsessed with our own personal demons?"

The Arch-Devils of Talislanta

Legend has it that the extra-dimensional entities known as the Shaitan once dwelt amidst the heavens, but were cast out by the gods for their scheming and pernicious ways. Consigned to the Lower Plane of Oblivion, the Shaitan were imprisoned within enchanted cities of brass, and given absolute control over that plane and the various devils which exist there.

According to mystics and theologians, only if a Shaitan is summoned by magic can he appear on any other plane of existence. The devils must reward those who give them temporary respite from Oblivion by rendering three services, but unless the summoner is clever and wields certain power, such requests may lead to disaster – Shaitan resent having to serve beings of lesser stature than themselves, and seek to thwart a summoner by twisting the meaning of any command in whatever way suits the devils' perverse nature.

If the Shaitan are in some way allied with the Savants of Nefaratus, it is not clear what their goal could be. The arch-devils are ultimately perverse, and their only known purpose is a negative one: they hate and oppose all demons.

The Black Ships

The Savants' midnight-black vessels are rumored to sail the cursed waters which lie at the edge of the world. Sailors who have encountered such vessels at sea claim that they are propelled by the efforts of demons, chained to the oars with silver shackles and driven on by giant copper-skinned devils. Others claim to have seen the black ships pull into certain Talislantan port cities on moonless nights, only to depart before the coming of dawn.

The Forbidden Straits

The narrow waterway which lies between the Chana peninsula and the island of Nefaratus is largely avoided by Talislantan sailors, and for good reason. It is within the territory claimed by the Black Savants, who patrol these waters in their ominous black-hulled vessels.

The Imrian slavers are rumored to have an arrangement with the Black Savants; in return for captive sea demons, they are supposedly allowed to pass through Nefaratan waters via certain prescribed routes. It is not known whether the Imrians deal with the Black Savants by choice, or because they were somehow compelled to do so.

OCEANUS

A waterborne city, Oceanus was established some centuries ago by wandering tribes of Sea Nomads. The metropolis is built entirely upon great plant-fiber barges tethered to each other in intricate fashion, and has no permanent location.

Though apparatus which allows the city to be moored to the sea-bottom can be employed, Oceanus is most often left to float freely on the waves. Besides increasing the productivity of Oceanus' food-gatherers (fishermen and kelp farmers), the deliberate drifting makes the city impossible to track, and acts as a precaution against roving pirate bands.

The Sea Nomads

The people who built Oceanus are a green-skinned, dark-haired folk of average height and slender build. Their style of dress is best described as eccentric: vests of iridescent scales, loincloths from the hide of the rainbow kra, and necklaces of colorful shells being most popular. Their warriors augment this basic wardrobe with shields of zaratan tortoise-shell and fierce-looking helms made from the skulls of sea demons. The most commonly employed weapons are barbed spears, swords fashioned from the bones of rainbow kra, and the flange-bow (a light crossbow that unleashes a half-dozen sea-anemone spines with a single shot) .

Customs

The Sea Nomads of Oceanus are superstitious to a degree that makes them unique, and perhaps even bizarre. According to their historians, the nomads once dwelt on land, but when a disaster of cataclysmic proportion caused their homeland to sink beneath the waves, the inhabitants were forced to flee in boats.

In their haste, or so the legends claim, the escapees left behind a certain hag named Jezem, noted as a practitioner of black magic. Out of spite, the witch placed a murrain upon her people, that they might never again dwell upon the land without invoking consequences of the most dire sort. Though the nature of these consequences was never specified, the survivors thought it best not to tempt fate by testing the efficacy of the hag's magics. Accordingly, they became nomadic seafarers.

At some later date, the Sea Nomads built Oceanus, deeming this to be a most clever way of foiling the hag's curse. To the present day, no Sea Nomad will set foot on land, believing that to do so would bring down some nameless doom.

An Oceanian Sea Nomad

The Floating City of Oceanus

The city of the Sea Nomads stands as perhaps the ultimate testament in all of Talislantan to an intelligent race's defiance of nature (or of common sense, depending upon one's point of view). Construction of the metropolis, begun some 300 years ago, remains an ongoing process; both to accommodate a growing population, and due to the ravages of wind, water and sea dragons.

The Sea Nomads utilize the ocean's natural resources to suit their needs. Materials used in construction include coral, sponges, the hide and bones of sea dragons and other aquatic creatures, and adhesives derived from the sticky secretions of various species of shellfish.

The primary source of building materials, however, is yellow aqueor, a giant species of kelp which grows to lengths of up to 500 feet. The plant's stalk, cut into sections and dried by exposure to sunlight, takes on a buoyancy and tensile strength similar to wood. The leaves are edible, and the fibrous stems can be used to make rope, parchment, mats, baskets, and even a type of coarse cloth. All of the products derived from yellow aqueor are greatly resistant to rotting and water-logging.

Though incapable of swift or precise movement, Oceanus is capable of movement through the water, and can be steered along a designated course. A great profusion of sails, masts and riggings is employed to give the city impetus. The shoulder-blade of an ancient sea dragon serves as a rudder.

PHANTAS

Cabal Magicus — home of the Phantasians

A small, semi-tropical isle measuring only 30 miles across at its widest point, Phantas is ringed on all sides by wavering cliffs of white stone. Its interior is cloaked in dense jungle, gradually thinning along the upper altitudes. A single river, the slow-moving Erutu, winds its way through the Valley of Dreams to the Azure Ocean.

Phantas is home to an uncountable number of strange plants, animals, fungi, and organisms which defy classification — many of which are to be found nowhere else in Talislanta. The astounding array of flora and fauna occasionally lures a few dedicated scholars and naturalists to the island, who must usually suffer the company of mercenary warriors in order to make safe their journey to this faraway place.

Otherwise, the Isle of Phantas is seldom visited, as its rather isolated location serves as a deterrent to all but the most determined voyagers. The Imrians once invaded the isle, but the slavers fled upon encountering certain of Phantas' bestial population.

High above the island, tethered to the ground by unbreakable chains of adamant, is a singular structure: a great castle built in the clouds, called Cabal Magicus. Here in the sky dwell the last descendants of an ancient race of magicians and thaumaturges, known as the Phantasians.

The Phantasians

A pale-skinned people, the Phantasians are tall and very thin, with delicate features and hair of the color of amber. They dress in long trailing robes, and wear conical caps and necklaces of colored crystals. The Phantasians claim to be descended from the Elande, a race of magicians which supposedly lived in fabulous floating cities during ancient times.

Customs

Believed to once have been amongst the most skilled practitioners of the magical arts, the Phantasians have forgotten nearly all of the fabled knowledge possessed by their ancestors, who built Cabal Magicus and fostered the strange and unusual plant and animal species which populate the island. Among the few secrets left to them are the talents associated with the building of windships, and the art of distilling dream essence. Phantasian Astromancers also continue to be in demand throughout Talislanta as windship pilots and navigators.

It is the ability to concoct dream essence which provides the Phantasians with their livelihood, such as it is. By the utilization of certain ancient magical operations, the mages are able to capture the stuff of which dreams are made, and to contain the distilled fluid in amberglass vials. These the dream merchants pack in velvet-lined chests and transport in their windships to such places as Cymril of the Seven Kingdoms, Thaecia, Zandu, Faradun, and the Quan Empire.

Because dream essence sells for as much as 900 gold lumens per dram, only the wealthiest of individuals can afford to partake of this exotic substance. Many Talislantans consider dream essence to be over-priced and frivolous, especially since it has no practical use whatever.

The dream merchants seldom retain the profits of their wares. Most of their earnings must be used just to keep Cabal Magicus afloat, maintain their windships, and feed their families. Nonetheless, the Phantasians continue to ply their trade, resolute in the pursuit of their dreams.

Cabal Magicus

Built upon a disc-shaped platform measuring approximately one mile in diameter, the castle of the Phantasians is composed of solidified cloud-stuff, covered with a plating of magical quicksilver – perhaps fashioned utilizing the same manner of construction which was used to create such legendary places as the City of the Four Winds. The foundation is over three feet thick, and equally resistant to harm from projectiles, magical energy, and the elements.

The Phantasians have long since forgotten the secret of manufacturing such materials. Now it is all they can do merely to keep Cabal Magicus from descending permanently.

Four great adamant chains anchor Cabal Magicus to the isle below, and channel the harmful energies from lightening and electrical storms to the ground below. A system of wind-powered winches can raise or lower the flying structure as desired, up to a maximum altitude of 2,000 feet. A gondola, suspended by chains from the bottom of the platform, is available for low-altitude reconnaissance.

An observation tower rises from the top of this flying castle, allowing sentinels to keep watch for hundreds of miles in all directions; smaller towers mount catapults and fire-throwers, and would be used to defend the flying fortress if it were attacked.

Cabal Magicus is defended by the Guardians, an elite military order which has been in existence for untold generations. However, the decline in the fortunes of the Phantasians has led many of the Guardians to seek employment elsewhere as mercenaries. The Wizard King of Cymril maintains a contingent of Phantasian Guards (on his personal windship), as do certain private concerns in both Cymril and the City-state of Hadj.

Inside the hollow interior of the castle are vast storage areas, facilities for recycling garbage and waste products, giant levitationals, and an immense gyroscopic mechanism which helps keep Cabal Magicus hovering at an even pitch. Fin-shaped apparatus on the exterior also work to maintain the castle's stability, and can be adjusted to take advantage of the prevailing winds.

Cabal Magicus was designed to be entirely self-sufficient. The same wind funnels which supply power to the winches also separate moisture from the air, providing the floating castle with an ample supply of fresh water.

The wind is also thaumaturgically captured in the form of wind crystals, which are then used to provide arcane power for such devices as gyroscopes and levitationals. An abundance of hybrid fruits, vegetables and herbs is grown in glass-domed gardens.

Some facilities for the construction, repair and docking of windships remain available, but most of the docks have fallen into a state of disrepair. Though the early Phantasians commanded a great fleet of wind vessels, it is doubtful if their descendants have more than a hundred windships in good working order.

Among these are perhaps two dozen warships, plated with magical quicksilver and armed with catapults, incendiary spheres, and rams. These vessels are always kept in excellent condition, and are ready to respond to any attack by forces hostile to the Phantasians.

This attention to military concerns is considered curious by some, for the people of Phantas have no known enemies, and are not normally inclined to warlike behavior. One possible explanation is that the Phantasians fear a reemergence of the Baratus – fierce raiders of the skyways, and dire enemies of the Phantasians' ancient ancestors, the Elandar.

THE THAECIAN ISLES

A visitor to the Isle of Garganta poses a question to a Monolith.

A string of islands situated in the Azure Ocean off the southwestern coast of Talislanta, the Thaecian Isles consist of dozens of islands in a chain, some little more than rocky atolls sprouting tufts of tropical vegetation.

The islands are surrounded by the Azure Ocean, a great expanse of deep-blue water which compasses the whole of the western and southwestern coasts of Talislanta. This ocean is traversed by the ships of many lands, including Zandu, Aaman, Gao-Din, Imria, Parthene, and Faradun. Sea dragons are not unknown in its currents, and storm demons may be encountered in these waters, particularly during the months of the spring and fall.

Thaecia

The island after which the group is named, Thaecia is a place of rare and splendorous beauty, located at the far-eastern tip of the island string. Here, shimmering waterfalls cascade into shaded lagoons, and fields are filled with flowers swaying in the warm ocean breezes. Myriad species of avir songsters fill the air with subtle melodic variations. To the west,

the other Thaecian Isles curve northwestward in a graceful arc. Visitors from all of the Talislantan races and nationalities are welcomed here, provided they come in peace.

The island is home to an advanced and prosperous people known as the Thaecians. Slender and graceful in stature, they have silvery complexions and hair of a deep shade of blue. Like the Muses of Astar, to whom they may be related, the Thaecians dress in diaphanous robes, and show an aversion to hard work of any sort. They are partial to the nectar of rainbow lotus flowers, a secret distillation of which is used to create "Thaecian nectar," a drink noted for its exhilarating properties.

Thaecian Customs

Renowned throughout Talislanta for their hedonistic appetites, the Thaecians are devout pleasure-seekers who enjoy indulging in all manner of stimulating pastimes. The drinking of Thaecian nectar, the consumption of rare delicacies, and the pursuit of various romantic confluxes occupy much of the Thaecians' leisure hours.

When not relaxing in this manner, each Thaecian practices an art or craft of some sort. Some are weavers of gossamer, and others create the scintillant spheres of amberglass called Thaecian Orbs. These items and others the natives sell to traders at substantial prices, or proffer as gifts to the most respected of their people.

The island's enchanters and enchantresses are highly regarded for the wondrous images and illusions which they confine within glassine Thaecian Orbs. By placing these devices to the forehead, the holder is able to experience unequaled panoramas of color and sound. The Thaecians are also able to store spells within these spheres, which can be released by breaking the orb. The enchanters are also skilled in the making of philtres, powders, rare fragrances, and vivid-colored inks, all of which possess fascinating magical properties.

The Thaecians have no army or navy, and in fact disdain violence, which they consider an over-strenuous form of physical activity. They depend upon their enchanters to protect Thaecia from aggressors, a task that has proven to be well within the capabilities of these potent spell-casters.

The islanders live in elaborate pavilions constructed of translucent gossamer fabric, artfully stretched over frameworks of silken cords. They build no cities, but simply erect pavilions wherever they wish to live. As such, small "colonies" of Thaecians are scattered across the main island and certain of the smaller isles. The sole settlement of noteworthy size is Caprica, which is located along the southern coast of the isle.

The Festival of the Bizarre

An annual Thaecian exhibition of oddities and diversions – the Festival of the Bizarre – is attended by diverse peoples from all over Talislanta. To gain entrance, one must be attired in costume or make-up. Wearers of the most outlandish garb are awarded a silver goblet, entitling them to drink for free while at the Festival.

Multi-colored tents and pavilions litter the festival grounds, each housing some sort of attraction or entertainment: a duel of spell casters for wagers, abominations from the Aberrant Forest, illusory panoramas, romances, sensations, or improbabilities and other things which defy description. The visitor is invited to observe, partake of, or otherwise experience as he or she desires. Rare delicacies from all over the known world are available, as well as more standard fare, at nominal cost.

The climax of the festival is the awards ceremony, where valuable prizes are awarded in several cate-gories. For those entries judged to be the "Most Unique," "Most Provocative" and "Most Absurd," the prize is 10,000 gold lumens. The final category, appropriately entitled "Most Bizarre," carries with it a prize of 100,000 gold lumens. A committee of twelve Thaecian enchanters judges the entries, registering varying degrees of approval or disapproval by means of magically exaggerated facial expressions and gestures.

Orb Island

This isle is uninhabited save for such noxious entities as water raknids and the spawn of giant sea scorpions. A rare and exotic variety of crystal dendron grows here, the globular "fruit" of which is employed in the making of the finest Thaecian Orbs. Thaecian enchanters commonly offer up to 50 gold lumens apiece for these crystalline objects, which they are understandably somewhat reluctant to gather for themselves.

Nearwan

This small tropical isle has traditionally been a place of exile for individuals convicted of crimes in Thaecia, including thieves, interlopers, and individuals rendered insane as a result of dabbling in unsafe magical practices. Thaecia claims Nearwan, and has declared the isle off-limits to outsiders.

There are perhaps 40 criminals consigned to Nearwan at any given time, each imprisoned in a web of perdurable force 100 feet in diameter. The convicts subsist on fruits and vegetables, which the exiles are allowed to grow within their enchanted prisons. Thaecians assigned to monitor these pariahs check the facilities daily, either by windrigger or in person.

Garganta

Largest of the Thaecian Isles, Garganta is a great and irregular mound of volcanic rock. Here live the gigantic stone beings known as Monoliths, who some experts believe to be the most ancient living creatures in the known world.

Generally silent and implacable, Monoliths can sometimes be persuaded to reveal a portion of their knowledge, which is said to be quite comprehensive. Normally a period of several days or even weeks is required before a Monolith will deign to respond to any query; less, if the Monolith is one of the few demented sorts who are occasioned to acts of violence. As fewer than one in five of the Monoliths is predisposed to such irrational behavior, the chances of attaining enlightenment at little cost are fairly good. The traveler should beware of wind demons, however, which come here to mate during certain times of the year.

Peridia

A small and rocky isle, Peridia would be of little interest if not for its massive subterranean grotto, known as Caverncliff. Accessible only by means of an underwater entrance, this cavern is adorned with spectacular ceilings which glitter with encrusted gems and crystals. Climbing the slick and jagged walls is a difficult task, and the rumored presence of sea demons has given many entrepreneurs pause to consider another means of attaining affluence.

Twin Islands

These two rocky isles lie off the north coast of Garganta. Each is actually an ages-old Monolith, worn and weathered by untold centuries of wind and water. On rare occasions, the two can be heard conversing with each other, their rumbling voices carrying for many miles in all directions.

It is said that one of these two Monoliths can utter nothing but the truth, while the other — a deviant sort — speaks only lies. Opinions differ as to which one is which, as neither of the two behemoths is particularly talkative, or cooperative with idle visitors.

Dalia

Like so many of the Thaecian Islands, Dalia is a place of scenic and peaceful vistas. Of particular note are a series of bluffs overlooking the ocean, located on the isle's western coast: the view at suns-set is said to be unsurpassed anywhere in the known world. Unfortunately, the occasional presence of neurovores (or "brain leeches," as these small, winged parasites are sometimes termed) can detract from the visitor's appreciation of nature's wonders.

Farique

There is an enchanted fountain on this mystical island, high atop a peak surrounded by dense jungle, the waters of which are purported to confer continued youth and longevity. A single ounce of the "Waters of Farique" sells for as much as 500 gold lumens in some lands, but is difficult to obtain; the fountain emits but a trickle of liquid, and the dense jungles of the isle are rife with ravengers, aramatus and water raknids.

Eros Isle

This sylvan atoll is one of the most beautiful islands in the Azure Ocean. A hedonistic cult of violet-skinned Men, the Thiasians (not to be confused with the Thaecians) live here in fanciful dwellings constructed of woven vines, shells and bits of colored coral. The natives enjoy merry-making of all kinds, and are especially fond of their pets — quaal, dractyl, and the like. The Thiasians are extroverted, and justly renowned for their exotic dances and other colorful performances. However, they lack interest in most practical matters.

As both male and female Thiasians are exceptionally attractive, they are greatly favored as consorts. The islanders have often been victimized by Imrian slavers, who seek to capture Thiasians for sale in Faradun or the Quan Empire.

Cella

This pleasant tropical isle is reputed to be home to a Thaecian temptress known only as the Enchantress of the Shoals. Reliable reports verify the potency of her magics, which are perhaps the most efficacious in the region. It is said that the Enchantress will grant a wish in return for a favor. The nature of the favor required by the Enchantress is, alas, a matter impossible to determine short of inquiry in person at her manse.

Sorcerer's Isle

This insignificant-seeming island has long been avoided, due to its proximity to the far-western isle of Parthene. It is here that the fabled Kabros, sorcerer-king of ancient Phaedra, is purported to have settled following his hasty departure from that strife-torn land. A few eccentric Talislantan scholars maintain that Kabros lives here to the present day, in an enchanted castle of his own making.

Parthene

Here, at the furthest stretch of the Thaecian Isles, dwell the mysterious beings known as the Parthenians — a metallic-skinned race of seafarers, of whom little is known. The Parthenians are rumored to sail the unknown waters which are beyond sight of the coasts of Talislanta, across regions which many scholars believe lie at the very edge of the world.

Aloof and untalkative by nature, the Parthenians refuse to discuss such matters under any circumstances. Their strange sailing vessels, fashioned in the form of giant idols, are occasionally known to stop in such ports as Zir (in Zandu), Tarun (Faradun), Caprica (Thaecia), Tian (the Quan Empire), Oceanus, and — according to some reports — a mysterious anchorage on the island of Nefaratus.

The Parthenians are said to offer no wares for trade, but put into foreign ports only to obtain provisions and supplies, which they pay for in five-pound ingots of gold and silver.

Scale: 1" = 75 miles.

ALCEDON

The Flying Continent of Alcedon

Alcedon is a large landmass which floats some 10,000 feet above the surface of the world of Archaeus. It follows no set orbit, but travels at random on the winds, held aloft by aberrant magical forces. The floating continent encompasses an area little more than 300 miles in diameter at the widest point, and includes the ancient ocean bed which supports the Sea of Dread.

History

Prior to the Great Disaster, the territories which comprise Alcedon were contiguous with the continent of Talislanta, and were part of the Kingdom of Elande (in the region known to Talislantans of the New Age as the Sinking Land). The rulers of the kingdom were the Elandar, a cabal of Archaean magicians renowned for their knowledge of windships and levitationals.

When they divined the impending Disaster, the Elandar fled south in their windships, leaving behind their flying metropolis (the City of the Four Winds) and abandoning those who had served them — including various neomorphs, servitors and individuals of lesser status. Only one of the Elandar chose to stay — the magician Archimandias, who took pity on those who had been left to die, and helped them to escape the drifting city.

When the Disaster struck, much of the Kingdom of Elande was torn loose from the Talislantan continent, and hurled into the clouds. Here it remained, arcanely suspended high above the surface of the world of Archaeus.

Many of the former servitors of the Archaeans perished in the cataclysm. Those who survived followed Archimandias to the east, searching for a new home. After a long and harrowing ordeal, they came to a line of cliffs overlooking a dark, foreboding sea.

The magician cast a divination, determining that passage across the waters was infeasible — nothing lay beyond save the end of the world. From this, Archimandias concluded that Archaeus had been destroyed, except for this small portion of land and sea. Informed of these findings, the mage's followers decided to travel no further. They erected a shelter of stone and mortar which came to be known as Sanctum. In memory of days gone by, they named the land Alcedon (meaning: "halcyon").

The Present Age

Obscured by a dense layer of clouds, Alcedon cannot be discerned from the world below. Talislantans of the New Age know nothing of the mobile continent, though reported sightings of the *City of Four Winds* are no doubt based upon chance sightings of Alcedon by windship pilots. (The abandoned Archaean citystate was no doubt destroyed during the Great Disaster.) Nor are the denizens of this continent aware that a world lies beyond the clouds which encircle their domain.

Sanctum

Originally a modest stone fortification, the sanctuary of the escaped servitors has become a gigantic castle which stands over 2,000 feet in height. It is composed of hundreds of towers, turrets, domes, spires, and cupolas, connected one to the other by networks of passageways, stairs and walkways. Constructed over thousands of years, the edifice ex-

hibits a baffling variety of styles, reflecting the changing tastes of generations of engineers. The interior is dark and gloomy, with the sole illumination provided by racks of tapers and flambeaux.

Castle Sanctum is divided into a hundred levels, built one atop the other by successive generations of Alcedians (as the former servitors now call themselves). Each level houses a single Guildclan, and includes quarters for extended families, work areas, training areas, and storage facilities. Stairways, wagon ramps and vertical shafts (for winch-operated cargo lifts) provide access from one level to another.

Laws and Customs

The Alcedians are a conservative folk, governed by age-old customs and superstitions. They abide by a set of laws and traditions posited by Archimandias, whom they credit with saving them from destruction during the Great Disaster. These strictures, known collectively as the *Archaean Pandects,* form the ba-

Castle Sanctum.

sis of Alcedian thought and culture. Scripted upon 100 stone tablets, the original Pandects are stored in the castle archives, where they have lain undisturbed for thousands of years.

Among the many entries listed in the Pandects:

"The Kingdom of Elande was destroyed by the Great Disaster, along with all the rest of the Archaean world except for Alcedon."

"The world is flat — a great disk suspended in the void. Those who travel too far in any direction risk falling off the edge of the world."

(This *is* essentially true, at least from the Alcedian perspective.)

"The only known place of safety in all of Alcedon is Sanctum. To venture beyond the walls of Sanctum is to risk death."

"The lands which lie to the west of Sanctum are haunted by the ghosts of those who perished in the Great Disaster."

"All Alcedians are prohibited from practicing more than a single skill, to ensure that every inhabitant of Sanctum will always have a job and a purpose."

(In practice, this has led to the evolution of what is perhaps the most unusual facet of Alcedian society — the Guildclans.)

"The construction or use of windships is proscribed, as voyagers in such craft risk sailing off the edge of the world. The windship is to be remembered as a symbol of the cowardice and treachery of the ancient Elandar."

The Guildclans

Alcedian society is fragmented into numerous groups called Guildclans, each of which specializes in a single field of expertise. Each clan is composed of members of a unique sub-race, superbly equipped both mentally and physically for the tasks which they are born to pursue.

Generations of intra-clan breeding have led to the evolution of ever more specialized physical characteristics. Thus, members of the Porter Guildclan have become permanently stooped in a lifting posture, the Indagators (spies) have developed new organs of vision and hearing, and several of the labor Guildclan races have lost the ability of speech and communicate solely by signs.

A Guildclan consists of a community of small family units. Marriage outside of one's clan is frowned upon, and in many cases would be anatomically absurd — mixed-clan romances are a rarity.

Alcedian Society

Though well-intentioned, Archimandias' Pandects had an unintentionally stifling effect on Alcedian society. Originally fearful of venturing beyond the safety of Sanctum, the Alcedians have become fearful of change in any form. They have no creativity or individual impetus — the Alcedians have lost the ability to adapt. This situation is reinforced by the presence of the Indagators, spies who monitor every action and report all deviant behavior.

Those who question the ancient traditions are ostracized, accused of being non-conformists — a condition generally considered equivalent to lunacy, or worse, heresy. Individuals who fail to adhere to the law as prescribed in the Pandects are subject to imprisonment, execution, or in extreme cases, banishment to the Wastelands.

The Alcedians regard all outsiders with suspicion. Any stranger who would seek sanctuary within the walls of Sanctum must first allow himself to be examined by the Chief Guildmasters, whose duty it is to determine whether he is a carrier of misfortune, ill humors or some other threat. If the Guildmasters rule in his favor, the visitor may be allowed to stay...though the Hierarch always has the final say in matters of this sort.

The Hierarch

The rulers of Sanctum belong to the Administrator Guildclan, whose members are trained in all fields of bureaucratic decision-making. The Chief Guildmaster of the Administrators, known as the Hierarch, is the patriarch of all the Alcedian Guildclans. The Council of Chief Guildmasters acts as his circle of advisors, though it is the Hierarch who wields absolute authority within the precincts of Sanctum.

The Sea of Dread

The largest body of water in Alcedon, the Sea of Dread lies east of Sanctum, and is overlooked from the mainland by sheer rock walls up to 1,200 feet in height. The cliffs are dotted with caves and crevices, which the Pandects claim were once home to a now-extinct race of man-like avians called the Aeriad. Now only creatures such as terrax, dracs and chasm vipers reside in these places.

The Sea of Dread is ringed by an undersea mountain range known as the Archaean Ridge. The waters are named for the terrible creatures — such as giant Rahab — said to dwell within their depths. The Alcedians have a deathly fear of waterborne craft of all sorts, and so have never sailed the Sea of Dread. They believe that any ship which traverses these waters will be propelled to a certain and sudden doom.

According to the Archaean Pandects, the Sea of Dread terminates at *World's Edge* – the end of the world. It is thought by the Alcedians that nothing lies beyond World's Edge except a void, and the mysterious phenomenon known as the Maelstrom.

The Maelstrom

A perpetual storm of swirling blue mists, the Maelstrom lies just beyond World's Edge. Its cause has been attributed to aberrant magical forces unleashed by the Great Disaster, and which (unbeknownst to the Alcedians) have kept their continent airborne for several millenia.

Alcedian Aeromancers claim that the Maelstrom affects weather patterns across the face of the continent, and is the source of all storms and tempests. Archimandias believed that the high-altitude winds made passage by windship highly perilous.

The Unfortunate Isles

This group of small islands lies off the coast of Alcedon, adjacent to the Straits of Ill Fortune (the traditional mating grounds of the legendary Rahab). This proximity is most unfortunate for the isles' inhabitants, who are coveted as food by the newborn monsters. The loud and incessant arguing of a colony of Misanthromorphs – an obnoxious species of avians – acts as a beacon to the predators.

According to the Pandects, the island natives employ only primitive stone tools and weapons, and dwell in rude cliffside dwellings. Strict vegetarians, they feed off seaweed which washes ashore.

The Wastelands

The territories which lie west of Alcedon have been deserted for thousands of years. The region is littered with the stone cairns of Alcedians who died during the exodus east, and the ruins of forgotten civilizations moulder beneath thickets of tangled vegetation. The Alcedians fear this region, believing it to be haunted by the ghosts of lifeforms which perished during the Great Disaster.

The Wastelands are home to a variety of unpleasant plant and animal species, including arbolests, pheroids, stranglevine, and the manx – a creature believed by modern Talislantans to be extinct. Alcedians who have been convicted of breaking the most important proscriptions of the Alcedian Pandects are sometimes banished to the Wastelands, from which none have ever returned.

The Phalanyx Mountains

Situated several hundred miles to the west of Sanctum, the Phalanyx Mountains lie past the farthest edge of the Wastelands. A single trail – the same route by which the ancestors of the Alcedians made their eastward exodus from ruined Elande – is the only passage through this imposing and otherwise impassible barrier.

According to the Pandects, these "peaks" are actually gigantic stone warriors. The giants reportedly were once capable of movement and speech, and acted as the guardians of the Kingdom of Elande.

Located south of the Phalanyx Mountains, the *Uncharted Isles* are thought by the Alcedians to be the heads of additional, submerged stone giants. The location of the isles was discerned by Archimandias, who scryed them magically and recorded them on the most ancient maps of Sanctum – no Alcedian has ever ventured among the isles in person.

The Wilds of Alcedon

This gloomy woodland lies north of the Wastelands, and is composed of misshapen trees capable of moving freely across the land. An evolved form of tanglewood, these deciduous plantforms are incapable of great speed, but possess an evil cunning. They move silently, so subtly that it is nearly impossible to tell that any movement has occurred. Whiplike branches seize any prey which strays too near, drawing it into the upper portion of the tree to be slowly strangled.

The Ruins of Elande

Unbeknownst to the Alcedians, not all of the Kingdom of Elande was destroyed during the Great Disaster. The City of the Four Winds is long gone, but beneath the city in former times stood a second metropolis, the home of the most junior of the Archaeans' servants and minions. The remains of this city are precariously perched at the far-western edge of the flying continent of Alcedon, just beyond the Phalanyx Mountains.

Though still relatively intact, the once-gleaming towers of *Lesser Elande* exhibit the effects of eons of wind and weather. Many of their curved surfaces have been scoured of the plating of chromar which formerly gave them their resplendency, and thus the towers are no longer capable of reflecting the suns' rays in the delicate pageant of light which so enraptured the ancient Archaeans.

Though Lesser Elande is not the equal of the lost City of the Four Winds, the wondrous devices which can be found here would astound modern Talislantans.

The wizard Tamerlin in his tower keep in Castle Sanctum, circa 586 N.A.

Sanctum

Due to the intricacies of Sanctum's three-dimensional laby-rinth, keying a one-view map of the castle in any useful way is impossible. Hence, the map is unnumbered, and the entries which follow have simply been arranged in order from the lowest levels of the structure to the highest.

1) Drudges Guildclan
This guild, quartered here, is responsible for cleaning the halls, stairways, gutters, and animal pens of Sanctum. While these guildsmen are of low status, without their services (and those of the similar Refuse Engineers Guildclan), Sanctum would soon become an unlivable rubbish heap.

2) Peddlers Guildclan
These sellers of trinkets and gewgaws lack the status of the Merchants Guildclan, and so are relegated to these lowly domiciles within the castle. Despite this, Peddlers can be found throughout Sanctum, although they are often ejected from the upper levels.

3) Thief-Takers Guildclan
Members of this guild, whose function is to capture thieves and ne'er-do-wells, are not considered entirely trustworthy by their fellow Alcedians. All the same, other Guildclans do not hesitate to call on the Thief-Takers' services when and if they are victimized.

4) Refuse Engineers Guildclan
These vital but unpopular Guildsmen are responsible for the removal, storage and disposal of garbage. Due to their characteristic odor and grimy clothing, the Refuse Engineers are shunned by other Alcedians.

5) Animal Handlers Guildclan
Individuals who breed, cross-breed, raise, and train animals reside on this level. Hundreds of corrals, pens and cages are located here, as well as an extensive menagerie which draws many visitors from the upper levels.

6) Butchers Guildclan
Alcedians who slaughter animals for food reside here, conveniently close to the pens of the Animal Handlers. The slaughter chambers and blood-disposal channels are marvels of engineering, although few citizens have the stomach to observe these wonders in operation.

7) Warehousers Guildclan
This officious Guildclan is in charge of Sanctum's extensive storage facilities. Guild members maintain copious inventories of items stored and their locations.

8) Tanners Guildclan
Working closely with the Animal Handlers and the Butchers, the Tanners cure and cut hides for all leather goods used within Sanctum. The acrid fumes from this level are so pungent that they sting the eyes and make breathing difficult.

9) Artisans Guildclan
Descendents of those who originally built Sanctum, these craftsmen are skilled in the working of stone, wood and black iron. They are intensely proud of their work, and their handiwork may be seen throughout the castle.

10) Brewers Guildclan
Intoxicants consumed on every level of Sanctum are created here. Extensive storage facilities for grains and other ingredients are located in the outer rooms, while the inside chambers are used for fermentation and distillation.

11) Weaponsmiths Guildclan
This level houses the extensive workshops where bombasts, blades, crossbows, and other weapons are manufactured. The cacophony of the smiths' labors is such that members of this Guildclan can communicate only through elaborate hand gestures and by passing written messages.

12) Armorers Guildclan
The makers of all types of ceremonial and common armor reside here. Only Journeymen and Masters are allowed to wear armor within Sanctum, and each prospective customer's rank must be verified before an order is filled.

13) Hostelers Guildclan
Aside from the Dancers' and Thespians' halls, these inns are the center of Alcedian entertainment. Rank is carefully observed, with the best seats reserved for the Masters.

14) Healers Guildclan
The Alcedians believe these guildsmen to be skilled in the diagnosis of bodily ills; actually, without the cooperation of the Apothecaries Guildclan, the healers are impotent. For many patients, it is a short trip from here to the next level.

15) Morticians Guildclan
This level houses mortuaries and crematoriums, as well as those responsible for the disposal of the dead. Deceased Hierarchs repose here in ornate vaults.

16) Porters Guildclan
Elaborate sedan chairs and palanquins are located adjacent to every major passageway, where the Porters await the opportunity to serve; others of this Guildclan carry baggage from one level to another. Sturdy, squat individuals, Porters justifiably have a reputation for being rather dull.

17) Artificers Guildclan
In the large outer rooms, junior Artificers tend fires for melting the metals used in crafting fine jewelry; elsewhere, a Journeyman assembles the framework of each piece, which is then finished by a Master. The Artificers of Sanctum are very dexterous and have superior close-vision, but are terribly nearsighted. This is one of the most brightly-lit levels of Sanctum, thanks to the Pyromancers Guildclan.

18) Limners Guildclan

Here, all manner of documents, scrolls and texts are illustrated with pictures and designs by the Limners. The inner chambers of this level are where the pungent lacquers, solvents and paint compounds are mixed and stored.

19) Culinarians Guildclan

This level of Sanctum is divided into kitchens, pantries and dining halls. All of the Guildclans dine here – seated according to rank, not by trade.

20) Gladiators Guildclan

An immensely popular coliseum is located here, along with the training grounds of the warriors (male and female) who "perform" within. Opulent barracks house the most successful Gladiators and their families.

21) Myrmidons Guildclan

This level accommodates the warriors responsible for the defense of Sanctum. Myrmidon patrols traverse the castle at regular intervals, ever alert to possible danger.

22) Merchants Guildclan

The elaborate, ostentatious quarters of Sanctum's Merchant Guildclan double as places of business. Masters from every Guildclan may be found here, negotiating deals with the Merchants. The professional middlemen handle all of the trading among the Guildclans – for a sizable fee.

23) Money Lenders Guildclan

These lenders provide the money which finances the Guildclans and allows them to remain in business. They also operate the gambling concessions at the Myrmidon Coliseum. Lucre, a coin fashioned from the curious alloy known as jade-gold, is the official currency of the Alcedians.

24) Toolsmiths Guildclan

Nearly as loud as the Weaponsmiths' quarters, this level of the castle is the home of the Toolsmiths Guildclan, whose members produce all of Sanctum's tools. Most of the area is taken up by a large foundry, where metal brought from subterranean mines is smelted. The remainder of the Toolsmiths' district is comprised of workshops and living quarters. To ensure quality, each Guild member specializes in the creation of only one type of tool.

25) Curio Dealers Guildclan

Many small shops and stalls are found on this level, where oddities, antiques and collectibles are displayed for purchase. The cries of the craftsmen, and the often loud arguments of hagglers disputing with Merchants, makes this level a noisy one. Since Sanctum is a closed society, the discovery and sale of a new relic is a rare event.

26) Draymen Guildclan

This level is devoted to housing the Draymen Guildclan's burden beasts, wagons, and the tools of their trade – tarps, ropes, barrels of axle grease, and spare wheels. Drayage fees are determined by the weight of the cargo, the number of wagons required, and the distance to travel.

27) Glassmiths Guildclan

These quarters are the home of the craftsmen who cut, blow and polish glass. The huge furnaces used to make glass are found in the center chambers, while the small workshops where Masters shape their intricate works are located just beyond the Guildmaster's offices.

28) Potters Guildclan

This level is devoted to the production of fired-clay products. The pottery furnaces are maintained under the careful supervision of the Pyromancers Guildclan, which gets first pick of all products in return for its assistance.

29) Scribes Guildclan

Thousands of warmly-glowing tallows and flambeaux illuminate this level's cavernous scriptorium, where the Scribes – Alcedians skilled in cuneiform and other forms of writing – live and work. Save for the scratching of innumerable quill pens, this level is completely silent.

30) Weavers Guildclan

Hundreds of looms cover the floor of this immense work area, which fills an entire level of the castle. Barriers of cloth delineate storage areas for spindles of thread, bolts of cloth, and other supplies necessary for the creation of rugs and fine cloth; open bins contain the plant fibers (obtained from the Horticulturists Guildclan) from which common cloth is woven. Gold and silver threads, used in ceremonial vestments and burial shrouds, are provided by the Alchemists Guildclan, while the opalescent threads in the investiture garments of each Hierarch come from Crystal Moths in the Animal Handlers' menagerie – gathering sufficient filaments to create a single chasuble takes decades. The Weavers sleep beneath their looms at night.

31) Costumers Guildclan

Closely allied to the Weavers Guildclan, the members of the Costumers Guildmembers produce clothes using the raw cloth provided by the workers on the level below – creating everything from the meanest Drudge's smock to the Hierarch's ceremonial vestments. Costumers have long, dexterous fingers, and excellent near-sight.

32) Locksmiths Guildclan

Skilled in the making and repair of all sorts of locking mechanisms, the members of the Locksmiths Guildclan reside here. A huge iron-bound tome – written in Locksmith code – is kept in the Guildmaster's office, detailing the construction of all of the locks and mechanical traps known to the Alcedians. Locksmith Masters take their oath of office with one hand placed on this massive volume.

33) Gaolers Guildclan

Over 500 cells of varying sizes and types (including special quarters for spell-casters and other troublesome types) grace this level of Sanctum. The degree of comfort offered varies, depending upon the rank of the prisoner and the severity of his crime. The Gaolers – an ugly and brutish subrace, with long, muscular limbs and beady eyes – practice their trade with great relish.

34) Torturers Guildclan

The members of this Guildclan specialize in obtaining information by interrogation and torture. Numerous torture chambers are found on this level, each equipped with a variety of grisly instruments. Other Alcedians — even the Gaolers — avoid this level if at all possible.

35) Executioners Guildclan

Alcedian Executioners — including specialists in such fields as hanging, poisoning, beheading, and other forms of institutional killing — live and work on this level, which is usually the last part of Sanctum that a condemned prisoner sees. The Executioners of Sanctum are noted for their efficiency, and take pride in their work.

36) Tattoo-Makers Guildclan

Body ornamentation is especially popular among the warrior clans and the Courtesans. Each Journeyman and Master Tattoo-Maker has a salon in the outer circle of rooms.

37) Stylists Guildclan

The Alcedians born into this Guildclan are trained in the arts and science of hair care. High-ranking Alcedians come to the Stylists' level to obtain fine wigs and perukes, which denote rank within Sanctum — the higher and more ornate, the higher the position.

38) Litigators Guildclan

Sanctum's legal system (based on the Pandects of Archimandias) is complex in the extreme, as is evidenced by the numerous law books and scrolls which fill the Great Library here. Litigators of all specialties study in the central quarters, and dwell in the outer chambers.

39) Herbalists Guildclan

This part of the castle is crowded with vats, drying racks, and shelves laden with glass jars. Herbs are grown, dried and powdered here by the Herbalists of Sanctum, who cultivate a wide variety of medicinal and culinary herbs.

40) Perfumers Guildclan

Alcedian fragrances are concocted and distilled in these quarters. The Perfumers Guildclan has close relations with the Apothecaries and Herbalists Guildclans.

41) Apothecaries Guildclan

Skilled in the production of purgatives, curatives, hair restoratives, tonics, and other remedies, the Apothecaries of Sanctum are truly masters of their trade. Working according to formulae passed down verbally from one generation to another, the Apothecaries continue to treat the ails and misfortunes of their people.

42) Exorcists Guildclan

Most Alcedians avoid this section of Sanctum out of superstitious dread. It is said that the Exorcists bind spiritforms to their altars as part of the warding which protects the castle from the spirits of the wastes. These guildsmen also dabble in anti-magics, excelling in the removal of curses, mordets and murrains.

43) Theologians Guildclan

Small temples located on this level are dedicated to the ancient deities, including many of those whom modern Talislantans call the "Forgotten Gods" — Bajan the Merciless, Lisilis of the Many Veils, Xrrgh of the Damned, Sarille the Temptress, and so forth. The Theologians are always eager to discuss religious matters, although their conversations tend toward the abstract.

44) Cryptographers Guildclan

Codes, cryptograms, and symbological communication systems are catalogued and stored in this area. The Cryptographers of Sanctum dedicate their lives to the study and the invention of cryptomancies.

45) Indagators Guildclan

The castle is rumored to be riddled with secret passageways, peep-holes, and spy-conduits used by the members of this Guildclan. Locked cabinets on this level contain files on each current or former resident of Sanctum. The Guildmaster possesses the only keys to the central repository, which is known as the Room of High Secrets. Due to the nature of their work, the Indagators are best avoided.

46) Archivists Guildclan

This dimly-lit level is the storehouse of Sanctum's vast collection of ancient books and scrolls. Record retrieval is a haphazard chore, since only the Guild member who cares for a particular section knows what is in it.

47) Artists Guildclan

The works of this Guildclan grace the upper levels of Sanctum. In their studios on this level, Alcedian painters and sculptors practice their trade, monitored by representatives from the Aesthetes Guildclan (see below).

48) Musicians Guildclan

The large concert halls on this level can seat most of the castle's population. Instrumentalists, balladeers and troubadours of Master rank perform here, while Musicians of lesser rank entertain on the Hostelers level.

49) Dancers Guildclan

The Dancers of Sanctum teach, catalogue and preserve the dances of the Archaean Age. Journeymen from the Musicians Guildclan perform for the dancers.

50) Courtesans Guildclan

Trained from birth in the art of seduction, the members of this Guildclan (both males and females) wait on this level to cater to the needs and desires of the other residents of Sanctum. They avoid emotional involvement with clients.

51) Harlequins Guildclan

The fools, jesters and mimes of Sanctum learn their trade in schools on this level. Visitors are discouraged, as the inexpert lampoons performed by apprentice Harlequins might prove offensive. The Guildmaster of the Harlequins is tradiionally one of the few Alcedians admitted into the Hierarch's chambers (the Courtesan Guildmaster is another).

52) Acrobats Guildclan

Jongleurs, tight-rope artists, and tumblers live and train in these quarters. A representative from the Healers Guildclan stands by to treat injuries.

53) Hazarders Guildclan

Sanctum's many betting parlors and houses of chance are found on this level. The Hazarders run the games, and take bets on all manner of contests or business transactions.

54) Horticulturists Guildclan

This region of the castle is the domain of Sanctum's farmers. The castle's food supply is grown in huge liquid-filled vats which almost fill this level. One storage room holds nutrients obtained from the Alchemists Guildclan, waiting to be mixed into the solutions that feed the plants. This Guildclan is also responsible for tending Sanctum's many roof-top and terrace gardens, as well as the mushroom grottos sometimes found between levels.

55) The Vaults of Sanctum

This level contains the treasury vaults of the Hierarch, which are guarded by members of the Myrmidons Guildclan. The relics to be found here – ancient coinage, the account books of Lesser Elande, and other records of monies possessed or owed to the Elandar from before the Great Disaster – are of little practical use to modern Alcedians.

56) Steeplemen Guildclan

Closely allied with the Artisans and Architects Guildclans, the Steeplemen of Sanctum are responsible for maintaining the structural integrity of the castle's expansive roof.

57) Illusionists Guildclan

Members of the Illusionists Guildclan create illusory panoramas for the entertainment of Sanctum's upper classes. The Guildmasters also find the Illusionists useful during the debates of the Council of Guildmasters.

58) Curators Guildclan

The Museum of Lost Archaeus occupies the majority of this level. Hundreds of ancient artifacts – pre-dating the Great Disaster, brought by Archimandias on the exodus east – are stored and catalogued here. Many of the uses and functions ascribed to the items are incorrect or incomplete, the original documentation having long since been lost. The Curators are regarded with awe by most Alcedians.

59) Alchemists Guildclan

Makers of potions, powders and elixirs, the Alchemists reside upon this level. Their workshops are heavily shielded, a precaution against explosions and other mishaps.

60) Architects Guildclan

The extensive suites and studios of this level house the Architects, who are responsible for overseeing the continuing construction and renovation of the castle. Their instructions come from the Hierarch – although technically phrased, the convoluted missives lack all logic. The obedient guildsmen have turned Sanctum into an architectural nightmare.

61) Appraisers Guildclan

This is one of the most richly appointed areas in all Sanctum. These Guild members, for an exorbitant fee, can determine the worth of any individual. It is fashionable among upper-class Alcedians to be appraised by these guildsmen.

62) Thespians Guildclan

Three large theaters take up most of this level. Plays, operas and other dramatic productions – most dating from before the founding of Sanctum – are performed here by the Thespians. The most popular are the twin epics, *The Saga of Archimandias* and *The Cowardice of the Elandar.*

63) Literati Guildclan

Poets, romancers and chroniclers live here, using the comfortable workrooms to write, recite and discuss their works. Nightly readings of poetry and other works are well attended by upper-class Alcedians, particularly when the subject matter is controversial or titillating. However, should a Literati transgress the Pandects, he may find himself in trouble with the Indagators Guildmaster. Brawls between rival sects of poets are not unknown, and often require the intervention of the Myrmidons.

64) Talismancers Guildclan

These guildsmen craft beneficial charms, periapts and fetishes, each designed to avert a specific calamity. Alcedians of every rank wear as many as their Guildmaster allows. It is common practice for Talismancer Masters to ward an area prior to an important event, or after an accident.

65) Sages Guildclan

This quiet level is rarely visited, as the Alcedians find it a dull place. The Sages are renowned for their comprehensive knowledge, and when not questioning the Archivists, spend most of their time engaged in study and reading. Their chambers are well lit and are provided with padded, comfortable furniture. The Sages are eager to share their knowledge with others, and usually cooperate with the Litigators and Adjudicators when a mystery must be solved. The Sage Guildmaster is one of the Hierarch's closest advisors.

66) Venturers Guildclan

The members of this Guildclan are the only citizens of Sanctum permitted to travel beyond the walls of the castle. As such, the Venturers are regarded with a mixture of awe and horror by their fellow Alcedians. The Indagators are particularly vigilant in monitoring this level, and each returning party is questioned at length by the full Council of Guildmasters to ensure that no corruption is brought in from the outside. The Venturers make one expedition each year, under the direct guidance of their Guildmaster.

67) Pyromancers Guildclan

The Pyromancers of Sanctum are responsible for magically maintaining the castle's flambeaux, as well as all hearth and brazier fires. A secondary function of the Guildclan is to extinguish accidental fires, using the appropriate counterspells. Although greatly revered, the fire-mages are also viewed with apprehension by common Alcedians.

68) Hydromancers Guildclan

Responsible for maintaining Sanctum's water supplies, artesian wells, and sewage system, the Hydromancers are mage-engineers. A stylish mural covers the walls of their Great Hall – close inspection reveals it to actually be a diagram of the castle's water system.

69) Geomancers Guildclan

This level is dominated by a colossal model of Sanctum and its environs, used to monitor erosion around the castle. The Guildmaster updates the model annually, after the latest Venturer report. The Geomancers also monitor a magical web which envelopes Sanctum's interior buttresses. Geomancer Masters oversee whatever efforts are required to stabilize the castle.

70) Aeromancers Guildclan

The libraries of the Aeromancers are stacked with tomes of weather information, dating back for several millenia. The Aeromancer Journeymen laboriously create a monthly *Expectation Chart* for the Hydromancers Guildclan, predicting the rainfall according to the data from previous decades.

71) Enchanters Guildclan

These guildsmen are responsible for the creation of such cogent arcane adjuncts as magical swords for the Weaponers Guildclan, singing locks for the Locksmiths Guildclan, and scintillant girdles for the Courtesans, to name but a few of the wonders the Enchanters' workshops produce.

72) Oracles Guildclan

In these small, plushly-appointed chambers, soothsayers, prophets, mantologists, and augurs scry the future for Alcedians of all ranks. This is the only level, aside from the Hierarch's chambers, that is free from being monitored by the Indagators – their spying is discovered too easily by the prescients who dwell here. Whether the Oracles' pronouncements are accurate or even useful is questionable, but their influence on Alcedian society is not. The Oracles Guildmaster is often called to consult with the Hierarch.

73) Dream Readers Guildclan

Members of this Guildclan may be consulted in the privacy of their curtained sleep-chambers. The Dream Readers are skilled in the art of deciphering dreams, and should not at all be confused with those other practitioners of bedroom arts, the Courtesans. Visitors who come to this quiet, dimly-lit level are required to remove their shoes – to be exchanged for the soft-soled slippers handed out by the Journeymen.

74) Adjudicators Guildclan

The Low, Middle and High Courts of Sanctum are found on this level. Myrmidon patrols routinely stop the Scribes, Gaolers, Causidians and Harlequins who pass through this area – anyone lacking the proper paperwork indicating that he has business here will find himself in dire trouble. The Adjudicators are a sequestered Guildclan, in order that they might remain impartial and unbiased. They are the only Alcedians (excluding the Hierarch) who do not venture beyond their assigned level.

75) Aesthetes Guildclan

A showcase of Alcedian artwork, this level gives off such an aura of culture that even the living quarters seem like museums. The Aesthetes are responsible to see that acceptable standards of art, style and fashion are maintained in Castle Sanctum. As such, they are generally accompanied by a great crowd of would-be art critics and fawning devotees. Not surprisingly, few of the Aesthetes possess artistic talent. Hopelessly conservative and provincial, the Aesthetes wield their considerable power without really understanding their function – and an unfavorable decree from this Guildclan could mean the ruination of an artist's career, and result in the destruction of his works.

76) Emissaries Guildclan

The Hierarch seldom answers the petitions of the Guildmasters in person. Instead, his reply is carefully set in writing by his associate Administrators, then sent to the appropriate recipient by a member of this Guildclan. The Emissaries each specialize in a particular Alcedian clan, and pride themselves on knowing the swiftest route by which to deliver their assigned messages.

77) Administrators Guildclan

The level is where the ruling Guildclan of Sanctum maintains its luxurious quarters. All of the bureaucrats, minor officials, ministers, and vice-regents of the castle are members of the Administrators Guildclan. Without these functionaries, nothing can be accomplished in Sanctum.

78) Sycophants Guildclan

Members by birth of the Hierarch's entourage, the Sycophants are found in distressing numbers in their upper level domain. In return for gifts from the various Guildclans, the Sycophants use their influence to attempt to win the Hierarch over to whatever view the gift-giver desires. The quarters of these guildsmen are plush to the point of being decadent, particularly those of the Master Sycophants. Curiously, most members of the Sycophants Guildclan have never even glimpsed the Hierarch, but are satisfied merely to bask in the light of those who are called to consult with Sanctum's ruler.

79) The Hierarch's Chambers

By law, the Hierarch must reside on the uppermost level of Castle Sanctum. Unknown to the general citizenry of the castle, however, is the fact that the palatial chambers of the Hierarch are not the only rooms on this level – here is also found the secret sepulchre of the Alcedians' savior, the magician of ancient Elande, Archimandias.

Millenia ago, when the elderly mage lay on the verge of death, the Master Healers, Alchemists and Artisans of Sanctum thought to devise a means by which the ailing magician could remain with his people forever. Their plan was only partially successful – the great mage never died, but he cannot truly be said to be alive, either. Archimandias now floats in a liquid-filled crystal, forever preserved from decay and the other effects of time.

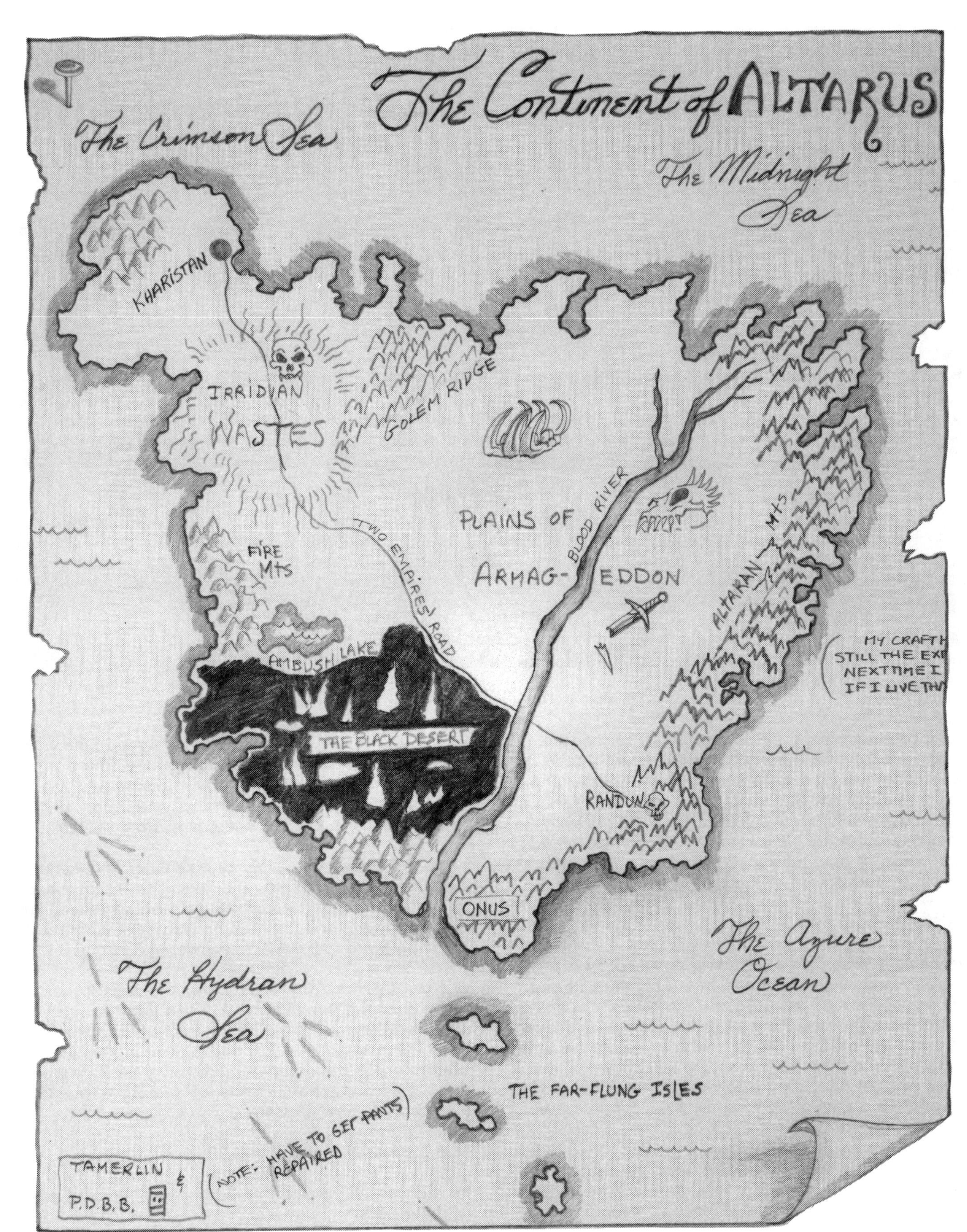

Scale: 1" = 75 miles.

ALTARUS

Vandar Warrior on the Plains of Armageddon

The continent of Altarus is situated far to the west of Talislanta, beyond the waters of the Azure Ocean. Its existence is hinted at in certain Talislantan legends, such as those of the Sunra mariners, but this land has traditionally been confused by scholars with the mythical continent of Alhambra — partly for this reason, little of any substance is known of this distant locale by Talislantans of the New Age.

History

In ancient times, Altarus was the site of two prosperous Archaean communities — *Kharistan,* located to the north, and *Randun,* to the south. Each was ruled by a Sorcerer-King of great abilities and even greater aspirations. When the two rulers became embroiled in a dispute over the affections of a female enchantress, they resolved to settle the matter through the use of surrogates, in accordance with the First Law of the Archaeans.

First, armored warriors were sent to fight, then groups of soldiers, and at last, armies. The conflict escalated to include cavalrymen mounted on arcane steeds, beast-drawn artillery, massive siege engines, and finally, giant golems designed solely for making war. Still locked in a stalemate, the Sorcerer-Kings resorted to ever more destructive methods, sending plagues, murrains and rains of fire down upon one another's forces without surcease.

In the end, the citystates of Kharistan and Randun were reduced to rubble, and their citizens perished. At some point the Sorcerer-Kings also vanished, but whether they died or merely went elsewhere is a question which remains unanswered.

The continent of Altarus is today much as it was at the end of the Surrogates' War — a land ravaged by the effects of over a thousand years of constant warfare. The cities of Randun and Kharistan are piles of rubble where not even a blade of grass can grow, due to the lingering effects of sorcerous plagues, maledictions and firestorms.

The Plains of Armageddon

In the central regions of Altarus, the once-fertile fields are now a vast desert. Here is the charred and blasted battleground known as the Plains of Armageddon, a great expanse of blasted soil littered with shattered siege-engines, discarded weapons and armor, and hunks of twisted metal. Also found here are giant siege and battle golems, some of which are still functional to some degree...and thus, extremely dangerous.

Now little more than a dried-up riverbed, the *Blood River* winds across the plains. During the war, it is said to have run red with the blood of thousands of surrogate warriors. In modern times, the river is choked with dust and subject to flash floods.

Sheets of black rain fall periodically from the sky, covering the plains with layers of soot and ash, and killing any form of greenery which might otherwise grow here. Columns of smoke cast a constant haze over the landscape, which is dotted with craters filled with stagnant water and debris.

Yet even in this scorched and barren land, nature struggles to regain a tenuous foothold, as evidenced by the occasional patch of wireweed, lichen or iron-needle. Fleet-footed terrax — resembling a cross between reptile and rodent — infest the battlefield wreckage by the thousands. Larger creatures such as the spiked arbolest and the scaly-skinned rath are also found here, though with less frequency than the terrax. The fiercest of all who come here, however, are the barbarian Vandar.

The Vandar

The descendents of the arcane warriors employed in the Surrogates' War, the Vandar are a nihilistic and savage folk who have engaged in inter-tribal warfare for countless centuries. The war-clans roam the Plains of Armageddon, searching for enemies to engage in battle — any creatures which venture into their domain are considered fair game.

Customs

Although primitive and warlike by nature, the Vandar abide by certain laws and customs which are instilled in them at birth. Warriors of the same clan never fight among each other, except when a member of the clan wishes to challenge the authority of the Warlord (Vandar chieftain). A combat of this sort always results in a fight to the death, and the victor is recognized as the sole leader of the war-clan...until the next challenge, that is. This process is known among the Vandar as the Law of Succession.

There are over a hundred Vandar war-clans, each with its own battle standard made from hide, bone and metal. Every war-clan marks a portion of the Plains of Armageddon as its territory. Some of the largest and oldest clans include the Reaver Clan, the Dractyl Clan (whose members ride winged dractyl into battle), the Beast Clan, the Dragon Clan, the Demon Clan, and the Rath Clan.

When in its own territory, a war-clan spends much of its time preparing for battle — fashioning weapons, armor and missiles from scrap iron and other materials, gathering rations, repairing damaged battle-golems, and breeding new warriors. At such times, Vandar may trade with the Nomad clans for supplies, or enter into an alliance with another clan.

When a war-clan is ready to do battle, it ventures onto the plains with its standards displayed from its war-towers, siege golems, and mounts. Vandar thus encountered are searching for a fight, and will attack any creatures which cross their path. When two clans meet, the battle lasts until one of the Warlords is slain, at which time the leaderless clan surrenders, and joins forces with the victorious war-clan.

The Vandar utilize numerous engines of war, including armored war-machines, siege engines, catapults which launch rock or incendiary missiles, and a giant device called the bombastion. Some of the larger clans possess battle golems salvaged from the ancient battlefields. While the constructs give a clan a distinct advantage in battle, most of the golems are extremely unreliable due to their age.

The Black Desert

A vast expanse of onyx sand, the Black Desert is broken only by outcroppings of knife-edged obsidian and a few small oases. The dark, wind-swept dunes rise to heights of over 200 feet, forming ever-shifting peaks and valleys of sand. In the daytime, the heat may exceed 120 degrees, but temperatures plunge after suns-set. It seldom rains here more than once or twice a year, but raging sandstorms are all too common.

There are perhaps a dozen oases in the Black Desert, and these provide the only respite from the harsh conditions of this region. Each sanctuary possesses an ancient stone well, a grove of desert palms laden with dates, and a wide variety of thirsty (and often hungry) lifeforms. The Black Desert is inhabited by desert palms, several varieties of unique cacti, rath, sand dragons...and the Altaran Nomads, the only other man-like inhabitants of the savage continent of Altarus.

The Nomads

This race of dark-skinned, man-like beings is of an indistinct origin — they could be the descendents of refugees who fled from Talislanta following the Great Disaster, or the Altaran Nomads may have always dwelt here. Their tribes range far and wide, across the Black Desert and beyond.

The Nomads customarily wrap themselves from head to foot in grey-black linen, a necessary precaution against sandstorms. Owing to the scarcity of water in this region, they have also adopted the practise of "washing" themselves with sand — for this reason, it is difficult to ascertain if the Nomads are truly dark-skinned, or whether their coloration is due to accumulated dust and grime.

Traders by profession, the Nomads of the Black Desert are also scavengers and opportunists at need. They habitually scour the ruins and wastelands for usable pieces of scrap metal, wood, glass, and so on. From these items, the Nomads make many useful products, including excellent blades, a peculiar type of sand-goggle, and a seemingly endless variety of pack-wagons.

The Nomads' eccentric conveyances are bizarre in appearance, each being decorated according to the tastes of its owner. Goods carried in the pack-wagons include sequins, scrap iron, caged beasts, artifacts exhumed from ancient ruins, and — the most precious of all commodities in the desert — water.

There are a dozen different Nomad tribes, ranging in size from a little over a hundred to as many as several thousand individuals. Each tribe is led by a Cara-van Master, whose traditional symbol of authority is an iron staff. Although they are generally friendly to each other, disputes over salvage rights occasionally lead to skirmishes between the trading clans.

A doctrine of strict neutrality is practiced by the Nomads; they trade with anyone who will meet their terms. This should not be misconstrued into a belief that the traders are weak-willed or unwilling to stand for their rights. On the contrary — the tribesmen are all heavily armed, and are ready to fight at a moment's notice.

The Forgotten One

The Nomads are a devoutly religious people who worship a god so ancient that they cannot recall his name — he is referred to only as "The Forgotten One." Followers of the Forgotten One believe that he rewards the faithful among his followers with rich and plentiful salvage, from which the tribe may grow and prosper.

Priests of the Forgotten One are known as Seers. Though they know little true magic, these clerics possess an ability — known as "the Sight" — which allows them to divine the location of water, salvage, and riches of all sorts. Only a handful of individuals

Altaran Nomad at the reins of his pack wagon

in any tribe have this rare power, which is considered to be a sign of favor from the Forgotten One.

A Seer may use the Sight to locate a specific person or place, or any single type of substance (i.e., water, iron, etc.). The person who is to be located must be known by the Seer in order for the Sight to function. The talent then reveals to the Seer the direction in which the person or item is to be found, but no idea of distance is communicated. Furthermore, the indicated direction makes no allowance for intervening terrain, and so may lead toward impassible peaks or treacherous gorges, rather than showing the best and safest (though perhaps circuitous) route.

Kharistan and Randun

The shattered ruins of these once-great citystates serve as a dismal reminder of the folly of war. The sites are nothing more than piles of rubble — the giant siege golems employed by the opposing armies barely left one stone standing upon another.

Both the Nomads and the Vandar keep their distance from these ruins, which they believe still radiate hostile sorcerous and necromantic magics. Evil mists from the dead cities are said to turn their victims deaf and dumb, and the Vandar tell of glowing lights which pursue the unlucky and turn flesh into a soft and pliable mass.

Ancient devices of war, some of sorcerous make, may well remain buried beneath the debris, though no one knows for certain. Also to be found in the ruins, according to the legends of the Nomads, are ancient weapons ensorceled with fabulous enchantments, aerial palanquins and windships of war (imported long ago from ancient Elande), a library of magical tomes, stones which could see and hear, and automatons of various and marvelous types and arcane abilities.

The Mountains of Altarus

Formerly known as the Western Mountains, the *Fire Mountains* were renamed after the peaks caught fire during one of the more brutal battles of the Surrogates' War. The mountains were totally defoliated, and even now are barren of life.

Nearby is the largest source of potable water on the continent of Altarus: *Ambush Lake,* which is fed by crystal-clear streams from the Fire Mountains. Many creatures come here to drink, as do the Vandar warclans — hence the lake's name.

The jagged heights of the *Altaran Mountains* were thrust through the soil by forces unleashed during the Great Disaster. Lichen and mosses are the only types of vegetation to be found on the rocky outcroppings. Raths occasionally venture into this forbidding region to hunt for dracs and other prey. Wind Demons can also be seen among the knifesharp peaks, riding the storm clouds bred by Altarus' sorcerous emanations.

Two Empires' Road

This road anciently connected the citystates of Kharistan and Randun, and was paved with slabs of golden-veined marble. The roadway now lies in ruins — in some places, its massive shards protrude from the earth like rows of teeth; elsewhere, the marble was pounded into dust by rampaging battle golems.

Golem Ridge

The site of a great clash between the forces of ancient Kharistan and Randun, Golem Ridge's battle resulted in a stalemate. The blasted wreckage of hundreds of battle golems — most long since stripped of any salvageable materials — are strewn along the slopes and gullies of the ridgeline, some still frozen in poses of attack or defense.

The Irridian Wastes

During the Surrogates' War, this region was repeatedly blasted by potent magical spells and incantations, and to the present day it has continued to radiate aberrant energies. The entire region glows with a faint red illumination at night, and the hills constantly grind within themselves as if some great movement were occurring in their depths.

It is said that travelers who sleep in this place risk having their minds dispossessed by the restless spiritforms of soldiers who died in the ancient war.

Onus

This far-southern locale within the Black Desert is infested with sand dragons and other predators. The Nomads consider it cursed, and the trading clans therefore avoid it.

The legends of the desert traders tell of a terrible demiurge who lives here in a domus of black glass, with a menagerie of lifeforms from many ages, all of which are held in stasis within enchanted cages of a crystalline material.

The Far-Flung Isles

These islands are rumored to be the domain of several avian species, including ravengers, misanthromorphs, winged demons, and others. It is said that the skies above the Far-Flung Isles echo with the sounds of violent aerial clashes between these predatory avian species.

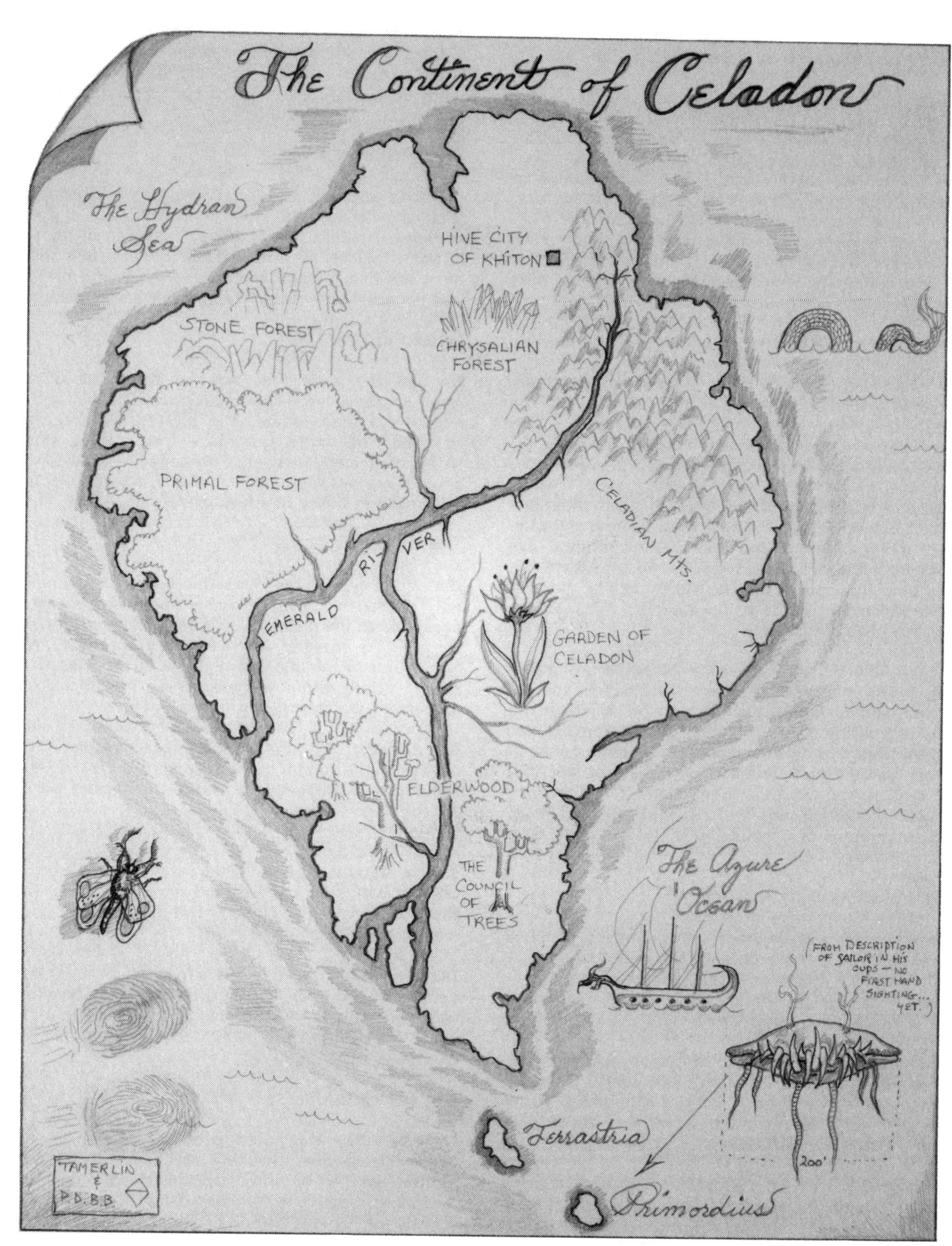

Scale: 1" = 75 miles.

CELADON

The Green Mandarin and his subjects

Celadon is located southeast of Talislanta in the Sea of Madness. The continent is rife with countless varieties of vegetation, from ancient deodars towering over 500 feet in height, to lush gardens overgrown with hanging vines and wildflowers. Thickets of giant thornwood, spiny creepers and giant mantrap dominate much of the land.

Innumerable varieties of insects, avians, and other types of living creatures are found on the continent. Some of the more notable examples include manx, arbolests, silk-wyrrms, and dragon-flies.

History

In ancient times, the Archaeans established a settlement in Celadon, known as *Imperion*. The citizens of the citystate were opportunists and fortune-seekers, interested only in personal gain. They came to cut down the forests for timber, to decimate the herds of wild beasts so that fresh meat might be sold to other lands, and to strip the soil of precious stones and metals. The Great Disaster resulted in the destruction of Imperion, and the demise or displacement of its inhabitants.

In the present age, the continent of Celadon is a veritable paradise which nature has reclaimed from the depredations of the ancient Archaeans. Its forests sweep over hills and vales worn smooth by the passage of time, inundating the ruins of the forgotten civilization in a blanket of greenery.

The Dendrads

Among the most unusual of the lifeforms of this world, the Dendrads appear by day to be plants, rooted in the soil. Yet at night, they undergo a weird metamorphosis. Adopting fantastic man-like and semi-man-like shapes, they uproot themselves and gather together to engage in the strange rituals of the Plant Kingdom.

There are many different sub-species of Dendrads, all of which exhibit a great diversity of colors, shapes and sizes. The more common types include the lovely but vain Purple Narcissus, the mysterious Hooded Mystic, the winged Snap-Dragon, the despondent Weeping Willow, and two musical varieties – the syncopative Cinnabarian Castanetta and the dulcet-toned Wandering Minstrel.

The nominal ruler of this loosely-knit community is the Green Mandarin, an organic entity of unknown origins. His home is a fabulous topiary palace situated in the center of the Garden of Paradise.

The Green Mandarin holds court within the Council of Trees, where he is surrounded and aided by the eldest and wisest of the race of Dendrads. He is said to have no love for the ways of the so-called civilized races, and is swift to exact vengeance upon any who commit crimes against Nature.

All of Celadon's indigenous lifeforms adhere to the Green Mandarin's dictates, and live in harmony with the environment. Even hostile beasts such as the manrak are careful to serve only a useful purpose here, such as to keep the population of an over-abundant species in check.

The Chrysalids

A cross between Man and the insect races, the Chrysalids have inherited certain traits associated with both of these species. It is not known whether the race was deliberately created by the Archaeans through sorcerous hybridization, or whether the natural and arcane processes of evolution are responsible for these aberrant lifeforms.

The Chrysalids have their own language, and are adept at a simple style of cuneiform writing and other talents usually associated with more civilized peoples. Unlike Men, however, Chrysalids enjoy a symbiotic relationship with their environment, and by nature are neither wasteful nor destructive.

The quasi-insectoids live in elaborate hive-cities which resemble great step-pyramids or ziggurats. The Chrysalids have domesticated such species as the snael and the dragon-fly, which they employ as burden beasts and airborne steeds, respectively.

The largest of the Chrysalids' hive-cities is *Khiton*, an immense structure which stands over 200 feet in height. The city is constructed of a fibrous substance composed of fallen leaves and dead bark, chewed into mulch and mixed with a liquid secreted by Chrysalid workers. The material is malleable so long as it remains moist, allowing it to be easily shaped into blocks. When dry, it exhibits great tensile strength, yet is lightweight and extremely durable.

The species' insectoid tendencies are reflected in the structure of their society. Chrysalid colonies are carefully organized, with each individual having a specific function. Heredity, rather than free choice, is the primary factor determining which function a member of the colony will have. Efficiency and cooperation are of primary importance to all members of this species.

The Manrak

A highly aggressive species distantly related to the Chrysalids, the Manrak resemble a hideous cross between Man, demons and raknids. Their social structure is similar to that of the Chrysalids', though it is much less sophisticated and designed primarily for warfare. Manrak hive-colonies are crude fortresses, built of dried mud and daubed into strange and eerie forms – convoluted towers, bridges, ramparts, and machiolations.

The Manrak Queen resides deep within the fortress, protected from her enemies. She is attended by several dozen male consorts, who feed her and assist in removing eggs from the royal chamber. All others in the hive are warriors, whose sole purpose is to annihilate all lifeforms which might be construed as a threat to the propagation of the Manrak species.

The Manrak have waged war on the Chrysalids for centuries, seeking to expand into their territories. To date, their plans have yielded little reward, but have served only to deplete the Manrak population.

Wildernesses of Celadon

Of the forests and gardens of this continent, the following are especially noteworthy:

Once the site of the Archaean settlement of Imperion, the *Chrysalian Forest* has enveloped the city's ruins for many thousands of years. Towering deodars threaten to block out the light of the twin suns, while far below the leafy canopy grow fan-shaped ferns and club-mosses in shades of muted pink, blue-grey and ochre. The Chrysalian Forest is populated by scaly-skinned dragon-flies, giant snaels, and hundred-foot-long mosswyrrms.

The most ancient Dendrads in Celadon, some of whom claim to be old enough to recall the time before the Great Disaster, reside in the grove known as the *Council of Trees*. They converse with each other in hushed tones, speaking in the secret language of plants.

The oldest woodland on this world, *Elderwood* has remained virtually untouched for thousands of years. The dense forest is home to countless varieties of flora, many of which are found only in this primordial forestland.

A riot of color and perfumes assaults the senses in the lush paradise known as the *Garden of Celadon*. Because of a peculiar soothing quality found in the surrounding flora, the creatures which inhabit the area are incapable of offering violence to strangers or one another. Accordingly, a feeling of peace and serenity pervades the garden.

Chrysalids defending the hive-city of Khiton from attack by Manrak.

Everything in the *Primal Forest* grows to immense proportions, including both plants and insects. Chrysalid hunters come here to capture giant dragon-flies and snaels, and to harvest several varieties of giant fungus, some of which are believed to possess magical properties.

The *Stone Forest* is replete with strange growths: shrubs of land-coral, rock-like trees which bear "fruits" of precious stones, and crystalline flowers. Megaliths – elemental entities which resemble animate statues – sometimes come here to muse about days past.

The Celadian Mountains

Erosion has softened the peaks and cut deep valleys in this ancient mountain range, but the Celadian Mountains still appear majestic, draped in their forest robes of greenery. Many species of flora and fauna are found here, particularly species of predatory and ambulatory plants.

The most unusual specimen of flora to inhabit this elderly mountain range may be the Sunstalker, a plant mentioned in the annals of Viridian. This animate bush is said to seek out sunny meadows and clearings amid the woods, whereupon it laps up the light of the suns and plunges the area in darkness.

Viridian never acquired a Celadian Sunstalker, and Talislantan naturalists of the New Age regard tales of the remarkable plant as mere legends.

Emerald River

A swift-moving river of shimmering green water, the Emerald River nourishes the central continent. The river waters are credited by some with wondrous properties – a vial of the green water reportedly makes any plant grow to its full size overnight.

The Southern Islands

Off the southern coast of Celadon, the island of *Terrestria* is populated entirely by para-elementals of earth, stone and mud. The inhabitants are quite young, in elemental terms – perhaps only one or two thousand years old.

The adjacent island, *Primordius*, is not an island at all...he claims to be the oldest Monolith in the world, and may well have existed since the Time Before Time. Sunra legends claim that such a Monolith in the southern seas possesses the answers to mysteries which have puzzled Talislantan scholars for centuries, but the same tales warn that the Monolith takes longer than a single lifetime to give its answer to such questions.

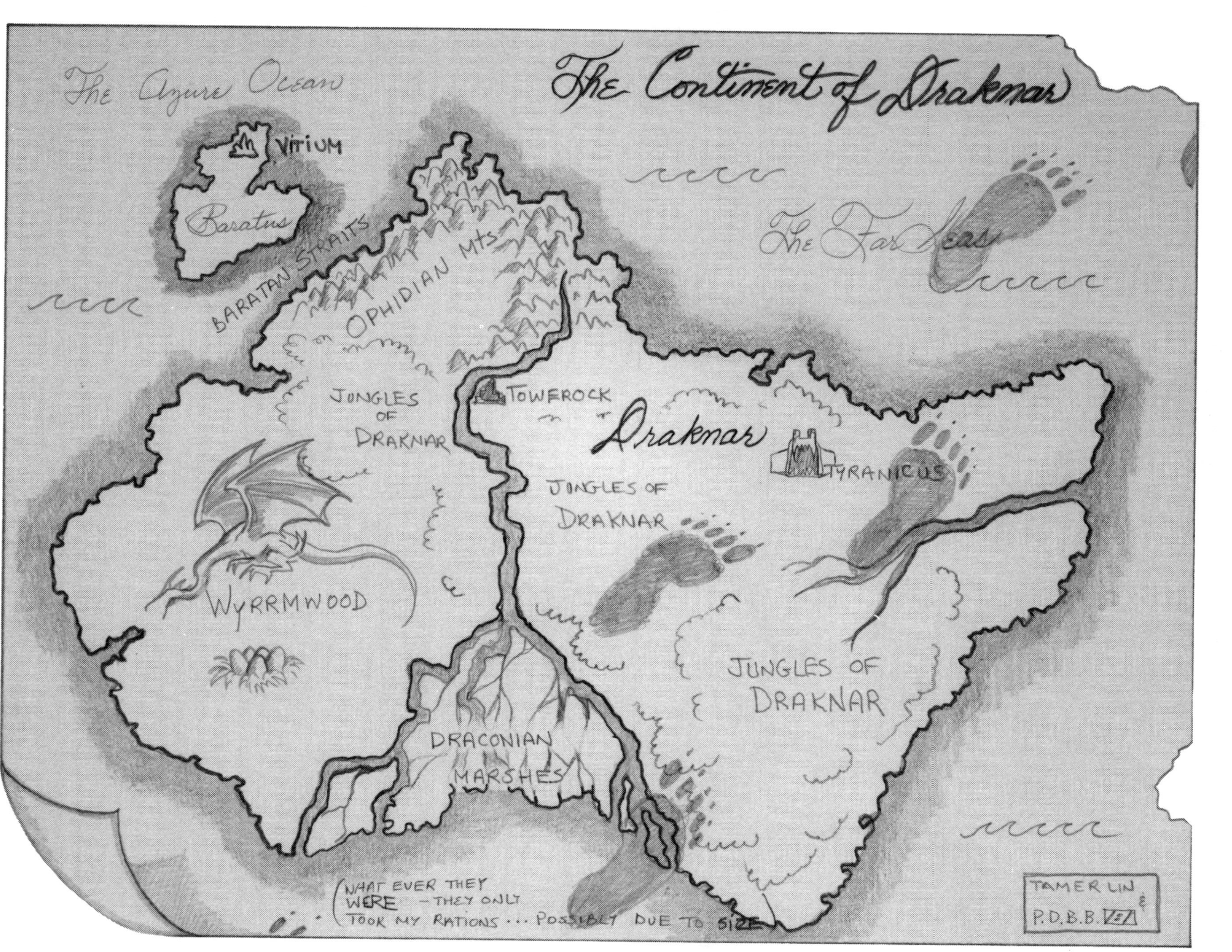

Scale: 1" = 75 miles.

DRAKNAR

Drakken standing guard at Towerock

Draknar is a continent of steaming jungles and swamplands, located far to the south of the continent of Talislanta, in the Far Seas. This land is home to a race of intelligent, reptilian giants .

The Drakken

In ancient times, the giants known as the Drakken were the masters of the Talislantan continent. They built a great empire, erecting such impressive structures as the City of Kharakhan (in the Wilderlands of Zaran, now in ruins), the Watchstone (on the Plains of Golarin), and various other now-ancient megalithic monuments.

The rise of the Archaeans signalled the downfall of these great reptilians. Unable to withstand the powerful magic of the new arrivals, the Drakken were driven south over a now-submerged land bridge, eventually arriving and settling in what is now known as the continent of Draknar.

The Giants of the Kharakhan Wastes of Talislanta are degenerate descendants of the last of the Talislantan Drakken, and it is possible that the Saurans and Sauruds are likewise related to the reptilians. Similarly, the races of dragons may somehow be kin to the Drakken — indeed, the dragons may be the source from which all of the reptilian races sprang.

Drakken Culture

The Drakken are the most intellectually-developed of the reptilian races, being skilled in the making of weapons, armor and stone fortifications, and possessed of a highly-developed language and a complex alphabet.

Their symbology is three-dimensional, and can only be expressed if carved in high relief upon wood, stone or metal. Different meanings are expressed simply by varying the depth at which a symbol is carved. This secret is unknown to Talislantan scholars, which is why they have been unable to interpret the hieroglyphs of the Kharakhan ruins. The Kharakhan Giants have an instinctive understanding of this symbology, but they do not comprehend the full meaning of the ancient writings, or realize what has become of their forefathers.

Drakken are herbivorous hunter-gatherers by nature; they only hunt destructive creatures (such as behemoths) if the animals present a threat to one of their settlements. The reptilians harvest edible plants from the swamps and jungles, transporting the food back to their settlements using young land dragons not yet mature enough to be trained as cavalry steeds.

Though Drakken have domesticated land dragons for use as burden beasts, they consider these slow and ungainly creatures to be of limited use as cavalry beasts. For military mounts, Drakken prefer Crested Dragons, which they capture in the wild and train for use in aerial combat.

These creatures are fierce fighters, but their great weight retards their maneuverability and range (a mere 150 miles, or less if bearing a heavily-armored rider), though they can develop astounding speed in a dive. The relatively rare steeds are also valued for their ornamental appearance, an individual dragon's worth being determined in part according to the color and richness of the creature's scales.

One reason why the Drakken have never attempted to return to Talislanta is the short range of their dragon-steeds. Certain of their breeders have attempted for some time to breed Crested Dragons with greater endurance, but the results have been disappointing to date.

Many of the reptilians are skilled metal workers, able to fashion high-quality weapons, armor, tools, and jewelry. Drakken fabric is woven from plant fibers, and is more functional than ornamental — good fabric is rare and a valued trade item, and the wearing of cloth robes is a sign of status among both male and female Drakken.

The Drakken possess a superstitious loathing of water travel, and know nothing of ship-building.

A Hostile Attitude

Drakken clans trade among each other, and occasionally vie for control of each other's territories. However, the reptilians are united in their hostility toward the race of Men, making no distinction between them and the ancient foes of the Drakken, the Archaeans. The reptilians, who have no talent for magic, are especially contemptuous of magicians and their minions.

The written histories of the Drakken are filled with accounts of the many atrocities performed upon their species by the Archaeans — in fact, the Drakken charge the Archaeans with causing the Great Disaster in an effort to drive their race into extinction. The eldest of the living Drakken are survivors of that catastrophe, and their tales of the ensuing destruction are well known among all of their people.

A Code of Honor

The Drakken have always been a warrior race. Both the males and females receive training in mounted combat — including aerial combat, for those lucky enough to receive dragon-steeds — and the use of siege weapons. Though the reptilians relish battle, they live by a Warriors' Code of Honor which prohibits them from killing vanquished or captured opponents, and forbids acts of wanton violence against non-combatants such as immature young, the very old, or the infirm.

Breaking the Code of Honor brings great shame on the transgressor, even if the victim is a hated foe. For instance, several decades ago, a Drakken warchieftain (Tyranicus) and his followers were banished in disgrace after they slaughtered a group of Zandir sailors (from Talislanta) who were shipwrecked on Draknar.

To the Drakken, the most honorable form of warfare is one-on-one combat — especially dragon-rider versus dragon-rider. Rival clans often engage in aerial duels to settle arguments or territorial disputes.

The Abandoned God

Like the Saurans of Talislanta, the Drakken once worshipped Satha, a reptilian goddess associated with volcanos and fire elementals. In the lore of the reptilians, however, Satha is a Drakken, not a giant dragon as the Talislantan reptilians believe.

The goddess' popularity diminished rapidly after the Drakken were driven out of Talislanta — the Drakken King proclaimed that Satha had forsaken his people. However, shrines dedicated to the diety can still be found in remote areas of Draknar, tended by very elderly and extremely devoted priestesses.

The Fortress of Towerock

The mountain fastness of the Drakken King and his minions is actually the cone of an ancient, inactive volcano. Over the years, the mount has been cunningly shaped into a conical obsidian tower — the walls are 200 feet thick at the narrowest point, and rise to a height of 1,500 feet. The surface is studded with the peculiar three-dimensional glyphs of the reptilian alphabet.

When Towerock's massive doors are closed, the entrance is virtually undetectable. An ingenious arrangement of ramps above the doors allows the defenders to rain stones down upon besieging troops without exposing themselves to danger.

Castle Tyranicus

This jungle fortress is home to the outcast Drakken war-chieftain, Tyranicus, the sworn enemy of the King of Draknar. His castle is built in the likeness of a Crested Dragon, and the main gate consists a set of gaping jaws over 500 feet in height.

Tyranicus has vowed to take possession of Towerock and usurp the throne of the Drakken King. His followers constantly raid the settlements and forts of the loyal Drakken, preceding their acts of belligerence by issuing gouts of smoke from the mouth of Castle Tyranicus.

The rebel war-chieftain has gained a large following by promising to unite the Drakken, then to launch an invasion to retake their ancestral Talislantan homeland — conquering Baratus, then Imria, and finally assaulting the mainland.

Geography of Draknar

The following sites are among the more noteworthy on the continent of Draknar:

The dense, primordial *Draconian Marshes* are inhabited by dangerous predators, both plant and animal. Scarlet sporozoid and violet creeper thrive here, and deadly venin and exomorphs pose a constant danger to hunters and explorers.

The *Ophidian Mountains* rise out of the jungles of Draknar like the blackened bones of a fire-blasted foe. The slopes are shattered lava flows, littered with sharp and treacherous hunks of igneous rock. Howling winds and torrential rains pry away even the most stubborn of plants.

The swift-moving *Ouros River* is fed by tributaries from the Ophidian Mountains. Named for its winding, snake-like appearance, the waterway's color and flow depend upon the time of year: During Ardan and Drome, it is bright yellow and swollen with early rains. By Laeolis, the Ouros is orange and sluggish in the mid-year heat. In Talisande and Zar, the river turns vivid red, and becomes frantic with blood-crazed spawning chang.

Wyrrmwood is an ancient forest inhabited by Crested Dragons. Drakken scouts come here to capture the young wyrrms, which they train for use as aerial steeds. As for the dragons, they seem to view the hunts as an interesting and equal contest.

The Island of Baratus

A rocky isle fringed in jungle, Baratus is an inhospitable place, crawling with alatus, aramatus, vexx, and stranglevine. Submerged reefs, jagged rocks, and creatures such as echinomorphs and sea demons make navigation through the Baratan Straits (between Baratus and Draknar) most treacherous.

Unbeknownst to Talislantans of the New Age, this sub-continent was once the home of the now-legendary Baratus, a race of infamous pirates who roamed the seas and skies of Talislanta prior to the Great Disaster.

An Ancient Menace

A sea-faring race of savage sub-men, the Baratus were the dire enemies of the Archaeans from the earliest days of the arcane empire. The mages finally succeeded in defeating the Baratan tribes, thanks in large part to the invention of the windship (created by the Elandar, the ancestors of the modern-day Phantasians). The surviving barbarians were forced to flee into the unknown waters of the Far Seas.

Fortunately, the Baratus knew of a secret sanctuary — the southern isle which they claimed as their new homeland. Dwelling in these jungles, the sub-men built a city cunningly concealed from magical surveillance: *Vitium*, an impregnable stronghold protected by a dome-shaped web of magical energy, reportedly maintained through the use of a fabulous crystal stolen from the Elandar.

The sub-men had a simple plan: to remain in exile long enough for the Archaeans to forget about them, and then to strike Talislanta in force. The problem which bedeviled the pirate chieftains was how to offset the tremendous advantage which the windships gave their enemies.

Then one day, an Elandar windship lost in a storm made a forced landing in Baratan territories. The sub-men seized the vessel, and used torture to extract the secret of the craft's operation from the captain and crew. Employing the captured windship, the crafty Baratus stealthily captured further windships until they amassed a sizable fleet.

The Rebirth of Piracy

At last, the Baratus struck against their ages-old foe. Their powerful skyfleet ranged far and wide across the Talislantan continent, preying on Archaean shipping, raiding the citystates, and reestablishing the Baratan reputation for ferocity in battle. The Elandar led the Archaean campaign against the airborne marauders, but without notable success, since the Baratan homeland could not be found.

The Baratus – fierce raiders of the skyways

The pirates developed many specialized weapons: arrows with heads designed to cut rigging; a halberd with a blade-and-hook apparatus, used during boarding operations; and various types of long-range harpoons fired from deck-mounted arbolests and siege engines.

The Baratus were similarly innovative in dealing with Talislantans who fell into their hands. The pirates' victims might be killed on the spot, made to walk the plank from a high altitude, or taken captive, all depending on the whim of the Baratan captain and his crew.

To Talislantans of the late Archaean Age, mysterious Vitium was the heart of all that was depraved and evil. The Baratus were said to practice all manner of atrocities against their victims: impaling, boiling in oil, and pressing victims beneath piles of stones. The use of live Elandar captives for aerial archery practice was especially common.

The Fate of the Baratus

Following the Great Disaster, the Baratus disappeared from history – apparently destroyed by the cataclysm. The pirates' last known act was to attack Elandar ships fleeing southward from the City of the Four Winds. The entire Baratan fleet was purportedly brought out for this massive assault, which resulted in the decimation of the Elandar – an act which the Baratan pirates viewed as final revenge against their hated foes.

However, vengeance had its price – the Baratan fleet was most probably destroyed by the savage convulsions of the Great Disaster, before it could return to its secret haven. If this is true, the Baratus who remained in Vitium would have been dealt a severe blow, for the pirates were never able to master the secret of constructing their own windships. Without stolen ships, the pirates would become once more powerless to sail the skies.

The modern descendants of the Elandar, the Astromancers of Phantas, believe that a resurgence of the Baratan threat after all these millenia is well within the realm of possibility. Whenever a windship is reported missing, the Phantasians speculate that the event may be evidence that the Baratus are once again gathering their forces for an attack against their age-old enemies.

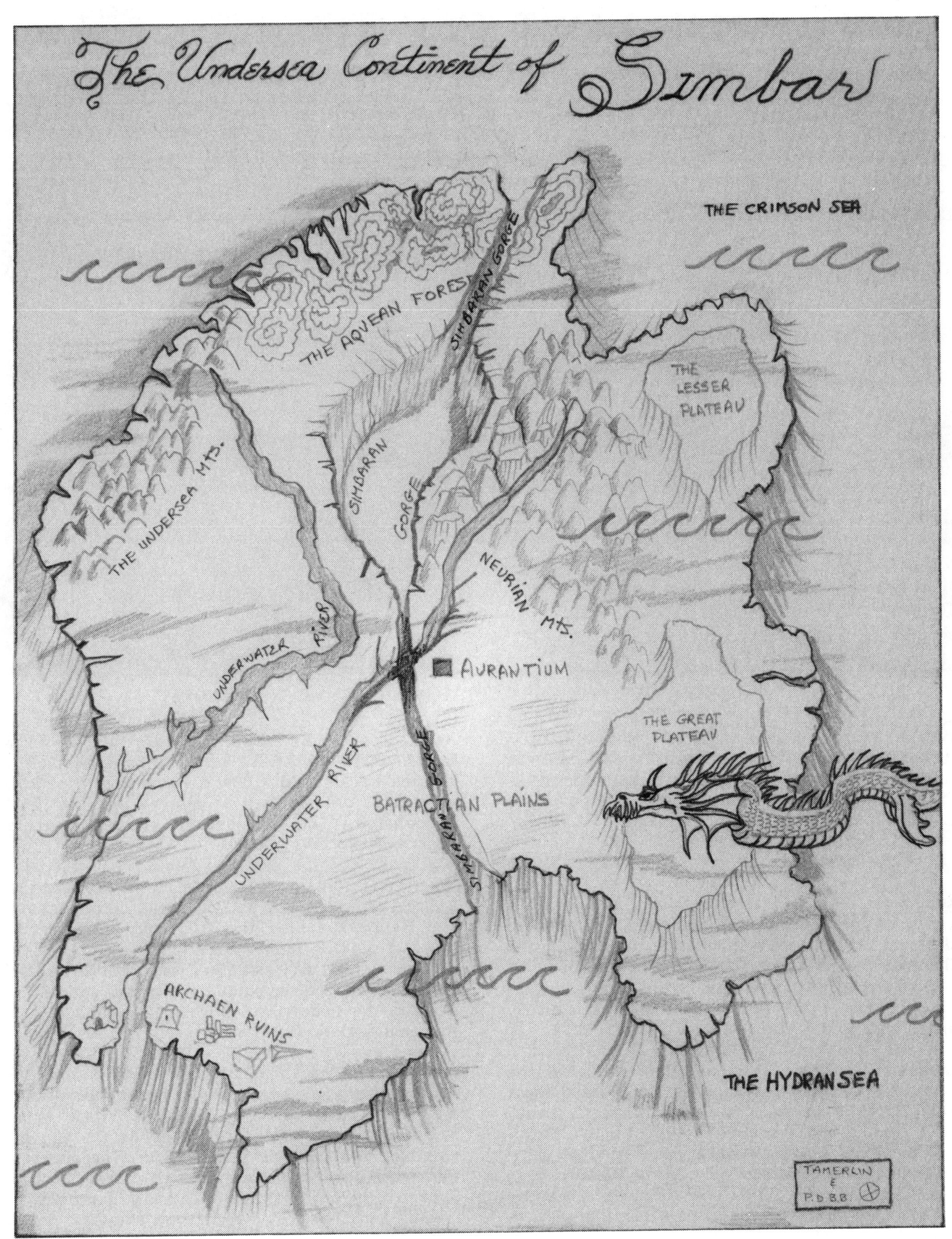

Scale: 1" = 75 miles.

THE LOST CONTINENT

A Batrachian nomad wanders the ruins of the Sunken City of Aurantium.

Referred to on ancient maps as Simbar, this now-sunken land — the "Lost Continent" — was once the center of a great kingdom. This was the homeland of the Neurians, a race of dual-encephalons possessed of extraordinary intellectual capabilities.

The Neurians

Known for their skill as alchemists (particularly as experts in the transmutation of metals), the Neurians also had an advanced knowledge of metaphysics. The walls of *Aurantium,* their capital city — known to Talislantans of the New Age as the legendary Lost City of Auran — are said to have been alchemically plated with gold.

Fascinated with the study of the Omniverse, the Neurians' unfamiliarity with magic prevented them from traveling between the dimensions to pursue their studies. Undaunted, they constructed elaborate pyramids of crystal which were used as viewports into other realities. Scholars of the Archaean Age speculated that the Neurians may have been refugees or exiles from one of those other dimensions, though this theory was never substantiated.

Archaean explorers arrived in Simbar during the latter part of the Archaean Age. Finding the Neurians to be their equals (and in some ways, their superiors), the mages entered into an alliance with the dual-encephalons. The two became trading partners, dealing in precious metals.

When this arrangement proved to be profitable for both races, they embarked on further joint ventures. The Neurians served the Archaeans as windship navigators, using their knowledge of metaphysics to help design the first astral galleon. With this vessel, the races planned to explore the planes and dimensions of the Omniverse, utilizing a combination of Archaean and Neurian lore.

The onset of the Great Disaster halted these plans and brought about the untimely destruction of Simbar, which sank beneath the waves. Many of the Neurians refused to abandon their homes and belongings, and perished in the floods. The ghosts of these drowned victims are believed to still haunt the Sunken City of Aurantium, jealously guarding the wealth and treasures which they amassed during their lifetimes.

According to the legends of the Sunra, a party of Neurians and Archaeans escaped in the prototype astral galleon – but where they went, no one knows. Others escaped in windships, one of which crashed in western Talislanta, resulting in the loss of its sophisticated levitational devices and those who understood their maintenance. Stranded, the Neurians were forced to wander the continent along with other survivors of the Great Disaster. As time passed, these Simbaran refugees have been able to keep the secret their origin. They are known by Talislantans of the New Age as the "Sindarans."

The Hydrans

The most intelligent species now dwelling in this submerged region are the Hydrans, an ancient and malign race of aquatic beings. They live in glass colony-towers, and ply the Hydran Sea in crystal submersibles, hunting both for food and crystals. The sea emerald, the rarest of these sea crystals, is employed by the Hydrans as a power source for their crystalline ships. The amphibious creatures known as Batrachians are enslaved by the Hydrans, and forced to cultivate the kelp beds which surround their underwater towers.

The Hydrans once ruled the seas and oceans of Archaeus, but this was a long time ago – perhaps during the Time Before Time. The Archaeans, who fought the aquatics and wrested mastery of the sea lanes from them, theorized that the Hydrans must have originally come to this world from one of the Elemental Planes.

The last vestiges of the aquatic empire collapsed following the Great Disaster. Since that time, the Hydrans have warred among themselves, and have been unable to recapture the mastery of the seas enjoyed by their ancestors. Yet they still consider themselves the masters of the Hydran Sea, and dislike intrusions into their domain.

Gods of the Hydrans

The Hydrans are ritual users of crystal lotus, a plant which reportedly has profound narcotic and mind-expanding properties. Through the use of this substance, they are said to make contact with the spirits of their ancestors, whom they revere as gods.

Curiously, Talislantan naturalists do not know whether the crystal lotus is capable of actually producing such effects, or whether the Hydrans have simply been deluded into believing that they are in contact with beings from the Underworld. The Hydrans make little distinction between the subconscious and conscious states, considering dream experiences to be as valid as those which occur during the waking state.

The Batrachians

The other intelligent race known to dwell amid the ruins of lost Simbar are the Batrachians. These amphibians possess both gills and rudimentary lungs, and can survive for long periods of time out of the water. They are heavy-set, with scaly skin, and a dorsal fin which extends along the length of their newt-like tail.

The clans of the Batrachians traverse the underwater plains of Simbar in packs of up to 60 individuals, carrying their possessions on their backs in sacks of woven sea-vines. They collect artifacts and precious stones from the Neurian ruins, which they trade among themselves or with the Drakken.

This race of nomadic amphibians may be the progenitors of the modern-day Imrians and Sunra. On the other hand, some scholars speculate that the Batrachians are descended from Oceanians who defied Jezem's Curse by stepping foot on land.

The Seas of Simbar

Two great bodies of water are separated by the shallows above the Lost Continent of Simbar: the Crimson and the Hydran seas.

The blood-red water of the *Crimson Sea* stretches north of Simbar, almost reaching the southernmost cliffs of the Midnight Realm. The coloring comes from red aqueor, a variety of giant kelp which grows in abundance in this region. Swirling currents have formed a massive floating island of kelp in the stagnant waters of the central sea, and the rotting hulks of many storm-lost sailing vessels lie tangled among this mass of flotsam.

The Crimson Sea is known for its unpredictable weather. Sudden downpours of scarlet rain are not uncommon, and violent tempests frequently sweep down from the far north. The Hydrans avoid this sea, which they regard as cursed.

To the south of Simbar lies the *Hydran Sea*, of which little is known by Talislantans of the New Age – chiefly because the Hydrans do not let intruders escape with their lives. These waters are the home of icthyons, anthocephali, and other strange lifeforms.

Geography of Simbar

The *Aquean Forest*, an immense sea-bottom kelp bed, was once a mighty forest before the continent was submerged. It is now populated by numerous species of aquatic flora and fauna. Some of its denizens, such as the zaratan, are benign. Others, like sea dragons and sea scorpions, are definitely not. The Batrachians come here to harvest kelp.

The ancient city of *Aurantium* is now buried under a deep mantle of silt and sediment. Neurian and Archaean artifacts may still be found here. So may the Batrachians, who regularly hunt for food here, and the Hydrans, who come here to prey on the Batrachians. The pyramids of the Neurians also draw Parthenian salvagers, who dive here to exhume the vast stores of alchemical gold and silver contained within these ancient structures.

Other ruined Archaean settlements lie in southern Simbar. Some were coastal villages, and once contained shipyards and commercial warehouses. Other communities included the inland retreats of Archaean mages, who came to this land to study in the Neurian libraries. Among the secrets to be discovered here may be the lost principles behind the creation of the first astral galleon.

Home of the amphibious Batrachian nomads, the *Batrachian Plains* are crowded with colorful varieties of aquatic life. Giant mollusks and scavenger-crabs favor the large coral formations which spread across the plains, while predators such as echinomorphs, devilrays and sea demons prowl the grottos in search of an easy meal.

The *Neurian Mountains* were often visited by the dual-encephalons in former days, who said that the upper altitudes seemed oddly familiar to them. The highest peaks now form treacherous reefs.

The yawning crevice known as *Simbaran Gorge* was created as the continent sank beneath the waves, when Simbar nearly split into two pieces. The sheer cliffs of the gorge descend hundreds of feet below the surface of the sunken land. The Hydrans believe ancient sea monsters such as the Rahab make their home in the lower depths. Consequently, the aquatics will not venture into the gorge.

The imposing peaks of the *Undersea Mountains* once constituted the coastal barriers of Simbar. Now, however, they are little more than a vast pile of broken stones — their sudden descent beneath the waves caused them to crumble, toppling mountain against mountain. Echinomorphs find the caves formed by this cataclysm an attractive home.

The Underwater River, formerly known as the Simbar River, is a riverbed which the Batrachian clans follow on their seasonal migration from the Aquean Forest to the Batrachian Plains.

A Hydran aquamancer in his crystal tower

The Midnight Realm
Hells Gate
Pandemonius
Mountains of Midnight
Vale of Shadons
Shadowmoor
River of Iron
Seas of Frozen Fire
The Midnight Sea
Castle Porpharon
Castle Minauron
Thanatius
Castle Maladon
Castle Agathon
Castle Colothon
Castle Averon
Castle Othyron
Tamerlin and reluctantly P.D.B.B.
THE MIDNIGHT REALM
Scale: 1" = 75 miles.

THE MIDNIGHT REALM

A Night Demon battles a Tarteran demon hunter.

The Midnight Realm is a land of continual night, located far to the north of the continent of Talislanta. Here, rivers of molten iron flow across a nightmare landscape of twisted ice spires and frozen ravines. Few sensible folk willingly venture into these territories, which have long been considered the domain of malefic spirits. Common throughout the Midnight Realm are such creatures as moondracs, shadow dragons, reavers, gellid, and fantasms.

The Night Demons

This northern territory is also home to the race of Night Demons — four-armed demonoids whose bodies are comprised of quasi-elemental darkness. They are ruled by a supernatural entity known as the Lord of the Night Skies, a creature whom some Talislantan scholars believe to be an avatar of the Demonlord, Aberon.

Night Demons are chaotic, maniacal and dangerously unpredictable. They live in nightmarish fortresses of twisted stone, with convoluted spires, towers that lean at odd angles, spikes and other protrusions, and walls which look as though they've been warped by great heat.

Pandemonius, a nightmarish city, is the seat of power within the Midnight Realm. From within his Obsidian Palace, the Lord of the Night Skies holds sway over his domain. Blood-curdling screams and wails can be heard throughout the environs, and a foul stench pervades the city.

The demons rise into the skies in droves, eager to attack whenever an intruding ship is sighted in the waters of the Midnight Sea, or when careless devils (whom all demons instinctively hate) expose themselves on the mainland.

The Night Demons wield immense weapons of stone and brass, and wear bracers and thick plates of brass armor. Although the demonoids consistently outnumber their enemies, the Night Demons' disorganization and lack of discipline work against them. These same factors may prevent them from achieving their ultimate goal: to bring darkness and entropy to Talislanta.

The Isle of Thanatus

A bleak and foreboding land located at the edge of the Midnight Sea, Thanatus was once home to a great kingdom whose ships spanned the world's oceans. The rulers of this ancient land were the Thane, a tall and saturnine strain of Archaeans whose interests centered around the study of death and the necromantic arts.

Thane ships sailed the waters of the Midnight Sea, and may have ventured into such waterways as the Lost Sea of Talislanta (then known as the Northern Sea) and the Dead River. Some chronicles record that their ships were driven on horrific errands by captive demons; others, merely that the Thane were dealers in funerary wares, such as urns, sarcophagi and ceremonial masks.

Unfortunately, the civilization of the Thane — like that of the other Archaean races — was destined to come to an end. Learning from occult sources of the impending threat posed by the Great Disaster, the Thane apparently abandoned their cities of black stone. Following the Great Disaster, their civilization vanished without a trace, and the mystery remains unsolved to the present day.

Like much of the Midnight Realm, Thanatus was ravaged by aberrant elemental forces during the Great Disaster. This mountainous land is today characterized by incessant volcanic activity, lakes of frozen fire, constantly shifting masses of ice, and raging elemental storms.

Aberrant weather produces such phenomena upon the island as frozen lightning, firestorms of burning rain, ice quakes, and poisonous clouds of black mist. Travel across Thanatus is a perilous endeavor, recommended to none but the most reckless and foolhardy of individuals.

The Tarterans

The current inhabitants of Thanatus are the Tarterans, a hybrid of Man and Devil believed to have been created long ago by Arkon, an Archaean sorcerer known for his reckless innovation. The devils are man-like in form, with skin of a deep and glistening shade of red, raven-black hair, bat-like wings, and diabolical features.

Legend has it that Arkon created this race in order to protect his manse and property from an infestation of minor demons, knowing of the instinctive dislike which all devils feel toward demons. He named his creatures "Tarterans," after that part of the lower planes from which he obtained the grisly components utilized in their creation.

As is often the case with regard to sorcerous hybridization, Arkon's experiment yielded less-than-satisfactory results. In the end, the sorcerer was forced to banish the Tarterans from his home. During the confusion of the Great Disaster, the devils fled to far-distant lands, and a number of Tarterans found the conditions in Thanatus to their liking.

The Tarterans eventually established seven mountain-top settlements, each ruled by a Tarteran Prince: Agathon, Avernon, Colothon, Maladon, Minauron, Othryon, and Porpharon. The petty rulers continually compete against each other, forging pacts and alliances as suit their needs, and betraying their former allies at every turn.

A Tale of Nine Princes

According to a legend known to the Sarista of Talislanta, there were once Nine Princes of Thanatus, until one became so powerful that he threatened to take control of the entire island. The other eight rulers, fearing the consequences of such an occurrence, formed an alliance under one of their number, the Prince of Valek. Combining forces, they succeeded in banishing the Ninth Prince and his followers to another dimension.

No sooner had this been accomplished than seven of the remaining Princes turned upon Prince Valek, treating him to a similar fate. The seven devil-lords then agreed to divide the spoils of the two deposed Princes equally between themselves. Unfortunately, negotiations arrived at an impasse, resulting in a civil war which continues to this very day (or so say the Sarista) among the devils of Thanatus.

Diabolical Society

Each of the Tarteran Princes resides in an imposing castle, and is personally served by a legion of devils attired in ceremonial battle armor of argentium (an enchanted silver of alchemical origin). Representatives of the subject fiefs journey to the royal palace each month, bearing the required tribute of black diamonds, casks of wine, and ingots of silver.

Tarteran society is hierarchical, and is very tightly structured. The *Ministers* serve as advisors, adjudicators and administrators to the Princes, and are infamous for their involvement in devious and often sinister court intrigues — which, after all, is typical of the devilish temperament. The most successful of these ministers have been known to become princes themselves, while those who are less skilled at plotting meet a traitor's end — it is truly a wise Tarteran courtier who lives to die of old age.

Ambassadors act as emissaries in all dealings between the Princes of Thanatus. This position is one of high esteem, but it is not without certain risks; Tarteran Princes have been known to slay the bearers of bad tidings.

The *Tarteran Knights* are the sworn protectors of the realm. Some stand guard in the watchtowers, ready to defend their prince's castle against attack from any quarter, while others serve as personal bodyguards to their liege lord.

The highest honor to which a Knight can aspire is to be granted the rank of *Demon Hunter*. These Tarterans have the special responsibility of assassinating demons wherever they can be found, and their task gives them a status which transcends even the authority of the Seven Princes.

Given the nature of all of the races of devilkin, it is not surprising that a Tarteran might occasionally betray his master and begin to work for another devil lord, perhaps even doing so in secret. The Princes do not quietly abide such treachery — when a traitor is revealed and caught, he is bound with chains and drowned in a cauldron of molten silver.

War Against the Demons

Like all of the various races of devils, the Tarterans hate demonkind. They make war on them, however, not only for dogmatic purposes, but for profit. The Princes trade the black diamond "heartstones" of slain demons in exchange for imports of argentium, wine and other goods.

In battle against the Night Demons of the mainland, the Tarterans wield enchanted weapons of silver (or, more rarely, argentium) and wear silver chainmail or suits of silver plate-armor. A few of the devils know magic or possess potent magical artifacts, but most rely on their strength and native abilities. In contrast to their demonic foes, the Tarterans are well organized, being both methodical and cunning.

Geography of the Midnight Realm

The annals of Talislantan scholars of the New Age record the following geographical information about the mysterious continent to the north:

The strange phenomenon known as *Hellsgate* resembles a bottomless pit, but this is only because its true nature cannot be seen with mortal eyes. The

Tarterans believe that the chasm is a magical gate to Nihilus, the region of Cthonia from which they claim the Night Demons spawn. The River of Iron (see below) originates from Hellsgate.

The jagged range of the *Mountains of Midnight* is inhabited by moondracs and reavers, both of which prey on the Night Demons. This region is known to be unstable: The obsidian peaks often crumble without warning, sending black avalanches of razor-sharp shards hurtling down the slopes, and entire mountains sometimes rise or fall in the space of only a few hours.

The *River of Iron* is not a real river, but is actually an extra-dimensional anomaly which defies all of the laws of nature as understood by modern scholars. The liquid substance which flows in this waterway resembles molten iron, but is an alien essence which is both boiling hot and freezing cold — the Night Demons call it "freezing fire," and the Tarterans refer to it as "hellfire." Horrible entities such as Void Demons occasionally bathe in the depths of this river.

The so-called *Seas of Frozen Fire* are small lakes found throughout the southeastern regions of the Midnight Realm, fed by the strange waters of the River of Iron. A monumental building built of blue-green rock stands next to one of the lakes, and is probably a Thane ruin of some sort.

A dark and frozen swampland, *Shadowmoor* is inhabited by unclean spirits, predatory gellid, and other unpleasant entities. Also found in this place is the rare black moonblossom, the only form of plant-life capable of thriving in a realm which never sees the light of the twin suns. The wind moans across the rolling landscape, carrying the cloying perfume of the sable blooms with it for leagues.

A deep valley, the *Vale of Shadows* is haunted by spirits and shadowforms of all types. Shadow Dragons, an immense and frightful variety of shadow wight, are a constant threat in this region. Night Demons sometimes come here to capture wandering spiritforms, which are imprisoned in amberglass and presented for the entertainment of the Lord of the Night Skies.

The Midnight Sea

The dark and ominous body of water lying to the north of the Talislantan continent is the one which sailors of the New Age fear the most. Icebergs and frozen straits pose obvious hazards to vessels attempting to ply these waters, but these are not the only risks — the legends of nearly every land tell of the sea dragons, demons and phantom ships which prowl the Midnight Sea.

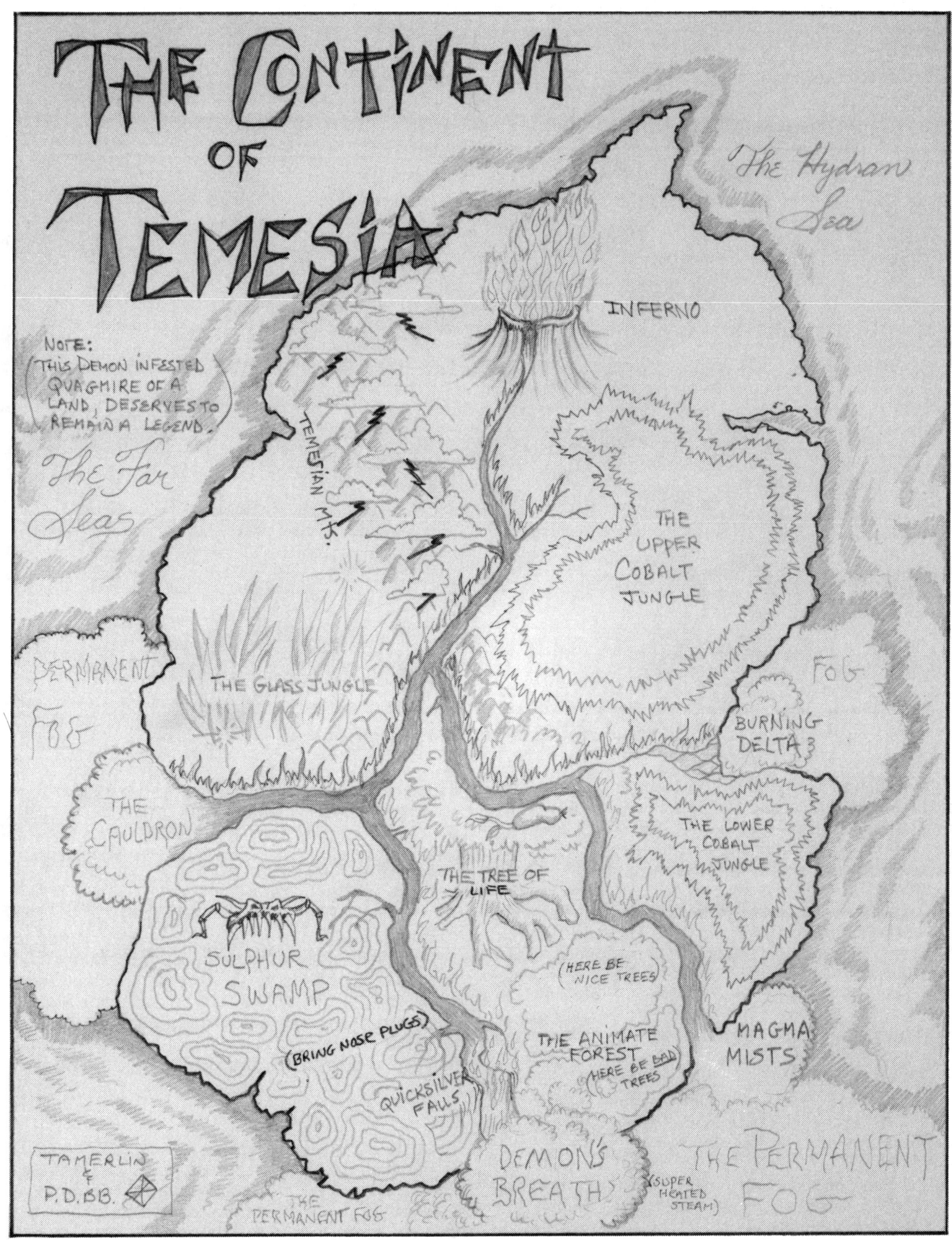

THE CONTINENT OF TEMESIA
Scale: 1" = 75 miles.
NOTE:
THIS DEMON INFESTED QUAGMIRE OF A LAND, DESERVES TO REMAIN A LEGEND.
The Far Seas
The Hydran Sea
INFERNO
TEMESIAN MTS.
THE UPPER COBALT JUNGLE
THE GLASS JUNGLE
PERMANENT FOG
FOG
BURNING DELTA
THE LOWER COBALT JUNGLE
THE CAULDRON
THE TREE OF LIFE
SULPHUR SWAMP
(BRING NOSE PLUGS)
(HERE BE NICE TREES)
THE ANIMATE FOREST
(HERE BE BAD TREES)
MAGMA MISTS
QUICKSILVER FALLS
DEMON'S BREATH
(SUPER HEATED STEAM)
THE PERMANENT FOG
THE PERMANENT FOG
TAMERLIN & P.D.BB.

TEMESIA

A panic demon perches in a silverthorn tree

This volcanic, mist-hung continent is thick with fields of acid plants and jungles of cobalt-blue iron trees. Silver dragon-flies glide overhead, on the same winds which drive the iron-tree leaves to clash and send crimson sparks into the night sky.

Such a place would seem to be forbidding to members of the animal kingdom, but the forces of Nature have bred lifeforms which survive and prosper amid these hazards — glass terratoids and panic demons, for instance.

The Panic Demons

These hideous avians are the dominant species on the continent of Temesia. Circling on high with their leathery wings, these one-eyed demonoids avidly seek creatures of flesh and blood on which to feed.

It is the habit of Panic Demons to nest in the mouths of dead volcanoes, from which their horrible, shrieking cries can be heard for miles in all directions. The shriek of the demonoids is said to have the effect of amplifying the deepest fears and phobias of any creature hearing them. "To hear the call of the Panic Demons," say the Zandir, "is to know the meaning of fear." The Corsairs of the Mangar Islands claim that the only way to resist the impulse is to flee as far as possible from the sound.

Panic Demons prefer to feast on intelligent prey, and perhaps gain as much sustenance from their victim's terror as from their flesh. Fortunately, the demonspawn exhibit the sort of chaotic behavior typical of most demons, being prone to fighting among themselves and cannibalizing their offspring — they are unlikely to spread beyond their current domain.

A Lost Race

There is some doubt among Talislantan scholars as to whether the Panic Demons should be categorized as true demons, or as aberrations. For most, the question is moot; since few naturalists of the modern age even believe that Temesia exists, other than in legend and the writings of the Zandir poet, Rajni

Rajim. But for the purposes of theoretical discussion, the scholars have noted the similarity between the description of the Panic Demons and several of the more advanced avian races (such as the Stryx and Ardua), and several theories of devolution have been put forward. The Savants of Mandala even suggest that the demonoids of Pana-Ku may be an aberrant form of Panic Demon.

The histories of the Archaean Age complicate the matter further. According to the ancient scribes, the continent of Temesia was once a fertile place, home to a race of steely-winged avians known as the Aeriad. The species vanished following the Great Disaster, the only evidence of their existence now being a few metallic skeletons kept in the vaults of the Xanadasian Savants.

The Mountains of Temesia

An intermittently-active, aberrant volcano of gigantic proportions known as Inferno dominates the northern landscape of Temesia, and has been known to spew forth a variety of substances: white-hot sulphur, boiling acid, molten brass, thick strands of a mysterious organic substance, spheres of poisonous gases, and even geodes containing young Megaliths. The legends which refer to the peak as the "Mountain of Brass" allude to the ten-foot-thick layer of copper which covers its slopes, though several eruptions of magical quicksilver have threatened to change the volcano's coloration.

The magical elements which pour from Inferno's crest flow into the bed of an ancient river shattered by the upheavals of the Great Disaster. Ash from the volcano has sealed over the ruined waterway, creating a sluice. At the river's mouths, sheets of quicksilver cascade over the cliffs at the *Quicksilver Falls,* plunging hundreds of feet into the sea below.

Because of Inferno's continual eruptions, it is impossible to determine the true composition of the *Temesian Mountains* — the range is buried beneath a bizarre patchwork of metals and alchemical substances. Eerie green lightning dances among the mountains, produced by the acidic condensation from the clouds interacting with deposits of aberrant alloys on the slopes. Panic Demons find the atmosphere pleasant, and nest here.

The Junglelands of Temesia

The tropical *Animate Forest* is home to a species of ambulatory plants which could well be related to the mandragores and mangs of Talislanta. The sentient trees near the Tree of Life (see below) are inclined to be helpful, but those found further from the tree's benign influence are spiteful and predatory, hungrily stalking any creature that enters their domain.

The flora of the *Cobalt Jungle* — which includes steely-blue iron trees, copper deodars, acid plants, silverthorn, and creeping mantrap — make this among the most dangerous regions of the continent. When the metallic branches are blown by the wind, the clashing foliage sends great showers of sparks leaping into the night sky in a dangerous display of pyrotechnics. Metallic creatures populate this jungle, such as iron wasps and silver dragon-flies. Glass terratoids, which are immune to acid, often come here to feed on the crystal foliage.

Delicate-seeming crystalline plants and trees infest the *Glass Jungle.* Although the wilderness appears fragile, it has withstood centuries of storms and eruptions. A strange vibrating hum is created when winds blow through the transparent foliage, and suns-rise and -set here are nearly blinding as the light is refracted into thousands of rainbows.

Panic Demons prefer to avoid the Glass Jungle, for their shrieks cause the crystal vegetation to shatter, producing explosions of razor-sharp leaves. However, the demons find the indigenous glass terratoids to be quite tasty. Likewise, glass dragons — the jungle's other primary inhabitants — regard Panic Demons as something of a delicacy.

The Tree of Life

This great tree is believed to have existed since the Time Before Time. According to the Ariane, the tree's roots extend throughout the world. Once a year, the Tree of Life produces a single fruit, the juice of which can supposedly be used to concoct a potent elixir which will restore life — no matter how long the recipient has been dead. If eaten by a living creature, the fruit is said to produce startling and evolutionary changes.

This Tree of Life may be the same "Elemental Tree" which is integral to the legends of the Ardua. The Sindarans of Talislanta are also aware of the legendary tree, which Sindra sometimes seek in the hope of reuniting their divided mental faculties.

Sulphur Swamp

This poisonous swamp is inhabited only by the worst sorts of predators — neurovores, venin, swamp demons, and pseudomorphs, to name only a few. Somewhere in these boglands are the ruins of the sole Archaean settlement ever established in Temesia. The scholars of Cymril's Lyceum Arcanum are in possession of a logbook from an Elandar windship, sent to rescue the settlers prior to the Great Disaster. An eruption forced the rescuers to abandon their mission, but the navigation notes are revealing. However, the mages mistakenly believe the log to be fraudulent.

GUIDE TO PRONUNCIATION

Aabaal (ah-BAHL)
Aaman (ah-MAHN)
Aberon (AB-er-on)
Agathon (AG-ah-thon)
Ahazu (ah-HAH-zoo)
Ahrazahd (ah-rah-ZOD)
Akbar (AK-bar)
Akmir (AK-meer)
Al Ashad (ahl ah-SHOD)
Alcedon (AL-seh-don)
Alchahest (AL-kah-hehst)
Altan (AHL-tan)
Altarus (ahl-TAHR-uhs)
Ammahd (ah-MOD)
Anasas (a-NA-sus)
Andurin (an-DUR-in)
Aquean (OK-wee-uhn)
Aramut (AHR-ah-moot)
Araq (AH-rak)
Arat (ah-ROT)
Archaeus (ahr-KAY-uhs)
Archaen (ahr-KAY-eßn)
Archon (AHR-kon)
Ardan (AHR-dan)
Ardua (AHR-joo-ah)
Arial (AIR-ee-al)
Ariane (ahr-ee-AN)
Arim (AH-rim)
Ashann (a-SHAN)
Astar (AS-tar)
Auran (ahr-AN)
Aurantium (ahr-AN-tee-uhm)
Avar (AY-vahr)
Averon (ah-VEER-on)
Bahahd (bah-HOHD)
Baratus (bar-AH-tus)
Batrachian (bah-TRAY-kee-uhn)
Batre (BA-tray)
Bodor (BOE-dore)
Borean (BORE-ee-an)
Boru (BOE-roo)
Callidian (Cal-ID-ee-uhn)
Caprica (CAP-rih-kah)
Castabulan (cas-TA-byoo-lahn)

Celadian (sel-AY-dee-uhn)
Celadon (SEL-uh-don)
Cella (SEL-ah)
Chakos (CHAH-kose)
Chana (CHAW-nuh)
Chrysalian (krih-SAY-lee-uhn)
Cicz (SIZ)
Cinnabar (SIN-ah-bahr)
Colothon (coe-LOTH-uhn)
Cthonia (kah-THONE-ee-ah)
Cymril (SIM-ril)
Da-Khar (dah-KAHR)
Dalia (DAH-lee-ah)
Danuvia (da-NOO-vee-ah)
Dhuna (dah-HOO-nah)
Djaffa (JAH-fah)
Djaffir (ja-FEER)
D'Oko (DO-koe)
Domal (Do-MAHL)
Dracarta (dra-KAHR-tah)
Dractyl (DRAK-til)
Draknar (DRAK-nahr)
Drome (DROME)
Druas (DROO-uhs)
Druhk (DROOK)
Duar (DOO-ahr)
Durne (DUHRN)
El Aran (el AH-rin)
Elande (eh-LOND)
Equs (EHK-wuss)
Erastes (ehr-ASS-tees)
Erendor (AIR-ehn-dore)
Erutu (air-OOH-tooh)
Fahn (FON)
Farad (FAH-ruhd)
Faradun (fah-rah-DUNE)
Farique (fah-REEK)
Farnir (fahr-NEER)
Ferran (FAIR-ehn)
Gao-Din (gow-DIN)
Garganta (gahr-GAN-tah)
Gnomekin (NOME-kin)
Gnorl (NORL)
Golarin (Go-LAHR-in)

Gramayre (GRA-ma-ree)
Gryph (GRIF)
Gwanga (GWON-gah)
Hadj (HOJ)
Hadran (hah-DRAHN)
Hajann (hah-JAHN)
Harak (HAHR-ak)
Hydran (HIGH-druhn)
Ikarthis (ih-KAHR-this)
Imria (IM-ree-ah)
Irdan (eer-DAN)
Irridian (eer-IHD-ee-uhn)
Isalis (ISS-ahl-is)
Ispasia (iz-PAY-see-uh)
Jabutu (jah-BOO-too)
Jacinth (jah-SINTH)
Jaka (JAH-kah)
Jalaad (jah-LAHD)
Jamba (JOM-bah)
Jezem (jeh-ZEHM)
Jhang (JANG)
Jhangara (jan-GAH-rah)
Kaliya (KAH-lee-yah)
Kangir (kang-GEER)
Kang-Tu (kang-TOO)
Karang (kah-RANG)
Karansk (kah-RANSK)
Karfan (kahr-FAN)
Kasir (kah-SEER)
Kasmir (kaz-MEER)
Kasraan (kas-RAHN)
Kha (KAH)
Kharakhan (kahr-ah-KON)
Kharistan (KAHR-iss-tan)
Khazad (kah-ZAHD)
Khiton (KI-ton)
Khu (KOO)
Kiru (KEE-roo)
Kragan (KRAY-gehn)
K'tallah (kah-TAH-lah)
Laeolis (lay-O-lis)
Lahsa (LAH-sah)
Lal-Lat (lahl-LOT)
L'Haan (lah-HAHN)

Lir (LEER)
L'Lal (ehl-LAHL)
Maladon (MAL-uh-don)
Malum (MAL-uhm)
Mandala (man-DA-lah)
Mandragore (MAN-dra-gore)
Mandu (man-DOO)
Manik (MAN-ihk)
Mangar (MAN-gahr)
Manra (MAN-rah)
Maruk (MAH-rook)
Matsu (MOT-soo)
Mazdak (MOZ-dak)
Minauron (min-OR-ahn)
Mirin (MEER-in)
Mogran (MOG-ran)
Mogroth (MOG-roth)
Monad (MOE-nad)
Mondre Khan (mon-druh KON)
Moorg-wan (moorg-WAHN)
Morphius (MORE-fee-us)
Myr (MEER)
Nadan (nay-DAN)
Nadir (nay-DEER)
Nagra (NOG-rah)
Na-Ku (NAH-koo)
Narandu (nah-RAN-doo)
Nauticus (NAWT-ih-cuss)
Nearwan (neer-WAHN)
Necron (NEK-ron)
Nefaratus (neh-fahr-AH-tuhs)
Neurian (NOOR-ee-uhn)
Oceanus (o-see-AN-us)
Ogriphant (OG-reh-font)
Ogront (OG-ront)
Ophidian (o-FID-ee-uhn)
Orgovian (or-GO-vee-uhn)
Osmar (OZ-mahr)
Othyron (OTH-eer-ron)
Ouros (OOH-ros)
Pana-Ku (pa-na-KOO)
Pandemonius (pan-duh-MOAN-ee-uhs)
Parthenian (pahr-THEE-nee-uhn)

Peridia (peh-RID-ee-ah)
Phandir (FAN-deer)
Phaedra (FAY-drah)
Phantas (FAN-tas)
Phantasian (fan-TAY-zee-ahn)
Pharesian (fahr-EE-zee-uhn)
Porpharon (por-FAIR-on)
Primordius (pry-MORE-dee-uhs)
Quaga (KWAH-gah)
Quan (KWAHN)
Quaran (kwahr-ON)
Rahastran (rah-HOSS-tran)
Raknid (RAK-nid)
Randun (ran-DOON)
Rasmirin (rass-MEER-in)
Rhin (RIN)
R'ruh (AIR-roo)
Sahar (sah-HAR)
Sardonyx (sahr-DON-ix)
Sascasm (SASS-ka-zehm)
Satada (sa-TAH-dah)
Sathir (sa-THEER)
Sathra (SATH-rah)
Sauran (SORE-uhn)
Saurud (SORE-uhd)
Sawilu (sah-WEE-loo)
Shadinn (shah-DEEN)
Shaitan (SHY-tin)
Shalihan (SHAL-ih-han)
Shattra (SHOT-rah)
Shonan (SHO-nan)
Silvanus (sil-VAN-uhs)
Simbar (SIM-bahr)
Sindar (SIN-dahr)
Ska-wae (SKAH-way)
Stryx (STRIX)
Sunra (SUHN-rah)
Tabal (ta-BAHL)
Talisande (tal-is-AND)
Talisandre (tal-is-AND-dre)
Talislanta (tal-iss-LAN-tah)
Tamar (ta-MAR)
Tamaranth (TAM-ar-anth)
Tanasian (tan-AY-shee-uhn)

Tantalus (TAN-tahl-uhs)
Tarun (tah-ROON)
Temesia (tehm-EEZ-ee-ah)
Terrestria (tear-ESS-tree-ah)
Thaecia (THAY-shah)
Thalia (THAH-lee-ah)
Thanatus (THAN-a-tuhs)
Thaumaturge (THOW-mah-turj)
Thiasian (thee-AY-see-uhn)
Thrall (THRAWL)
Tian (tee-AHN)
Torquar (tore-KWAHR)
T'sai (SIGH)
Tyranus (TEER-an-uhs)
Urag (YUR-ag)
Urmaan (UHR-mahn)
Valanis (va-LAN-is)
Vashay (VA-shay)
Vajra (VAHJ-rah)
Vardune (vahr-DOON)
Vird (VERD)
Viridia (ver-ID-ee-ah)
Vishana (vih-SHA-na)
Vitium (VIH-shee-uhm)
Vodruk (VO-druk)
Vulge (VULJ)
Xambria (ZAM-bree-ah)
Xanadas (ZAN-a-duhs)
Yaksha (YOK-shah)
Yitek (YIHT-ehk)
Yrmania (eer-MA-nee-ah)
Yassan (YAH-sahn)
Zadian (ZAY-dee-in)
Zagir (zah-GEER)
Zar (ZAHR)
Zandre (ZAN-drah)
Zandu (zan-DOO)
Zantil (zan-TEEL)
Zantium (ZAN-tee-uhm)
Zaran (ZAH-rehn)
Zaratan (ZA-ra-tan)
Zir (ZEER)
Zodar (ZO-dahr)
Zoriah (zore-EYE-ah)

Fantasy Art

in the fine

art tradition

BY
P.D. BREEDING-BLACK
ARTIST/ILLUSTRATOR
ASSOCIATE J.G. TORRES
580 DEVONSHIRE LN.
CRYSTAL LAKE, IL 60014
815-459-5175